The Ransomed Crown

The Saga of Roland Inness

Book 4

Wayne Grant

For Lewis and Cleo

Contents

Map
The Saga of Roland Inness

Part One: The Danes

Wayne Grant

Rumours of War

*I*t was an hour past dawn when a single scream came from inside the town. A moment later there was a second cry, cut off as sharply as a thread being snipped—or a throat being cut. The two men who lay in the tall grass on the treeless knoll overlooking Sheffield did not flinch at the sound.

They had been shadowing the mercenary army on its slow march north from Nottingham for over a week and such sounds had become commonplace. As Prince John's Flemish and Irish hirelings entered each village along their route, they helped themselves to whatever they fancied. When a place was being pillaged, screams were the order of the day.

Sheffield was clustered around the outside bend of the River Don with a timbered palisade atop a motte at the town's centre. That fortress would not have lasted three days against the rams and trebuchets in the army's siege train, so the locals had bowed to the inevitable, opened their gates and hoped for the best. Those hopes were not realized. From the hill above the town, the two men watched as some of the more prudent inhabitants fled at the mercenaries' approach. Those who stayed would regret that decision—if they lived. Meeting no resistance, the outriders of the army entered the town, and the screaming began.

The men who entered Sheffield had spent six long months laying siege to the castle at Nottingham. The town that clustered beneath that fortress had been picked clean long ago and the men were eager for new plunder—and Sheffield was untouched. But

3

no longer. For two days the mercenaries drunkenly took their liberties with the town.

At dawn on the third day, wisps of smoke still rose amid the charred remains of burnt buildings. From their hilltop, the hidden watchers could see a dead horse in its paddock at the edge of town and bodies in the surrounding fields, ripening in the August heat. The single scream that had broken the morning calm was the only sign that anyone was stirring in the town below.

After a time, the larger of the two men on the hill plucked a blade of grass and began to chew on it. Magnus Rask was a tall, broad-shouldered man with thick bands of muscle across his upper back—a sure sign of long practice with a bow. He had a golden braid tied in back with a bit of rawhide and looked every inch the Dane that he was.

He rolled toward the burly monk beside him. He'd got to know Father Augustine well in the months they had fought together to hold the castle at Nottingham and had come to appreciate both the nimble mind and the sword arm of this friar they called Tuck.

"I think they're all dead drunk," he said with disgust. "Two hundred men could walk in there and butcher the lot of them before they woke."

"We've only got eighteen," Tuck reminded him, dryly, "and this lot might be sober by the time we fetched Robin and the lads from Sherwood. What's puzzling is why they are still here. Sheffield is hardly worth three days' plunder."

Rask gave a noncommittal grunt. When the mercenary army had moved north, they had watched it from the edge of the forest. There were well over two thousand men in the column and they'd counted thirteen siege engines loaded on wagons and hauled by teams of oxen. There was no other force in the land to match it. The likely target of this army was York, but here they still sat.

Rask scratched himself idly and sat up. Tuck did the same, there being little chance that the drunken rabble in the village would notice two men sitting on the hill. Rask had an intricately carved silver ring around one huge arm and a short sword at his side. Resting across his lap was a longbow made of yew.

Viking, thought Tuck.

4

Magnus Rask had once been Master of the Sword for Sir Thomas of Loxley. He had trained the young Robin of Loxley in sword and longbow and, with Sir Thomas dead, had given his loyalty without hesitation to his master's son. Tuck had followed them both, along with fifteen others, over the wall of Nottingham Castle the night before the surrender of the fortress. Had they stayed, they would have had a choice—swear fealty to Prince John or face the gibbet. They chose to go.

By the dark of the moon they had climbed ropes from the south wall to the top of the steep bluff that plunged another two hundred feet into the River Leen. It was a miracle that none of them died on that rocky slope in the pitch dark. Once down, they slid into the shallows of the river and slipped unseen through the cordon of enemy troops.

Their refusal to bend a knee to John had made them outlaws in these parts, so they'd struck north to the favoured refuge of such men—the ancient forest of Sherwood. Outlaws they might be, but they still had their honour—and their heads.

As Tuck and Rask continued to watch the town, they heard a whoop from inside the cluster of hovels that clung to the outside of the fortress palisade like piglets around a sow. A girl burst from one of the narrow lanes and ran like mad straight toward the hill where they sat. She had gathered up her skirt and her long white legs flashed in the morning light. Behind her, five men came streaming out of the alleyway like a pack of hounds on a hare.

For a bit, it looked as though she would simply outrun the lot as she cut through a field of ripe barley. The men who shouted and hooted behind her were stumbling over the uneven ground, but one man, who looked to be hardly more than a boy, was gaining rapidly on the girl.

Tuck sighed. He was a practical man and had steeled himself to the sights and sounds of terror as this foreign plague moved north from Nottingham. He knew that two men alone could not save the unfortunate folk caught in the path of destruction. Robin had sent them to watch and report on where this pack of Irish and Flemish war dogs would turn next and that is what they had done.

5

But the mercenaries appeared to be going nowhere and Tuck had reached the end of his patience. He looked at Rask and rose to his feet. Rask arched an eyebrow and waited to see what the monk would do next. Tuck drew his short sword just as the girl in the field below let out a curse that carried in the still air to the top of their hill.

Rask leapt to his feet, an eager smile on his lips. He drew five arrows from his quiver.

"We keep one alive," Tuck insisted, "long enough to tell us why they are just sitting here in Sheffield."

Rask grunted an acknowledgement and set off down the hill at a lope. Tuck gathered the hem of his brown robe in his free hand and ran to catch up. They reached the bottom of the hill as the rest of the baying pack converged on the girl. The young soldier had caught her and pinned her to the ground, the golden stalks of barley smashed down around them. His companions were hooting and urging him on.

The girl had not given up. She managed to get one hand free and clubbed the boy's left ear with a closed fist. For a moment he drew back, surprised and stunned that the girl had struck him. In that moment, she drove her other fist into his groin, doubling him over in pain. Groaning, he rolled off her. The girl immediately seized the opportunity and scrambled to her feet. Before she could take a step, one of the four remaining pursuers grabbed her arm and drew back his fist.

But the blow never came. For a moment, it looked as though the man had frozen with his fist cocked. He gave an odd grunt and lowered his arm, a look of confusion on his face. He reached around his body with his other hand and pawed at his side. Only the feather fletching of the longbow shaft showed where it had entered there. He tried to say something to his fellows but blood frothed at his mouth and he toppled face first into the barley.

The three mercenaries still on their feet looked up to see a tall man fifty paces away with a bow in his hand. They were veterans of many campaigns and knew what a bow could do to men standing in the open with no shields. They began to back away from the girl and would have run, but then they saw the big

6

man drop his bow and draw a short sword. A burly monk had come up beside the bowman and he also carried a sword.

With no bow in play, the odds had shifted. The younger man had managed to stagger to his feet, though he was still bent forward at the waist and clutching at his crotch. The other men drew their swords and fanned out. The girl was forgotten as they edged toward the two intruders who had interrupted their fun and killed their comrade.

Unexpectedly, the tall man and the monk began to lope across the field to meet them, looking for all the world like wolves about to fall on a flock of sheep. The mercenaries stopped their advance and cast uneasy glances at each other. For months men and women had fled at their approach. No one in the villages had dared to raise a hand to them. Now these men were coming at them on the run.

But there were only two...

Magnus Rask increased his speed to a near sprint, his long legs eating up the ground. He headed straight for a beefy man on the far right of the line. The big Dane raised his sword and the mercenary braced to parry, but the blow didn't come. Rask pivoted and lunged at the man to his left. The move was so sudden his victim could not bring his own sword into play. He feebly flung out his left arm in defence. It did not stop the point of Rask's blade from slicing into the base of his neck. The man fell like a puppet whose strings had been cut.

Tuck was cursing to himself for not keeping up with the long-limbed Rask as he came across the barley field. He would have to pray to St. Bernard to forgive his blasphemy—when his work here was done. He noticed that the youngest man in the group, the one the girl had struck, was standing stiffly, the discomfort still with him.

You're lucky. You, I'll let live.

He feinted toward the boy who lurched backwards, falling on his backside, then turned on the man next to him. This one was no novice swordsman and, whatever the effects of the drink he'd had the night before, the sight of a man coming at him with a blade and death in his eyes sharpened his focus.

Tuck came forward slowly, rolling up the sleeve on his sword arm as he came. The man saw a tracery of white scars there, but his eyes were fixed on the monk's blade that moved in a slow weave. The mercenary watched him like a bird watches a snake. Tuck moved closer and the man lunged.

He thought the stocky monk would be slow, but his blade found nothing but air. He whirled to find Tuck had danced off to his right, still moving his blade as though to entrance him. The man was Irish and a fair swordsman. He had made a good living killing men with his blade, but now he felt a chill in his spine. He had never faced someone like this monk. The man in the brown robe moved faster than seemed possible for his age and girth. The Irishman leapt at Tuck and took a wide sweeping stroke, but all his blade found were a few stalks of barely.

He swung around in a panic to find the monk closing in. His fear was now a cold knot in his stomach. Sweat coursed down his face and stung his eyes. In desperation he charged at the monk, attempting to close with his tormentor and negate the man's fearful speed. But he was off balance and too slow. His world went black as Tuck sidestepped and slammed the hilt of his sword into the man's temple.

At the other end of the line the beefy man had watched the man next to him go down in a welter of blood and now saw another of his comrades clubbed to the ground by a monk. Of the men who had chased the wench into the field, he was the only one left standing. He thought of running, but he would never make it to the safety of the village before the big man retrieved his longbow.

He would have to stand and fight, but now this blonde giant with the bloody blade was coming for him. His throat was dry and he wished for one more gulp of the fine ale they had found the night before. He looked into Rask's eyes and shuddered at what he saw there. He wished they'd never found the damn girl!

He came forward swinging his blade hard—too hard. The big Dane simply stepped back as the man's stroke whistled by his nose, six inches short of its mark. He stepped forward, driving his blade up under the soldier's ribs. The man gave a strange whining cry then twitched twice before hitting the ground. Rask wrenched his blade free and drove it into the earth to clean the blood. It had all taken less than a minute.

He turned to see the final soldier, the boy who had pinned the girl, rise from his posterior and lunge at Tuck from behind with his sword. His shout of warning died in his throat as the boy flung his arms out and crumpled to the ground, a blade protruding from his back.

It was the girl. She had found a fallen sword and put it to good use. She stood over the boy waiting to see if he would move. He didn't. She kicked the lifeless body, then looked around, unsure of what to do. For the first time since she had burst from the alleyway, nothing moved in the barley field. Tuck looked anxiously at the town, but nothing stirred there. They had killed quietly and quickly. There had been no clash of steel to alert the town. He glanced at the girl, who looked more angry than frightened. He returned his sword to his scabbard and gently took her arm. She jumped, but then settled as he spoke gently to her.

"You can't go back, miss."

She looked back at the little town of Sheffield and slowly nodded her head.

"Never liked the place anyway," she whispered.

"Very well then," Tuck said, glancing once more at the town. "We should go now."

The girl nodded and let the monk lead her back toward the hill that loomed above the barley field. Rask caught up with them.

"The one you clubbed—he's still breathing. Shall I drag him along?"

Tuck stopped.

"We still need to know why they are not moving, Magnus. Do you think his skull is split or is he just out?"

Suddenly the girl spoke up.

"I know why they don't move."

The two men looked at her. Tuck cocked his head and gave the girl a gentle smile.

"And what is your name, my dear?"

The girl managed a small smile in return.

9

"It's Marian, Father. Thank you for killing those men."

"Ah, it was no trouble at all, child—and thank you for doing your part." He jerked his head back toward the bodies in the field. "That boy might have split me if you hadn't done him first."

"They were pigs," she said with disgust.

Tuck shook his head sadly.

"They were men, miss, and some of them are worse than pigs. Now tell us why the mercenaries are still here in Sheffield."

Marian told.

***

Walter of Coutances, the Archbishop of Rouen and Justiciar of the Realm, stared across the table at the exhausted face of Earl William Marshal and wondered if his own countenance looked as grey and drawn. The Lord of Striguil and his fellow Justiciar had just returned to London from his mission to the north of England. He had left for York three weeks before to bolster the resolve of the northern barons and had arrived back in the city just this morning.

He'd gone because of Nottingham. The castle there had held out heroically for six months but when Marshal's relief force had failed to lift the siege in early June, its doom was sealed—and the barons of the north knew it. He had arrived in York just two days ahead of the news of the garrison's surrender. That same day, the richer merchants and nobles of York began to discreetly move their families out of the city.

The loss of Nottingham was a huge blow. In May, Ranulf of Chester, newly declared innocent of treason, had retaken his city from John's man, the Earl of Derby. Word of his daring assault had spread like lightning throughout the country and had given pause to those who would turn on their King. Earls and lesser barons came forward to confide in Marshal and the Archbishop that they were happy that John's ambitions had been checked. But now, with Nottingham threatened, those same Earls and barons had gone silent. So Marshal had undertaken his difficult and dangerous journey. That a Justiciar of the realm had to travel backroads between London and York to avoid foreign mercenaries said much about the current state of affairs in the kingdom.

Dust still clung to the man's clothes as he gratefully downed a cup of wine. The Archbishop studied him. For years he had maintained a casual acquaintance with William Marshal as they had both risen in stature and influence under the patronage of King Henry. But it had only been in the last year, when both had been thrown together as the appointed Justiciars for King Richard, that he had come to fully know and appreciate Marshal's many qualities.

Adversity had a way of revealing character in a man, and there had been a surfeit of adversity since Richard's departure on crusade. Over the past two years, they had watched many of the English nobles go over to the King's brother. Prince John had worked relentlessly to undermine Richard's throne, but Walter of Coutances had not wavered from his sworn loyalty to the King—nor had William Marshal. That loyalty could be trying at times. In many ways the Archbishop thought the King rash and bull-headed—and quite capable of fumbling away his crown to his brother. And if that happened, men who had kept faith and remained loyal to Richard could expect little mercy from the new King John.

In truth, his loyalty to Richard was more loyalty to the man's mother, Queen Eleanor. He knew that Marshal felt the same. He often thought that the kingdom would have been better served if she had simply been made the monarch, but that was not the way of things. Nevertheless, he and the Earl had cast their lots with Eleanor and hoped that it would not cost them their heads. As Marshal returned his empty wine cup to the table, the Archbishop saw worry etched in every line of the man's face.

"William, you should rest awhile. There are chambers prepared upstairs. Can your report not wait a few hours?" the Archbishop asked gently. Both men had long ago dispensed with the honorifics of "my lord" and "your excellency." There was simply too much business to attend to when they met to waste time on puffery.

William Marshal looked up at the Archbishop. He appreciated the man's concern for his health, but knew how anxious he was for news. Walter of Coutances had been chosen by Eleanor to run her spy network in England and Marshal had soon learned that the churchman was far from ignorant of secular affairs. The man soaked up information like parched earth soaked up rain, and he had a remarkable way of sorting through tangles of rumour to get to the truth.

"Walter, I could hardly take my ease knowing you would be down here, pacing about and waiting for me to rise," he said with a wry smile, "so let's get on with it. First the good news—as I passed through Lincoln, word came that John's army made it only as far as Sheffield before stopping, I expect, to loot the place. So they have not moved on York—yet."

"Well that is a blessing—at least for the people of York, though not to the poor folk of Sheffield," the Archbishop said and crossed himself, "but what is the temper of the barons in the north? Are they with us? Will they resist John?"

Marshal shook his head.

"All say to my face they are loyal to the King, but we can be sure some are lying. I believe the Northumberland nobles are with us. They look to Richard to protect them when the Scots come howling over the border and they have no faith that John is up to that task. But, of course, they do not control the gates of York. The Sheriff of Yorkshire does that and he seemed a bit *overeager* in his protestations of loyalty. I cannot be certain how he stands. It does not help that the King has not yet started for home."

The Archbishop nodded. Richard had sent word—had *given* his word to the Queen—that he would sail by the end of July from Acre, but no messenger confirming his departure was likely to reach them much in advance of the King himself. Provided Richard did not tarry on the way home, a habit he was prone to, he should reach these shores before Christ's Mass. At the moment, beset as they were, five months seemed like an eternity.

"Did you remind these fence-sitters in the north that choosing wrongly might put their heads on the block when the King returns?"

Marshal grinned. The Archbishop was no doubt a Christian, but he had a backbone of steel and no great surplus of Christian forgiveness—particularly when it came to treason.

"Aye, I did, and pretty bluntly, but they are more fearful of the wolf pawing around their door than the lion half a world away."

The Archbishop grunted. Marshal's report on the mood of the northern barons did not surprise him, but the news that the mercenary army had stopped dead at Sheffield was unexpected. In hindsight, it should not have been. The siege of Nottingham Castle had taken six months and the town outside the castle must have been thoroughly looted in the first few weeks.

Sheffield would have fresh spoils that should occupy mercenaries for at least a day or two, but then, which way would they turn—north or west? The nobles in the north seemed susceptible to coercion and York would be a rich source of plunder, but there was also Chester. John had lost sizable revenues when Earl Ranulf had retaken his own city in a brilliant coup. The Prince, no doubt, wanted it back and the revenue that came with it. Mercenary troops did not march for free! This thought prompted another.

"William, you may be pleased to learn that news of Ranulf's recapture of Chester has spread wide and has had an effect in the south. Roger Mortimer, who I had counted as firmly in John's camp, paid me a visit here in London last week. He was inquiring about the health of the King and when we expect him back."

"So my neighbour along the Welsh Marches has gone from likely enemy to fence-sitter!" Marshal said with a sneer.

"It's progress, my friend," the Archbishop said earnestly. "With the first positive news of the King's approach, he will leap off that fence onto our side—and we shall welcome him as though he was there all along!"

"And when will that be? Has the Queen heard nothing more of the King?"

"Nothing since early June. I send couriers to her weekly and she to me. While we wait for news of Richard, the Queen spends her time putting backbone into our Norman lords along the border with France. Only a fortnight ago, King Philip marched an army to Gisors and demanded its surrender. Claimed to have papers signed by Richard granting the place to him! But Eleanor was there ahead of him. The commander sent the King and his army packing."

This made Marshal smile.

"The Queen can always inspire a man to his duty. She probably had the fellow puffed up and believing he was Achilles by the time she was finished with him."

"Or more frightened of her than of Philip!" the Archbishop said. Marshal nodded and refilled his wine cup.

"So tell me, what is the temper of things here in London?"

The Archbishop sighed and spread his hands helplessly.

"London is London. The mayor and the aldermen are cautious, but hardly bother to disguise their preference for John. The Prince has taken up residence in the Tower, which he's strongly garrisoned. To the merchants and tradesmen, he's promised virtual immunity from taxation if they support his claims to rule. And the place is rank with spies like fleas on a dog. My house is watched day and night and so is yours. I've had two of my staff approached in the past month to spy on me for money. I've yet to determine if the approach came from agents of John or agents of King Philip, but I am working on that."

Marshal rubbed his chin.

"I trust the members of my own household, Walter, but it does seem as though John has been more than lucky in countering our plans. When I marched north to relieve Nottingham in the spring, only you and the Queen should have known my plans, but John was waiting for us at Leicester." There was a note of bitterness in Marshal's voice as he harkened back to the beating he'd taken at the River Soar. He paused, then reached out and touched the Archbishop's sleeve.

"Walter, we cannot let these people win. John would be the ruination of the kingdom—not to mention of us!"

Walter of Coutances laid a hand on his friend's shoulder.

"I still have hope, William. The merchants and nobles may see Richard's crusade as a folly, but for the commoners, his victories at Acre and Arsuf have made him the greatest English king since Alfred! The day he sets foot back in England, this foolishness will end."

The Archbishop paused, searching his memory for another item he had stored away for Marshal's return.

Ah, yes.

"And, William, you will be pleased to hear that these loyal commoners are delighting in the exploits of your Invalid Company. The news that a band of half crippled Englishmen nearly annihilated a troop of Flemish mercenaries has gained them a reputation for daring and ferocity. Minstrels have composed a rather bawdy ballad in their honour that does little for the reputation of the Flemings—but is most popular with the common folk of London."

William Marshal laughed. It was the first time he had done so in weeks and it felt good. He had held out little hope that the wounded veterans of the crusade who had washed up on England's shores would be of much use when he pulled them out of the gutters of London in the spring and sent them off to find the Earl of Chester. They had proved him very wrong and he was glad of it.

"I shall have to learn this ballad myself, so I can sing it in my bath! But tell me, Walter, has the Archbishop of Rouen actually been patronizing taverns here in London?"

Walter of Coutances smiled a slightly evil little smile.

"More often than you might think, William."

Saint Oswald's Priory

*T*wo men sat their horses in the tree line watching the monks preparing for harvest. It was early July and the day promised to be hot. The two had ridden for five days to get to the priory of Saint Oswald, keeping to the north of the high peaks of Derbyshire. They came on personal business.

The younger of the two was tall with broad shoulders and dark hair tied off in back with a strip of leather. There was a fresh red scar along his cheek—a reminder of the arrow that had grazed him during the taking of Chester. Over his shoulder was an unstrung longbow secured with a leather strap. The man beside him was huge and rode a massive black horse. He had a dark tangle of beard that looked like an approaching thunderstorm and a long-handled axe hanging from his saddle.

Across the fields of ripening barley and wheat they could see the plain structure of the priory itself. The building looked well maintained, as were the fields and barns that surrounded it. The monks were making good use of the dry weather, working industriously to sharpen scythes and clean out storehouses before the reaping began in a few weeks.

But as they bent to their labours, they did not lack vigilance. It was, after all, a dangerous world. So while their spirits looked to heaven, their eyes kept watch for trouble. They saw the two riders emerge from the woods and all but one man began to move back toward the shelter of the priory walls. That man, an elder, put down his basket and came forward to greet them.

"Welcome, my sons, to our humble priory. Can we offer water and feed for your horses? It is an hour until the midday meal and it is plain fare, but you are welcome to join us."

Sir Roland Inness dismounted as did Sir Edgar Langton. The sight of the huge bearded knight caused the priest to unconsciously take a small step backwards.

"Father, we thank you for your offer and can pay for the fodder for our horses," Roland said with a reassuring smile.

The priest nodded happily.

"Wonderful—and the meal? Will you join us?"

"Perhaps, Father, but we are not passersby. We have come here on business."

"Business?"

"Aye, my name is Sir Roland Inness and my companion here is Sir Edgar Langton. Three years ago, my friend, Father Augustine, brought two children to this place—a boy and a girl. They are my brother and sister. I've come to see them."

The priest looked shocked—then nervous.

"Children, you say?"

Roland did not like the way the man had started to wring his hands. He took a step toward the priest, who shrank back.

"I've sent you gold, through Father Augustine, to pay for their care. It would not do, Father, for me to find I'd not got my money's worth. Where are my kin?"

"My lord, it was not our fault...I swear to you. We tried to raise the boy as a good Christian, but he...he was difficult from the start."

Now Roland closed the distance to the priest and grabbed the collar of his robe in his fist. He pulled the man close.

"What have you done with Oren?" he growled.

"No...nothing, my lord. He was a high-spirited lad with no discipline in him. We applied the rod, as I'm sure you would have wanted us to, but it had no effect on the boy's behaviour. He would not read scripture or sing hymns and when he was set to work in the fields, he was more trouble than help. And now, my lord, he's run away. It was in the spring. We searched the

17

grounds and for miles around, but there was no sign of him. When we asked his sister where he might have gone, she just said 'home.'"

Roland eased his grip a bit, but did not let go of the priest.

"Lorea—she is here?"

"Aye, lord. She is here, and a more wonderful child never there was."

"Take me to her!" Roland said, releasing his hold on the priest's robe. The man straightened himself, relieved to be released by this surly young knight. With as much dignity as he could muster, he pointed toward the stone priory.

"Of course, my lord. This way."

They found her in a sunny courtyard with a fountain at its centre. The rest of the space was filled with carefully cultivated herbs and flowers, leaving narrow paths between. Tall sunflowers, heavy with seed, seemed to be bowing their heads under the weight, or perhaps from the sanctity of the place.

The girl was laughing at something an old priest was telling her. She had golden hair. She was six years old. When the old priest saw the two knights he laid his hands gently on the girl's shoulders and turned her toward the men. He seemed to know, without being told, that they had come for her. His old eyes held genuine sadness.

"Father Pipin, this man is Sir Roland Inness. He has come— for Lorea...and Oren."

Roland took a step forward and studied the girl. She had their mother's eyes. Lorea had been hardly more than a babe when he last saw her, walking away from their homestead, holding Oren's hand. He recalled that his brother had looked up to the rocky outcrop where he had hidden himself and waved farewell as he led the little girl to safety. Thankfully, they had been spared the pain he had endured watching the murder of their father.

He took another step forward and looked into his sister's bright blue eyes. She was watching him intently, but had said nothing. He went down on one knee.

"Lorea. It's me. I'm Roland. I am your brother."

The bright eyes of the girl lit up even more. She took a hesitant step away from the old priest, then ran the remaining way and threw her small arms around him.

"They said you would come," she murmured into his ear. "You look like Oren…"

Roland folded his arms gently around her. He wanted to hold her tightly, but was afraid he would frighten the girl.

He let her cling to him for a long time. She was crying, but it seemed a happy cry. Finally, he pried her arms from around his neck and held her at arm's length. He took his thumb and brushed away the tears on her cheeks.

"You were so small when Father died and I had to go away. I know you cannot remember me, but I remember you! You've grown so much, I can hardly believe it," he said. That seemed to please her.

"Have you come to take me home?" she asked.

"Lorea, I have found a new home for us. It's away over the mountains you see to the south. It's a lovely place called Shipbrook and you will be happy there, but we cannot go just yet."

"Why not, Roland?" she asked.

Roland wondered how to tell her about the destruction of the pretty fort by the Dee. He would not lie to his kin.

"Some bad men burned it down, Lorea, but we are going to build it back, better than ever."

Lorea considered this new information solemnly.

"They told me bad men killed my father. Are they the same ones?"

Roland rose to his feet.

"Yes, little one. They are the same ones, but don't be afraid. I promise we will make an end to these bad men who kill and burn. And when we're done, I will come back for you. Can you wait a little longer?"

Lorea turned back to the old priest.

"Father Pipin, can I stay a little more? Roland can't take me now."

The look of relief on the old man's face would have been answer enough. Here was a childless man who had discovered late in life the simple joy that a child can bring. He could scarce bear the thought of this little golden-haired girl leaving.

"Oh, of course, my dear. You can stay as long as your brother needs us to care for you."

She turned back to Roland.

"Roland, I can stay, but I will be waiting for you. I'll watch those mountains to the south to see when you come back."

"Aye, sister," he said and took her back into his arms. "You keep watch. And as sure as the sun comes up, I will be back and we will be a family again."

"Oren too?"

"Yes, Oren too. The priest said you told him that Oren had gone home. Where is that, Lorea?"

The little girl looked at him with surprise.

"You know where home is, Roland—Kinder Scout."

***

As the forest closed in on the narrow path ahead of them, Tuck, Magnus Rask and the girl Marian dismounted and walked the horses forward. They had ridden for most of the day to reach this place. It was a section of Sherwood that had burnt years ago, allowing bracken and white birch saplings to spring up thickly amid the blackened skeletons of holly, hawthorn and small oaks that did not survive the blaze. Here, a man could not hope to see more than twenty feet ahead.

For a quarter mile they followed the path as it wove through the thicket, until at last it led them to a copse of ancient oaks that fire could not kill. Under the shade of the big trees, the saplings and undergrowth ended.

No sooner had they emerged from the narrow path than Tuck heard a loud bird call. He grinned and waved toward the sentry he couldn't see, but knew was there.

"Run! Go tell Robin that Tuck and Rask have come home!" he called cheerily to the unseen watcher. A man dropped from a low branch a hundred feet up the trail and waved back, smiling.

"Aye, Friar, I'll let him know yer back and just in time. We've a boar roasting on coals."

20

They walked their horses through the towering trees until they came to a lovely little clearing that bustled with activity. It was their camp. On the far side, rough lean-tos had been built and from one of these came Sir Robin of Loxley with a huge smile.

"Tuck! Rask! I had begun to worry about you two!" he said, as he hurried forward and embraced each man in turn. Then the girl caught his eye.

"I see you've brought a new recruit with you, and a right lovely one at that. Welcome to Sherwood, Miss..."

"Marian," Tuck said with a pointed look. He had spent most of his journey back from the Holy Land advising the young knight to stop charming the tavern maids. It drew too much attention. So it was hardly a surprise that Robin would be taken with this girl. She was a pretty thing Tuck had to admit to himself.

"It's a pleasure to meet you, Miss Marian," he said and gave a short bow. "Sir Robin of Loxley, at your service."

The girl looked at the young knight with a sceptical eye. She was a serving girl from a Sheffield inn and had no illusions about men—especially handsome and charming men.

"Thank you, my lord. Friar Tuck and Master Rask saved my life, or at least my honour, and I am in their debt," she said. "As for a service you could do for me—a bucket of clean water would be nice."

"Of course, miss," he said, then turned and shouted across the clearing.

"Hubert!" A man Tuck had not seen before jumped up from the fire where the boar was roasting and came at the run. Robin nodded toward the girl.

"We have a guest and she looks tired and thirsty."

Hubert grinned happily.

"Oh, I'll fix 'er right up, my lord. Come this way, miss. There's some nice shade and we got lovely spring water so ye can wash yer face. Not that it's dirty, mind ye, just a bit of dust from the trail." He prattled on merrily as he led her across the clearing. The man's obvious pleasure in making her comfortable was hard to resist. Marian gave him a small smile.

"That would be lovely, Master Hubert."

Robin watched her go, tall and straight-backed across the clearing, and shook his head. She was truly a lovely girl. He turned back to find Tuck and Rask giving him knowing looks.

"What? Can't a man admire a pretty girl?"

"For the moment, no," said Tuck, a little sourly. "But come, we've much to report and I see you've been fruitful and multiplied while we've been gone." Tuck had noticed that the sixteen men they'd left in this place a week ago were now two dozen.

"Aye," said Robin. "They started showing up the day after I sent you north. More come every day. They're desperate."

Tuck looked around. Every man in the clearing was painfully thin, including Robin, but the new arrivals were the worst. The men who had gone over the wall at Nottingham had endured months of short rations and then starvation, but these new men had seen worse horrors from the look of them.

Robin read his face.

"Things were as bad in the countryside these past months as they were in the castle. While John's army was starving us out, his new Sheriff was seizing everything of value from the farms and villages. These men have seen their children die, Tuck. They are weak, but if we can get a little food in them, they're ready to fight back."

Tuck saw the grim look on his friend's face and gazed around the clearing at the forlorn farmers who had edged close to the bed of coals where the boar was being turned on a spit, drawn to the smell of food. Some had staffs and some had pruning hooks in their hands. None had a proper weapon.

Fight back? These men?

"Robin... what are you thinking?"

Robin was looking at the hungry men too, and shook his head.

"Tuck, I'm done with whatever squabbles our royal masters may have with one another. Six months defending Nottingham Castle paid whatever debt I owed to Richard. But I will not stand by while these people starve to death. We were outlawed the moment we went over the wall. I think it's time we acted like

22

outlaws. I plan to steal back food from the Sheriff and feed the villages."

Tuck blinked, started to protest, then stopped. Robin's plan could hardly hope to succeed, but he'd seen the look on his friend's face. It was a look he had seen on the faces of the Danes and his fellow Saxons when they had risen against Lord Robert de Ferrers years ago. That uprising had failed and most of his comrades had been hunted down and killed, but he had never regretted his decision to join them. He looked again at the starving farmers huddled around the cook fire.

"Very well. Where do we start?"

Robin grasped the monk by both shoulders.

"I knew you would agree! First we will get some pig into these men, then we will need to teach them how to fight and find out where the grain stores are being held, but tell me—what of the mercenaries? Are they marching on York?"

Tuck shook his head.

"They reached Sheffield after a week and looted the place. Not surprising, but after three days they hadn't moved and that *was* surprising. Sheffield can hardly have three days' worth of plunder to loot! They were still there when we rode out yesterday."

Robin shook his head.

"That hardly makes sense. When they started north, York must have been their objective. Why linger in Sheffield?"

"We had the same question," Tuck said, "and the girl gave us the answer. The Flemings and the Irish haven't been paid in a month. They are refusing to go any further until they are. It seems John is running out of money."

***

Roland and Sir Edgar stayed at the priory for the evening meal and watched as a score of solemn priests doted on Lorea. Tuck had surely known what he was about when he brought the children to this place. He inquired after the monk, but none had seen Father Augustine since he had returned to the priory two years past with the golden arrow Roland had won at King Richard's coronation. Over their simple meal, Roland learned that his gift had fed hungry mouths in southern Yorkshire for miles around and that the monks lifted up daily prayers for his soul and his safety.

At this news, Sir Edgar leaned over and whispered in Roland's ear.

"Can't tell about yer soul," he said dryly, "but ye've been to the dungeons of Jerusalem and back again, so the prayers for safety seem to be havin' an effect."

Roland wondered why Oren had chafed so under the care of these kind men, but recalled that his brother was always ready for a scrap. When they were boys, he had more than once rescued Oren from fights his brother had started, often with older and bigger boys. He had even had to thrash the boy himself on a couple of occasions when Oren had challenged him. For all that, his brother had been a kind lad, and brave. Now he must find him.

For once, duty and family obligations did not seem to be at odds. His duty was sending him into the high country to find the Danes and fate had sent his own brother in the same direction. Find the Danes and he would find Oren—if the boy had made it that far. Between the priory and the high peaks was some of the same country he had travelled while on the run from William de Ferrers. He knew there were many ways a boy could meet a bad end there.

The next morning they left at dawn. Father Pipin had Lorea up, dressed and brushed for the farewell. She waved to them until they were out of sight.

"Beautiful child, that," Sir Edgar said. "Looks nothing like you."

Roland smiled to himself.

"Do ye think yer brother made it up into the hills?"

"I don't know, but we are bound for the high country in any event, so we will know soon enough."

"We'll pass near to Peveril Castle."

"Aye, we have to pass within a few miles of the place. I like it not, but it's the only way to get to Kinder Scout, save climbing more ridgelines than you would care to."

Edgar snorted.

"Why don't we just ride up to Peveril and see if that bastard William is at home? I wonder if he's recovered his senses?"

William de Ferrers, the Earl of Derby had been dragged unconscious from the approaches to Chester the month before, after Roland struck him in the helmet with an arrow at over two hundred yards. Word had reached them that the Earl survived, but was not quite himself.

Roland grinned. Sir Edgar's barely banked hatred for the Earl of Derby nearly matched his own.

"In time, friend, in time. For now I need to find my brother and the Danes—and I wish to visit the graves of my mother and father. Can your feelings for de Ferrers keep for now?"

"Oh, aye. I said I would follow ye, and I'm a man of my word. This brother, he looks like you?"

"So says my sister."

"Then it's a very ugly lad we seek. That will make the quest easier."

***

Riding south, they forded the River Dearne and skirted the village of Barnsley. Topping a low ridge, they stared off at the southern horizon and saw a ragged procession of people coming up the road from that direction. They had the familiar look of people fleeing from danger. Behind the column of refugees they saw smoke rising in the distance.

"Woods burning?" Sir Edgar wondered.

"Could be a town," Roland replied. "Prince John's army was heading in that direction a week ago."

John's mercenaries.

One day they would have to be beaten if the King was to keep his crown and if there was to be any security for him and the people he held dear back in Chester. This journey was meant to even the odds when that reckoning came—just not too soon. They were not ready yet. Roland turned his horse's head to the west and rode down off the ridge. Ten miles on, the country rose up to meet them.

***

Two hours after Roland and Sir Edgar rode down from the ridge, a dozen riders appeared on the road pressing south through the mob fleeing from Sheffield, cursing and striking anyone who did not make way for them. The men were heavily armed and all wore mail. They had ridden out at dawn through the Micklegate Bar at York, pausing only to water their horses in the Dearne.

As the lead rider forced his way through the column of human misery flowing up the road, the sight of it lent new energy to his mission. This scene would *not* be repeated at York! William Marshal might preach loyalty and threaten dire consequences upon the King's return, but Marshal was gone and of the King, nothing was heard.

The Sheriff of Yorkshire spurred his horse. He had to get to Sheffield and buy off the Prince's army.

Return to Kinder Scout

As shadows lengthened, Roland and Sir Edgar followed an ancient trail that wound its way southwest through the high country toward Castleton. In the narrow mountain valleys, night fell quickly, even during the long days of summer. When the sun dropped behind the peaks to the west, they followed a small stream away from the road and made camp.

"Tomorrow we stay south along this trail," Roland said, as they unsaddled and tethered the horses. "This valley will broaden out until we meet the main road that runs from Sheffield to Castleton."

"I know that road," Sir Edgar said. "Our fief was east of Sheffield and we travelled that road often when the old Earl was in residence at Peveril Castle."

"There will likely be patrols along the road."

"Boys, with spears," said the big Saxon, hoisting his battleaxe. "Short work."

"We are not looking for a fight—not yet," Roland warned. Edgar shrugged.

"Very well, we avoid trouble—but if trouble finds us..." He hefted his axe again and gave Roland a wide grin. Roland laughed and nodded.

"If the way is clear, we travel the Castleton road west until we reach a stream coming in from the north. It flows from Kinder

Scout mountain. We follow it as far as we can, then we leave the horses and climb."

Sir Edgar struck some sparks and got a small blaze going.

"I know the stream you mean," he said, "but where it meets the road is scarcely more than two miles from Peveril Castle. You're sure you don't want to ride up there and knock on the gate? De Ferrers would piss himself."

Roland shook his head and laughed again.

"Yes he would, just before his men killed us."

Edgar snorted.

"Probably torture us first."

"And we'd deserve it for being stupid."

Edgar did not respond immediately, but threw more wood on the fire and watched the embers fly into the dark sky. Finally he spoke.

"Are we any less stupid climbing up into these hills uninvited? These Danes we seek—they use the longbow. We both know what one of those can do. We have no shields," he hefted the mail shirt that he had removed in camp and dropped it in a heap, "and this will be worthless, if they aren't glad to see us."

Roland knew Sir Edgar spoke the simple truth. There were a thousand places on their path ahead where a man with a longbow could kill them, but the men he had known as a boy would not kill another man simply for climbing their mountain. But things might have changed. He looked at Sir Edgar and shrugged.

"We'll know that by the end of tomorrow."

***

At dawn, they rode slowly south through morning fog that clung to the valley floor. By midmorning it had burned away and the day looked to be clear and hot. It was nearing noon when they struck the main road to Castleton. From the trees they watched the road for a long time, but no one passed by.

Strange.

The road from Sheffield into the mountains should not have been empty at harvest time. Finally, Roland clucked to his horse and trotted down to the road. Turning west, they rode toward Castleton. Still, they saw no one. At this time of year, there should have been men in the fields at dawn, but there was no one—and for good reason. Most of the fields were overgrown. If crops had been planted in the spring, they had been abandoned and weeds had choked out any grain that had been sown. The few huts they passed in the valley all appeared to be deserted. It was an eerie landscape and it seemed to unsettle Sir Edgar.

"Where is everyone?" he asked with an edge in his voice.

"I don't know. This is a fertile valley. When I was a boy, my father and I would hunt in the high ground over yonder. We could look down and see these fields—so green and thick with grain it would make you want to weep. Nothing like the rocky patch we worked on our farmstead higher up."

They rode on for another hour until Roland reined in his horse and signalled to Sir Edgar to be silent. For a moment, no sound reached them beyond the buzzing of insects and the cries of angry crows heckling some unseen hawk in the distance. Then there was something else—a low rumbling that echoed up the valley from around the next bend.

Riders.

"Off the road!" Roland spurred his horse toward the nearest trees with Sir Edgar close behind. The dust of their passage had just settled when a patrol of a half dozen riders came around the bend. Had they been vigilant they might have seen the tracks left by two horses in the soft dirt of the field, but, heedless, they thundered on down the road toward Sheffield. Edgar snorted after they passed.

"Boys with spears."

When the patrol was out of sight, they returned to the road. The sun was inclining toward the west when they reached the stream leading north into the higher hills. There was no road here, just a rugged path hardly wide enough for a farm cart. They had to dismount and lead their horses in places. As they made their way north, they passed small fields and clusters of huts that should have been the centre of midday activities, but were still and silent.

The Midlands bleed.

Millicent had said those words to him and here was the evidence, but could it be bad enough to empty the land like this? He had grown up among peasant farmers who tilled the poor soil of the high country. Such men did not leave their hard won plots willingly—and to have left good land on the valley floor? Something had driven these people away.

After another hour of scrambling along the edge of the stream, they led the horses into a thicket and made a cold camp. It would be unwise to enter the hills where the Danes held sway at twilight. The next morning they rose at dawn and continued north up the valley. Three miles on they saw a thin column of smoke rising from a wooded ravine off the trail. Had there been any breeze, the wisp of smoke would not have been visible, but the day was calm and in the still air, it was like a beacon.

Dismounting, Roland and Sir Edgar led their horses up a path into a dense copse of trees. There they found a tiny hovel of wattle and daub, its thatched roof black with age. A thin swirl of smoke drifted up from a hole in the roof. Without being told, Sir Edgar quietly circled around behind the dwelling. Roland stepped forward and pounded on the oak door. No answer. A sound came from the rear of the hut and Sir Edgar soon came around the side, leading an old man by the arm.

"He had a little bolt hole out the back," Edgar said with a grin, as he released the man in front of Roland. The old man was trembling with fear and would not meet Roland's eye.

"What is your name, grandfather? We are not here to harm you," Roland said gently.

The old man lifted his eyes and spoke. His speech had the familiar accent of the Saxon peasants in these parts.

"Godric, my lord."

"Godric, I am Sir Roland Inness and this man is Sir Edgar Langton. We hoped to find stabling for our horses, but the valley is deserted. Where are the people? Has there been a plague?"

"No plague, my lord."

"Then where have they gone?"

Godric shook his head. He still trembled, but a look of defiance was in his rheumy eyes.

"I'll not tell."

Roland sighed and looked at Edgar.

"Very well, Godric. But we have business hereabouts. May we leave our horses with you? We'll pay with good coin if you will feed and water them until our return." He held out a silver coin in the palm of his hand.

Now Godric's gaze turned from resolute to a mixture of greed and worry.

"Aye, my lord. I can keep the beasts for ye, but be warned. They may be taken by the Earl's patrols. I can't be held to account fer that, can I now? They take anything of value they find. They took the seed fer grindin' and when that wasn't enough fer 'em, they took our seed for planting. So you can see the fields are empty."

The Midlands bleed.

Roland handed the man his coin.

"No, old man, we'll not blame you if the horses are taken, but hide them as best you can. If soldiers come, leave the horses and hide yourself. And Godric, put out that fire—it's how we found you."

For the first time the old man grinned.

"Aye, lord, that I can do. But tell me, where are ye bound? I would stay clear of Castleton. Strangers are not welcome there these days."

Roland turned and pointed towards the looming mass of Kinder Scout to the west.

"We go to Kinder Scout."

The old man looked puzzled.

"Nothin' but heathen Danes up there, my lord, and they're no kinder to strangers than the folk in Castleton."

Roland nodded.

"I appreciate the warning, Godric, but I am no stranger to the Danes."

***

They left the horses with the old man and headed up the valley on foot. There were more deserted farmsteads along the way and an unnatural emptiness hung over the land like a pall. The silence was only broken by a lone pig that had somehow been left behind when its owner fled. It happily grunted and rooted down by the stream, unconcerned by their passing.

Soon after they left Godric's hut, Roland sensed they were being watched. Once, as they rounded a bend he caught a flash of movement high on the wooded slopes overlooking the valley. Whoever the watchers were, they were careful. For another half hour they hiked with no sign of anyone on the trail or the heights, but he knew they were there.

Around the next bend, the valley broadened out into a wide meadow. Roland stopped. He knew this place. This was where he had missed his best chance to take revenge on the man who had killed Rolf Inness so many years ago. He had pursued William de Ferrers to this very spot after killing three of the Earl's men-at-arms. The Earl's son had bolted in a panic, but Roland had caught up to him here. As he looked at the meadow, now covered with summer grass and wild flowers, that day came back to him vividly.

He had burst from the woods just in time to see de Ferrers disappear over the small rise in the middle of the meadow. He began to sprint toward the top of the rise and would have had a clean shot at the man, but a patrol of the Earl's men had appeared, coming up the valley road. He had been forced to retreat into the woods. That was where Tuck had found him.

Roland suddenly realized that his heart was pounding and he was breathing hard, almost as though he was still pursing the man he had sworn to kill. He forced himself to turn away. Sir Edgar was looking at him oddly. He took a deep breath and pointed to the eastern slope.

"We go up here," he said.

They crossed the meadow and started to climb. It had been over three years since he had killed that roebuck on the side of this mountain—three years since he had set foot on Kinder Scout, the mountain of his boyhood. When they had climbed for a while, they struck a game trail. He knew this trail—knew where it ran to in both directions. He turned west and followed it.

A little ways on, the trail broadened and showed signs of regular use by the people who lived up here in the high country. Around a bend, they came to an opening in the trees where a small patch of level ground had been cleared. The field was barren now, and there were only a few blackened stumps where a farmer's hut had once stood. This place was nearer the valley than most, but the Earl's men had rarely ventured this high up the mountain in the past.

It was an ill omen.

They passed the abandoned place and followed the trail higher. To his surprise, Sir Edgar kept pace with him. For a huge man with a crippled leg, he was surprisingly nimble, though Roland could hear him sucking in air like a bellows behind him. He wondered how far they would get before the watchers in the woods made themselves known. It wasn't long.

They had just crossed one of the many rivulets that ran off the flanks of the mountain, when an arrow buzzed by Roland's head and imbedded itself in a nearby tree. Sir Edgar reached for the axe at his belt, but Roland put a hand on his arm. If the hidden watchers had meant to kill, they would already be dead. He took a step forward and opened his arms wide. He called up the slope, speaking in Danish.

"I appreciate the warning shot. Now if you would have the courtesy to show yourself—my bow is unstrung and my friend here can't throw his axe that far. We are no threat."

For a long moment, there was no response, no movement in the trees ahead. Then a man stepped out from a tangle of deadfall. He was tall and lean and moved with the easy grace of a man at home in these woods. He held a longbow in his hands with an arrow nocked. He moved down the trail toward the two men,

"We'll judge if you be a threat or no, stranger," the man said. He spoke in English but with a recognizable Danish accent. "I see you have a longbow and you speak our tongue, but you dress as a Norman." He gave a disdainful sniff. "Smell like one too. Who are you then?"

Roland bristled at the man's insult, but checked himself.

"I am Roland Inness—the son of Rolf Inness. I grew up in these mountains. I've come to visit his grave and that of my mother. I also come to find my brother."

There was a long silence.

"We heard the son of Rolf Inness was dead." This came from a second man who had quietly emerged from a cluster of bushes upslope and to his right. He too had an arrow nocked in his longbow. "Killed by Ivo Brun they said."

"As you can see, they were mistaken." Roland called back. "I'm alive—and it's Brun that's dead."

Roland saw the man cast a surprised glance at his companion who did not return it. The first man spoke again.

"Perhaps he is or perhaps not. Brun hasn't troubled these parts for a long time, but no one knows what became of the bastard."

"I do."

"And I suppose you killed him?" the man asked with a sneer.

"No, but I saw him die."

The tall man seemed to contemplate that for a moment, then gave a small signal with his hand. Two more men with half drawn bows emerged from the trees on the left.

Roland tried to place the bowmen, but couldn't. The scattered farmsteads of the Danes stretched over many miles in the high country of the Pennines and large gatherings were rare. If he'd seen any of these men before, he did not recognize them.

"It's been three years or more since we heard Rolf Inness was dead—killed by the Earl's men I'm told. We heard his son ran. Is that true? Did you run away, boy?"

Roland gritted his teeth, but held his temper, barely.

"Aye, I ran, but not before killing three of the Earl's men. It would have been four if I could have caught up to the Earl's son."

The leader of the group started to reply, but one of the other men spoke first.

"Odo Kjeldsen once told me he found three of the Earl's men-at-arms dead on the high trail—one arrow in each."

"Odo was our nearest neighbour," Roland said. "He would have been the one likely to have found those bodies." The leader shot him a dark look. "If you are who you say you are, where have you been these past three years?"

"I've been to war and now I'm back."

"War? What war are you speaking of?"

34

"King Richard's crusade to take Jerusalem back from the Mohammedans. My friend and I," he jerked his head toward Sir Edgar, "fought there for two years, but have come home."

"Crusade!" the man spat on the ground as he spoke the word. "Your father is killed by the Normans, so you join up with the bastards to fight their wars?"

"I did not. My master was ordered to go and it was my duty to follow him. I'll not apologize for that—or for serving a Norman knight. He's a better man than anyone I see here."

There was an angry murmur from the men who surrounded them and Roland could hear the familiar creak of yew being bent. Once more, Sir Edgar slid his hand toward the handle of his axe. Roland could feel that bloodshed—probably theirs—was near, but civility did not seem to be working.

"Think of me what you will, but you should hear me out. I've come here to honour my parent's graves, but also to make an offer to the Danes. It's an offer that you should consider."

The leader of the group looked at him sceptically.

"Offer? From you, or from the Normans? Or perhaps there is no difference. We don't make bargains with the Normans. They come into our mountains—we kill them."

"I'm a Saxon," Sir Edgar observed, to no one in particular.

"We kill Saxons as well," the man said.

Sir Edgar slowly drew forth his wicked battleaxe.

"You'd better shoot straight then, or I'll be takin' a few of you with me."

"Hold!"

It was a voice that had the bark of long-practiced command to it and was close enough to startle. A wiry older man stepped out from a tangle of deadfall not twenty feet away. His hair was long and grey and there were talismans woven into its strands. He had blue ink tracings on one cheek and down an arm. He looked as though he had stepped out of the Viking past all of the Danes shared.

"Put the axe down, Saxon," he ordered.

Sir Edgar scowled.

The man looked at his fellow Danes and made a palm-down gesture with his hand. They lowered their bows. The tall man started to protest, but was stopped by a hard look from the older man.

"These men have not threatened us, Svein. Would you kill them for sport? Are we no better than Normans?"

Svein locked eyes with the older man, and for a moment Roland thought he was going to disobey. Then he shrugged and slowly lowered his bow. Satisfied, the grey-haired man came down to the trail where Roland stood. He moved with a spring to his step that belied his age.

"I am Thorkell. I fought with Rolf Inness twenty years ago when last we rose against de Ferrers," he said. "He was a clever war leader and a brave man. Now, the Danes must defend themselves once more—we've been forced to it, I am sad to say—and they have chosen me to be their war leader." He stepped closer and looked intently at Roland.

"You do favour Rolf Inness a bit. On the chance that you might be his son, we'll not kill you, but we'll have your weapons, here and now."

Sir Edgar growled behind him, but Roland did not hesitate. He swung his bow forward and handed it to Thorkell. He unbuckled his sword belt and drew Ivo Brun's dagger from his boot and handed them over. Thorkell passed the weapons to Svein. Sir Edgar was slower to comply, and was swearing oaths under his breath as he passed his axe forward.

They were now prisoners of the Danes.

The Danes

*T*horkell gave a hand signal and headed up the trail as easily as he had bounded down it. Roland and Sir Edgar hurried to follow. Svein jerked his head toward two of the bowman who fell in behind the captives.

They were still miles to the north of the Inness steading high on the eastern slope of Kinder Scout, but it was country Roland knew well. As they hiked, they passed the familiar profile of an old rock slide and snaked through a narrow clough that sheltered an ancient, misshapen oak. It was land he had hunted as a boy and hunters paid attention to such things.

As they moved further up the slope, they came to one of the many trails that wound along ridgelines linking the isolated farms of the Danes. This trail headed due north, away from the Inness place. As they marched, they skirted a farm perched on a small piece of flat ground. Unlike the abandoned steading further down the mountain, this one was still being farmed.

A man was standing in a small patch of oats with two young boys nearby. They all stopped to watch the procession pass by on the trail. Thorkell gave them a wave and they waved back. Whoever had burned out the farm lower down had not penetrated this high into the hills—not yet.

They hiked in silence until they reached the crest of a ridge overlooking a high valley. From this height, Roland could see smoke rising from camp fires below. As they descended through

37

the trees he saw a sentry who nodded to Thorkell as they passed, but kept his gaze fixed up the trail toward the ridge.

Roland recognized this place. It was a narrow valley on the western side of the long ridge that ran north from the summit of Kinder Scout. Sometimes deer remained in this sheltered spot well into winter and he had hunted them here with his father. The valley was isolated and well-hidden, but the sentry's vigilance told its own story—trouble, it appeared, had been no stranger to the Danes. They did not feel secure, even this deep in the mountains.

As they emerged from the woods into a clearing, he could see at least a score of men spread around the open area. All had longbows near at hand and were looking at the new arrivals with interest. In the years he had spent on Kinder Scout, he had never seen such a gathering of men, and certainly not at harvest time. That they were here and not tending to the crops on their farmsteads was more evidence of trouble.

The Midlands bleed.

Thorkell led them past a long low hut that seemed to be a sort of rude dormitory for those not on patrol. As they moved into the clearing, the men in the encampment drifted toward the group. By the time they reached the far side, a dozen men had converged on the place. Some stood and others took seats on fallen timbers. None looked friendly.

Thorkell halted them at last. There was a low buzz of hushed talk from the gathered men. Roland looked around in vain for his neighbour Odo, but did not see him. Then he noticed a boy standing in back who was watching him intently. He was tall, thin and dark haired and was leaning on a longbow. It had been three years, but there could be no mistake.

It was Oren Inness, his brother.

The boy made no move to greet him as Thorkell raised a hand and the buzz of conversation fell silent. The war leader of the Danes pointed to Roland and Sir Edgar.

"We found these two over the ridge and three miles east. They were coming our way, so we thought it best to escort them. The tall one says he is Roland Inness, son of Rolf Inness. The big one is a Saxon."

There was a renewed buzz as more men drifted into the clearing. Thorkell raised his hand again to silence the crowd.

"Inness says he has come to visit the grave of his mother and father and to find his brother, but he comes here as an oath man to a Norman and says he has an offer for us. So what are we to do with them?"

Whatever good will may have been conjured up among the Danes by his kinship to Rolf Inness vanished with the news of his allegiance to a Norman. The buzz now had an angry, threatening tone to it.

Thorkell frowned.

"First, let's confirm if he tells the truth about his name." Thorkell turned and spoke to the boy in the back of the crowd.

"Is this your brother, Master Inness?"

Oren Inness gave a small nod.

"Aye, it's him," he said. There was an edge to the boy's voice, but Roland could not conjure its meaning and his brother seemed to have nothing else to say.

Thorkell again quieted the crowd.

"Well then, we will hear what Roland Inness has to say, and then decide what to do with him and his Saxon friend." He turned to Roland and motioned him forward as he stood back.

Roland stepped to the centre of the clearing and nodded toward Oren. The boy did not return the gesture. He glanced over at Sir Edgar, who was scowling back at the hostile faces in the crowd. He looked ready to sell his life dearly if the Danes wanted it. He took a deep breath.

"Here is what I have to say. Three years ago William de Ferrers came to our farm and had my father killed. I saw it happen and killed three of his men in return. I would have killed de Ferrers, but he escaped me that day. He will not escape me forever, this I've sworn."

For the first time, there was a rumble of agreement in the crowd.

"But I've not come here for any private vengeance. That must wait. I've come because there is a war in the land—a war between the Normans to determine who shall rule. You've seen this war in the abandoned farms and deserted valleys at the foot of your mountains. And even the high country hasn't been spared. Some of your own steadings have been lost, and your men, men who should be taking in the harvest, are patrolling the approaches. It's well they do, because these mountains will not save you from what is coming."

He paused, looking at the silent watchers, sensing their unease at his blunt words.

"In this war, Prince John seeks to wrest the crown from his brother, King Richard. I care little for either, but know this—if John prevails, William de Ferrers will become the most powerful baron in England. And what will become of the Danes then?"

He saw that some of the men were starting to lean in, to truly listen to what he was saying. It was time to make his offer.

"I come to you from Ranulf, the Earl of Chester. Ranulf is a Norman, through and through—but a man of his word—a man who, like you and I, counts William de Ferrers as a mortal enemy. He is the only baron in the Midlands that stands against the Prince and de Ferrers. He offers you an alliance against this man who would starve your children and make of Derbyshire a desert. He offers each man who joins him a hide of good farmland in Cheshire to bind the alliance."

Svein leapt to his feet.

"And why should we trust an offer from a Norman? The truth is not in them." He spat on the ground and pointed at Roland. "If this man was ever a Dane, he is no longer. He is a creature of the Normans and this is a trick. He would coax us from these hills that protect us so his Norman masters can slaughter us. I say we treat him as we would any Norman who trespasses on our mountain. I say we kill him—and the Saxon oaf he brought with him!"

Roland bristled, but kept a leash on his anger. Thorkell stepped forward and raised an arm. He looked weary but unbowed.

"There will be no killing," he said, first staring at Svein, then turning from man to man, looking for a challenge. Roland could tell that some sided with Svein, but none were ready to challenge their war leader's authority.

"These men committed no offense against us. Perhaps Svein has the truth of it. Making common cause with a Norman lord goes against every instinct that I have, but this is a matter that cannot be decided by the few men here now. Your offer, if genuine, is generous, but it is a hard thing you ask of us—to give up the mountains that have been our defence for generations, to give up the farms we have sweated blood over. I will send runners to fetch the men who are not here now. By the end of tomorrow, most should be here. Then we will give you an answer."

Svein leapt to his feet to protest, but Thorkell snarled at him.

"Sit down. You will have a chance to have your say along with the others." He turned back to Roland.

"You are welcome here until our decision is reached. You said you wished to find your brother and visit your parent's graves. The one is there," he said gesturing toward Oren across the clearing "and I expect you know the way to the other."

He jerked his head toward Sir Edgar who stood with his arms crossed, scowling at anyone who met his gaze.

"Keep your Saxon friend close. He doesn't speak our language and he seems eager to have a misunderstanding with Svein. I will hold you responsible for his conduct."

Roland nodded.

"And I hold you responsible for Svein. Sir Edgar will not start any unpleasantness with any here, but he will not suffer insults, nor will I."

Thorkell stared at him for a moment, seeming to revise his estimate of the young knight before him. Then he nodded back.

"Fair enough. I will have my eye on Svein. Good luck with Oren. He's a good lad and more than a fair shot with the bow, but he is quick to start a scrap."

Roland grinned.

"It was ever so, Thorkell."

Oren Inness

*T*horkell called out half the men in the clearing and gave them terse instructions for summoning the Danes to council. Men left in every direction, following the paths that linked the isolated farmsteads of the high country together. Generations of Danes had followed these trails and Roland wondered if this would be the last to do so. He noted that Svein was one of the messengers and was relieved to see the man trot off to the north. The rest of the men in the clearing drifted off, back to whatever duties engaged them.

As Thorkell's messengers moved off, Roland stole a glance at his brother. The boy had made no move to come to him and gave nothing away in his face. This would not be the warm welcome he had got from his sister. He walked across the clearing and Oren watched him come, his eyes wary. As Roland drew near, it was the boy who spoke first.

"I used to wonder what I would say to you—if you ever came back," he said. "I didn't think you would."

Roland studied his brother. Oren was almost his own height, but was very thin. He had the broad shoulders of an archer, but it was the eyes that struck him. They were pale grey like their father's. He had not remembered that. It was like having Rolf Inness staring back at him.

"It's been a long road, brother, but I am back now. It's good to see you, Oren."

"Have you been to the priory?"

Roland nodded. "Aye, Lorea is well and she misses you."

Oren turned his head away for a moment and Roland thought the boy's eyes looked shiny when he turned back.

"I hated to leave her there, though they all loved her. I had to go, but it would have been selfish—and dangerous—to bring her with me."

"Why did you run, Oren? Tuck was only trying to protect you and our sister."

The boy shrugged.

"Did the monk tell you I refused to go with him, until Odo and Thorkell made me? And that I ran away twice on the journey to the priory?"

Roland arched an eyebrow.

"No, he left that part out."

Oren nodded.

"Your friend Tuck is a hard man to escape from. He whacked me good with that staff of his. I had a knot on my head for a week."

Roland fought to keep a smile off his face.

"You've no idea what I've seen that friar do with a staff or a sword. You got away lightly with a knot—and Thorkell tells me your head is hard."

"Thorkell has also given me a bump or two up there, so he would know. Your friend the friar meant well, but I did not want to leave here with him. They made me go—said it was too dangerous to stay."

Roland could tell from the boy's voice that his forcible exile by the Danes still rankled.

"The monks at St. Oswald's—they were not bad men—they loved Lorea from the start, but me? They were pious and I was not. I wished to roam and they would not abide it. Odo had given me a bow and I spent all my time fashioning arrows and practicing with it instead of feeding the pigs and chickens."

For a long moment, neither brother spoke. Then Oren locked eyes with Roland.

"I need to know what happened after I took Lorea away from the farm that day. I know father was killed. Odo told me and took me to his grave later. You say the Earl had him killed—but why? No one here seems to know. So tell me, brother, what happened?"

Roland had known that one day he would have to confess to his kin what had happened that dreadful day on Kinder Scout. Now that day had arrived.

"It was my fault," he began.

***

He left nothing out. He told of poaching a roebuck far down the mountain in direct disobedience of their father, how the Normans had stumbled on his crime and how he had fled in a panic. He told of hiding far up the mountain above their farmstead as William de Ferrers had Rolf Inness murdered while he watched helplessly. Finally, he told of killing the three soldiers on the trail and chasing the Earl's son into the valley, only to lose his chance at revenge.

Roland paused and stared at his brother who had been listening intently. The boy spoke.

"I remember that morning. I was gathering wood at the pile of deadfall on the far side of the field. I saw you come out of the woods, but took no note of it. By the time I got back, Father was handing you a parcel of food and then you were gone—up the mountain. Father wouldn't tell me what had happened, just that I must take Lorea to Odo's and stay there until he came."

The boy stopped for a moment, his eyes shiny.

"But he didn't come," Roland said, hot tears stinging his own eyes. Oren shook his head mournfully.

"No, he didn't. I remember looking up as we were leaving—at the big rock above our place. I couldn't see you, but I knew you were there. I waved."

"I remember, Oren. You were holding Lorea. I didn't wave back."

Oren nodded and was silent for a while. Then he spoke.

"That spring—I remember crying at night from the pain in my stomach because there was no food."

"I heard you—and Lorea too. I couldn't stand it."

44

"So you went down the mountain to hunt—where Father told you not to."

Roland could only nod. There was no escaping his guilt for that fatal mistake. When Oren spoke again, there was sadness in his voice, but kindness too.

"It's just the sort of thing the monks of St. Oswald's beat me for. If I had been the older brother, Roland, I expect I would have done what you did."

Once more Roland had to fight to keep tears from springing to his eyes. He had longed for and dreaded this day for three years. He had borne the guilt of their father's death for all that time. Now, the brother he had made an orphan had heard his confession and with a few words had lightened his burden.

Oren Inness had forgiven him.

***

They stayed up for hours around the flickering coals of the fire as Roland told his story and Oren peppered him with questions. He spoke of his new life at Shipbrook, his travels to the strange lands of the Crusade. He told of the terrible attack on the breach at Acre and of being knighted by the King himself. He told it plainly, but it sounded like some kind of wild folk tale—even to him. Oren had listened, a little wide-eyed at his brother's account.

"This knight that is your master, Sir Roger—he is a Norman, yet he made a Dane his squire. That seems strange. Mostly they kill us."

"Aye, Sir Roger is an uncommon man, though not the only Norman or Saxon I've met that I would trust my life to. He cared not that I was a Dane, and he appreciated my skill with the bow. Sir Roger is first and always a soldier. You will find none better to stand with you when swords are drawn or arrows nocked. As for me being a Dane, he already had an Irishman as a squire, so…"

Oren's eyes showed his surprise.

"The Irish—I've heard they are a dangerous and unpredictable people. Your friend…Declan you called him, is he of that sort?"

Roland had to smile. How to describe Declan O'Duinne?

"Yes—dangerous and unpredictable." He would let Oren reach his own conclusions about Sir Declan, but the boy did not dwell for long on the nature of Irishmen.

"The King, they say he is a great warrior. Is that so?"

Roland nodded.

"I did not see him in a pitched battle. When they fought at Arsuf, I was in Saladin's dungeons, but men I trust—warriors all—say that none could stand before the King that day. So many fell to his blade that brave men in the enemy host fled at his approach."

Roland could see the fascination in his brother's eyes.

"Oren, the King is a man who loves glory and has the bold heart to grasp it, but he is a man after all, not a god and all men are flawed."

"How do you mean?"

Roland poked at the fire and rearranged some coals with a stick. He was silent for a long time and Oren was about to speak again when he replied.

"There were things done in that war—things ordered by the King—things that should not have been done. Do not ask me to describe them. They brought no honour to our cause. I think Tuck said it best. 'Richard is a bad man, but a strong king, and England needs a strong king.'"

"And the King's brother, John—he is weak?"

"Yes, but dangerous in his own way and it is John and those that support him like William de Ferrers that put us in our present peril. The Danes should consider this—if Chester falls, it will move John closer to the throne and put more power into the hands of de Ferrers than has ever rested with the Earls of Derby. For the Danes, nothing could be more dangerous."

"It seems neither Danes, nor Saxons, nor even Normans, are safe these days," Oren said.

Roland looked up at the sky that was now full of stars. The fire had slowly died to a soft blanket of ashy coals.

"We live in dangerous times, brother, but a man still needs to sleep. We will speak more of this tomorrow. Will you go with me to visit the grave?"

"Aye. I go on Sundays, when I can."

***

The next morning they climbed the ridge that formed the long north-south spine of Kinder Scout and dropped down along the eastern flank of the mountain. Thorkell had consented to returning their weapons and Sir Edgar seemed particularly happy to have his battleaxe at his side once more.

The day was hot and, in clearings, pink, honey-scented heather and bracken crowded into the sunny openings among the trees. On this day, in deference to Sir Edgar, they spoke in English as they made their pilgrimage.

"The monks at St Oswald's showed me the golden arrow that Father Tuck brought from London," Oren said. "They said you won it at a great archery tournament. It was a thing of beauty, but they melted it down and used it to buy food for the priory. Those monks might be too holy for my tastes, but they fed many mouths that winter with the food that gold bought."

"Aye, I had no need of a golden arrow."

Oren gave a sly smile.

"You must be very good with that bow of yours to win such a tournament."

There was no disguising the subtle challenge in the boy's comment.

"Well, I believe there is a man from Loxley who is my match and I have seen archers among the Welsh who can hit a mouse in the eye at a hundred paces, but I am good enough."

"I've been practicing," the boy said.

Roland stopped on the trail and Sir Edgar, who had been admiring a pair of songbirds fluttering about in the heather, almost ploughed into him. He looked around the clearing and pointed to a single white birch sapling on the far side, its trunk no bigger than a man's forearm.

"Can you hit that, brother?"

Oren gave a small hoot.

"Can you, brother?"

Roland had to smile. This was the little brother he remembered. He drew an arrow from his quiver and nocked it.

47

There was a slight breeze rising up from the valley far below them and moving from his left to his right. He gauged the distance to be one hundred and fifty paces to the birch. He drew the flax string back to his ear as he elevated his longbow. With a slight adjustment for the breeze, he loosed the arrow. It arched across the clearing and struck the narrow trunk of the sapling in the centre.

Oren did not seem impressed. He nocked his own arrow and drew. Roland studied his form. Someone had been teaching the boy well. Oren paused as his draw brought the string back to his cheek, then released. A moment later, his arrow struck the birch a few inches above his brother's. He turned and gave Roland a look of triumph.

Sir Edgar who had been watching patiently spoke up.

"If you two pups are done pissing on trees, I suggest we continue. The day is growing hot."

Oren swung around to confront the big man, pointing at his axe.

"Is that just for ornament?"

Roland thought Sir Edgar would bristle at such a taunt, but he gave the boy a charitable smile and walked over to another birch sapling that was growing nearby. This young tree had the girth of a man's leg.

He slid the heavy oak handle from a loop on his belt and with hardly more than twitch of his massive shoulders swung the gleaming blade at the trunk. There was a soft ripping sound, but the sapling hardly moved. There was a brief shudder that disturbed the leaves and Roland wondered if the big man had aimed poorly. Then a breeze caught the upper branches and the birch toppled over into the clearing, its trunk cut clean through. Sir Edgar returned the axe to his belt without ceremony.

Oren laughed and spoke to Roland in Danish.

"I like him—for a Saxon."

***

They followed the trail for another two miles to reach the small patch of level ground that had been the Inness farmstead. The tiny field where Rolf Inness had scratched out food for the family was overgrown now with heather and patches of golden gorse.

Little grew in the blackened circle that had been their wattle and daub hut, burnt so long ago by the Earl's men. Roland's eyes rose to the rocky outcrop where he had watched as Rolf Inness died. Oren led him to the base of the slope where two stone mounds with weathered crosses marked the resting place of Rolf and Mara Inness.

Roland sank to his knees. He thought that enough time had passed—that the rawness of his loss had been worn smooth with its passage, but now it all came back to him with a sharp bitterness. A sob caught in his throat and he felt a hand on his shoulder. It was Oren.

"I come here often. It doesn't hurt so much now. It takes time, brother."

Roland wiped his eyes with a shirt sleeve and stood up. Sir Edgar stood a little ways off and tactfully looked away. Oren had gathered up a bunch of pink heather and gave it to him. He laid the blooms on his mother's grave, then turned slowly to take in this place that had been his whole world not so long ago. He doubted he would ever return.

He looked up at the cloudless sky and saw that the sun had passed its highest point.

"It's time we were getting back."

They made their way back to the trail and headed north. Roland spoke to Oren as they retraced their steps.

"What will the Danes decide?"

Oren shook his head.

"I don't know. A hide of land—it is almost beyond belief, but these mountains have been their home since the Normans came. They feel safe here. It will be hard to leave."

Roland nodded.

"Will you speak at the council?"

"It is my right. I am of age."

"And what will you say?"

Oren shook his head.

"I don't know, brother. I don't know."

The Ransom of Yorkshire

William de Ferrers drummed his fingers nervously on the table. The room where he sat was in the finest house in Sheffield and it had mercifully been spared arson, though the smell of burnt wood hung like a pall over the town. They had been here for four days and should have long since marched on York, but the army would not move.

This was an embarrassment. He had been given command of this force of Flemish and Irish mercenaries by the Prince himself, but these hard-bitten warriors paid him little heed. They had refused his orders to march north until all of their back wages had been paid, but he had nothing to pay them with. His entreaties to the Prince for funds had brought only further embarrassment.

"I'd have the funds to pay the men, if you had not lost Chester," the Prince had said to him. John had promised to find the money, but his payroll had grown painfully large over the past months as more barons sought to dine at the royal trough. It seemed these nobles could not be bought, only rented, and their appetite for silver seemed limitless. So the great mercenary army sat in the despoiled town of Sheffield and refused to move.

De Ferrers got up and paced around the room. It had taken him a month to recuperate from the blow to the head he had received outside the walls of Chester, though he still had occasional bouts of dizziness and blinding headaches. His physician had assured him these would pass, but he had little faith in the man with his bleedings and noxious potions. He would be damned if he let these afflictions rob him of his role as John's chief baron in the Midlands!

He had ridden to London as soon as he was able after the fall of Chester to meet with the Prince and John had received him warmly. When he passed through the outer gate of the forbidding Tower by the banks of the Thames, the Prince had actually come from the keep itself to greet him at the top of the stairs.

"My lord, William—I am most gratified to see you returned to good health. I have had my priests praying for your recovery every day!"

"Your grace is too kind. I would have come sooner, but the physicians treat us all like old women."

John chuckled and placed a hand on his shoulder.

"And the headaches and dizzy spells? These have departed?"

De Ferrers almost froze. He had forbidden any word of these episodes to be spoken of and had hoped to hide their existence from the Prince.

How did he know?

"Yes, your grace. They are gone entirely and I am ready to be at your service."

"Good, good, my lord," the Prince said as he led him into the arched entrance of the Tower keep. "Come with me. I would have you tell me how we lost Chester."

John led de Ferrers across the first floor of the Tower with its guard quarters and armorers workshop and up the winding stair to the sumptuous royal residence on the second floor. He waved de Ferrers toward a soft chair as they entered a richly appointed parlour. The Prince settled himself opposite the Earl of Derby. De Ferrers felt the first pulse of pressure in his temples as he looked into the eyes of Prince John and saw no warmth there. Nervously, he began to give his account of the loss of Chester.

"Your grace, the traitor Ranulf crossed the Dee with a large host of Welshmen, hundreds of men—cutthroats all. I led my garrison out to meet them and we would have beaten them in a fair fight, but turncoats inside the city stabbed us in the back.

They treacherously opened the gates to Ranulf's henchmen and barred them to us when we returned. We assaulted the walls, but when I sustained my wound leading a charge, the men lost their nerve."

The Prince raised a hand.

"My lord Earl, your account differs somewhat from others I have received," he said, his voice soft, but with a steely edge, "but I suppose these other reports could be mistaken. No matter—the city is lost and must be taken back. Your neck and mine are at stake in this. I know not if or when my royal brother may return to these shores, but if we do not wrest the crown away before he does, our heads may be keeping company above the gates of London!"

John leaned forward and placed a hand on de Ferrers' knee.

"We have lost a great deal of money with the loss of Chester. That money buys loyalty and it buys men. We must get it back. Do you understand? *You* must get it back!"

De Ferrers recognized the blunt threat in the Prince's words and was determined not to show weakness, though the throb in his temple was quickly growing into one of his pounding headaches.

"Aye, your grace. It's why I've come here at the first opportunity. Give me the army you have laying siege to Nottingham and I will take back Chester."

John slapped his hands together.

"Ah, my mercenaries! They are the best money can buy and you shall have them shortly. I have prepared an order placing you in command of my army—once Nottingham falls. You will use it to take back the city you lost, but before you do, my lord Earl, you will march my men to the gates of York. I would remind the barons in the north where their interests lie."

"Of course, your grace. I will not fail you!"

"See that you don't, William."

The Prince rose, signalling the end of the conversation.

De Ferrers rode away from London that day with pounding temples and a knot in his stomach. He arrived at Nottingham the day before the garrison surrendered and presented the Prince's orders to the senior mercenary commander. Pieter Van Hese was a Fleming and a veteran soldier with a reputation for both bravery and cruelty—traits not uncommon among the men who sold their swords for silver. He was a gaunt man with a milky eye from some old wound. He looked at the scroll briefly and tossed it on the table with a grunt.

"The Prince has ordered us to move on York," de Ferrers said.

"Aye, I can see that," Van Hese said, irritation in his voice. "Your Prince is more prompt with his orders than with his pay. But we will move north as he asks—after we've settled with these bastards at Nottingham. But you, my lord, had best find some money soon, or my boys will go where they will."

That threat had come almost a fortnight ago. Van Hese had ordered his men as far as Sheffield and here they had sat for three days, refusing to move. He had called the leaders of the Flemings and those of the Irish together the night before and they had been barely civil to him. Several of them, he concluded, were drunk. They had made their position clear—the army would not move until paid and, in the event no further payment was forthcoming, they might simply march to ports on the Channel or the Irish Sea and go home. Or perhaps they'd march to York on their own accord and plunder the place.

"We'll not be leaving England without a profit," the Irish commander slurred, "and if all else fails, we might see what price you'd fetch as a hostage."

De Ferrers had little doubt this threat was real. The men had filed out and he had listened to another night of revelry punctuated by screams. Now, as he paced about the room, he could barely control his despair. A sharp knock on his chamber door brought him back to the present.

"Come."

It was the clerk he had elevated to replace Father Malachy. Young Jacob Booth was clever enough and knew his letters and figures, but de Ferrers found he missed the crafty priest—if a priest he had ever truly been. Malachy always had a strange ability to know what was happening in the Midlands and beyond and a gift for plotting. This new man had no such qualities and de Ferrers missed that.

The priest had been called away in late June, supposedly on some ecclesiastical mission. De Ferrers had little understanding of the church and less respect for the men who laboured in its service, but Malachy…there was a man he understood and in this burnt-out town he could have used the cunning priest.

"My lord," young Jacob began. "There is a man downstairs claiming to be the Sheriff of Yorkshire. He demands to see you."

De Ferrers felt a small throb over his right eye.

What now?

"Bring him up, Booth, and do not leave us. Are you armed?"

Booth looked nervous.

"I have a blade with my things in the next room, my lord."

"Bring your blade when you bring the Sheriff."

"Aye, my lord," the young man said and hurried away. A few minutes later de Ferrers heard footsteps on the stairs. Booth opened the door and announced the visitor.

"My lord, Sir Hugh Bardolf, High Sheriff of Yorkshire."

A big man with a red face and a strong jaw strode into the room. His hair was mussed and his clothes were coated with dust, though attempts to brush his tunic had clearly been made. He had two leather bags slung over a shoulder. He made a short bow to de Ferrers, stepped forward and dropped the bags on the table. They made a sound that could only mean they were heavy with coins.

William de Ferrers smiled, his headache forgotten.

"My lord Sheriff. Welcome to Sheffield."

***

The bargaining had been hard. The Sheriff of Yorkshire had brought enough silver to pay off the back wages of the mercenaries and a month more. De Ferrers had flatly rejected the offer.

"My lord Sheriff, do you not smell the burnt homes and shops of Sheffield? Did you not see the bodies growing ripe in the fields around the town? We would not want that for York, would we?"

Sir Hugh looked like a man caught between a fire and the frying pan.

"My lord, the people of York have scraped together all they could. It is a generous offer!"

"Twice this would be generous," de Ferrers said as he hefted the bags and dropped them with a sneer. "And twice this you will pay. It is common knowledge there is a fortune in silver in the vaults under the York Minster. You'd best squeeze your Archbishop and get it! In one month, you will deliver this same weight of silver, or, so help me, wherever these war dogs are, I will sic them on York! Am I understood?"

De Ferrers had hardly finished speaking when a heartrending scream floated up from the streets below. Sir Hugh Bardolf thought of his daughters.

"Yes, my lord. I understand. I will have the silver for you a month from today. Just keep these animals away from York."

"I knew we could reach a meeting of the minds," de Ferrers said and slapped the Sherriff on the shoulder. The man looked ill.

***

The Earl of Derby mounted his horse and looked at the long column of men forming up west of Sheffield. With back pay delivered, the mercenary leaders had suddenly become more agreeable to his leadership. The silver from York had bought its safety—for a time. No need now to frighten the northern barons—the silver proved they were already cowed.

With York subservient, Chester was now the prize he must gain for the Prince. The road to Chester ran west through the narrow valleys and passes of the high country of Derbyshire and he had unfinished business there. De Ferrers smiled as he saw the sergeants move up and down the line, bawling at their men to close up the ranks.

These were just the men he needed to pluck an old thorn from his side.

The Choice

*T*he sun was low in the sky when they reached the sheltered valley on the western slope of Kinder Scout. As they came down the trail toward the clearing, Roland could see that over a hundred men had already gathered there and more could be seen coming in from the north and further west.

"I've never seen this many of the men in one place," Oren said. "It's good. All will be affected by what is decided here, so the more the better."

They found Thorkell sitting on a stump and running a sharpening stone over an ancient broadsword. Oren left his brother with the war leader and went off to explore an appetizing smell coming from a cook pot across the clearing.

"Your blade takes a good edge," Roland said, looking at Thorkell's work on the old sword. "You don't see many of those here in the mountains."

Thorkell looked up and grinned at him.

"I took this off of one of Lord Robert's men when we fought them twenty years ago. I wrapped it in oilcloth and buried it in one of the caves north of here. Hoped I'd never need to dig it back up, but…"

Roland watched the man draw the stone over the blade with long steady strokes.

"My father never spoke to us about the rising twenty years ago. Tell me about it. Tell me about him."

Thorkell stopped his labours and looked up at Roland, his expression somewhere between pride and sadness.

"We rose back then for the same reasons we now go armed for war in our own land. The Normans would not leave us be. Lord Robert was a young man then, and headstrong. He controlled all of Derbyshire with an iron hand, except these mountains. It irked him, so he sent men here to enforce his will. They did not come back, so he sent more men with the same result."

"And my father?"

Thorkell's face looked pained.

"I was angry the people chose your father to be our war leader over me. If Earl Robert was spoiling for a fight back then, I was more than ready to give it to him. I was young and bold, with a thirst for glory. I thought I could lead the Danes to victory. Your father had a new bride—your mother, Mara. He was troubled by what war might bring to our people. I was spoiling for a fight and thought him a coward because he counselled caution, but the people chose him to lead us, not I."

"I didn't know."

Thorkell nodded. "We few who survived among the fighters never spoke much of those days after it was all over. We just went back to our farms and families—those that had them."

Thorkell paused once more. His eyes seemed to look beyond the valley and the present.

"You know, your father and I became fast friends. Rolf was a brave and clever man. He seemed to understand, better than any of us, how the Normans fought and he used that knowledge to help us kill a great many of them. He was not a bloodthirsty man. I think he felt sorry for the poor Saxon lads Lord Robert sent into the hills to catch us. In time we actually came down out of the mountains and took the fight to them. The farmers in the valleys, most of them Saxons, joined us. We besieged Peveril Castle for two months."

"Friar Tuck said he fought with the Danes back then."

"Aye, he was one of the youngest of us. He was the miller's son in Castleton. His name was Bernard as I recall, but all called him Tuck—I'm not sure why. When the King sent his men in to rescue Lord Robert and break the siege, we had to scatter. We never knew if Tuck survived until he appeared as Father Augustine many years later. I was surprised to see him as a churchman. As a boy, he was deadly with a blade."

"He still is," Roland said.

Thorkell stood up and touched the edge of his sword with a thumb. Satisfied, he slid it back into a leather scabbard.

"Most of the men should be here before nightfall," he said, gazing around the clearing and doing a quick estimate of the numbers in the valley. If you count the boys of twelve and older among the men, we are a dozen short of two hundred fighters in all."

"Enough to save Chester," said Roland.

"Enough to defend our mountains as well. The Earl's men have ravaged the valleys and have come further into the mountains than at any time since your father and I fought them twenty years ago. They've burned a few farms, but we have always turned them back. They are not over fond of our bows—but you know that."

Roland nodded.

"Aye, in this the Normans are fools. The King once told me that if he had five thousand longbowman he could conquer China, but they only see the bow as a danger to their rule. They are blind."

"True enough, lad. With only twenty or thirty good bows we almost beat Lord Robert and his men. Now we have five times that number."

"Enough to make a difference when Earl Ranulf meets Prince John's men. It's why he is willing to grant you the land. He needs you."

Thorkell nodded.

"That's clear enough, but do we need your Earl? That is the question our men will answer tonight. All have been told the gist of your offer, but I will allow you to speak a last time to make your case."

"Will you speak, Thorkell?"

"No. The men must decide for themselves and I will abide by their choice. No doubt Svein will have something to say. He is angry with me for calling this gathering to consider your bargain. He is convinced you are false and we should have just killed you. That boy thirsts to kill Normans—as I once did."

"Stay or go, Thorkell, there will be Normans enough to kill I think. Perhaps I can convince him of that."

"Perhaps, but he is stubborn—has been since he was born."

"You know the family?"

"Aye, I know them all too well. Svein is my son."

"Your son...I didn't know." Roland started to say more, but a loud greeting from across the clearing stopped him.

"Roland Inness!"

Roland turned to see a tall lean man hurrying toward him. It was Odo, their old neighbour.

"Odo! It's good to see you, though I wish it was under better circumstances."

Odo grinned and placed two large, gnarled farmer's hands on Roland's shoulders.

"It's good to see you, boy, and damn the circumstances. It's been lonely over on the eastern slope since...well, since you left. Your father and mother were good people We heard from Tuck that de Ferrers had not caught you, but have only heard rumours since—most of them said Brun had killed you in York. Tuck took your brother and sister into his care and we thought that it was the end of the Inness clan on Kinder Scout—until your Oren came home in the spring."

Roland returned the man's smile.

"Oren tells me he stays with you when he is not patrolling these days. I hope you work him hard for his bread."

"Oh, you can be sure of that. He eats a lot, but he earns his keep. We had hoped to clear some of the weeds from your farmstead next spring and put in a crop. The boy has his heart set on farming your old place, but now..."

Oren hadn't mentioned that.

***

It was full night when the last of the men trailed into the camp. Roland stood with Oren and Odo at the edge of the clearing and watched them come. A few of the new arrivals who had known the Inness family in earlier days came forward to greet him, but none offered an opinion on the issue to be decided this night.

Three sizable fires had been started to provide light for the assembly and Thorkell stepped forward to begin the proceedings.

"You men have been summoned to decide upon a matter of great weight. My messengers have given you the gist of the offer that has been placed before us, but you should hear it directly from the man who has brought it to us."

He turned to Roland.

"Present your offer, sir."

Before he stepped forward, Roland saw Svein separate from a knot of men and walk into the circle of light from the fires. A low buzz rippled through the crowd and the young Dane raised a hand for silence.

"I will speak!" he said, his voice thick with passion. "We must not take this bargain, for to my eyes it is nothing more than a trick to lure us from these hills to the lowlands where we will be cut down like sheep. Has any man here cause to trust the word of a Norman?"

The soft buzz of the crowd had swelled to an angry hum.

"I trust the word of a Norman." Roland shouted above the uproar and the crowd quieted a little.

"I have as much right as any to hate the Normans. They killed my father and almost killed me, but it was a Norman who saved me."

"And now you've become a Norman yourself," Svein sneered, "and a traitor to your own people!"

Roland flushed.

"You call me traitor? I would watch your tongue—or is that the only weapon you are willing to draw against me?"

Svein reached for the long skinning knife at his side, but Thorkell seized his wrist. He looked between the two young men who stood glaring at each other.

"There will be none of that here!"

The crowd had grown quiet as the two men faced off. Thorkell turned to them.

"Inness will have his say. Let him speak and we will then decide amongst ourselves." He turned to his son and snarled in his ear. "Sit down and shut up." Furious, Svein elbowed his way through the crowd and out of the circle of firelight.

Roland gathered himself as he got his temper under control. He took a deep breath and began.

"We Danes once ruled here—from York to Oxford. We fought the Saxons for control of this island for generations, but we lost that fight. The longboats stopped coming from across the North Sea and we were forced to make our peace with the Saxons. Then the Normans came and pissed on Dane and Saxon alike. They drove the Danes from rich farmsteads in the fertile lowlands into these barren hills an age ago. Since then, we've scraped out a living on the fringes of this country."

Roland paused. It was a history they all knew, but he saw that men were leaning in.

"It is easy to love these mountains," he said, "but it is time that we, like our fathers' fathers found a better land—a better place to feed our families. A hide is five times the land any of you can claim here in the high country. It's land enough to raise your children where famine does not take them. The Earl of Chester is a Norman, through and through, but he is a man of his word. The land he offers is rich land and he offers it because he needs us. Now is the time for the Danes to come down from the hills."

He paused once more and pointed into the darkness outside the ring of firelight.

"There is a war out there. Till now, it has barely touched you, but I believe that it will. You can wait for it to come to the foot of these hills or you can take this offer from Earl Ranulf. Come down while the Normans fight amongst themselves. We may not be able to throw off their rule but we can prosper from their war. You know what William de Ferrers has to offer— oppression and death. Ranulf of Chester has given you another choice. You should take it."

He had had his say and stepped back. Thorkell stepped up and spoke quietly to him.

61

"Take your Saxon friend and find a place out of earshot. I will call you when a decision has been reached."

Roland nodded and walked away from the circle of light, motioning for Sir Edgar to follow. Oren caught up to him.

"You spoke well, brother."

"I am no talker, Oren, but the offer is an honest one and I hope the men take it. On which side will you speak?"

Oren stopped.

"Roland, I have no desire to leave here. I've had it in mind to work our farm, once the trouble is passed."

"Odo told me."

"But listening to you, I fear trouble may never pass by the Danes—as long as a de Ferrers is the Earl of Derby. I will speak in favour of your offer, but whatever is decided…I stay with the Danes."

Roland put his hand on his brother's shoulder.

"Oren, you are a man now and must make your own decisions. Whatever you decide, I will always be your brother."

To his surprise, Oren threw his arms around his neck and hugged him.

"And I, yours."

Then he was gone, back into the circle of light to decide the fate of the Danes.

The gathering lasted late into the night with the sound of voices rising and falling—some pleading and others angry, though the words were not plain. Near midnight Thorkell stopped the debate. Roland could not hear what the man said, but when he had finished men moved off into two groups on opposite ends of the clearing. They were choosing sides. A count of heads would not be necessary. One group was twice the size of the other. He saw his brother and his heart sank. Oren was in the smaller group.

Thorkell spoke once more and the men began to drift away to find someplace to curl up for the night. The war leader came across the clearing with Oren alongside him. Roland rose to meet them.

"The Danes have spoken," Thorkell said. "The answer is no."

The Ransomed Crown

***

Oren and Roland stayed up into the small hours of the morning as Sir Edgar snored peacefully beside the banked fire. Oren had made his decision to stay with the Danes, and would not waver from it. Roland's efforts to convince him to leave were half-hearted. He understood loyalty.

Oren, in turn, tried to convince his brother to stay.

"Roland, Thorkell is a good leader, but he is not young. When he grows too old, others, like Svein, will make their claim to leadership. I think that will be bad for the Danes. He itches for a fight—a fight I doubt we could win. You have been to war. You know the Normans like no one here. You, brother, should be our next war leader."

Roland nodded. He agreed with all Oren had said, but he had his own loyalties.

"Oren, I am the sworn man of Sir Roger de Laval. God knows where he is in the world, but until he releases me from my oath I must act in his interests. All that is dear to him is threatened by the war between the Normans and I must do what I can to protect those things. And Oren, there is a girl, Sir Roger's daughter..."

He saw his brother's eyes widen in the firelight.

"Tell me about this sweet maiden, Roland," he said with a touch of sly humour in his voice. "Is she beautiful?"

Roland laughed.

"If you called Millie de Laval a sweet maiden, she might try to cut out your liver—but beautiful? She's the most beautiful girl in England, I'd warrant."

Oren slapped him on the shoulder and sighed.

"I might have talked you out of your allegiance to this Sir Roger, but the most beautiful girl in England? I can see it is a lost cause. I will go with you and Sir Edgar on the morrow—as far as your horses. What will happen is in God's hands."

***

A heavy fog blanketed the hidden valley at dawn as Roland and Edgar gathered their kit and weapons and prepared to climb the ridge to the east. Oren watched their preparations morosely.

63

"I know the place you left the horses," he said, looking up the slope covered in thick grey mist. "I've seen that old man. He sometimes comes up the mountain to avoid the patrols in the valley, but he has never harmed anything of the Danes, so we leave him be."

"Let's just hope he managed to keep our mounts hidden. It's a long walk back to Chester."

Together they climbed the trail to the top of the ridge. Roland stopped at the crest and looked around at the four points of the compass. The tops of hills, covered in their summer green, could be seen for miles with grey layers of fog hanging in the valleys between. Toward the south, the rocky summit of Kinder Scout caught the morning light and seemed to glow.

He felt a tightening in his chest. This land was beautiful, but it was no longer his home. He looked off to the west. That was where his heart was now. His home was wherever a certain brown-haired girl was waiting. He would be heading back to her this day with crushing news.

The Danes would not be coming to the relief of Chester.

Chess Pieces

Walter of Coutances looked down at the chess board and arched an eyebrow. The young priest who sat across from him had played cautiously early in the game, but now he moved his knight into an exposed forward position. Was this a blunder or a trap? The obvious response was to block the knight's escape with his rook and take the piece with his queen. It would open up an entire file and expose the white king to attack.

But was it too easy? He had not played this young man before and had seen nothing in his early moves to suggest subtlety, but the Archbishop of Rouen was no novice at this game. He looked at the board carefully. He surveyed three moves ahead, then four.

No danger.

Five moves forward.

Ah, there it was!

A trap had been set that would snare his queen and even threaten his king. The Archbishop felt a twinge of disappointment. This priest was good—just not good enough for the delicate thing he needed done. For that, he needed someone who could think more than five moves ahead.

Still, the boy was clever and could be put to good use on some lesser task. The Archbishop ignored the knight and moved a bishop to near the centre of the board, then rose and walked to a window while the younger man contemplated the collapse of his careful gambit.

Looking out into the garden behind his lodgings, he saw a dog curled up in the shade of a fruit tree, its tail occasionally thumping contentedly against the ground. The Archbishop sighed. He didn't much like dogs, but envied them their single-minded pursuit of comfort and lack of care.

Would that men could be as content with their lot as were dogs! But the nature of man was to strive, and in their striving, men were capable of the most admirable feats and the most appalling wickedness. His recognition of this simple fact had helped to raise him up from a lowly clerk in King Henry's service to Justiciar of England—in service to Henry's son, King Richard.

In his many years of observing the character of men, he had developed no illusions about his own nature. He was no dog thumping his tail in the shade. He relished the prestige and power that came with his current position and did not intend to lose either. Ultimately, power, prestige and position all flowed from the King—but from which king—John, who acted as though he was already crowned or Richard, crowned but absent?

John's aggressive assertion of his position was forcing men of rank all over England to choose. Neither man was a prize as a king, so the Archbishop had chosen neither. He had chosen the most capable ruler he knew. He had cast his lot with Eleanor of Aquitaine. The Queen had given him the burden of extending and strengthening the spy network she had started to build, a challenge he found both intriguing and frustrating.

Over the past winter, one of his own spies had been discovered in the employ of William de Ferrers, Earl of Derby, and John's primary supporter in the Midlands. He'd heard that his man had died painfully. In the spring, two ladies, recruited by the Queen, had been unmasked within Prince John's court and were even now held under close arrest in John's new possession—Nottingham Castle.

Both Philip of France and Prince John had agents at work in England. John's spies were more numerous but not as skilled. One had recently been uncovered working as a clerk for the Earl of Oxford, Lord High Chamberlain of England. The boy confessed all before they hung him and disposed of the body in the Thames. It was the French who worried him.

The plot to use Earl Ranulf's wife to implicate him in treason had been very clever and was very likely hatched by Philip's agents. The priest who had suborned Lady Constance was connected to the Earl of Derby, but there was strong evidence his real master was not William de Ferrers. That nobleman, the Queen had assured him, had neither the brains nor the bollocks to conjure up such a brilliant manoeuvre. It had to be the French.

Then there was the matter of the attempt to relieve Nottingham in June. William Marshal's plan had relied heavily on surprise and only the Archbishop and the Queen had been informed of his intentions. That John's mercenaries were perfectly placed to fall on the relief column as they crossed the River Soar was simply too convenient. Somehow, the Prince had been warned that a relief column was coming. The warning could have come from John's own agents, but he strongly suspected the information had been passed to him by the French.

The compromise of Marshal's plan raised suspicions on all sides. Was there a spy in his friend's household or that of the Queen? He dismissed the idea of a traitor close to the Queen. Eleanor's closest companions were women who had shared fifteen years of captivity with her when her husband, King Henry, had locked her away. And with these loyal women, she never discussed affairs of state.

But what of his own people? Most of his staff had been with him for years, and he had tested them—had laid clever traps to reveal any who might be betraying his secrets. None had been snared. No, the traitor must be among William Marshal's household and associates here in London. The Archbishop had enormous respect for his fellow Justiciar, but felt the man had a blind spot. Incapable of treachery himself, Marshal had difficulty seeing it in others.

The man would no doubt bridle at the thought that any of his people were traitors, but in the end he would see the need to confirm their loyalty. The Archbishop had made a point of deferring to Marshal on all things military and his fellow Justiciar had granted him the same deference on all things concerning the Queen's spy network. In the end, Marshal would trust him.

The Archbishop watched as the dog got up and extended its front legs to stretch and yawn before trotting off in search of whatever it might find on a warm summer day. For all of its cold and damp much of the year, London's weather could be rather pleasant in July. He would have to follow the dog's example and go for a stroll after his midday meal, but first, he had to consider what to do with the young priest. Five moves ahead was not bad.

But it would not do.

He turned away from the window and spoke to the young man who was still pondering a new strategy.

"My son, I fear we will need to continue our game another time."

"Of course, excellency. I would like that."

The Archbishop came forward and laid a hand on the priest's shoulder.

"Come to me tomorrow. I have a problem I think you can help me solve."

The priest nodded eagerly.

"Anything, your excellency."

The archbishop smiled as the priest withdrew and looked down at the chess board. He sat down heavily and sighed. This had been his third interview of the day and only this boy looked promising—just not promising enough. He would find a use for the young priest, but knew he was not up to the more delicate task he had in mind.

Mary Cullen, his most trusted servant, entered the room quietly and brought his mid-morning indulgence—fresh cider and sweet cakes. He had brought Mary with him when he left Rouen for London. She was young with short brown hair and intelligent eyes. Alone among his staff and servants, he trusted her to be a part of the real work he did for the Queen.

Mary was a clever girl and, had she not been well known as a member of his household, he might have used her for this task. But her appearance struck a spark. There was another girl—the one from Chester—the one who had saved Ranulf's head. That one had a keen eye and a level head and was brave in the bargain.

She was someone who thought more than five moves ahead.
What was her name? Ah, yes.

Millicent de Laval.

The Harrowing

As the morning sun rose higher, the fog began to burn away. The trail down the eastern slope of Kinder Scout switched back and forth following the contour of the mountain. The three men came to the farmstead Roland and Sir Edgar had passed two days before as prisoners. The man had not yet returned from the meeting on the opposite side of the ridge, but a woman and the two young boys were already at their labours.

The older boy was pulling weeds from the barley crop and the younger was helping his mother with repairs to a small pen where the family pig was confined. It was a peaceful scene. The boy weeding the field looked up and waved as they approached, but the mother and her younger son, intent on their task, never noticed them pass.

They were still well above the valley floor when Roland saw first one, then three more crows rise up from below, loudly cawing at whatever had disturbed them. He scanned the skies for a hawk they may have been heckling, but saw none. Something in the valley had disturbed the birds. Then a sound reached him that made him freeze. It was the faint, but unmistakable, sound of metal on metal. He grabbed Oren's arm and turned to Edgar, raising a finger to his lips for silence.

The sound came again, clearer this time, then yet again. It could have been the sound of a farmer's billhook scraping against a scythe or some other metal tool, but they had been in this valley three days before. There were no farmers left there.

Roland started forward, moving with more urgency than before and the others fell in silently behind. To get a look at what was in the valley, they would have to get much closer and find a safe vantage point. They came to a small game trail and Oren touched his arm, pointing down the path to the right. Roland nodded and let his brother take the lead. The sounds in the valley grew louder. Now the snorting of horses and the distant shouts of men could be heard below.

They came to a place where part of the hillside had collapsed, leaving a scar of bare earth and a debris field of rocks and downed trees below. From just above the lip of the slide they could see the road clearly without being seen. It was a sobering sight. A large force of infantry was marching along the muddy track that hugged the opposite bank of the stream at the bottom of the valley.

"De Ferrers." Oren whispered.

Roland shook his head. He could tell by their weapons and style of dress that these were no local men-at-arms employed by the Earl of Derby. These men had a distinctive look about them that he'd seen once before. In the winter just past, men such as these had tried to ambush the Invalid Company on the road from Shrewsbury to Chester.

"Flemish mercenaries," he whispered back. "They were moving north toward York last I heard, but it seems they've turned west."

They watched from hiding as a continual stream of men passed by. There seemed no end to the column. Then an officer on horseback rode up and signalled a halt. Sergeants shouted orders and men split off from the path. A few seemed to be engaged in setting up a camp, but the rest crossed the stream and moved into the woods below the slide.

Roland rolled onto his side.

"We've feared they'd march on Chester, but if that was their goal, they would not be on this trail. The main road from Castleton to the west is well south of here." He looked down the slope as a hundred or more men emerged from the band of trees by the stream. The group split to either side of the tangle of rocks and trees in the debris field and began climbing the slope toward them.

"They aren't marching to Chester," Roland said with finality.

"They're coming for us," said Oren, his voice bleak.

For another minute they watched the men labour up the hill toward them.

"How large is this force?" Oren asked. "I counted five hundred as they passed this point, but I don't know how much further the column stretches."

"Last month our scouts set their number of foot soldiers at three times that or more," Roland said. "They have over four hundred heavy cavalry, but mounted troops would be of little use here."

"We have to warn Thorkell and gather the men," Oren said.

"Aye, but let's slow them down and give them something to worry about before we go."

Roland stood and nocked an arrow. Oren scrambled up beside him and did the same. Roland wondered whether the boy had ever drawn his bow in anger before. This was not a white birch he was aiming at. It was a man's chest. The brothers drew together.

Oren loosed before he did. A sharp cry from below announced that the arrow had flown true as one of the men on the slope below toppled over backwards. Roland loosed his own shaft and a second man went down. The line of men below now scrambled to find shelter behind stumps and fallen timbers.

Roland looked at Oren. The boy turned away quickly and retched into the bushes. When he'd finished emptying his stomach, he turned back to face his brother.

"Your first?" Roland asked.

Oren nodded mutely.

"It gets easier with practice," he said grimly, "and those men down there have a lot more practice at killing than we do. They'll be circling around on either side of us soon."

He looked at Oren again. His brother still looked stunned at what he had just done. But now was no time to contemplate the right and wrong of such things or to offer comfort.

"Oren, take the lead. We have to get to Thorkell." The boy blinked and seemed to come out of his daze.

"Right, follow me," he said, and headed back up the game trail, back to warn Thorkell.

War had come in earnest to the Danes.

***

Roland and Oren dove behind a cluster of deadfall trees as two crossbow bolts buzzed over their heads. They landed beside Sir Edgar who had staked out this spot for their next defensive stand. They had been fighting almost continually for three days as the troops of the mercenary army slowly pushed up the slopes of Kinder Scout.

The longbowmen had taken a heavy toll on the invaders, but these Flemish and Irish soldiers were not fools. They quickly adapted their tactics to the steep terrain and the threat posed by the lethal longbows of the Danes. The mercenary troops had pushed relentlessly up every trail, the lead ranks of infantry carrying shields to protect the crossbowmen who were assigned to each assault group.

Behind the deadfall, Roland's chest heaved as he took in great gasps of air. Sweat stung his eyes and, beside him, Oren was sucking in air. They had bolted from their hiding place a hundred yards down the trail having been flushed out by troops sent to circle around them.

"Any sign of flankers?" he gasped to Sir Edgar who was peering cautiously over the trunk of a huge fallen oak.

The big Saxon shook his head.

"Not yet, but soon I'd wager." He sank down and jerked a thumb back over his shoulder. "The game trail just to our front— I think some of the Danish lads are down that way. By the looks of it, they should be along any minute."

Roland nodded wearily. Thorkell had organized his men to guard the main trails, but they could not keep watch on every approach. Time after time, the Danes were forced back when the enemy found a way around them. It had become an exhausting routine of fight, then run, then fight again. By the third day, the thin line of bowmen had been forced to retreat to just below the long north-south ridge that led up to the summit of Kinder Scout. Another day of this and they would be swept off the crest of the mountains and lose the advantage of the high ground.

The families of those who worked farms on the eastern side of the mountain had already fled as the danger crept closer. Roland, Oren and Sir Edgar had retreated past the farm they had seen three days before. The woman, her two sons and the pig were gone. Soon after, a column of black smoke rose from where the abandoned steading lay. To the north and south, other black smudges in the sky marked other farms being burnt.

Roland heard a shout in Danish from below, then movement off to their left front. The three men huddled in the deadfall grasped their weapons and eased into position to see what was coming toward them from down the slope. There were three of them. One man watched back down the trail with his bow half drawn. The second dragged the third who had a crossbow bolt imbedded in his calf. The wounded man was Svein.

Roland rose from cover.

"Here! Bring him here!"

The man dragging Svein swerved off the trail and almost tumbled his burden to the ground, but Sir Edgar reached out a massive hand to catch the wounded Dane. Svein looked more angry than injured as he was lowered to the ground.

"Pull it out!" he ordered.

Roland squatted to examine the wound. The steel head of the bolt had passed clean through the calf muscle and protruded a full inch from the exit wound. He drew his dagger from his boot. Svein eyed the weapon with its jewelled hilt.

"Fancy blade there," he said.

"It was once Ivo Brun's," Roland replied. "Someone hold him still. This will hurt."

Svein waved off the man who reached to steady him, but gave an involuntary gasp of pain as Roland took hold of the head of the bolt and began gouging the wood of the shaft. He had learned how to deal with such a wound in the Clocaenog forest when Millicent de Laval had taken an arrow from his thigh.

He cut halfway through the wood, then with a quick twist of his wrist, he broke off the head, tossing it aside. Svein's jaw was clinched shut to cut off any cry as the jolt of pain hit him, but his face was covered in sweat as Roland grasped the five inches of shaft that protruded from the other side of the man's calf. He looked at Svein, who nodded.

In one motion, he yanked the bolt back through the passage it had made in the man's flesh. Fresh blood seeped from the wound, but slowly. No major vessel had been hit. Sir Edgar had been watching the proceedings and handed him a length of rag. It was filthy, but it would stop the bleeding. Roland tied it firmly around Svein's calf.

"Can you walk?"

Svein nodded and hauled himself up gingerly. He winced but was able to put weight on his injured leg.

"They were already behind us when I took this," he said gesturing at his leg. "They'll be around us by..."

His words were cut off by the sound of movement up the slope behind them. They turned to see five men with shields and lances charging down the trail from above with two crossbowmen following. They'd been flanked.

A crossbow bolt flew by just to Roland's left and dug itself into the great fallen oak behind them. Three longbows came up as one and, in an instant, both crossbowmen were down. But the five men to the front were committed now. For three days they had endured death and wounds as they watched the lightly armed Danes flee whenever they sought to close on them. Soldiers for hire they might be, but this fight was no longer about money. The wild, wailing Gaelic war cry that burst from their lips was filled with genuine hatred.

Sir Edgar sprang forward to meet them. Seeing the huge shaggy warrior rise up with axe in hand, the mercenaries hesitated, but it was too late to check their headlong charge. If these hireling warriors had been frustrated by the long distance nature of the fighting, the big Saxon was even more so. With an evil smile he swung his axe in a slow sweeping arc from side to side as he waited to finally strike a blow at the enemy.

The narrow trail could only give passage to two men abreast and the two leading the charge sought to use their bulk and momentum to bludgeon the lone man blocking their way. They were not prepared for the thundering impact of Sir Edgar's big war axe, which splintered one of the shields and drove its owner into the man next to him. Unbalanced, the two tried to recover, but staggered off the trail into thick brush.

Trusting that his companions would deal with them, Sir Edgar moved up the trail to meet the three men who followed. These men had now stopped dead on the trail. The mercenary in the middle was almost as big as Sir Edgar, with heavily muscled shoulders and a neck like a bull. He edged forward, his shield held high and his lance resting easily on its top edge. While the others might hesitate, this man had earned his living for fifteen years killing other men and was not overawed by the big man to his front. He had killed bigger.

Sir Edgar grinned at the man. He had heard a brief clash of steel followed by groans behind him and knew without looking that the first two mercenaries were no longer a threat. He beckoned the big Irish warrior forward.

The man was happy to oblige. He thrust with his lance, but it was a feint meant to draw his enemy out of position. Sir Edgar did not take the feint and as the mercenary drove the lance at the big man's stomach, he twisted to the side, swatting the weapon away with a massive paw as though it were a bothersome insect.

The Irishman's momentum had taken him inside the killing arc of Edgar's axe. He desperately swung his oaken shield up but it could not save him. It splintered as the razor sharp steel did its work and the man felt his entire left arm go numb from the blow. He swung the lance around in a final effort to defend himself, but knew he had drawn his last pay for killing men.

The two remaining men on the trail had watched in horror as their comrades fell, their thirst for revenge now replaced with raw fear. They began backing away, keeping their shields high. When they reached the game trail they had crept down to get behind these Danes, they turned and ran.

"Let them go," Roland said. "There'll be others behind us 'for long. We need to move." He looked at the downed mercenaries around them. "Take their lances and retrieve your arrows, we may have need of those—and get that wound cleaned out before it festers," he said, pointing at Svein's leg.

Svein moved forward, gingerly at first, but the pain was manageable and he shook off help from his companions. He nodded to Roland.

"I'll be back before nightfall."

Roland nodded back.

"Good, we need you."

As the day wore on, they were forced further up the slope. It was only a few hundred yards now to the crest of the ridge as they watched the trail below them. A sound came from behind and all three men whirled around, expecting trouble from the rear once more. But it was Thorkell, coming down the trail from above at a crouching run. The war leader ducked as a well-aimed crossbow bolt flew overhead. He looked at their exhausted faces and Roland looked back at a man who looked beyond weary.

"We can't stop them," Thorkell said flatly. "There are too many."

Roland nodded.

"These are not de Ferrers' men, but I see his hand in this. The mercenaries have no interest in us or this land and I doubt the Prince does either. There is no loot here. They are doing the Earl's work for him. The Danes have plagued the de Ferrers family for generations and he wants us dead or driven from Derbyshire. This is his chance to do it."

Thorkell gave a weary nod. Roland studied the older man. He'd seen the wiry strength that had kept the war leader moving at a killing pace throughout the long days of fighting as they tried in vain to throw back the enemy. But no man could sustain that effort forever. Now, for the first time, Thorkell looked old.

"So what are we to do?" he asked, but Roland could sense he already knew the answer. He spoke the word that now was their only hope.

"Chester."

Thorkell sighed and shrugged his shoulders. "I did not speak at the gathering, but I favoured your bargain. I feared a day such as this might come. Now it has and the Danes must seek refuge where they can. Can we reach the city before we are overwhelmed?"

Roland wiped the sweat from his eyes and considered the distance from these mountains to the walls of Chester. The Danes were hardy, but there would be women and children and the mercenaries would press them hard.

"I don't know, Thorkell, but we must try."

The war leader of the Danes seemed to gather himself.

"Aye, I see no other way. I will send runners to gather the people. We must hold this side of the mountain as long as we can."

Roland put a hand on Thorkell's shoulder.

"We'll hold them," he said, grimly. "Gather the people in the valley."

***

Night was falling around the flanks of Kinder Scout when the families assembled in the sheltered valley west of the summit. There were over eight hundred souls gathered there—grandfathers, babes being suckled in their mother's arms, skinny girls, dirty-faced boys—and all looked frightened.

It had been over a hundred years since the Danes had been pushed into these high hills. Generations had sweated and bled for their little patch of earth and none in this high valley could remember any other home. Most had never been more than ten miles from their farmstead and now they must march off into the darkness to find shelter in a place they had never seen. It was terrifying, but they knew what awaited them if they stayed.

Roland looked out over the clearing at the mass of people milling in the twilight and felt his gut clinch. These were his people. He had sprung from them and now they were staking their lives on his promise of refuge in Chester. A strong man could make the hike from these mountains to the gates of the city in a long day and a night, but it would take at least twice that for this collection of the young and old to cover the distance. The

Danes would leave no one behind and thus all would move at the speed of the slowest.

Their fighting strength was down to one hundred and seventy, though some of them were wounded and many were hardly more than boys. Twenty of the youngest who could wield a bow were given the task of staying close to the families on the long march to Chester. Sir Edgar would lead them. The rest would delay the advance of the mercenaries wherever they could and for as long as they could.

Roland had wanted to send Oren with Sir Edgar, but there were younger boys than his brother who could handle a longbow. Oren had given him a look of pure defiance that ended any notion of sending him with the women and children. Roland had watched his brother fight over the past five days. Had seen him struggle at first with the killing, but the boy had never wavered. He looked at Oren's lined and dirty face and had to admit that he was more man now than boy. His brother would stay with the rear guard and face the mercenaries with the other men.

Thorkell approached him as the twilight thickened.

"These are all that are coming. A few families could not bring themselves to leave their homes. They've gone into the caves and cloughs. We must pray they aren't found."

"Aye, leaving these mountains…it's hard. We must hope those who remain escape notice. Now we have to get the rest moving."

Roland turned and looked back to the east. As the night grew darker, the glow of campfires from the mercenary army could be plainly seen above the tree line that capped the ridge. His own men tended fires in the valley and would keep them burning through the night so that any enemy watchers would be unaware the Danes were preparing to flee. He turned back to Thorkell.

"They'll come in force up every trail and ravine at dawn," he said. "They know if they reach the crest of the ridge they will have won. We will hold them as long as we can up there, then fall back when we must. It's a good fifty miles to Chester. Every hour we hold them is an hour closer to safety for the families."

Thorkell nodded just as Sir Edgar hurried up, slightly dragging his bad leg. He saw Roland glance at it.

"All this clamberin' up and down the mountains has made it stiff," he said with an injured tone. "It'll be fine once we reach the flatlands."

Roland smiled at him. There was no gamer man than Edgar Langton.

"It's time to get them moving, Sir Edgar. God go with you and I'll see you in Chester."

"In Chester," he replied curtly and turned on his heel. In short order, he had his twenty boys with longbows assigned to their places in the column, some with torches that they lit from the campfires. A family at a time, the Danes began to rise and move off into the darkness.

The trail narrowed quickly as it left the clearing, making progress slow, but each family waited quietly until it was their turn to join the exodus. Thirty minutes after the order was given, the last of them had disappeared into the night. Men drifted to the western edge of the high valley and watched the faint points of light bob in the darkness as the moving column made its way toward the lowlands. Many were thankful that the darkness hid their tears.

Roland watched the flickering lights grow smaller and worried about what the morrow would bring. The Danes had seen the force arrayed against them. Over a thousand seasoned troops would be coming up every trail and along every ridgeline in the morning. They had to hold this army at bay as long as they could for the sake of their families.

Once the families were well on their way, Thorkell called the men together. He turned and nodded to Roland who faced those gathered around the largest bonfire. He saw Svein standing in the front rank, as dirty and weary as the rest. Before he could begin, the tall Dane stepped forward and turned to the crowd.

"You all know I spoke against the bargain Inness brought us. Had a thousand enemies not invaded our mountains, I would still speak against it! I do not trust the Normans, but our people must live and to stay here means death. If we must now stake our lives on the word of the Earl of Chester and that of Roland Inness, then we must." He paused for a moment, and looked back at Roland.

"I called Roland Inness a traitor to our people when first he came to us with this bargain," he said. "I thought him a creature of the Normans, but he has stood with us in this fight when he could have run." He stopped and gathered himself. "I take back my words," he said flatly. "Roland Inness is a Dane." With that, he limped to his place and nodded curtly toward Roland. Roland nodded in return, then spoke to the assembled fighters..

"Each man will hold his place on the ridge as long as possible," he began. "When the mercenaries began to break through, Thorkell will blow three blasts on a hunting horn. It's your signal to turn and run for the clearing in the valley. The enemy will not be far behind and if they run us to ground, we are all dead men." He stopped to let his words have their effect. "But that will not happen. Those men have shields and mail and even if they did not, they could never outrun a Dane."

"Not one who's running for his life!" someone called from the crowd to nervous laughter.

Roland smiled. Men who could jest were not yet beaten.

"Aye, we run for our lives, and we could outrun them all the way to Chester, but we won't. Your families cannot outrun them, so we must slow them. When these bastards think we are no more than hares to be chased, we must turn and show our teeth. You longbowmen, you will find the lowlands to your liking. There's not a man among you that can't drop a deer—or a man at two hundred paces, but here," he said, gesturing to the surrounding mountains and thick forests, "you rarely can see a man at more than fifty paces. Below, the land is flatter and there are open fields with nowhere for them to hide. There are a hundred places between here and Chester where we can strike at them and fall back before they can close on us. We might not be able to kill them all, but, by God, we will bloody them all the way to Chester if needs be."

He finished and looked at the tired faces of the men in the clearing. It was a simple enough plan, but he had not told them all the risks. If the infantry could get within lance and sword range, the advantage of the archers was lost and the foot soldiers would slice them to pieces. It was true that the Danes could easily outrun the more heavily armed infantry, but it was not the infantry that left him unsettled—it was the cavalry.

The Danes could not outrun cavalry.

If mounted men found them in the open they would close on the archers too quickly for their bows to save them. Declan's scouts had counted four hundred armoured knights among the foreign troops. If even a small part of that force caught them on the march, it would be a bloody slaughter.

Mounted troops were useless in the mountains and none had been seen in the valley at the base of Kinder Scout. Perhaps they had moved on toward York and were not a real threat, but with the foot soldiers engaged against the Danes, he doubted they were far off. The valley where Castleton lay had excellent pasturage for mounted stock and he guessed that this was where the cavalry was encamped, waiting for the infantry to clear the mountains.

He had held his tongue about the threat of cavalry. But once the foot soldiers fought their way to the summit of Kinder Scout and realized that the Danes had fled, they would send word for the mounted troops to take up the pursuit—if that force was as near as Castleton. Roland hoped to delay that until at least early afternoon. That would give the fleeing families a twelve hour head start. It was the best he could hope for.

The men left behind continued to feed wood to the flames so that the glow in the sky was visible to the men on the far side of the ridge. Roland wandered away from the campfires to think. He had done the same the night before he led the assault on the Bridgegate at Chester in the spring. That night, Millicent de Laval had found him standing in the dark and his life had not been the same since. He wondered what she would think when he led nine hundred Danes into Chester. She would have to figure out how to feed that many more mouths should the mercenaries lay siege to the city.

Let's cross one river at a time.

He turned to the east and looked off in the direction of the lowlands, toward the Irish Sea and Chester. It was a beautiful summer evening and in the high country the night sky was clear. Even with bonfires roaring behind him he could see a blaze of stars above. He turned back toward the clearing and saw Oren had already curled up to sleep. That was good.

Tomorrow would be a long day.

***

William de Ferrers stood outside his tent and looked to the west. All across the eastern slopes of the hulking ridgeline of Kinder Scout, there were points of light where fires burned. His mercenaries had almost reached the crest in the afternoon and had been ordered to hold their advanced positions even as night fell. They would spend the night under arms and continue the assault at first light.

Above the ridgeline a fainter glow could be seen that could only be the campfires of his stubborn enemy. The Danes were still there and that pleased the Earl of Derby. By sundown tomorrow, his troops would overrun what was left of the defenders on the mountain, then he would have his accounting with Danes.

The men he would hang as traitors—and the rest? They would be dispersed throughout Derbyshire as serfs to his favoured tenants. This high country that had been their redoubt for a hundred years would be scoured clean of them. The land was practically worthless and would be left for the deer and grouse to roam.

Turning away, he raised the flap of his campaign tent and entered. His servant had his cot prepared. The tent had been specially made for him and was far more spacious and well-appointed than the quarters of the mercenary commanders. Still, he hated sleeping out in this wilderness and would have preferred his accommodations at Peveril Castle, only a league away. But this was no normal night and he knew he would sleep well in these rough conditions.

For tomorrow he would put an end to the Danes.

Chester

Declan O'Duinne had just begun to wolf down his midday meal when a young man burst into the barracks at Chester. He was one of the boys from the city who had come forward to join the new garrison and he almost tripped over his spear entering the small room off the kitchen where the men took their meals. A month ago he had been a labourer at the tannery. Now he manned the Eastgate.

"Sir, armed riders at the Eastgate. Say they've come from London, sir. We closed the gate. Thought we should check with you before lettin' 'em in." All this he got out without taking a breath.

Declan finished swallowing a mouthful of leek pottage and wiped his mouth.

"How many?"

"I counted thirteen, sir"

"What were their horses like?"

This caused the young gate guard to pause. He was no expert on horses, having never ridden one, but he knew a spavined nag when he saw one.

"They looked to be of poor quality and hard used, I would say."

Declan nodded and picked up a chunk of black bread.

"Let's go have a look."

When he arrived at the Eastgate, there was a small crowd of garrison troops and idle citizens looking over the wall at the road below. He climbed to the wall walk and looked himself. There were, indeed, thirteen men in the group and they looked as worn out as their horses. All were armed, after a fashion. None had mail, but all carried a spear or sword. They looked nervous, but resolute. Declan sent the gawkers on their way and called down to the men outside the gate.

"Identify yourself."

A lone man urged his horse forward. He was small and lean and fatigue showed on his dust-lined face, but his eyes were keen.

"We've come from London. Been six days on the road to get here. We are soldiers—all of us—veterans who served with the King. We hear there are others like us who have done some proper soldiering out in these parts and we've come to join them. We've come to find the Invalid Company."

Declan looked more closely at the men on the dusty road outside the gate. The man who had spoken had a hook where a hand should have been. Another was missing an arm to the elbow. A man near the back appeared to have a disfigured face, covered in part by his hood.

More broken men.

"I have patrols out east watching the roads," he called down to the men. "Were you not stopped?"

The lean man rubbed his chin.

"We don't ride in strange country, my lord, without we keep a scout out ahead of us. He saw yer lads and they didn't see him. So we just went around. Plenty enough small roads and trails, if ye've a mind to use 'em."

Declan smiled. Patch had charge of the eastern approaches to the city. He would not be happy to hear these men had got around his boys. He turned to the lad who had fetched him from the barracks.

"Run, go bring me Patch. He's asleep in the barracks. Tell him to come to Eastgate. He has visitors."

The boy turned and ran down the steps to the street and off toward the centre of town. Declan turned back to the men outside.

"Drop your weapons on the road."

There had been too many unpleasant surprises at the gates of Chester for him to risk another. The men on the road looked nervously at each other.

"You'll get them back—after we've had a closer look at you."

There were harsh whispers between the men, but the wiry man with the hook hand drew his sword and dropped it in the dust. Then one-by-one the others dropped spears and daggers and bows as well.

"Open the gate!" Declan commanded and the men in the gatehouse began to crank the windlass that raised the portcullis. Before it cleared the arch of the Eastgate, Declan saw Tom Marston, known to all as Patch, hurrying up the street from the barracks. He arrived as the men from London rode in and dismounted. Declan met him beside the gatehouse.

"These men have come from London. They look for the Invalid Company."

Patch inspected the newcomers with a baleful look in his one good eye.

"Looks like they've spent the summer sleeping in the gutters of London," he said under his breath.

The Irishman smiled.

"You looked much the same the day we first met outside the walls of Oxford, Tom."

Patch hooted.

"Aye, true enough. I didn't get proper sober until we were two days on the march. So let's take a look at these men."

He turned and called to the group of thirteen men who stood beside their horses in the street.

"Who here fought with the King at Acre or Arsuf?"

The wiry man stepped forward.

"All save three of us fought with Richard in the Holy Land. Henry back there," he gestured toward the man with the maimed face, "took a crossbow bolt through the jaw outside of Messina when the King was chastising Tancred. John and Alfred," he pointed to the two tallest men in the group, "were badly wounded when the King seized Cyprus from the Byzantines. We all fought for the Lionheart, one place or another—every one of us."

86

"And why are you here? Did you grow weary of the hospitality in London?"

"Aye, ye might say that. I'll not deny we've partaken of the drink and the women of London, but that's what a soldier does when there's no fightin' to be done. We hear there might be work for men such as us in Chester. We hear that there are others— like us—that have done some proper soldiering out this way. We come lookin' for the Invalid Company."

Patch seemed puzzled by the man's answer.

"So Sir Declan informs me, but how did you come to know of the Invalid Company, or where to find us?

Now the reed-thin man smiled for the first time.

"Let me sing you a song makin' the rounds of the taverns in London."

***

A mile east of Chester, along the main road that ran from the city down to Wroxeter, Millicent de Laval sat on her favourite bay mare, a wide-brimmed hat on her head to gain a little shade in the blazing afternoon sun. She had ridden out that morning, both to see how the harvest was progressing and to simply get out of the city and *move*.

She and her mother had been tasked with replenishing the food stocks at Chester and there were endless issues to attend to—but none more important than getting in the harvest. William de Ferrers had taken the city through treachery the year before and had stripped the storehouses of grain. That grain had been shipped off to London or Ireland or France for gold—gold to fill Prince John's coffers—gold to hire a mercenary army.

Earl Ranulf had reclaimed his city in the spring, but now he had to defend it with too few men and no stores. The wealth stolen from Cheshire had paid the mercenaries who had captured the castle at Nottingham. Those same mercenaries could, on the Prince's whim, turn on Chester at any time.

Chester's walls had repelled many enemies over the centuries since they had been thrown up by the Romans. Britons, Welshmen, Saxons, and Danes had all tested those walls and had died bloody deaths in the ditch that lay at their base. In the early years of his rule, Ranulf had paid little attention to the defence of his city. The walls had fallen into disrepair and the ditch had eroded and become choked with weeds and brambles. The Earl's garrison had been undermanned, poorly trained and undisciplined. But Ranulf had learned a sobering lesson when de Ferrers had snatched the place from him.

Once he'd recovered his city, the Earl put the people of Chester to work repairing the walls and cleaning out the overgrown ditch, which was deepened and lined with sharpened stakes. Over the summer, a good four hundred men had been recruited from the town and surrounding countryside for the city garrison. They were green, but had been given sufficient training to man sections of the wall.

Those walls stretched for two miles around the city. A thousand men would have been needed to properly man them, but Chester was fortunate. It was nestled in a great bend in the Dee, making attack from the south or west nearly impossible. The garrison need fully man only the north and east walls. It was a thin force, but four hundred men, well led, could probably hold those walls.

Millicent had been pleased to learn that a new group of veterans had arrived just the day before to expand the ranks of the Invalid Company, the hard kernel of the Earl's fighting force. And in ways few had expected, Ranulf of Chester was finally growing into a leader of men—a true Marcher Lord.

Chester was prepared to withstand a direct assault, but it was a siege that worried Millicent. Without the harvest, the city would begin to starve in a fortnight. All summer she had watched anxiously as the crops ripened in the fields. The growing season had been kind. There had been enough rain, blowing in from the Irish Sea to the west and more than the usual amount of sun.

The harvest traditionally began the first week of August, but by mid-July the seed heads had turned golden and drooped with their weight. The yield promised to be better than she had hoped—more than enough to fill every grain bin in the city. As she watched the crops ripen, Millicent prayed they would be able to bring them in from the fields before John's army turned back toward Cheshire.

The day before, as though in answer to her prayers, those who tended the crops declared the winter wheat ready for gathering. It was a full fortnight sooner than expected and the spring barley was only a few days away from ripening. Overnight, Lady Catherine mobilized half the population to march out of the city and begin the reaping at dawn.

Millicent watched as rows of men and women bent low and rhythmically swung their scythes, leaving a foot of wheat stubble standing for the cattle to graze. Another row came behind gathering up the precious stalks into bundles and loading them onto wagons. Some of the reapers moved with the steady rhythm of long practice and others, more used to city occupations, cut and gathered clumsily, but all worked with an energy born of fear. They had heard of the starvation at Nottingham.

Once the wagons were filled, they trundled from the fields through the Eastgate and the Northgate—delivering the bundles of grain to barns within the city. There the grain was threshed and sent to the granaries or to the grist mills that took their power from the weir that held back and channelled the waters of the Dee.

The weather for harvesting was ideal, hot and calm. If they got the wheat in along with the barley, they could sustain a siege for five months, perhaps longer. It would be time enough for the King to return from the crusade and put a halt to his brother's plans. Time enough for her father to return.

Millicent looked through the haze at the far horizons to the east and north. She knew that Declan O'Duinne had sentinels watching every major road leading to Chester from those directions and patrols that ranged even further afield. If a mercenary army marched on Chester, they would not be surprised. The city had changed hands twice in the past year through surprise assaults and Earl Ranulf was determined that it would not happen again.

Satisfied that all that could be done was being done, she turned her horse's head and rode back toward Chester. She trotted through the Eastgate and slid from her saddle at the stables that stood a block inside the city wall. It had been a long hot day, but she was restless. She thought she would go to the wall at sunset to watch the river cascade over the weir. Watching the waters of the Dee made her think of her sunset strolls with Roland Inness on the walls overlooking the river.

He had been gone for almost a fortnight now. The days had not been so bad, caught up as she was in the whirlwind of her daily tasks. But come evening, her mind could not help but go to him. She wondered where he was and if he was safe. She wondered when he would come home. She wondered all the things a soldier's woman wonders when her man has gone in harm's way.

***

A lone rider arrived outside the Eastgate of Chester at sundown on the second day of harvesting. He announced that he was a courier, come from London with a message for Lady de Laval. The Corporal of the Guard escorted him to the castle where the evening meal was about to be served. The courier stood patiently while the Corporal spoke quietly to the Captain of the Guard who then ushered the man into the great hall.

There were only three people taking their meal at the table. They all paused as the courier approached. He stopped and bowed, then withdrew a rolled parchment from his tunic. It had an impressive red wax seal on it.

"My lord—and ladies, I bring a message for Lady de Laval from the Archbishop of Rouen, Justiciar of the Realm," he announced with a flourish.

After a moment, Lady Catherine stood and came forward. She extended her hand to receive the parchment, but the man suddenly reddened.

"Forgive me, my…my lady…the message is for Lady *Millicent* de Laval."

Lady Catherine stopped cold at the man's words. She let her hand fall then turned to her daughter who looked as flustered as the courier. The older woman tried to control her voice, but could not conceal a touch of fear.

"My dear, it seems you have a message."

Retreat

*T*hey came at dawn, moving up through the fog along every trail wide enough to allow a man to pass. Rough men from Ghent and Bruges, who had once been poor, gripped their weapons. Hardy farm boys from Roeselare and a hundred other hamlets in Flanders, who had grown weary of toiling in the fields, looked anxiously through the fog for some sign of an enemy. Men from Clare and Cork and Kerry, raised on the brutish wars between petty Irish kings, crept forward, shields held to the front.

These were hard men, long practiced at violence, and ready to finish this stubborn enemy who had torn gaps in their ranks and seemed to be always just out of reach. During the long battle to claim the heights, the Danes had been elusive as ghosts. Their bows could strike at impossibly long distances and an arrow to the chest was often the first and last hint a man got that there was an enemy somewhere ahead.

These men were veterans and their shields saved many, but not all. The bodies of dead and wounded men littered the steep slopes behind them as the sun climbed higher in the sky. They had managed to trap a few of the bowmen, and these they killed in an orgy of vengeance. They knew the end was near, and like dogs unleashed, they were ready to savage these troublesome Danes.

***

91

Roland and Oren had joined a dozen Danes who fought all morning to slow the mercenary advance up the main trail. But other trails were unguarded, and three times they were forced to fight their way past enemy troops who had got behind them.

Once, two swordsmen closed on them, charging down the slope to their rear, arrows bristling from their shields. Roland drew his own sword and as the first man reached him, he dropped low. The man could not check his headlong sprint downhill and was tumbled into the air, falling onto his back in front of Oren. The boy drew his skinning knife and drove it into the man's throat before he could rise.

Uncoiling from his crouch, Roland aimed a thrust under the second man's shield, but this man was a veteran and parried the attack. Using his shield as a ram, the mercenary aimed for Roland's head. Roland twisted his body and jerked his head back, but the shield slammed into his shoulder, unbalancing him.

He staggered backwards and his heel caught a root. Before he could recover, he was down and the mercenary moved in to finish his work. As his sword arm rose, he caught movement from the corner of his eye and glanced up to see Oren Inness with a drawn longbow twelve paces away. He tried to swing his shield around, but knew it was too late.

"Damnú air!" he cursed and died.

For a long moment, neither brother moved, breathing heavily from the exertion and the familiar battle fury that had swept over them. Then Oren walked over, extended a hand and pulled Roland to his feet.

"Perhaps you could teach me this manoeuvre where you fall on your backside," he said with a straight face.

Roland didn't know whether to laugh or cry at his brother's jibe. A week ago the boy had killed his first man and had been badly shaken by what he'd done. Now he had killed two more and could jest. Oren had shown the instincts of a warrior more than once in the long days of fighting and that would keep the boy alive, but...

Roland felt a wave of sadness wash over him. Another farmer—*another Inness*—had been turned into a fighter.

The Ransomed Crown

***

By noon, the hard-pressed Danes had been forced back to the very crest of the broad ridge that ran north from the summit of Kinder Scout. Here, the trees were sparse and stunted and in many places, nothing but bare rock and bracken covered the ground. If the steep wooded slopes to the east of the ridge had favoured the defenders, this level plateau swung the advantage to the hundreds of mercenary troops sweeping up from below.

Roland looked to the north and saw dozens of their own men being forced back onto the ridgetop. Some were starting to turn and run to avoid being overwhelmed by the enemy troops that seemed to emerge from every path and game trail. He heard a strange howl rise up, shrill and excited, as some of the Irish began to bay like hounds released for the chase. Above this wailing call, he heard three clear blasts from Thorkell's hunting horn. He grabbed Oren's shoulder and shoved him toward the west and their line of retreat.

"Run!" he shouted. They ran.

***

An Irish sergeant led a dozen men up a trail that switched back and forth as it climbed a spur. He was a veteran with grey flecks in his beard. It had been a long time since he had faced a foe this determined and he moved with practiced care, keeping his shield high and his eyes far up the slope looking for any sign of trouble. With his gaze fixed in the distance, he didn't see the tiny willow tit flush from a bush just ahead—but the man to his front did. Startled, the mercenary recoiled and dropped his shield half a foot. He never saw the arrow that took him in the throat.

The sergeant looked at his downed man and cursed. Gesturing to the rear, he raised four fingers and pointed to the left. Four Irishmen slid off the trail and began the practiced routine of circling the hidden bowmen. The sergeant waited. It took an hour, but finally he heard a call in Gaelic from above. The way was now open.

Slowly he moved up the trail, not entirely trusting the all clear signal. Three more switchbacks and they found themselves, for the first time in four days, on level ground. They had reached

93

the top of the ridge at last. Somewhere, off to the south they heard a hunting horn sound three blasts. The sergeant's instincts told him that signal meant the enemy was on the run. He gave a grim smile.

It was time to finish the Danes.

***

The long line of men ran in single file, each man holding his bow at his side and keeping his eyes fixed between the rocky path at his feet and the man to his front. The trail switched back on itself again and again as it headed down toward the flatlands. Roland ran near the end of the column and at one turn hopped off the trail and let those behind run on.

He looked back up the slope and saw no pursuit, but knew it would not be long before the mercenaries gave chase. He had told Thorkell to halt the retreat at the River Goyt. He and Sir Edgar had forded the river on their journey to Saint Oswald's. The ford was in a steep gorge where the river ran swift and shallow. The stream itself was no real obstacle, but the bottom of the gorge was wide with open lines of sight. The road dropped into the gorge on the eastern side, crossed a good forty paces through the shallows of the river and made two switchbacks coming up the western slope. It was an excellent place for an ambush.

He waited for a gap in the line, then jumped in, matching the pace set by the Danes ahead of him. Oren was somewhere in the middle of the column, but he had lost sight of his brother in the dash down the western side of Kinder Scout. He took a last glance over his shoulder and wondered if he would ever see these mountains again.

***

The Irish sergeant eased into the clearing with his shield held high and gave a hand signal that sent a half dozen of his warriors darting across flat ground to the tree line on the other side. This sheltered valley was tucked below the crest of the ridge to the east that they had just taken. He saw one of his men give the all clear signal and he lowered the shield a little and walked into the

94

open ground. As he crossed the clearing, he saw one of his men hurrying back from the tree line.

"They're on the run—the whole lot of 'em," the man said and pointed to the west. "From the ridge there ye can see all the way to the lowlands. I seen a whole string of 'em carrying those damn bows and running like deer."

The sergeant grunted and pointed back to the east.

"Get yerself back over the ridge and back down to the valley where we started," he said. "That's where the commanders will be. Tell 'em just what ye told me. And tell 'em we are pursuin.' Understood?"

"Aye, Sergeant!"

"Then go!" The man set off at a loping run back over the ridge of Kinder Scout.

The sergeant turned his attention back to the task at hand. He intended to latch on to the fleeing Danes like a wolfhound. He would stay on their trail and not let them shake loose. There would be a reward for him and his men for doing so, for, if contact were lost, their quarry might turn in any direction and vanish. The reward would be welcome, but after four days of brutal fighting his men would want vengeance as much as pay.

So they would stay close. If the Danes slowed, then the rest of the infantry would catch up and destroy them. If they stayed out of reach—well, no matter. There was always the cavalry.

***

By midafternoon, the first of the Danes splashed across the Goyt, and fanned out on either side of the road. By the time Roland arrived, Thorkell was positioning his archers in the trees on the western slope. The sides of the gorge were heavily wooded, but many trees had been cut back near the road and the ford. It made for an excellent killing ground. Roland saw Svein sitting on a stone letting his wounded leg recover. He had wondered whether the hot-headed Dane could make the run. Svein raised a hand in greeting but did not rise.

Tough bastard.

Roland caught up with his brother near the edge of the road.

95

"It's good ground," Oren said. "I counted eighty paces from the far side of the river to here."

Roland watched as the last men moved off the trail and into cover.

"Aye, I would not want to cross that ford with this many longbows aimed at me."

Thorkell came down the line checking each position. He had every man count what was left in his quiver. He ordered them to conserve their arrows, particularly the precious bodkin-head shafts that could pierce armour. Roland saw him come and did a quick count of his own supply as did Oren.

"Fifty-two, with twelve bodkins," he said as the war leader approached.

"Fifty-seven and fourteen" Oren added.

Thorkell nodded.

"That's better than most. I don't have to tell you to make every shot count. We won't be much use to the women and children if we have to throw our bows at the infantry."

Thorkell started to move to the next knot of men down the line, but Roland touched his shoulder.

"Do you have any among your men who can ride a horse?"

Thorkell rubbed his chin, surprised by the question.

"Two—that I know of."

"Do either of them know this country at all?"

Thorkell paused, unsure where Roland's questions were leading.

"Aye, I think young Gudbrand might. His family's farmstead was on this side of the mountains, and not far from here. They owned a horse, but it was taken and their farm burnt in the spring."

"He will do then. Will you send him to me?"

Thorkell started to speak, but simply nodded and went to the fetch the boy. He returned, trailed by a raw-boned lad with hair like straw and tired eyes. Gudbrand's face was dirty and his clothes ragged, but he had a ready smile.

Roland laid a hand on his shoulder.

"Gudbrand, do you know the road off to the south that comes out of the mountains from Castleton heading west?"

Gudbrand glanced at Thorkell. He was seeking the war leader's permission to speak and he received it with a small jerk of the man's head.

"Aye, I know that country well."

"Good! I need you to find a horse and ride out that way."

The boy frowned.

"A horse? We got no horses. They took ours in the spring. Where am I to get a horse?"

Roland smiled at the boy.

"You will steal one. I'd venture a guess that the hamlet a mile west of here will have one or two."

Gudbrand said nothing for a moment, then gave a small smile in return.

"I can steal a horse."

"Good lad! Once you have your horse, find you a good vantage point on the Castleton road and watch. If anything troublesome comes down that road heading west, you find us."

"Troublesome? Like what?"

"Like a lot of men on horses. I will need to know if any such are heading our way."

"Aye, men on horses. I can watch for them."

"Very good, Gudbrand. Now off with you!"

The boy gave an odd little wave and sprang off toward the road. Thorkell had patiently held his tongue throughout Roland's exchange with the boy, satisfied that he would learn what Roland intended soon enough. Now he knew and he wished he didn't.

"Men on horses? Cavalry you mean."

"Aye, cavalry, Thorkell. I expect they held them at Castleton while they sent the infantry into the hills."

"How many?" the older man asked.

"The Earl of Chester's scouts counted four hundred a fortnight ago."

Thorkell stared at him, his eyes blazing.

"Troublesome, indeed. You failed to speak of this when you offered your Earl's bargain to us."

Roland could see the look of anger and betrayal on the man's face.

"Thorkell, the last report I had was that the mercenaries were moving on York. On my honour, I did not know de Ferrers would send them into the mountains to attack the Danes. But once they pushed into the high country, the die was cast. You could not hold onto these mountains. You had to run somewhere and the only refuge left for the Danes is Chester."

Some of the fire went out of the older man's eyes as he considered the truth of what this young knight was saying. Roland Inness had not brought this plague down upon the Danes, and in the end, they would have had to flee—but to where? The son of Rolf Inness had offered them a haven, before they had even known they would need one. Now they knew.

"Very well, Chester it is, but God help us if the cavalry come."

***

Sir Edgar stood on the muddy bank of the River Deane and watched the last of the families cross. The water was knee-deep and a young mother leaned into the current holding an infant in one arm and pulling a small boy along with the other. The water was up to the boy's chest.

Tough people, these Danes.

He slid down the bank and sloshed through the muddy water to meet her. Without a word he hoisted the boy up on a huge shoulder with one hand and steadied the mother with the other. When they were safe on the bank, he turned back to see the final member of his party enter the water from the far bank. It was a twelve year old boy who had been assigned to make sure no one was left behind in this exodus. As he crossed the stream, he waved at Sir Edgar to signal there were no stragglers.

The big knight waited for this rear guard to reach him. The boy had a pudgy face smeared with dirt and eyes that were as innocent as a new born calf, but in his hand was a longbow and Sir Edgar had little doubt the lad knew how to use it. He clapped the boy on the back and took a last look at the ford.

There had not been rain for days and the water level was much lower than when he and Roland had crossed in this same place less than a fortnight ago. He wondered if Roland would try to make a stand here. The banks were low and the woods sparse. It would not be much of a barrier to the men who pursued them.

He looked up at the sun, which was directly overhead. They had been walking for twelve hours. He would keep them moving until they found a more sheltered spot, but knew the youngest and the oldest had to rest, and soon. When they had recovered a little, he would march them into the night. No one would complain. All knew the men on their trail would not be stopping to rest. He looked back over the stream and said another prayer that Roland and Thorkell would keep the war dogs from reaching him and the families he guarded.

***

Two men moved cautiously out of the woods that covered the steep eastern slope of the gorge at the River Goyt. They saw nothing on the far side of the ford, but there were plenty of signs in the soft sand and gravel that the Danes had passed this way. They expected there were at least some men concealed in the woods on the other side and they eased back into the cover of the trees. After a while, their sergeant arrived with the rest of the men.

"Ambush?" he asked his two scouts.

"Probable. Nothin' movin' on the other side, but they came this way fer sure and it's a good place for one."

The sergeant watched the trees on the opposite side of the gorge for a long time, then turned to his men.

"We wait until the rest come up. We should have three hundred men or more here within the hour." He turned to one of his scouts. "Get back to the rear. Find the captain. Tell him to send men north or south of the road. If the Danes are over there, we need to get our boys behind 'em."

The man set off back up the winding road that climbed out of the narrow valley. Two hundred paces across the gorge, hidden eyes watched them carefully. Thorkell had instructed every man to hold fire until he signalled. The enemy scouts across the way had seen nothing, but they were cautious. Cautious was good. Cautious was slow; and they needed the mercenaries to move slowly. For somewhere to the west, the families were moving at their own speed—the speed of the very old and very young.

***

The farmer had been turning over the soil of the fallow field to ready it for the autumn planting, but the day was hot and he was thirsty. He led the plough horse to a patch of shade beside the burnt over field and trundled off to a nearby stream for a drink. When he returned, he found his plough attached to nothing more than the severed ends of the reins and traces. Back toward the road, he saw a lingering cloud of dust. He sank to the ground and moaned, wondering how he would explain to his master the loss of a good horse.

Gudbrand was thrilled. The horse was a natural runner and deserved better than to be harnessed to a plough. When he had ridden out of sight of the field, he reined in the animal. Sliding off its bare back to the ground, he removed the horse's collar, leaving the reins attached.

He had stolen a ripe apple from an orchard a mile away and offered it to the horse. The animal took it and munched contentedly. Gudbrand patted its neck, grasped its mane and swung himself back aboard the beast. He leaned forward and whispered in the horse's ear.

"Let's go watch for trouble."

***

At the Goyt, an hour had passed with no movement to be seen on either side of the river. A hundred men were making their way north to find another crossing, while four hundred more gathered at the lip of the steep gorge waiting for the order to advance. Those with shields were ordered to the front. Once they had assembled, the command came to cross the ford and drive away any resistance on the other side.

The road that ran down to the river swept back and forth in three long switchbacks until it reached the bottom of the gorge. There was room for six men abreast on the rutted road and the order had been given to widen their front once they reached the river.

As they emerged from the woods and neared the bank of the river, men hurried forward to extend the front rank. By the time they entered the stream the front was eighteen men wide and was followed by two more ranks bearing shields. The men moved with care over the slippery rocks of the bottom. They were veterans, confident in their numbers and their tactics. The men had never failed to force a river crossing.

Then the arrows came.

The first found a small opening between the top of a shield and the exposed neck of its bearer. He staggered backwards but the line kept moving forward. Then a hail of longbow shafts whistled from the concealment of the trees on the opposite bank and more men fell.

The men in the back, having no shields, crouched low and closed up on the ranks in front as arrows began to land in their midst, trying in vain to find cover there. The mercenary crossbowmen had followed the infantry until they were in range of their attackers, but there was little to see and they had no shields to protect them. They shot wildly into the trees, but a dozen of their own number went down in less than a minute. The rest fled back to the opposite bank. A command rang out and the attack was broken off. Men edged back to the east bank of the river taking care not to expose themselves to the archers on the other side. Over a score of bodies lay in the shallow river that began to turn a sickly pink.

On the western slope of the gorge, there was little time to celebrate. Thorkell had sent a dozen men north and south along the river to watch for flanking attacks and those who had gone north now returned with the news that a large force of mercenaries were crossing the Goyt three miles downstream. They had bought a few hours delay here and it was time to fall back.

Thorkell passed the word and men began to ease back from their hidden positions and assemble on the road leading out of the gorge. They had been fighting since dawn and had run a league since noon. They were hungry and exhausted, but there could be no rest. The sun was low in the sky as they fell into the dog trot that would eat up the miles until sunset.

There would be no more bloodshed this day and they would march on through the night, reaching the River Deane before midnight. They would rest there and by first light be ready to bloody their pursuers again.

***

Roland cursed when he saw the ford at the Deane. It was a little before midnight and the water shimmered in the bright moonlight, but the river was only knee-deep and half as wide as when he and Sir Edgar had crossed it. He splashed across and found Oren and Thorkell waiting on the opposite bank.

"Not much of a river," Oren observed, as Roland climbed dripping from the shrunken stream. Thorkell said nothing.

"This ford was half again as wide and chest deep when we crossed it a fortnight ago. So I agree—bad ground to defend."

"The lads who crossed first found plenty of sign that the families passed this way," Thorkell said. "Our best tracker says they stopped a little ways on to rest."

Roland looked back at the river. The dry weather was likely to affect all of the small rivers between here and Chester. Only the River Weaver, over twenty miles to the southwest would still have enough flow to present a problem for the infantry chasing them. He looked at Thorkell.

The war leader of the Danes had the heart of a lion, but he was exhausted and out of his element here. The man was a master at fighting in the thick forests and steep slopes of the mountains against the Earl's men-at-arms, but the land here was flat by comparison, with long stretches of forest cleared for farming. And the men pursuing them were not the Earl's local soldiers. These were veteran warriors. Thorkell was a proud man, but he knew his experience was ill-matched for this fight. He looked at Roland with a plea in his eyes.

"You've fought in the crusade—against men like this. Do we strike them here?"

Roland rubbed his tired eyes.

"The next ford that will do us any good is at the River Weaver, twenty miles from here. Twenty miles beyond that are the walls of Chester. Between here and the river, there is a lot of open ground. We will use what the land gives us—tree lines, ditches, villages if need be—to turn and strike at the mercenaries. We force the infantry to stop and form up to clear the ground. It won't stop them, but it will slow them."

Roland said all this with more confidence than he felt. Sir Roger de Laval had taught him to never lead men into battle without a plan—even a flawed plan. The big Norman knight had also told him that any plan was doomed if men did not believe in it.

Thorkell was watching him carefully, judging whether this young veteran of the crusade believed in his own plan. This was no time for doubt. Roland returned Thorkell's searching gaze and smiled.

"How far can your men strike effectively with their bows, Thorkell?"

Thorkell blinked. Every Danish boy knew the range of the longbow.

"Two hundred paces at the least," he said, a question in his eyes.

"Aye, that's almost twice the range of the crossbows and short bows the mercenaries use. On Kinder Scout, you could rarely see a man further than fifty paces. But here?" he said pointing to the harvested field of winter wheat just beyond the stream bed. "Here we can actually see a man and kill him at two hundred paces and they cannot touch us."

Thorkell nodded now, beginning to see the running fight play out in his mind.

"We kill them until they are one hundred paces away," the Dane said, "then we run before they are in range with their damn crossbows. It could work..."

"It will work," Roland said, seeing the man's hopes rise. Then Thorkell frowned.

"Aye, unless the cavalry catch us."

Cavalry

It was midmorning when William de Ferrers reached the farmstead high on the flanks of Kinder Scout. Word had come the night before that the Danes had been pushed out of their mountains and were fleeing to the west. He was disappointed that the mercenary foot had failed to cut them off, but they had been flushed from the hills and the cavalry had been dispatched at dawn to complete the job of exterminating the vermin.

His own father had feared the Danes and he had his own grievance with them, but now they were gone and he wanted to see it for himself. He had climbed the mountain, surrounded by his own personal guard and led by a patrol of mercenary infantry left behind to root out any fugitives still hiding in the high country.

The stinking little plot of overgrown ground where he stood was a place that still appeared in his dreams. Those dreams had a dreadful sameness to them. The farmer is on his knees. His men strike the man down and arrows instantly sprout from their chests. He turns to run as they fall around him, but the mountains seem to grasp at him, holding him back as footsteps draw closer. Many a night he awoke, gasping and covered with sweat from this nightmare.

He looked around the place. There was nothing to fear now. He saw the burned circle where the hut had been torched. Walking across the field, now rank with bracken, he saw the two graves, covered with stones. He stopped as his escort gathered around.

William de Ferrers turned to the sergeant who commanded the mercenary patrol.

"Dig up these graves and scatter the bones!" he ordered.

The sergeant looked aghast. He'd happily kill his enemies, but trifling with graves was another matter.

"My lord? Ye want us to dig up the folk buried here?"

De Ferrers whirled on the man.

"You heard me!" he screamed. "Dig them up and scatter them across the field."

"Aye, my lord," the man said bowing his head. He ordered his men to begin removing the stones.

Satisfied, de Ferrers turned to his own guard.

"Damned Danes don't deserve a proper burial, lads. Now let's get down to the valley. We'll be riding west. I want to see our cavalry make an end to this."

He headed back across the field to retrace his steps to the valley below. As soon as the Earl disappeared into the trees, the sergeant ordered the men to halt their work.

"Let's put 'em back boys. We'll not be despoilin' Christian graves—no matter what that bastard says."

***

On a ridge overlooking the Castleton road, Gudbrand had tied up his new horse and found a good vantage point to watch to the east. He heard the trouble coming before he saw it. A low rumble to the east, out of sight around a bend, then the glint of sun on steel announced that trouble aplenty was coming his way.

The boy gasped. He had never seen such a thing. Even at a distance, the size of the horses was startling and the men who rode them looked like death coming to call. The column of horsemen bristled with armour and lances and stretched out of sight around the curve of the road.

He stopped counting at one hundred men. He had seen enough to know that eight score bowmen could not stop this mass of men. His fellow Danes should be somewhere south and west of the River Deane by now. Gudbrand climbed on the horse and turned its head in that direction. He gave the animal a kick in the flanks and the beast lunged down the trail and picked up speed.

Thank God I stole a plough horse that likes to run.

***

Connaught Kilbride was a veteran cavalry commander who had grown weary of the endless wars between the petty Irish kings that showed no profit and had long ago sold his sword to the highest bidder. For over a year, he'd been paid good wages by the English with little or no need to earn them. During the long siege of Nottingham the heavy cavalry had only been called upon once—to turn back a weak relief force. He did not object to easy money, but if the English decided they were not receiving value for the expense…That was another matter.

Word had reached Castleton late in the day that the Danes had finally been rooted out of the hills and were fleeing to the west. There had been arguments about what force to send after them, but the Earl demanded that half the mounted troops take up the chase and Kilbride had been chosen to lead them. He did not object.

This order to run down and slaughter a party of hill-country peasants would allow the cavalry to show its worth—and it would still be easy money. He'd been told there were only a few score archers able to put up any resistance, and for a force of two hundred heavy cavalry, that was no resistance at all.

By nightfall, they had ridden out of the narrow valley that wound west from Castleton and camped with the mountains to their backs. The next morning, they rode out at dawn and none saw the boy on the hill who watched them. Well before noon, they splashed across the River Deane. It was here they began to see the bodies.

Beyond that river, every open field along the southwest road held dead men. All of the corpses sported one or more arrows standing stiffly in the morning sun, like flags. Kilbride halted the column briefly to examine the first dead. He had seen arrows penetrate mail before, but only at extremely close range. He was surprised to find the bodies had fallen over a hundred paces from a tree line where the archers must have lain in wait.

He had heard about the longbows these Danes used but had given it little thought until now. The dead gave Kilbride pause, but he shrugged it off. These bows might be powerful enough to kill a man through his mail at a great distance, but the infantry's mail was of poor quality and most of his men had their vitals covered with plate armour.

Surely no bow could penetrate that.

The infantry had not stopped to tend the dead or to minister to the wounded. A steady trickle of casualties moved slowly along the road, back to the northeast. From these, Kilbride got a clear picture of what lay ahead. The mercenary foot had been chasing the Danes since noon the day before, but had not been able to close with them. Whenever they had to cross open ground, they were greeted with a hail of longbow shafts from archers hidden in the woods ahead.

One grey-haired veteran, his bloody arm wrapped in a rag looked at Connaught Kilbride and his column of armoured horseman with an evil light in his eyes. He waved the Irish commander to a halt and spewed out his frustration.

"Me brother lies dead two fields on," he said, his voice choked with anger. "We never seen a one of the bastards!" he said grasping Kilbride's reins for a moment. "Promise me ye'll kill 'em, Captain—kill 'em all fer me."

Kilbride nodded to the man and spurred his horse forward.

He would be happy to kill them all and he had no doubts his cavalry would be up to the job. And it would be easy money, indeed. He signalled the men behind him to pick up the pace. The Danes might be able to stay a step ahead of the infantry, but they could not outrun his cavalry.

***

Since before dawn, the Danes had fought and fallen back, again and again, staying outside the range of the enemy crossbows and taking a toll on the men who pursued them. The day had dawned cloudless and hot. As the sun rose higher in the sky, they picked their spots and made the stubbled fields of Cheshire a killing ground. By midmorning they had fallen back across the tiny Birken Brook, the bowmen stopping to quench their thirst in the muddy water. This stream was only ten miles from the Weaver. If they could get safely across it, Chester was less than twenty miles away.

Almost home.

Roland took a last look across the open fields to the northeast and saw men come out of the tree line he had passed through only minutes before. If they weren't so intent on killing him, he would have admired the tenacity of the Flemings and Irish who trailed them. As he entered the next strip of woodland, he passed through the line of archers who were already starting to loose shafts at the new targets in the field to their front.

This strip of woods was only fifty yards wide and he followed the Chester road south to judge the ground beyond. There was a large open field there, with the grain ripe and unharvested. The crop did not catch his eye, for there was a rider galloping up the road from the south. It was Gudbrand. The boy reined the plough horse to a stop and slid off the animal's back.

"Thank God," he gasped, out of breath. "I wasn't sure I could find you."

"Cavalry?" Roland asked. It was the only question that really mattered.

"Aye, sir. Over a hundred I'd say," the boy replied, his face reddening a little. "I did not stay to count the last one."

"No matter. How far do you reckon?"

"This is a good horse," Gudbrand said proudly, patting the sweating animal's neck. "He's fast, a lot faster than those brutes I saw. I had to circle around the infantry, but I would guess the mounted men are two hours away."

Roland nodded.

Not enough time to reach the Weaver.

"Gudbrand, see this road you came up? It runs all the way to Chester. You ride as fast as your good horse will take you until you catch up to the families. I hope to God they have already crossed the ford at the Weaver. Find Sir Edgar Langton and give him this news.

"Aye sir!"

Without waiting for a response, Gudbrand swung back up on the plough horse's back and headed south toward Chester.

Too late, Roland thought.

***

The guards at Chester's Northgate saw a boy running toward them a good distance off, but paid little heed until he stumbled and fell at their feet. The lad was drenched in sweat and he fought to keep his eyes from rolling back in his head as he gasped for breath. He finally managed to speak, but between the boy's panting and his odd accent they could not understand what he was so desperately trying to tell them. They sent for the Officer of the Watch.

Patch had the duty that day and hurried to the Northgate. By the time he arrived, the boy had been given water and had recovered a little but continued to be agitated.

"What is it lad? What's the trouble."

The boy spoke with an accent Patch had come to know. It had familiar cadences he'd first heard from Roland Inness. This boy was a Dane.

"I am sent by Sir Edgar Langton, sir. He is south of the Weaver with eight hundred women and children. We are pursued. He needs your help."

Patch needed nothing further. He turned to a gate guard and issued his order.

"Alert Sir Declan and the Earl."

"Aye, sir!"

"And call out the Invalids."

***

With the approach of the cavalry, Roland discarded all thought of slowing the infantry's advance. It would now be a simple race to the river. If they could cross, and if the river was deep enough to slow riders, they might survive. If the mounted men reached them first, there would be no hope. He ordered the men to run. He and Thorkell stayed until the last man loosed a final arrow at the advancing foot soldiers, then fell in at the rear of the Danes as they ran for their lives.

For the next hour they ran. Roland noticed that Svein had fallen back near the rear of the men, favouring his wounded leg. But the tough Dane managed to keep pace. They passed through a tiny group of huts clustered by the Chester road. The inhabitants, always alert to the approach of trouble, had fled.

Roland knew this place. It was less than three miles from the river. Another half hour and they would be over the ford. He stopped to look back up the road to the north. Surrounding the hamlet were open fields stretching a mile or more in all directions. For now, nothing moved on the road to the north.

Might they make it?

He turned to follow the Danes and was two hundred yards from the next patch of woods when he heard a new sound behind him. It was some distance off and faint, but there could be no mistake—it was the sound of iron-shod hooves. He turned to see his worst fears realized. Armoured knights poured out of the woods and into the open field, fanning out as they came.

He looked ahead and saw Thorkell had slipped an arm around Svein's waist as his son faltered. Roland caught up to the pair and grabbed the younger man from the other side. Ahead, he saw Oren disappear into the woods.

"They're here." he said. No need to say who he meant. Svein tried to struggle out of the grasp of the two men running beside him, but finally gave up and simply tried to match their strides. Behind them a hunting horn sounded. There was no point in looking back. The woods were now a hundred yards ahead. They would not be much refuge from what was about to fall upon them, but some men might be able to scatter and survive. They ran on, as the sound of hoof beats grew behind them.

Thirty yards now.

Roland released Svein and turned, drawing a bodkin head shaft from his quiver. He nocked it as the line of cavalry swept past the abandoned village and thundered toward him. They drew within two hundred paces and he saw they wore plate armour.

Wait.

At one hundred paces he loosed—too far to penetrate armour, but he could not tarry. He aimed at a big man on a coal black charger in the centre of the line. The shaft leapt across the distance and found the opening where the man had raised the visor of his helmet to gain a better view of the field. It was the last thing he saw. He toppled backwards off his horse, but the wave of heavy cavalry rolled on.

The sound of pounding hooves and snorting horses filled Roland's ears as he turned to run. His legs felt like lead and sweat poured into his eyes as he sprinted down the dusty road toward the refuge of the trees. He could still make the woods, but barely.

A barrage of arrows flew over his head. The Danes had not scattered in panic at the sight of the mounted onslaught. He saw Thorkell and Svein and his own brother at the edge of the field refusing to flee. They should have. He wanted to scream at them. *Run! Run!*

Another flight of arrows flew past him—this time closer to his head as the range shortened. He did not look back, but could hear the scrape of metal on metal as lances were lowered and swords drawn. Ahead, something moved in the tree line. He blinked the sweat from his eyes and saw a line of horsemen emerge from the edge of the woods. His heart sank. Somehow the mercenaries had got riders in behind them. He had led the Danes into a deathtrap.

He blinked again and his breath caught in his throat. A stirring of the breeze had caught a blue and gold banner, unfurling it. It was the flag of the Earl of Chester. Beside the banner was a knight standing up in his stirrups and shouting an order, his broadsword pointed toward the horsemen in the field. There could be no mistaking who this knight was. Declan O'Duinne had found them and he'd brought the Invalids with him.

Roland sprinted toward the trees as the Invalid Company spurred their mounts into a charge. They parted to let him pass, a chilling war cry rising up as the men urged their warhorses into a gallop straight at the charging mercenaries. He saw Patch on a dapple grey a little ahead of the line. As he rode past, Declan had a look of joy on his face. Roland reached the trees as the two lines met with a tremendous crash.

The mercenaries were shocked to find they were facing heavy cavalry when they had been expecting nothing more than a few archers to ride down and trample. Some tried to rein as this unexpected threat appeared, but a charge of warhorses is a thing not easily halted. Most of the Irish and Flemish warriors rode on, but any thoughts of easy money were now gone.

When the two lines met, a knot of horsemen around Declan and Earl Ranulf cut right through the enemy line leaving a ragged hole filled with downed riders and riderless horses. Without waiting for a command, they wheeled to the left and right, smashing into the rear of the enemy line and creating chaos in the centre of the field. The surprise and the ferocity of the attack checked the mercenaries for a moment, but with two hundred riders, their line overlapped the Invalid's and their riders began to swing around the flanks to take them in the rear.

Roland saw the danger and shouted at the Danes to train their arrows on the threat. The melee swirled barely a hundred paces from the edge of the woods and the bowmen began to abandon the cover of the trees to move closer. At one hundred yards they could pierce mail, but at twenty yards, they could penetrate plate armour. It was a dangerous thing to do, but they closed on the enemy horsemen. At this range they could not miss and the encircling horsemen, unaware of the threat, began to fall. Some turned to face their tormentors, but any mercenary knight who chose to attack an archer was instantly targeted by a score of bowman and went down in a blizzard of longbow shafts.

In battle, even experienced troops can lose their cohesion when taken by surprise. The Irish and Flemish knights were veterans, but the men they faced had learned their trade in a more unforgiving land. The Invalids were ruthless and the new men they had taken into their ranks were anxious to prove their worth. All fought with a battle rage that paid troops could not match.

First one, then a dozen, then a score of men jerked their horses around and fled up the road to the north. The others needed no order. They knew a rout when they saw one. Some of the Invalids started to pursue, but Declan and Patch screamed at them to a halt. A half mile across the field, hundreds of infantry began to pour out of the woods. There would be crossbowmen behind those ranks and, soon enough, the enemy cavalry would regroup there as well. It was no time for heroics.

The thunderous clamour of sword on sword and lance on shield that echoed across the field gave way to comparative quiet.

Warhorses stamped and snorted and men called to each other as the Invalids and Danes milled about on the field they had just won. Four of the Invalids were down and their comrades had dismounted to tend to them. Roland found Declan and Ranulf in the centre of it all.

"Very good timing, my lord," he said, giving a short bow to the Earl of Chester.

"Aye, Sir Roland. The families you sent ahead should be at the gates of Chester by now. I had to order your Sir Edgar to stay with them. He was eager to be a part of…this," he said, sweeping his arm across the field where dead mercenaries lay thick among the stubble. The Earl stopped as he faced south and saw scores of Danish archers watching him. On the ground in front of these men were dozens of dead mercenaries pierced with longbow shafts that armour did not stop. It was a sobering sight.

The Earl had learned much over the past two years about leading men. He had learned from Llywelyn, the young Welsh prince, what men would do for a leader who respected them. He had learned from the Invalids what men who had regained their self-respect could accomplish. He had lost and retaken his city, and in the doing of it, had remade himself. He rode out to meet the Danes.

The archers drifted closer to where Thorkell and Svein centred their line, Oren Inness among them. The Earl pointed to the dead Irish and Flemings.

"Sir Roland Inness told me that an alliance with the Danes would even this fight. I see with my own eyes the truth of it. If I had twice your number, I'd march on Derbyshire!"

Thorkell dipped his head. He was a man unused to bowing to Normans, but it had been this Norman Earl who had just ridden to their rescue.

"We will fight for you, my lord, but not to invade Derbyshire. We've been driven from our homes there and have been promised new homes in your lands. For that we will fight— if you are a man who is good to his word."

"My word is good. There will be a hide of land for every man who drew a bow here this day. That is a promise." He paused and looked at the broad fields they had just fought over.

"The River Weaver is two miles yonder," he said, pointing to the south. Between here and the river is rich farmland—some of the best in Cheshire. I give it to you. You may farm it and raise your families here—for as long as I am Earl."

"And after we clear it of mercenaries…" Thorkell said dryly, pointing at the mass of men continuing to form up across the way.

Ranulf laughed and most of the Danes joined in.

"Aye, I expect it would be hard to get a crop in under present circumstances, and for now, we will depend on the crops we have already taken in at Chester to feed your families, but I promise you this. We *will* drive these people from my lands—from *our* lands."

Roland stood behind the Earl and felt weary relief. Perhaps he had not led the Danes to their doom after all, but he did not feel like celebrating. He watched as more infantry arrived on the opposite side of the field. He saw that Declan was watching this movement warily. Behind the foot soldiers, the heavy cavalry appeared to have regrouped. A command rang out and the infantry began to move across the field toward them, toward the south and Chester.

Ranulf looked across the field and seemed startled to see the enemy advancing instead of retreating. He looked to his two young knights.

"Fight or withdraw?" he asked.

"I think Derbyshire may have to wait, my lord," Declan said. "Those people outnumber us and they know their business. We won't surprise them again, and if they follow, we will have to put the walls of Chester between us and them—at least for now."

Ranulf gave a quiet curse. His blood was up, but he'd learned to trust the advice of his young commanders.

"We'd hoped to avoid a siege…"

"My lord, I did not mean to bring the mercenaries back with me when I went to fetch the Danes," Roland said.

The Earl shrugged.

"Give it no more thought, Sir Roland. I hoped to escape a siege, but it was a very faint hope. Sooner or later they were going to turn on us." He paused and a grim look came over him.

"We are too much a thorn in John's side. He will have to dig it out if he is going to be king!"

Roland watched as the enemy drew nearer, almost into crossbow range.

"This looks to be but a part of their force, my lord, and they may not intend to invest the city, but for now—we should withdraw."

Ranulf nodded and Declan gave the order to fall back. The Irishman reached an arm down and pulled Roland up behind him.

"Welcome back, Roland. It's good of you to bring the Danes, even if you did bring the other lot with you."

Roland smiled as Declan turned his horse's head toward home. Nothing seemed to dampen his friend's wit.

"Believe me, they were not invited. Let's just hope they don't overstay their welcome. Is the harvest in?"

"Aye, all save a few hides west of town and those should be taken in by tomorrow. We were lucky with the weather and the yield this year."

"Thank the Lord for that, but there will be nine hundred new mouths to feed. How long will the food last?"

Declan shook his head.

"I expect Lady Catherine is at the Northgate counting heads right now and will know the answer to that by the time we get there."

"And Millie? She is well?"

There was an uncomfortably long pause.

"Declan?"

"Aye, she's well. She…she left for London two days ago, Roland. She was summoned by the Archbishop—the one who attended the Queen in Oxford. We sent a strong escort with her. Sergeant Billy will let no harm come to her."

"London?" Roland had thought the girl he loved was safe behind the walls of Chester. "To what purpose?"

"The summons did not specify, but the man is the King's Justiciar. She couldn't refuse."

They rode back to the woods in silence surrounded by the mounted men of the Invalid Company and the Danish bowmen. Once they'd reached the cover of the trees, Roland slid off

Declan's mount. One of the Invalids offered their commander his horse, but Roland refused. Other riders, without being ordered, began hoisting wounded men up behind them, Svein among them. Together the men of Cheshire and Derbyshire resumed the retreat to Chester.

Roland caught sight of Oren and was relieved to see him unharmed. They fell in together, both too exhausted to talk. Roland's thoughts were in a whirl.

Millie... gone.

He tried to convince himself that she would be safer in London than trapped inside a city under siege, but it was a half-hearted effort. Nowhere was safe in these troubled times and he wanted her near him. He knew the Archbishop would not summon a girl from the far west of England to pass the time of day. And whatever the Justiciar needed from Millicent would be more important to him than a mere girl's life.

As he trudged along, his weary mind made one plan after another to ride to London and bring her back, but the mercenary army had not broken off their pursuit and he had a responsibility to the Danes he had led here. He would not be able to ride to Millie's rescue.

He had Chester to defend.

Safe Haven

L ady Catherine de Laval watched them come—old men staggering from the weight of years, women with nursing infants, small children, weary and frightened, and young boys carrying bows taller than they were. Leading the vanguard of refugees was the huge Saxon knight, Sir Edgar Langton, his war axe slung over his shoulder.

The Danes had come to Chester.

She was as prepared as she could be, given the short notice. Ever since the Earl and Declan had led the Invalids out to the northeast, she had been frantically organizing Chester to shelter and feed the refugees. A cavernous vacant building that once housed a rope walk was found near the Shipgate. It could accommodate most of the families until less communal quarters could be arranged. Shelter would not be a major problem, but food?

The harvest was all in and the yields exceeded all expectations, but with the population of the city increasing by a quarter, the bountiful supplies would not last as long as planned. They had hoped to stretch the rations for six months if the city were besieged—more than enough time for King Richard to return and set matters aright in his kingdom, but now...food would begin to run out by early December without severe rationing.

Lady Catherine had townspeople posted at the Northgate with buckets of spring water and loaves of bread for the refugee Danes. All looked exhausted, but relieved to have reached this new destination. Most had never seen a city of any size and the children were wide-eyed at the huge stone edifice of the Northgate and the tight rows of buildings that crowded the streets inside the walls.

She beckoned to Sir Edgar who hurried to her side as the human flood poured through the gate.

"My lady, I've brung the families and didn't lose a one," he said proudly.

Lady Catherine gave him a warm smile.

"You've done well, Sir Edgar. The Danes will no doubt write a saga of the big man with the axe who led them out of danger."

Sir Edgar smiled sheepishly. He had come to know Lady Catherine a bit in the weeks he had been at Chester, and she overawed him.

"It was Sir Roland and the bowmen that kept the damned mercenaries off of us, my lady. All's I did was show this lot the way to Chester—and help along a few of the wee ones."

He had no sooner said this than a girl of no more than four tore herself loose from the clutches of her mother and ran over to where the big Saxon knight was standing. She wrapped her skinny arms around a massive leg and looked up at Sir Edgar with pure worship in her eyes. He smiled at the girl as he pried her arms loose.

"Get on back to yer mother, Freja. Get along now."

The girl pouted, but did as she was told.

"Seems you have an admirer among the Danes, Sir Edgar."

"Aye, my lady," he said, his voice a bit wistful. "I always thought I frightened small children—my appearance being what it is, but these little Danes…I guess nothing scares 'em much."

"Children are smarter than we think, Sir Edgar, and I wouldn't fret about missing the fight—I expect there will be work for you and your axe soon enough."

***

It was late afternoon by the time this wave of displaced humanity was sorted out and cared for. As the sun sank toward the Irish Sea, Lady Catherine returned to the Northgate and climbed to the rampart, studying the northern horizon. The fact that the refugees had made it to Chester unharmed meant that the men who had ridden out had managed to keep the pursuit at bay. That required fighting and no one could ever be sure of the outcome of a fight.

She had made ready as best she could. Soon after they had retaken Chester from William de Ferrers, she had sought out those women in the city and the surrounding villages who were skilled in the healing arts. These Lady Catherine organized to care for the sick and wounded should the city be attacked. She had also found space inside the walls of Chester Castle to fashion an infirmary. Before the Invalids had ridden out of the Northgate she had sent word for the women to gather at the castle and prepare for wounded.

The day had been clear and hot and a haze hung in the air. The flags that flew over the gate hung limp in the late July sun. To the north and east, she could see peasant families trudging toward the gates of Chester carrying bundles and pulling carts filled with what possessions they could carry. Word had spread quickly that an enemy force was approaching and all were seeking shelter behind the thick walls of the city.

She squinted into the distance and out of the haze to the north, men appeared. She bit her lip. These men were on foot and some of them were running. A few staggered and fell. All were stumbling down the road toward Chester and all were carrying bows—bows like the one Roland Inness had brought with him so many years ago when he had arrived, a mere boy, on her doorstep.

As the last of the bowmen left the cover of the trees, Catherine saw horsemen. Was it Ranulf and the Invalids—or the enemy? She strained to see through the haze. Then she caught sight of the bright blue banner of the Earl and the blood red banner of the Invalids. She exhaled and realized she had been holding her breath.

119

By the time she reached the street, the first group of exhausted Danes were trudging through the gate. Behind them, tired and dusty horsemen rode through, their heads high. These men were led by Patch and had wounded mounted behind them—about a dozen in all. Patch saw Lady Catherine approach and dismounted.

"Is this all the wounded, Tom? What of the dead?

"Only five dead, my lady—two of my boys and three of the Danes," he said with obvious relief. "A sight more Flemings and Irishmen are dead across the Weaver, I'd reckon."

"The Earl and Sir Declan?"

"Fought like demons," he said with a smile. "The mercs didn't know what hit them!"

"And Sir Roland?"

"Brought these bowmen," he said gesturing at the Danes who were gratefully accepting water from the locals, "just as he promised, my lady. I'd guess six or seven score of them and they made pin cushions out of the enemy cavalry. Deadly shots they are!"

Lady Catherine had known since early that morning that the Danes were coming and that Roland Inness was leading the rear guard. It was a dangerous place to be. She had been fond of Roland since he had saved Millie's life years ago in the Clocaenog Forest, but her daughter loved the boy. To lose him would break her heart and that made his safety all the more important.

Patch excused himself and Lady Catherine waited patiently by the gate. Finally, the last of the horsemen arrived. Roland had been ordered by the Earl to find a mount and was riding next to Declan. He slid off his horse, his legs weak and shaky. He had not slept in two days and had run and fought over ten leagues between the mountains and Chester. He had never felt as weary, but the sight of Lady Catherine buoyed him.

He and Declan walked over to their master's wife, but before they could greet her properly, she stepped forward, her eyes brimming, and hugged them both at once. She wanted to tell them that she had feared for them, that they both had become like family to her, but that was not Lady Catherine de Laval's nature. So she released them and stepped back.

"I'm happy to see you safe home," was all she could manage.

Declan saved them all embarrassment.

"We are simply too dangerous and bold to be killed, my lady."

Lady Catherine gave him a smile. His false bravado sometimes annoyed her, but she was grateful for it now.

"What is following you down the north road?" she asked, turning to Roland.

"My lady, I would guess about half of the mercenary army, with the other half likely to arrive before long. They were only an arrow's shot behind us when we cleared the ford at the Weaver."

She nodded. It was bad news, but not unexpected. There had been daily prayers said at St. Mary's on the Hill to deliver them from the spectre of a siege, but it appeared those prayers were in vain.

"My lady, I need to get up there," Roland said pointing toward the top of the Northgate. "I doubt they will be in a hurry to attack the city, but I would like to see how they deploy."

"Of course. I will see that your wounded are tended to and, when your labours are done, come to the castle. We must talk of Millie."

Roland bowed.

"Yes, my lady." He turned and Declan followed him up the stone steps, through the arched door to the second floor of the gate house and up the ladder to the top of the barbican. This was one of the highest points in the city. They turned their eyes to the north. They did not have long to wait.

From out of the distant tree line the cavalry came first. The lead riders reined in as the city came into view and they were soon joined by others. A small knot of them walked their mounts a little closer, then halted again. They seemed to be studying the approaches to the city. Satisfied with what they'd gleaned, a lone rider returned to the main body. Moments later, two groups of ten riders peeled off to the east and west.

"Scouting the main roads, I'd guess," Declan said. "They'll seal them off soon, I'd wager."

Roland nodded.

Below, the last of the nearby farm families straggled in and the Northgate was closed and barred. Roland watched as more mounted troops rode slowly toward a small hamlet at the edge of the woods. The place was abandoned, but they would be searching for any provisions left behind and fodder for their horses. By the time the last of the riders cleared the road, a thick column of infantry appeared. The column soon split into companies that followed the tracks of the cavalry. The mercenary army had come to Chester.

The siege had begun.

***

Connaught Kilbride was worried. He had been sent to slaughter lightly armed archers and round up any other Danes fleeing to the west and he had failed—miserably. No one had advised him that there could be heavy cavalry waiting in ambush for his men. The surprise had been complete and even seasoned troops do not fight well when surprised.

The greater surprise had been the number of his knights who had fallen to the Danish archers. He had seen a longbow before and knew of its range, but all of his men had worn mail and some had worn plate armour! It had been a shock to see so many of those men go down under the barrage of arrows. His own breastplate had been penetrated by two inches, but the angle of the shaft had prevented the arrowhead from piercing his chest. He'd broken the damn thing off and called the retreat before he lost even more of his men.

He would be judged for this failure, and not kindly. The men who paid his wages would not give a damn for the circumstances. He knew that the rest of the mercenary force was even now marching toward Chester, but he was the senior man present and would be held to account.

Perhaps he could salvage something—even his neck—by immediately sealing off the place. Victory in a siege was achieved by starving a place out and the sooner that began, the sooner it would be over. He hoped that would count for something.

He'd ordered his cavalry to cut off the roads to the east and north of the city. There was nothing to the west but the Irish Sea and little to the south but the River Dee and the wilderness of Wales. In time, the Dee and the approaches from Wales would have to be closed tight, but for now he would send his foot soldiers to watch the roads and fords. He knew the infantry was exhausted after the long pursuit of the Danes, but he didn't care. He had his neck to save.

***

Kilbride tried not to flinch. The face of the young English Earl of Derby was only inches from his own and the man was in a black rage. Kilbride knew it was coming—had known it the moment he rode out of the trees north of Chester and saw the empty road leading to the barred gate of the city. The Danes had eluded him and now came the accounting. He hoped to salvage his head, if not his command.

He told de Ferrers of the unexpected assault by heavy cavalry, just as they were about to savage the fleeing Danish archers. As he expected, the Earl did not care. He chanced a glance at his own leader. Pieter Van Hese was a veteran Flemish war lord with one blind eye and a reputation for ruthlessness. Earl William might be commander of this host in name, but this Fleming was commander in fact. Sadly, the man showed no interest in coming to Kilbride's defence.

I'm ruined.

He tried desperately to think of a way to salvage his position.

"My lord, when I saw these Danes had taken refuge inside Chester, I immediately sealed all the roads leading into the city. Nothing has gone in or out since."

"Damn the roads!" de Ferrers screamed. "I wanted them dead—not *inconvenienced!* And tell me, why did you not assault the city? You've been here three days and all I see are men sitting on their asses."

"My lord, the walls…"

"Walls?" de Ferrers spit out the word as though it was a piece of rotten meat. "Walls can be scaled! When I took Shipbrook we scaled the walls with ladders, man. Did you not think of ladders?"

Kilbride fought the urge to grasp this strutting idiot by his neck and squeeze the life out of him. Ladders? Had this bastard ever climbed a ladder with determined defenders hacking away at him from above? Kilbride had. He still bore the scars from a cauldron of scalding water tipped over a wall in Ulster that had burned right through his mail. Before the Irishman could fashion a reply to de Ferrers question, Van Hese interrupted.

"My lord, we used ladders at Nottingham Castle and suffered grievous losses. I know of your *victory* at Shipbrook, but the walls here are ten feet higher and there are far more than *twenty* defenders atop them. I wouldn't advise such an assault. I believe we can starve them out in due time. They've taken in hundreds of extra mouths."

De Ferrers turned on the man, unsure if he was being helpful or making jest of his victory at the small fort out near the Dee River ford. Had there been contempt in the mercenary's voice when he mentioned the number of defenders they'd faced at Shipbrook?

He started to rebuke the arrogant war lord, but hesitated. Van Hese was a stolid man, but de Ferrers knew the Fleming's bland countenance disguised a vicious streak deeper even than his own. He was more than a little afraid of the mercenary commander. The curse that was forming on his lips became a nervous cough.

"It is July," he managed, "and they've taken in their harvest. If they have food for five months, Richard could be home before they starve. The Prince will expect results long before then."

The Flemish commander shrugged.

"What the Prince expects and what the situation allows are not always the same, my lord."

De Ferrers studied the mercenary leader. He had learned during the siege of Nottingham that Van Hese had little fear of John and would not needlessly hazard his men, simply to please his employer. After a bloody repulse of their first assault on

124

Nottingham Castle, he had insisted on going over to a protracted siege. When de Ferrers had pressed him to move faster, the man had made his position clear.

"It's bad business to throw away lives. A dead fighter shows no profit."

But de Ferrers had learned in Sheffield that holding the purse strings had its own power. He had reminded Van Hese in that ravaged town that an unhappy client might look elsewhere for fighting men. That had got the army moving once more. It was time to remind the mercenary once more that John paid the bills.

"Very well, I will inform his grace that you are in no hurry to take Chester. Perhaps he will find someone who needs the gold more and will be willing to move with more urgency."

For a long moment the two men locked eyes, each judging the other's resolve. Finally, the Fleming shrugged his shoulders.

"Very well, the siege trains will take another ten days to reach here. If the walls are too high to climb over, we will knock them down. Then, my lord, you may have your assault on the city."

Part Two: Waiting for the King

The Ransomed Crown

Mare Tranquillus

Sir Roger de Laval sat in the sun and tested the edge of his broadsword with his thumb. He'd been working it with a whetstone, concerned that the sea air would dull the blade. Satisfied with the result, he slid it back into its scabbard and looked around the deck of the galley bearing the King of England through light swells toward Cyprus.

The sun felt good on his shoulders, the warmth easing some of the stiffness in his spine from the cramped sleeping quarters on board. There had been a time when he could have—and often did—sleep in worse conditions, but he had been younger then. Now, old wounds were quick to remind him of the insults his body had suffered over his long career as a soldier.

It felt good to be underway. It was late July and there had been fair winds and calm seas on the day they shipped anchor and left the accursed Kingdom of Jerusalem behind. The oarsmen had only been pressed into service when the breeze dropped off after sunset. The weather had held and on the morning of the third day the lookout sighted land. Why the King wished to stop on this island was a matter of quiet debate.

Richard had snatched Cyprus from its Byzantine Emperor on his outbound voyage the year before, and when it became clear that none of the Christian nobility in the Holy Land had confidence in King Guy as their leader, he had persuaded that hapless monarch to give up the throne of Jerusalem to become King of Cyprus.

The Ransomed Crown

Now it seemed, the Lionheart felt obliged to make a courtesy call on the new ruler on his way home to England. The King's close companion, Sir Baldwin of Bethune, had observed dryly that the last time his friend had stopped in Cyprus, he had stayed for two months. But Richard was determined to play out his role as kingmaker, despite the urgent need to see to his own realm.

Deep trouble was brewing back in England that might only be averted by the King's timely return. What's more, they would soon be entering a season when cautious sailors in these waters did not stray far from port. Savage storms were known to lash these peaceful seas with the onset of autumn.

Sir Roger could see two dozen men scattered around the deck, most wearing the red cross of the Templar Knights. Without doubt, the King expected trouble on his voyage home and was preparing for it as best he could. The extent of that trouble was made clear their second night on board, when Richard summoned Sir Roger and Sir Baldwin to seek their counsel on the planned route.

"Gentlemen, as you know, this journey is as fraught with peril as any battle. I have enemies who sit astride every path home. They would like nothing better than to have me in their power, but I have a notion of how to slip through their nets. The path I propose would take us to the head of the Adriatic, through the mountain passes to Bavaria, then on to Saxony. I would hear your thoughts on this plan."

Sir Baldwin spoke first.

"Your grace, let me begin by speaking of your enemies." The knight lifted his index finger. "The Holy Roman Emperor. Henry's domain covers everything from the Elbe to the lands of the Magyars. He hates you for allowing Tancred to stay on the throne of Sicily. He wanted that throne for one of his own vassals. We would be in his realm for most of the route you propose."

Richard snorted.

"Henry? He is a shadow of his father, Barbarossa! He should have taken up his sire's crusader shield when the old man drowned in Anatolia, but he sent that weasel, Duke Leopold, in his stead. Need I fear such a man?"

Sir Baldwin exchanged a glance with Sir Roger.

"Your grace, do not underestimate the Emperor. He is a man known for his cunning, if not his bravery." Baldwin then raised a second finger. "Duke Leopold. We must not forget his vassal, the weasel of Austria. Your route takes us near the southern border of Leopold's land and he will never forgive our defiling of his banner at Acre."

Sir Roger cringed at the memory of English troops dragging down the banner of the Holy Roman Emperor and trampling it in the dust the day after Acre fell. The Duke demanded that the offenders be punished, but the King was unmoved. Enraged, the Duke swore vengeance.

"That ass Leopold tried to claim an equal share in the victory, when there were hardly enough Germans left to fill a boot with piss," the King roared. "I should have wiped my arse with his banner!"

By now Sir Baldwin was getting exasperated. He was one of the few men who could do so in the presence of King Richard without fear.

"So, we should just promenade through Austria and Bavaria and Bohemia until we reach the safety of Saxony?"

Richard, his bluster expended, allowed himself a small grin. He had sought the views of these two men because they were the bluntest advisors he had. The others were all too cowed by him.

"Of course not, Baldwin," he replied calmly. "Even I am not foolhardy enough to enter Leopold's domain. That snake would love to humble me. But might we not disguise ourselves as simple soldiers returning from the Crusade and make our way unchallenged through the high passes of the Alpine mountains and into Bavaria? From there it is but a short way to Saxony— or would you prefer I simply go ashore in France and enjoy the welcome Philip would arrange for me."

Baldwin paid no attention to his master's sarcasm. He raised a third finger and then a fourth.

"France is out, on that we can agree—and Italy as well. The Venetians would sell you to the highest bidder in the blink of an eye, but disguising yourself as a simple soldier? You would fool no one, your grace."

Sir Roger now spoke up.

"Why not sail right across the length of the Mediterranean, through the Gates of Hercules and straight north from there to England. There are no kings or dukes with scores to settle on the sea."

Baldwin sighed and exchanged glances with the King, whose face had reddened a bit.

"Sir Roger, you were not with us on the outbound voyage from France. The fleet was caught in a gale and several vessels were lost with no survivors. That was in May, when conditions are best in this sea. Soon it will be the season for storms. Even a short voyage at this time of year is risky. If the King thought we could fight our way overland through the heathen Turks of Anatolia, we wouldn't be setting foot on this galley." Sir Baldwin turned back to the King.

"Does that sum it up, your grace?"

Richard gave his friend a sour smile.

"It's good that I like you, Baldwin, or I should have your head for that, but then I would only have Sir Roger here to goad me. So, yes, it is as you say. I will be most happy to set foot back on solid ground, which takes me back to the mountain route into Bavaria and on to Saxony. As difficult as that passage may be, it leads to our closest safe haven."

Henry the Lion of Saxony, was the King's brother-in-law and could offer protection. From the Saxon ports it was little more than a few days sail to England. There being no other options to put forward, the meeting was adjourned.

Now it was morning, and men were gathering at the bow to watch as the shore of Cyprus slowly came into view. Sir Roger glanced around at the battle-hardened men who clustered at the rail. The Templars were good men in a fight and more than adequate to deal with pirates or other brigands, but at no more than two dozen, they would be poor protection from the King's royal enemies—enemies through whose land they would be traveling.

As the shore drew near, he climbed down from the low sterncastle and made his way below decks to the tiny corner that was his spartan quarters for the voyage. He gathered his weapons

131

and kit to prepare for landfall and returned to the deck. It was a beautiful day and that lightened his mood a bit. With a bit of luck he would be home in three months.

Home.

He had managed to keep thoughts of Catherine from driving him mad during the long years of war, but now he let himself picture her—as fresh and beautiful in his mind as the day they had met. He thought of his daughter. Millie would be near grown by now—no longer his Little Lady. The thought left a lump in his throat.

He watched the sun glint off the cobalt water as the shore drew near. The day was indeed beautiful, but he could not shake off a sense of foreboding about this journey and a nagging thought would not leave him.

I should have sailed with my squires aboard the Sprite.

Game of Spies

Millicent de Laval clucked to her horse as she passed through the Newgate and into London as the sun was setting behind her. The arched gatehouse and the street just beyond were jammed with people and the animal was nervous. She was as well. The summons from Walter of Coutances had given her little indication of what he wanted with her and she did not like being in the dark.

Flanking her was William Butler, the one-legged soldier known to all as Sergeant Billy. Three other men from the Invalid Company rode with them, all veterans of the crusade. The Earl of Chester, her mother, and Declan O'Duinne had all insisted that she have a strong escort for the six day journey to the city and there had been a near fistfight amongst the Invalids to determine who would be her protectors on the trip.

Two of the men under Sergeant Billy's command had been with the Invalids from the start. The third was the youngest of the men chosen. Jamie Finch had arrived at the gates of Chester just a month before. Sergeant Billy picked the lad because he had grown up in the back alleys of London and knew it better than any man in the Company. He also wanted to see how the new man handled himself.

Finch was hardly more than a boy, but he was a boy with a past. He had an ugly scar along his neck and folks assumed it had come from wounds sustained on the crusade, but Sergeant

133

Billy knew it was from a barroom brawl in the dives of London. The boy had got it long after he'd returned from the killing grounds of the Holy Land.

Jamie Finch had brought a reputation as a drunkard and a hothead with him when he arrived in Chester, but that was no bar from joining the Invalid Company. Sergeant Billy himself had been barely sober that cold day when he and his mates had formed up outside the walls of Oxford town to ride to the relief of the Earl of Chester.

In the month he'd been at Chester, Finch had touched not a drop of spirits. For reasons only he knew, the young veteran had pulled himself out of the gutters of London and ridden alone across half the breadth of England to join their ranks. The scar on his neck might be a reminder of bad times and bad judgment, but none of the Invalids were saints. Few ever saw the true badge of Finch's service—a nastier scar on his left side where a Saracen blade had almost taken his life at Acre.

As they travelled down Watling Street from the Newgate, the looming bulk of St. Paul's cathedral appeared on the right, one side laced with scaffolding attesting to the continued expansion of the enormous structure. Two blocks on, they turned north onto Wood Street, which led up toward the Cripplegate. There were precise directions in the Archbishop's summons that led them to a rather shabby two-storey house near the London Guildhall.

Millicent dismounted, stiff from the long ride. She knew she must be a sight. Her light traveling cape was covered in the dust of the road and her hair had been blown into wild tangles. She absently combed at a few knots with her fingers as Sergeant Billy hammered on the front door of the place.

After a long wait, the door opened a crack. Whoever was inside took their time assessing the visitors, but then swung the door open. A bent old man stood in the entrance and looked right past Sergeant Billy to stare at Millicent for a long moment. He spoke something Millicent couldn't hear and Sergeant Billy stiffened. He hurried back to where she stood.

"He only wants you to come in, my lady."

Millicent furrowed her brow.

134

"You will come with me, William, regardless of what he may want. Have the others wait here."

She approached the open door with Sergeant Billy in tow and locked eyes with the man standing in the entrance. She may have answered the Justiciar's summons, but she was not going to be ordered about in this manner. The man was quick to read the look in her eyes. He shrugged in defeat and waved them inside.

"Yer just as his excellency described ye," he said, as Millicent came through the door. "Please, let me take your cloak."

Millicent shrugged off the garment and handed it to him.

"Is this the Archbishop's house? Is he home?" she asked.

"Oh, heaven's no, my lady. Heaven's no! This is a place we use—on occasion—when his excellency wishes to meet with someone...discreetly. He was not sure when you would arrive, but I see you have made good time. You may wait here," he said gesturing to a small parlour off the main hallway of the place. "I will fetch the Archbishop immediately. He has been anxious to see you!"

Millicent nodded and found a nicely stuffed chair to sit on. It felt good after five hard days in the saddle. Sergeant Billy sat on a bench opposite her and fidgeted.

"What do ye reckon this churchman wants with you?"

It was a question he had raised a half dozen times on the ride in from Chester. She smiled at him. He knew she did not know and he did not expect an answer. It was just his way of saying he worried about her.

"We'll know soon enough, William."

Soon enough came quickly. Within an hour, Millicent heard movement at the back of the house. She rose as the Archbishop of Rouen entered the room. He was a small man with quick, darting eyes that seemed to take in everything in a moment.

"Your excellency," she said, and did a quick curtsy.

"My lady, I am happy to see you again. I apologize for this rather—mysterious reception, but it is for good cause."

He turned to Sergeant Billy.

"I appreciate you safeguarding Lady Millicent on her journey, but if you could join your comrades in the street for a bit, I must speak with her alone now."

Millicent could see that Sergeant Billy wanted to protest, but she gave him a warning look and he simply nodded and walked out of the room. The old man opened the door onto Wood Street for him, then retreated to the rear of the house. She was alone with Walter of Coutances. He gestured to the chairs in the parlour and they sat.

"You must be anxious to know why I've sent for you, Lady Millicent," he said, his voice soft and solicitous. "Be assured, I would not have dragged you from your home and family unless the need was great. When we last spoke, I was most impressed by your quick thinking and courage in saving your Earl from a traitor's death. You saved Ranulf and now—your King needs you."

The Justiciar had all of the charm of a kindly uncle, but Millicent de Laval had not ridden six days to be charmed.

"Your excellency, let me speak plainly. I care little for what the King may need. He has already taken my father from me for two years and has left the rest of his kingdom to be preyed upon by traitors and villains. Why should I care what the man needs?"

The Archbishop frowned, surprised by the passion of her response, but was not deterred. If flattery and charm did not work on this girl...

"You've spoken plainly, miss, so let me do the same. Richard leaves much to be desired as King, I would concede, but if Richard's crown is not preserved, then John will have it. And if John has the crown, your young Earl will once more be outlawed and people like you—and I—will be trampled underfoot. Is that plain enough for you?"

Millicent did not flinch as the churchman changed his tone.

"Your excellency, I've left everything I love back in Chester to answer your summons. There is a good chance the city will be besieged soon and I feel my place is there, not here. But my father is the King's man and out of loyalty to *him*, I am here. Tell me what you want of me."

Walter of Coutances did not allow himself to smile, though he wanted to. This girl would do very well indeed.

"My dear, I'm afraid I need your talents as a spy once more."

***

They talked for an hour, then the Archbishop bid her goodnight and slipped out a back entrance of the house. In that hour, the Justiciar dropped entirely his façade of kindly uncle and bluntly outlined the role he would have her play. The spymaster was convinced there was a traitor among those nearest William Marshal—an agent in the pay of France who had done real damage to those defending Richard's throne. She was to find the traitor.

Walter of Coutances did not have to convince her of the gravity that such a threat posed for the kingdom. She had seen the damage that a single French agent could do when Chester had been taken by surprise and its Earl charged with treason. Father Malachy had brought down one of the most powerful men in England through guile, and only daring, luck and the lives of scores of men had restored Ranulf to his Earldom.

"Make no mistake, the French fear Richard and want John on the throne and they will stop at nothing to achieve that," he told her, his voice sharp. "Some of our closest secrets have been compromised and if they are privy to our every move, they will win in the end." He stopped abruptly and looked intently at the girl.

So young.

"I give you fair warning, my lady—they know the value of this spy and will use any means to protect him—any means. Is that clear?"

"Yes, your excellency. If they discover I am hunting their man, my life will be in danger, so I must fly a false flag and be on my guard. I have been a spy before."

"Indeed you have, my dear, and a good one. Will you do it?"

The Archbishop watched her carefully. The girl had an unsettled look in her eyes. She stood and turned away from him. For a moment the spymaster thought she was going to refuse him, but Millicent turned back, the unsettled look gone now. She simply nodded to the older man.

"How am I to become attached to Earl William's household?"

Walter of Coutances realized he had been holding his breath and now released it in relief. His instincts about this young woman had not been wrong.

"I have spoken with the Earl. You are to present yourself as the daughter of his cousin, come to London from Cheshire to escape the troubles there. Did you know that William Marshal has a distant cousin married to the Baron Malpas, one of the richest nobles in Cheshire, my dear?"

"No, excellency, I did not."

"That's because it's a lie, but none here will know that. To the people of London, Cheshire might as well be the moon. Many will know who your Earl Ranulf is, but of the other provincial nobility, they will be ignorant. You are to be Lady Millicent of Malpas, the daughter of Earl William's dear but distant cousin, Matilda, who is married to the Baron. I've chosen this particular deceit, my dear, because a Cheshire accent is quite distinct and you have one."

Millicent frowned.

"Then why cannot I simply be myself? As you say, I am from Cheshire, and if no one in London knows of the Cheshire nobility, then one noble family from there should be as good as any other. My father is a noble. Why can I not just be Millicent de Laval?"

The Archbishop steepled his fingers beneath his chin.

"Because there is one French agent who certainly knows your name."

For a moment Millicent did not take his meaning, then it struck her.

"Malachy!"

"Aye, your Father Malachy. I had a man, near to the Earl of Derby, who reported that this Malachy creature had disappeared not long after de Ferrers lost Chester and hasn't been seen since. Grievously, my man is now dead, and I've had no further word on the whereabouts of this false priest. He might even be in

London. I've alerted my own watchers and given them the description you gave me in Oxford, but this city is overrun with priests. It would be easy for him to hide in plain sight. If he is here, we cannot risk your name coming to his attention."

"I see," said Millicent. "So I am to be a distant cousin to Earl William Marshal—a country bumpkin sent to the city for safe keeping. What does my famous cousin think of all this?"

The Archbishop shrugged.

"He is not happy, but has agreed to my request. He is convinced that his people are loyal, but understands my need to be certain. You will stay here for a few days, then you will present yourself at William Marshal's London quarters in the east of the city—as though you have just arrived from Cheshire. You will need considerable freedom of movement and a noblewoman alone on the streets of London would draw unwanted attention. So Marshal agrees that you may keep one of your men, who will pose as your servant. Once you take up residence with the Earl, you may keep him informed of your work, but will report anything of note to me. There is a beggar who sits each day at the northeast corner of Saint Paul's. If you have information, drop a coin in his hat and I will meet you here an hour past sundown."

Millicent nodded.

"Other than myself and Marshal, only my most trusted assistant, Mary Cullen, will know your secret, my lady, and even Mary will not be told your true identity. I am often out of London and on those occasions it will be Mary who will be your contact. I will be sending her to meet you tomorrow. I believe she can be of assistance in preparing you for this task."

"Assistance, your excellency?"

The Archbishop looked slightly abashed.

"My lady, you will need a new wardrobe if you are to be the daughter of the richest man in Cheshire. Mary knows a good draper—one who caters to the wealthier families here in London. I'll provide her funds to buy new fabric and to hire a seamstress."

Millicent looked down at her frock and frowned. She had never thought much about her clothes, but she had to admit her dress was a bit faded and it was the best she had brought with her.

She might dress like a noblewoman, but a very poor one indeed. It struck her that there might be some advantages to this new role she was being asked to play.

Perhaps something in green…

***

Father Malachy closed the book of ornate Latin text and rose wearily to his feet. As a boy in Ireland, his local priest had taught him a little of the ancient language, perhaps hoping that his young student would follow him into the priesthood. But then the English had come to their village and he had been left an orphan with no place in his heart for a priest's grace or for Christian mercy—only hate for the people who had killed his father. He wondered what that parish priest would think if he could see him now in these robes memorizing the words of the Mass.

For three years he had masqueraded as a man of God. It was a simple subterfuge and one that granted him access to men of power. The Earl of Derby had recognized his talents and had given him important duties to perform, but rarely expected him to function as a churchman. Now it was different. He had been called away from Derbyshire to take up the position of priest at the small chapel within Westminster Palace.

The order had come from Archdeacon Poore. Poore was no counterfeit priest, having served for years within the hierarchy of the English church. The churchman knew full well that Malachy's priestly guise was a sham and that the Irishman was an agent of the French. He knew this for the simple reason that he was as well. The Archdeacon of Canterbury had been in the pay of King Philip of France for years and had slowly built the French spy network on the island. He was not driven by hate, as was Malachy, but by greed. Archdeacon Poore had very expensive tastes.

Poore had promised Malachy that his new post would offer him the opportunity to strike a blow against the English that would send them reeling, but had provided no specifics. The Irishman had waited eagerly for instructions from the spymaster for over a month, but none had come. With no guidance from the Archdeacon, he had focused on establishing his bona fides at the palace. With Queen Eleanor decamped to France to bolster the Norman defences there, only a few regular attendees came to his masses in the small chapel. Even so, he could ill afford for them to be suspicious of his status. Therefore he studied the words of the Mass and practiced them aloud in his room. But it was frustrating.

He was determined to wait until he received a summons from the Archdeacon, but after another fortnight he could not stand the idleness. He waited until dark then found his way to the fine house on the Strand that was Poore's London residence. A servant answered his knock, but before he was well inside the door, the Archdeacon appeared in the hallway. He seemed surprised but not unhappy to see his agent.

"Malachy! I was just thinking of you yesterday and here you are! What brings you to my door this night?"

Malachy had rehearsed what he would say to his master, but Poore's obvious pleasure at seeing him left him slightly flustered.

"Your excellency, it's been almost two months since I took up my post at Westminster and I have absolutely nothing to report. With the Queen absent, there are only clerks and servants about and they know nothing of value." He could not keep a note of frustration out of his voice.

The spymaster put a gentle hand on his shoulder.

"My son, this game we play rewards the patient as well as the bold. I have been at it for two decades and, if I've learned anything, it's that everything has its time. Rush a thing, and it slips right through your fingers! I know you chafe, Father Malachy, but I see noble deeds ahead for you. Believe me, you have not been forgotten, but, for now, you must wait—until your time comes round."

Malachy bowed.

"I will try to be patient, your excellency."

***

It was midmorning when Millicent heard a key turn in the rear entrance to the house. A young woman, only a little older than her came through the door and saw her standing there,

Sergeant Billy at her side. She gave them both a sunny smile and did a quick curtsy.

"I'm happy to meet you, my lady," she said brightly. "I'm Mary Cullen. The Archbishop tells me you're from Cheshire. I am from Normandy, so we are both fish out of water here in London!"

The girl voice had an infectious note of high spirits that was contagious. Millicent smiled back and found herself hoping that the Archbishop of Rouen would frequently find himself out of London. This girl would be much more interesting to conspire with than the churchman.

"So I am to help you put together a rich girl's wardrobe, I'm told."

Millicent flushed a little.

"The Archbishop thought it necessary."

Mary Cullen looked her up and down.

"Yours is a perfectly presentable frock, my lady, though a little worn." She winked at Millicent. "And since the Archbishop is paying—so much the better. It will be fun!"

Millicent didn't think so, but thought it churlish to object.

"Very well, Miss Cullen. Let's see if you can make a pheasant out of this country partridge."

Mary Cullen clapped her hands.

"I know just the place! And please, my lady, call me Mary."

***

The draper's shop was a long way from the Archbishop's town house, but Millicent welcomed the chance to walk through the teeming streets of the capital after days on horseback. She had a long stride and Mary Cullen had to hurry along to keep ahead of her. Finally, she touched Millicent's arm.

"My lady, forgive me if I give you a small piece of advice," she said, her cheeks reddening. "Your gait, my lady, is most...unusual. The fine ladies hereabouts don't tend to stride along at such a pace. It will draw attention to you."

Millicent felt her temper flare, but she checked herself. It did not profit a spy to be noticed and Mary Cullen was simply doing her job to point that out. And the poor girl was clearly embarrassed. She gave her a warm smile.

"Think nothing of it, Mary. I will try to mince along like a proper noblewoman hereafter."

Mary Cullen beamed at her, clearly relieved. They resumed walking—at a more refined pace. The two made their way up Wood Street then turned right to pass by the sturdy bulk of the Guildhall. They had almost reached Broad Street when the trade sign for the draper came into view. They entered the shop, which seemed quiet and cool after the heat of the August sun. Arrayed on tables and in bins around the walls were rolls of fabric—some plain, like the dress Millicent wore, but many of much finer quality.

Mary Cullen summoned the shop keeper and immediately began pointing out rolls of fabric she wanted to inspect. Millicent watched with interest. She had never been in a draper's shop and as the man brought forth roll after roll of fine cloth she marvelled at the rich colours and the sheen of the fabric.

She had seen good quality cloth before—when she had served as lady-in-waiting to Lady Constance, Earl Ranulf's wife, but that woman had always chosen drab colours. These rolls of cloth were anything but drab. Mary Cullen handed her a bolt of shimmering green. The cloth felt like the fine coat of a thoroughbred horse when she ran her hand over it.

"That colour suits you," said Mary, smiling brightly. "The green—it sets off your eyes quite nicely."

Millicent looked back down at the fabric.

"But what does it cost?"

Mary giggled.

"Too much for us—but not the Archbishop!"

***

For three days Millicent waited in the Archbishop's town house while a seamstress prepared her new wardrobe. The spymaster and Mary Cullen paid her a visit on the third night.

"Do you have any final questions, my dear?" he asked.

"No, your excellency, I'm as ready as I'll ever be—except for the new wardrobe, which I understand arrives tonight."

The Archbishop made a sour face and rummaged through his robes before producing a chit with the record of the cloth purchases from the draper's shop.

"You have expensive tastes, my dear!"

From behind the churchman, Millicent heard Mary Cullen speak up, with just a hint of censure in her voice.

"The fabric matched her eyes, your excellency."

***

At his townhouse on the Strand, Archdeacon Poore listened to the report from his most trusted agent in London.

"They suspect we have a spy near Marshal."

The churchman gave a soft chuckle.

"Well, we do. I would have been disappointed in the Archbishop if he failed to notice his secrets were being compromised. In any event, I would rather they fix their attention on Marshal's associates than probe elsewhere, though I'd hate to lose a man that close to the Justiciar."

"They've brought in a girl—from Cheshire, excellency. They're sending her to watch Marshal's men."

"A girl, you say? That might be a clever move. Women have a way of inducing loose talk from men, I think you'd agree."

"I would, though I doubt our man would be susceptible. Should we warn him or dispose of this girl?"

"As for our spy, give him no warning. It would only make him nervous—and if he's nervous, he will give himself away."

"And the girl?"

The Archdeacon shrugged.

"I hardly think a girl from Cheshire will be much trouble."

Marshal's Men

Five days after arriving in London, Millicent de Laval rode up to the house of William Marshal. It was on a rise north of the Tower and she could see the bulk of that enormous fortress off to her right. She wore a frock of shimmering green, fitted and sewn for her by the seamstress Mary Cullen had provided.

There had been heated arguments over who would remain behind with her, but in the end it was agreed that Jamie Finch, native of London, would become her servant. Sergeant Billy had argued for himself, but Millicent had gently pointed out that he hardly knew London at all and that, with his natural air of authority, he would not likely pass as a servant. With the issue decided against him, he turned to young Finch and fixed him with a menacing look.

"Master Finch, if a hair of Lady Millicent's head gets mussed on your watch, there are eighty Invalids who will hunt you down—understood?" There was no humour in his voice.

"Aye, Sergeant Billy. I'll keep 'er safe," the young veteran said.

All four of her escorts rode with her to Marshal's house. It was just past noon when Sergeant Billy climbed the stairs in front, his wooden leg tapping at each step and rapped on the door. An armed man cracked it open. There was a round of discussion accompanied by a bit of pointing in Millicent's direction. The man at the door nodded and Sergeant Billy returned to help her dismount. She could have easily managed that but her escort thought it unseemly for her to simply slide out of the saddle on her own—at least in sight of folks here in London.

"They are expecting you, my lady," he said as he helped her gently to the ground. He had a grim look on his face.

"Don't fret, William. I will be in good hands here. Why, they even have an armed guard at the door."

Sergeant Billy scowled.

"I'd like it better if we saw to your safety, my lady."

"As would I, William, but we all have our duty to attend to and yours is now back in Chester." As Jamie Finch was securing her baggage, she turned to the other men who had ridden with her all the way from the west country.

"Thank you all and God go with you. I think Chester will need you more than I."

These men had been there on the road from Oxford when this young woman had first won the hearts of the Invalid Company. She had come, unbidden, to their camp to greet them, outcasts and broken men all. Her simple decency had touched them deeply and from that night onward, they had all acted as though they were her favourite uncles.

The men helped her carry her things into the house. The young man at the door beckoned to one of his fellows who directed Finch toward the servant's quarters, then showed Millicent to her room. It was bigger than the one she had at Shipbrook. He told her that the Earl was out, but would meet her at the evening meal. Then he backed out of the room and closed the door quietly behind him.

For a moment, she stood there in the middle of the room, then she walked over to the window that looked down on the street below. She saw Sergeant Billy and the rest of the Invalids mount their horses and ride west, back toward the Newgate and Watling Street—back towards Chester and home. She felt a tightness in her chest.

She was on her own now.

***

Millicent heard a soft tapping on her door. She had sat alone in her room all afternoon and was beginning to wonder if she had been forgotten. She walked over and opened the door. A tall, fragile woman of middle years with a flushed face was standing in the hall and did a quick curtsy.

"Oh, my lady! I've just learned of your presence here from the dolts downstairs. I am Elizabeth Armfield, Sir William's..." The woman seemed to struggle for a moment with an explanation of her status. "I run the household here in London for Sir William. I was with the cook at the market and the young lads with the swords never thought to mention that the Earl's cousin had arrived in my absence! I am so sorry, my lady."

The poor woman seemed entirely flustered by this oversight. Millicent reached out a hand and touched her arm.

"Oh, please, Mistress Armfield, don't fret over me. I've taken advantage of the quiet and had a nice nap. It's been a long journey from Cheshire!"

The woman seemed genuinely touched that Millicent hadn't taken offense at her reception.

"Oh, please, my lady, you may call me Elizabeth!" The woman furrowed her brow and glowered back at the stairs. "You can be sure I gave those ruffians a hiding for such rudeness! They will be on their best behaviour henceforth."

Millicent smiled at her.

"Think no more of it, Elizabeth. I am from Cheshire, which is as far into the wilderness of the west country as you can get without stepping into the Irish Sea. I am more than used to a house full of rough gentlemen."

Elizabeth clucked in sympathy.

"The Earl told me you were coming because of trouble near your home." She sighed. "It seems the whole country is beset these days, but you will be safe here, my lady. The lads may be a rough lot, but they know their business."

Millicent nodded.

"I am from Malpas, and when Father heard that these awful mercenaries might lay siege to Chester, he thought it best I come stay with Cousin William here in London."

Elizabeth Armfield beamed at her.

147

"Well, you are most welcome, my lady. This house is far too full of men. They lounge about with their swords and track mud into the front hall. They pay me no heed, but perhaps having a lady present will improve their manners!"

Millicent laughed.

"I will do what I can, Elizabeth!"

The woman now seemed entirely put at ease.

"Thank you, my lady. I will be back in an hour to take you down to dinner. The Earl should be home by then. Please just call if you need anything—anything at all."

As the hour for dinner approached, Millicent prepared herself. She had met Marshal the previous winter when she had brought the news to Queen Eleanor that Earl Ranulf still lived. The encounter had been brief, but the man had made an impression.

He was almost a head taller than anyone in the room that day and, while he appeared to be at ease, his carriage radiated the look of a man born to authority. She had been told that Marshal had bested over five hundred knights in tournaments during his youth and, though he was older now, he still had the powerful build and the graceful movements of a warrior. She knew he had resisted the Archbishop's plan to place her in his household and hoped he would not make her task more difficult.

As promised, Elizabeth Armfield arrived to escort her down to the evening meal. She had not been exaggerating when she called Marshal's residence a house full of men, for there was not a woman among those who were gathered around the table. Eight men, mostly young, stood behind their benches on either side, trying to look courtly, but only succeeding in looking nervous. Mistress Armfield's tongue lashing must have been frightful.

Marshal sat at the head of the table and a gruff looking older man sat to his right. A place had been left for Millicent on the Earl's left. Marshal was engaged in an animated conversation with the man next to him when Millicent entered, but broke it off when he saw her.

"Lady Millicent!" he exclaimed, as he came around the table and took her hand. "Forgive me for not greeting you earlier, cousin. I've just arrived back here myself. Come, let's take some refreshment and afterwards you must tell me all about your dear mother and the awful situation in Cheshire."

Millicent gave the Justiciar a quick curtsy as he approached and let him lead her to her place at the table. She felt a wave of relief. Whatever the man's feelings about the job she had been sent here to do, he was at least making an effort to lend credence to her new identity. Before allowing anyone to sit, the Earl introduced her to each man in turn. She carefully memorized the names as she smiled at each new face.

The last introduction was to a Sir Nevil Crenshaw, the man sitting next to Marshal who was his long-time friend and commander of his personal guard. Sir Nevil had charge over these younger men, all of whom were engaged in securing the home and protecting the person of the Earl, save one, a clerkish young man who handled the Justiciar's formal correspondence.

During the meal, Marshal engaged her in conversation about the family of Baron Malpas—people that neither of them knew. Millicent took some satisfaction in describing her mother, and Earl William's cousin, as a scatter-brained woman with little knowledge or interest in things outside of the small town clustered around Malpas Castle.

This seemed to amuse Marshal who played along adeptly. The young men around the table were on their best behaviour and more than one was overly solicitous of the beautiful young woman who had suddenly entered their circle. Once the meal was concluded, Marshal dismissed his bodyguard and led Millicent into a private parlour next to the dining room. He closed the door behind him and turned to face her.

"I remember you from Oxford, my lady. We had little chance to speak on that occasion, so may I offer you my respects for saving the life of your Earl and seriously inconveniencing the King's brother."

"Thank you, my lord. My father is the Earl's man to his core, and I am my father's daughter. I could do no less."

Marshal smiled warmly at her and gestured toward a chair.

"I've never met your father, but I certainly know of him. I'm told he is a dangerous man in a fight and has risen to command the King's heavy cavalry on this latest campaign. England needs men such as your father these days."

Millicent did not return the man's smile.

"My lord, my mother needs her husband and I have not seen my father for over two years. What England needs is peace, or men like my father will all be dead. Tell me that all of this," she spread her hands, as though calling up all of her family's sacrifices, "will bring us peace."

Marshal's features, so warm before, grew pained.

"Lady Millicent, in this world, only a fool or a liar would promise you peace. I won't insult your intelligence by doing so. War is all around us and the best we can hope for is to keep bad men from winning the day."

"That is why the Archbishop has sent me here, my lord. He believes there is a bad man in your midst."

Marshal shook his head emphatically.

"There is no traitor here, my lady. My friend, the Archbishop, is suspicious by nature, but I suppose that is his job at the moment."

Millicent nodded.

"I hope you are right about your men, my lord, but secrets have been compromised, have they not?"

Marshal scowled.

"Yes. There is no other explanation for some of the Prince's actions. He has learned of our plans at critical times. But I do not believe he learned of them from one of my own."

"Perhaps my work here will lift that burden of suspicion, but I will need your help. For now I will do nothing but become familiar with your household and its routines. I will come to know everyone here and they will grow used to me. My hope is that I shall become such a part of the household that they will not notice I am watching them."

Marshal gave her a smile and a weary shake of his head.

"If I know these lads at all, my lady, they will hardly fail to notice you, however long you are here."

***

Sergeant Billy raised an arm and reined in his horse. They were six days out of London and half a day from Chester, having left Whitchurch behind them at noon. He had seen something out of place far down the road and had long ago learned to heed such things. It was early afternoon and the day was blazing hot. The air seemed to dance on the horizon, making it difficult to see clearly across the distance.

The road ahead swung down from the slight rise where they had halted and cut through a large cleared area. The fields had been ripe with grain when they'd passed this way a fortnight ago. Now there was nothing but stubble. On the far side, where the road left the open ground and rose up into a wooded slope, something was moving.

Sergeant Billy stood up in his saddle and tried to get a better look through the shimmering haze. It could have been plough horses, but he thought not. He turned to one of the younger man mounted next to him.

"What do you make of that?" he asked.

The man stood up in his stirrups and shielded his eyes from the afternoon sun with his hand. He studied the horizon for a long time.

"Those are warhorses!" he said, his voice eager. "And I see a bit of smoke above the trees. It won't be one of our patrols. We'd never stop at midday like this."

Billy nodded. It would not have been a surprise to see some of their own men scouting out this way. Sir Declan had used the mounted troopers of the Invalid Company to screen the approaches to Chester ever since they had retaken the city. But having strangers camped athwart the road ahead could only mean one thing.

"They'd be mercenaries and they're sealing up the main roads into the city. It appears that Chester is besieged."

"I count only five of them," the younger man said, grimly. "Not enough to stop us."

Sergeant Billy shook his head.

"We've nothing to prove here, lad. We'll take the backroads until we're near to Chester."

He saw the disappointed look on the young man's face and leaned over to slap the boy on the shoulder.

"Cheer up! If Chester is besieged, ye'll have all the fightin' yer heart desires. I promise ye' that."

***

Two weeks into August, word reached London that Chester had been cut off and was now under siege. Marshal did not keep the news from Millicent, but tried to comfort her in his own way.

"The walls of Chester are thick, my dear. Your people will be safe inside. Please don't fret."

But she did fret. In her short stay, she had come to like Marshal. He had a friendly, slightly formal manner that put people at ease, but she sensed he did not take her seriously. His assurances about Chester were like a pat on a child's head, but her worries were far from childish and never far away.

The walls of Chester might be thick, but the contents of the granaries were not endless. She knew there was food enough for the people of the city to last until the end of the year. Her mother had seen to that. The city was well prepared for a siege, but so had been Nottingham Castle—and it had fallen. And what if the King failed to return? These were not the worries of a child.

Then there was Roland Inness. She could not stop her thoughts from dwelling on him. He had ridden away from Chester in early July and there had been no news of him since. She prayed he had made it back into the city ahead of the mercenary army—for Chester's sake as much as his own. Siege or no, he would be safer inside Chester's walls and the city would be safer for his presence.

She knew Roland was a gentle man at heart—a farmer, really, but she had also seen how he had taken command of the Invalids. She had seen him in battle. Earl Ranulf might be growing into a Marcher Lord and Declan O'Duinne was a man to be feared when swords were drawn, but Roland Inness was the man they all now looked to when it came to a fight. Chester would need him.

This fretting over a man was new to Millicent. Her mother had warned her that worry was the price a soldier's woman paid and, as always, Lady Catherine had the truth of it. She sometimes wondered when she had first thought of Roland as something more than just another of her father's squires. He had come to them as a half-starved boy who sat a horse like the peasant he was.

Thinking of those early days when she had tried to teach him to ride still brought an amused smile to her lips. A bond had been formed when he had risked everything to track her into the Clocaenog Forest where she had been taken by Welsh raiders. They'd been drawn even closer together during the desperate struggle to regain Chester for Earl Ranulf.

She had no doubts now regarding her feelings. She was a soldier's woman—Roland's woman—and worry came with that. But to her, Roland Inness was worth the worry.

Assault

*I*t was the second week of August when the first stone overshot Chester's north wall and landed in the middle of Barn Lane, scattering a flock of geese in every direction. It was just past dawn and for a long moment those few early risers who shared the lane with the geese stared dumbly at the object, as though it might have fallen from the hand of God. Then they ran, adding their shouts and screams to the honking of the geese. The siege of Chester had begun in earnest.

For more than a fortnight, the encirclement of the city had meant nothing more than forced idleness for the hundreds of peasant farmers who had taken shelter inside the walls. There was enough to eat, though food was carefully rationed. But there were none of the usual chores that would have occupied them on their little plots of ground as autumn approached.

For part of each day, except Sunday, the men drilled with spears provided by the Earl's garrison and seemed to enjoy playing at being soldiers. Boys and girls climbed up to the ramparts and gawked at the mercenary camp that had spread across the fields to the north and east. It seemed like a grand adventure.

Then the bombardment began.

The second stone fell into the dry moat near the Northgate with nothing more than a dull thud, but the men who worked the trebuchets knew their business. The third stone hit the top of the north wall just west of the gatehouse, smashing a part of the crenelated battlement into rubble. The sound of it set babies to squalling and caused horses to startle.

Roland was on duty as Captain of the Guard when the first stones began to fall. If the actual sound of the bombardment had not reached him near the Eastgate, the sudden stream of people headed south down Northgate Street was enough to alert him to trouble in that direction.

He ran north along the wall walk. As he neared the tower that marked the northeast corner of the city's defences he saw a stone, tiny in the distance, arc lazily into the sky, then grow larger as it plummeted down. It disappeared behind the Northgate, but the sound reached him, a sickening rumble of stone smashing stone.

It was a sound he had grown accustomed to during the long siege of Acre, but there it had been the English battering the walls. After a month-long bombardment, they had smashed a breach in those great ramparts, but the Saracen defenders had fought with fanatical courage to keep the Crusaders from passing through it. He wondered how his own garrison would acquit itself defending a breach in Chester's walls. As another stone struck the north wall, he could feel the vibrations in the stone beneath his feet.

"Roland!"

The call came from below him. He looked left to see Declan O'Duinne running up the stone steps near the northeast tower, hurriedly strapping on his sword belt. He had had the night duty and Roland had relieved him at dawn. The two met at the top of the stairs and Roland slowed to a walk. There was no need to hurry. If there was to be an assault, it would only come after weeks of this pounding.

"I'd begun to think they would just sit there and wait till we starved," Declan said, "but it seems our mercenary friends have decided to move things along."

The Irish knight grinned as he spoke, as though having huge stones falling about was hardly a bother. Together, they continued to the Northgate and climbed to the top of the barbican. In the distance, they counted thirteen siege engines arrayed in a shallow arc facing south. All had been carefully placed to aim at a single point on the north wall of the city.

"I liked them better at Acre when they weren't pointed at us," Roland said. He had barely spoken the words when a volley of four stones were released and converged on the wall just to the west of them. Both men watched until a moment before impact, then ducked behind the merlons on the top of the Northgate. Fragments of stone buzzed by overhead.

"They must have worked through the night to assemble them," Declan said as he straightened up. "Someone over there is in a hurry!"

"So it would seem," Roland said. He walked over to the left edge of the barbican and peered over the side. He saw that a merlon on the north wall had been demolished and another was cracked and stood askew. There were two distinct dents halfway up the outer wall. He looked back to the north, studying the enemy machines, then walked back to the trap and called below for the Danish archers.

Four men scrambled through the hatch from the gatehouse below and Roland was pleased to see Oren among them. His brother had continued to lodge with Odo's family once they'd reached the refuge of Chester, but the brothers had been taking their evening meals together. There had been much lost time to recover. When the last man reached the roof of the gatehouse, Roland pointed to the new siege machines.

"I think our guests have been incautious in their haste. It seems they have not come to appreciate the range of our longbows. I reckon the distance to be about two hundred paces. It's a long shot, but any Dane worth his blood should be able to hit a man at that distance." The Danes all grinned like wolves and drew arrows from their quivers.

"On my command," Roland ordered. The four archers spread out along the wall, picked their targets and nocked their arrows. Roland paused as another man emerged from the trap in the roof of the Northgate. Roland motioned for the archers to hold. Earl Ranulf had come to see for himself this new threat to his city.

"My lord," Roland said in greeting.

"Sir Roland, what is the situation?" the Earl asked. His voice was calm, but he looked to the north with some apprehension on his face.

"Thirteen trebuchets, my lord—assembled overnight. They are targeting the north wall just there," he said, motioning the Earl toward the western side of the roof. The Earl peered over and saw the damage to the wall.

"It doesn't look too bad."

"Not yet, my lord," Declan offered, "but they can keep this up for months if need be. With thirteen of those beasts all chippin' away at this one spot…I give it a month, two at the most, before there's a breach."

The Earl nodded grimly.

"So what's to be done?"

Roland gestured toward the four archers standing ready.

"I was about to show those men the error of their ways, my lord," he said, pointing toward the men operating the trebuchets. "While our bowmen were killing their infantry and cavalry in the retreat from the mountains, the siege engineers were safe at Castleton. It seems no one bothered to warn them to beware the range of the longbows before they set up their engines."

Ranulf looked at the distance and nodded. "By all means, proceed, Sir Roland."

Roland raised his arm.

"Draw!"

The men, in perfect unison, drew their bowstrings to their ears and leaned back, elevating their longbows. Roland waited two heartbeats and dropped his arm.

Four shafts, all tipped with bodkin heads, arced northwards. Four men who had thought they were safe this far from the walls, fell to the ground. Others froze for a moment—shocked that the defenders of Chester could reach them at this distance. Another volley of four arrows took down two more men and the rest scattered for cover.

Roland called to Oren as the other men continued to shoot.

"Go fetch all the archers. They will be moving those machines back a hundred paces. Let's see how many we can kill while they do that."

Oren nodded and scrambled back down the ladder. Within ten minutes, over a hundred archers were ranged along the north wall, raining death down on any man who tried to approach a trebuchet. Finally, the enemy engineers gave up and moved a respectful half mile away to wait for darkness. There were clusters of dead bodies by each of the thirteen machines.

"Well done," the Earl said.

"They'll still be able to reach the walls once they move them back," Declan observed. The Earl shrugged.

"Aye, but they won't be as accurate. Still—it's a problem I need you two to think on."

Both men bowed as the Earl turned and climbed down into the hatch in the roof. Declan followed him, giving Roland a small wave as he disappeared inside.

"Think well!" he called up. "I'm going back to bed."

***

"We have to burn them," Roland said.

It had been two days since the trebuchets had begun battering the north wall. He sat beside Declan at the long rough table that served as the mess for the Invalid Company. Both men yawned between bites of black bread. Declan had just come off duty as Captain of the Guard and Roland was preparing to take up the post. They always met for breakfast here in the guard barracks.

"Excellent idea," Declan said. "How? We can't just walk out there with lit torches and we don't have Greek fire like the Saracens did at Acre."

Roland nodded as he washed down his morning bread ration with a cup of mead.

"There's the problem. How do we burn the damn things?"

"You said you'd think on it."

"I have, and burning is the thing to do. I just don't know how yet."

Declan finished his breakfast and rose to go. He leaned across the table and slapped his friend on the shoulder.

"Just keep thinking, Roland. It's what you do best!"

It took another two days for the solution to come to him. He grabbed Declan as he came into Invalid's mess. The Irishman was barely awake.

"Fire arrows."

Declan yawned.

"Fire arrows?"

"Aye, Dec. We shoot fire arrows into the trebuchet's. They haven't been covered with vinegar-soaked skins as we did with our siege engines at Acre. If we can hit them with enough fire arrows, they'll burn."

"Have you ever shot a fire arrow?" Declan asked.

"No," Roland admitted, "nor have any of the Danes I talked to last night, but I know the Saracens used them at Acre. I just regret not paying closer attention to how it was done."

"I assume you're going to try to fashion a few—for testing?"

"Aye, this very day. I'll let you know how it goes."

Declan frowned.

"I'll have men standing by with buckets of sand."

***

Roland stood in the large open field in the northwest corner of the city. Word of his plan to use fire arrows against the siege engines spread quickly, and he was soon joined by Oren, Svein, Thorkell and a dozen other Danes. None in the growing group of spectators knew how a fire arrow was made, but all freely offered suggestions on how one might be fashioned.

There was general agreement that a woollen cloth should be tightly bound just behind the arrow head, but what the cloth should be soaked in or smeared with was the subject of much debate. Oren obligingly built a fire at the edge of the open field while Roland dabbed pitch on his first test arrow and soaked the second in resin. The third, he covered with rendered pig fat. There was lively betting among the Danes on which method would work the best. In the end, no one collected.

The test was a dismal failure.

When Roland nocked the first arrow and held it over the fire, the pitch-soaked cloth erupted in flames and promptly burned through the thread used to bind it to the arrow. The entire flaming mess fell apart and briefly set fire to the dry grass of the field. Roland's curses were drowned out by the laughter of the Danes. Undeterred, he nocked the second, resin-soaked, arrow and lit it.

This flame was less intense and he carefully did a three-quarters draw to keep the burning end of the arrow from igniting his bow. He loosed the shaft and there was an appreciative murmur from the crowd as the arrow made a low arc across the open field. The murmurs quickly turned to groans as the woollen rag, buffeted by the wind and the acceleration of the arrow, slid back towards the fletching, causing the arrow to wobble drunkenly then fall out of the sky forty paces away. The pig fat arrow fared no better. It flew further, but the rush of wind snuffed out its flame almost immediately. Roland threw up his hands in disgust.

"Have ye ever seen a fire arrow up close, lad?"

Roland thought someone was making jest of him and turned with a frown to see who had spoken. He recognized the man standing at the edge of the crowd. It was Sir James Ferguson. Ferguson might have been the oldest man bearing arms within the walls of Chester, but he was no native to the place. He was a veteran soldier who had faithfully served the Earls of Derby for thirty years. He had finally got a bellyful of William de Ferrers' arrogance and cruelty when the nobleman tried, in vain, to destroy Earl Ranulf, losing Chester in the bargain. After Chester fell back into Ranulf's hands, Ferguson abandoned de Ferrers' service and offered his sword to the Earl of Chester.

Sir James and Declan had frequently kept company over the summer. They had much to talk about. Ranulf's bold return from exile in the spring and occupation of Shipbrook had goaded de Ferrers to rashly lead the Chester garrison out of the city to retake the small fortress on the Dee. But Shipbrook had been nothing but a lure.

Declan was to hold the fort long enough for Roland and the Earl to lead an assault on Chester itself—and he might have held it forever, except for Ferguson. De Ferrers' commander had launched three piecemeal assaults on the gate with little success and high casualties, before seeking the old soldier's advice. Sir

James orchestrated the coordinated attack from three sides that finally overran Shipbrook's defences.

The old soldier and the young Irish knight seemed to delight in exchanging thoughts on how that small but deadly battle had unfolded—enemies, now friends.

"Sir James," Roland said sheepishly, "sorry you had to see this."

The old knight smiled, but quickly turned serious.

"Ye mean to burn the siege engines?"

"Aye, if we don't, there'll be a breach in the north wall."

Ferguson nodded sagely.

"How long do you reckon."

It had only taken a month to breach the walls of Acre, but then they had hundreds of engines flinging stones.

"Three months—perhaps."

"I've been watching the bombardment. I'd say closer to two. So the machines must be destroyed, or we will have to defend the breach."

"Aye, I've fought in a breach before, Sir James. I've no wish to fight in another."

"Nor I," said Sir James and beckoned him closer. He took out his sword and began carefully scraping a figure in the dirt at his feet. "Look here, I've seen the Pisans use fire arrows and they fashion a kind of metal cage as part of the arrow's head. It keeps the burning material from falling off or sliding down and unbalancing the shaft."

Roland looked at the man's scratching in the dirt. There was the familiar triangle of an arrowhead, but with barbs along the edges to prevent the shafts from being easily dislodged. Behind the tip was a small egg-shaped metal cage to hold the flammable cloth.

"This could work," he said.

"Aye, it should, but the shaft will need to be heavier for balance and you can't do a full draw—as I think ye've seen. Your archers will have to be close—no more than one hundred paces, I'd guess. How will you do that with a thousand mercenaries watching the north wall?"

Roland shrugged.

"I don't know, Sir James, but come with me to the smith. I want you to draw this for him. We are going to need hundreds of these shafts. By the time we have them, I will know how to get close enough to use them."

***

The second trial, with the new shafts constructed to Sir James' specifications, drew another crowd, but the results were much different. The smith had produced four arrows with the new tips and Roland first tested them without fire. To compensate for the new weight at the tip, the fletchers had fashioned a thicker and longer shaft that would allow a man to take nearly a full draw.

His first shot flew true, with little of the previous wobble, and as Sir James predicted, it travelled just over one hundred paces, landing beyond a heavy oak post placed in the middle of the field. Now it was time for a true test. A resin-soaked wad of cloth was threaded between the openings in the oval cage. Roland nocked the arrow and held the tip of the shaft over the fire. The resin ignited and he drew the string back to his cheek.

He exhaled and loosed the flaming arrow. It flew true, trailing sparks but holding its flame until it struck the base of the post. The crowd rushed forward and watched as the flames licked at the oak. The heavy post did not catch, but this was only one arrow. A dozen arrows striking a wooden frame should have a more dramatic effect.

"By God, I think this will work," said Svein. Men were slapping Roland on the back now and admiring the new arrow. Sir James caught Roland's eye.

"It's a start, but we'll need hundreds of these to burn thirteen of those infernal machines."

Roland grinned.

"There are four smiths in this city, Sir James. I'm sure Earl Ranulf will agree that they should all stop making horseshoes and door hinges and turn to making these new arrows. We could be ready in a fortnight."

Sir James arched an eyebrow.

"And how will you get your archers within a hundred paces—without getting them all killed?" he asked.

Roland frowned.

"I'm still working on that, Sir James."

The older man nodded.

"Be sure you get it right, lad."

***

By the middle of September, the smiths had done their work. While the city waited, a furrow eight feet deep and thirty wide had been gouged out of the top of the north wall. It looked as if some giant out of a child's tale had knelt down and taken a huge bite from the barrier. From the Northgate, the city's defenders could see a steady stream of wagons bringing new stones forward to feed the trebuchets. The enemy engineers kept the machines busy from first light until darkness made it impossible to see where the stones were striking.

The height of the north wall, from the bottom of the ditch to the top of the rampart had been twenty feet. Now it was only twelve. Still a formidable barrier, but the ditch was beginning to fill up with rubble and another fortnight of bombardment would open a proper breach.

While the smiths and fletchers of Chester toiled day and night to produce the four hundred fire arrows Roland had requested, he spent his days and some of his nights atop the Northgate watching the enemy. He could see where his archers would have to stand to reach the machines with their heavy arrows and despaired over how to protect them long enough to finish their task.

In the time it took to cover the open ground and get within a hundred paces of the machines, the mercenary infantry could be put into motion, or worse, their cavalry. If even half of the enemy's mounted knights closed on the archers before they could get safely back into the city, it would be a slaughter.

On the morning of Michaelmas, he arose at dawn and made his way toward the Northgate. There was a first hint of coolness in the air after a long summer of heat. Wisps of fog swirled in the street. The slight crispness in the air was like a tonic and he breathed it in as he walked up Northgate Street.

So distracted was he by the change in the weather that he hardly noted something else different about this dawn. He had almost reached Barn Lane when he noticed the quiet. For forty days, first light had brought the sound of stones striking the north wall of the city. This morning there was silence. Puzzled, he hurried to the top of the gatehouse and looked out on a sea of grey. He found Sergeant Billy on duty there.

"It rolled in around midnight," the veteran said. "It reminds me of the fogs we get in Suffolk when the seasons change—so thick ye could cut it and serve it up on a plate! I expect it will burn off by noon." Roland turned away from the grey curtain and felt like hugging the older man.

"Midnight, you say?"

"Aye, sir, about then," Sergeant Billy said and knitted his brow, suddenly nervous. He joined Roland at the front of the barbican. He strained to make out anything moving to the north, but could barely see objects fifty feet from the wall.

"Do ye think the bloody mercs will use it to slip in close and attack?" he asked. Roland shook his head, hardly able to contain his excitement.

"No, Billy—just the reverse."

Suspects

August in London had turned oppressively hot with hardly a hint of the usual breezes from the west. In this swelter, Millicent was grateful for the distraction the Archbishop's task provided her. But after a month of watching, she had little to show for her efforts. For the men of Marshal's guard, it had taken most of the month for the novelty of the new houseguest to wear off. In the first weeks, there were numerous awkward bows and offers of assistance from the young men who hovered about. For her part, Millicent simply tried to fall into the routine of the place.

Marshal's prediction had proven true—every man in the bodyguard fussed over her, save Sir Nevil and young Andrew Parrot, the clerk. It was annoying, but did give her a perfect opening to learn more about each man.

There were twin brothers, sons of one of the Earl's oldest oath men, a cousin of Marshal's wife and three young knights that had, at various times, been squires to the Earl. Some were friendly and some a bit dour, but all showed more than a passing interest in the lovely young lady who had come to dwell in their midst.

Millicent was not unfamiliar with the behaviour of young men—even the shyest among them showed a bit of swagger and stood up straighter when she was near. And they talked, some shyly and some full of braggadocio, but all prattled on happily about themselves. Millicent listened carefully to their stories, but none of the young guards betrayed any hint of treason. She sensed no hidden grudges, no unhealthy rivalries and no animus, whatsoever, toward William Marshal or the King. Still, she was determined to not rush her judgment and continued to keep an eye on the young men as the weeks passed.

Then there was Sir Nevil Crenshaw. He was an interesting man. The knight had first encountered William Marshal as an opponent in a tournament at Caen. Both were young men then and Sir Nevil had already built a reputation as a skilled competitor. But like most who faced Marshal in the jousts, he lost the contest—though not before giving Marshal a broken collar bone and a concussion. The two men had been fast friends ever since. Crenshaw was Marshal's closest confidant and therefore privy to more secrets than the others. As such, he was the man she most wanted to get a sense of.

But Sir Nevil paid no attention to Millicent at all. He was deferential when in her company, but seemed wholly uninterested in getting to know her or letting her get to know him. She had tried to engage with the man as much as possible and he had always been polite, but Sir Nevil always found the first opportunity to excuse himself. It was frustrating.

The Earl tried to be helpful, even if he did think her task was a fool's errand. He told her that he did all his state business in the single small room off the parlour on the first floor. He always locked the door behind him when he was absent. Only he and Parrot, the clerk, had keys to the office. While his guards were often present when he was working there, the servants were never allowed to enter unsupervised. She had asked Elizabeth about this. The older woman shook her head.

"We've no business nosin' into what the Earl does in there, my lady. He's a great man, he is, and will save the country yet, but he don't need our help to do it. We just see that he's fed and cared for. The Earl will do the rest."

A month after arriving at Marshal's house, she had Jamie Finch escort her to mass at Saint Paul's and dropped a coin into the beggar's hat. That night, the Archbishop met her at his house by the Guild Hall. She reported on her observations and noted, with frustration, that none of the men she'd come to know seemed a likely spy.

"My dear, these things take time," the Archbishop said gently, "and that is something you have an abundance of now. You can scarcely go home with a thousand or more mercenaries encamped around your city."

Millicent clinched her fists, but held her tongue. Something told her the Queen's spymaster was not sorry that she had no way to return home—but his words were true nevertheless.

"Give it another month or two," he said, "If our spy were clumsy, we would have found him by now! You must be patient."

But patience was not one of Millicent de Laval's best qualities. As September brought the first suggestions of autumn to the city, she began to pay more attention to Andrew Parrot, Marshal's clerk. He was very young, but was often at Marshal's side and, like Sir Nevil, was privy to a great deal that went on in the Justiciar's small office.

He was the shyest of the men in the house and rarely looked her in the eyes. In fact, he seemed to avoid her almost as much as Sir Nevil did. But in this, she was not an exception. The skinny clerk did not socialize with the men of Marshal's guard and took no part in their easy banter. Thus it was easy for Andrew Parrot to fade into the background, while the other young men jested with each other and preened about.

It was the clerk's very blandness as well as some of his unusual habits that drew Millicent's attention. Both she and Jamie Finch had noted that, when the Earl was absent overnight, Parrot sometimes left the house in the evening. He was never absent for long on these outings. On other nights when Marshal was away, the clerk could be found alone in the first floor office late into the night. He did neither of these things when Marshal was home—odd behaviour to be sure, but hardly proof of treason.

Millicent resolved to find out what the skinny clerk was up to. When next Marshal was away overnight, she peeked down from the second floor landing and saw candlelight coming from the parlour office. She lit a candle of her own and came quietly down the stairs.

Without knocking, she opened the office door to find Parrot hunched over a small desk, scribbling away with a quill. He looked up, startled .

"Oh, Master Parrot, forgive me for barging in like this!" she said, feigning surprise at seeing him. "I thought the Earl had returned."

Parrot scrambled to his feet, his eyes shifting between Millicent and the papers in front of him. He began to stammer, all the while shuffling the sheets, then slipping them into a small drawer in the desk.

"My...my lady, you gave me a start!"

"Oh, I am sorry, Andrew—may I call you Andrew? But I'm glad it's you. I've been here over a month and we've barely spoken. I see you working away, night and day, keeping the Earl's affairs in order and I wanted to say how much I admire your dedication and your learning. I've always thought it would be grand to be able to read, as you do, but I guess that is of little use to someone like me."

Parrot seemed to relax a bit as she prattled on. When he spoke again, his voice was calm.

"It is an honour to serve Earl William, my lady, and I only do my duty." He reached over and picked up a bound volume, one of dozens in the office. "And it is grand to read!" he said, his eyes a bit dreamy. "It is like having another world at your fingertips."

"Perhaps you could teach me, Andrew. I would be obliged if you would."

"Why I would be happy to, my lady. It's really not that difficult. I'm sure you could pick it up straight away!"

"That would be very kind of you, Andrew. Send for me tomorrow when you have a moment to spare." She gave an entirely unnecessary curtsy and left the young man alone.

What had the clerk been scribbling and why had he hid it?

It was the first suspicious thing she'd seen since her arrival. It might be nothing, but...

***.

168

The Ransomed Crown

Through September, Andrew Parrot met with Millicent for an hour most afternoons to teach her the rudiments of writing and reading. She could do both at least as well as he, but easily disguised her ability. In those sessions she drew him out about his own history. The clerk had learned to read and write while studying for the priesthood, but for reasons he would not reveal, he had abandoned that career. He had been with Marshal for four years and appeared to esteem his master.

In their first sessions, Parrot brought only a copy of the Bible to use in his lessons and Millicent dutifully practiced reading the verses. But in the second week, he had a slimmer volume with him.

"My lady, I thought you might find this work appealing," the clerk said, his eyes shining. "It is a book of poetry--mostly the words of troubadours taken from the ballads they sing. But such words! It sometimes takes my breath away to read them."

He opened the small book and hovered a finger above the text, careful not to touch the fine paper of the page.

"Listen to these words, my lady," he said, and began to read.

> In good faith do I love
> And without deceit
> The fair lady in my dreams
> Whom I shall never meet
>
> But the day shall come
> When from dreaming I awake
> To find fair lady waiting
> For my heart to take."

Parrot raised his eyes from the text and looked at her.

"Did you like it, my lady?" he asked eagerly.

For a moment Millicent had the sinking feeling that this young clerk was trying to woo her, but when she met his gaze he dropped his eyes back to the page, scanning the words that had so affected him. It was the words that enchanted—not her.

Andrew Parrot is a romantic!

It was a startling thought. The shy clerk had seemed unlikely to be moved by love poems, but the heart can hide many secrets.

"It was lovely, Andrew. Read me another."

For the remainder of the hour, Andrew Parrot read the words of troubadours to Millicent and truly seemed to be connected to another world entirely.

Twice more in September, she saw candlelight showing under the door to the parlour office late at night. She was tempted to go to Marshal with what she had seen, but what did it really amount to—a clerk working late? She resolved to not bother the Earl unless there was more evidence to present, but she felt her frustration growing.

She summoned Jaime Finch.

"Jamie, the next time our clerk goes for one of his evening walks, I need you to follow him. He's much less likely to notice you than me. Tell me where he goes and try to see who he talks to—if anyone."

"Aye, my lady, and thank you. Life as a servant is dreadful borin'. It will be good to visit some of my old haunts."

Millicent furrowed her brow.

"Jamie, Sergeant Billy told me that you had struggled with drink. You will need a clear head for this."

Finch scowled.

"Billy is like a nursemaid, but have no concern, my lady. I'm done with spirits. I'll find out what yer clerk is about and that's fer certain!"

***

Jamie Finch stood before her, his face red.

"It was a…a…bawdy house, my lady."

"A what?"

Finch's face grew redder.

"A bawdy house, miss. A place where men go…some men…to take pleasure with the girls."

"A brothel?"

Finch let out a reflexive breath, relieved that Lady Millicent was not entirely unfamiliar with the kind of place he was describing.

"Aye, my lady, a brothel."

"Andrew Parrot sneaked out to go to a brothel?"

170

The Ransomed Crown

"Aye, miss. I followed him close, though I'm certain he wasn't aware. I saw him go in the place."

"How do you know it was a brothel?"

Once more Finch's face reddened.

"I know that establishment, my lady. It's been there since I was a boy."

Millicent recognized her questions were making Finch uncomfortable, but there was no help for it.

"Could you tell who he met with there?"

Finch shuffled his feet.

"No, my lady, I couldn't very well follow him in." He paused a moment and his shoulders slumped. "Beggin' your pardon, my lady, but I'm too well known at the White Mare…from the old days. They'd have made a fuss if I'd gone in."

Now it was Millicent's turn to flush a bit.

"I'm sorry, Jamie. I didn't mean to pry. How long was he there?"

"Oh, I'd say the usual amount of time. Half an hour or so."

Millicent nodded. Parrot may have been meeting a contact at the White Mare or simply doing what most men did in such establishments. Once more, the clerk's behaviour had raised suspicions, but provided no proof of treachery.

"We need to find out what he's doing for certain in that place, Jamie. Can you talk to the owner?"

Finch shook his head sadly.

"I could try, but I doubt she'd talk to me. There is bad blood between us. I'm sorry, miss—maybe ye shoulda kept Sergeant Billy with ye. I know London, it's true, but I'm afraid, London knows me as well."

"You needn't apologize to me, Jamie Finch. None of us is perfect."

"Thank you, my lady," Finch said, clearly relieved. He paused for a moment, then spoke again.

"It has set me to wonderin' though. Ye told me about the clerk and his love ballads. I'm thinkin' the man may be in love."

"In love? With who, Finch?"

Finch shrugged.

"One of the girls at the White Mare, my lady. He wouldn't be the first man to fall in love with a whore."

***

The next day, Millicent dropped a coin in the beggar's hat and this time it was Mary Cullen who met her at the shabby house on Wood Street. She was glad it was the young woman and not the churchman. She poured out her frustrations.

"Nothing seems amiss, Mary. I've been watching them all discreetly for two months now. Marshal's guards seem ill-suited to treachery. There is a clerk with slightly odd habits but nothing that comes close to proof of treason."

Mary patted her hand.

"You are right to move slowly and get to know these people, my lady. Whoever is false among them must get no notion that you are watching."

"I'm careful, Mary, but I don't feel as though I'm making progress."

"Tell me more about this clerk."

"There isn't much to tell. One time I surprised him in the Earl's office late at night and he seemed to hide some papers. He goes in there on some nights when the Earl is away. On other nights, it appears he patronizes a brothel. I had Jamie Finch follow him two nights ago. He went to the White Mare."

Mary Cullen did not seem shocked in the least.

"I've seen the place, my lady. There are a dozen more like it within a mile and they do a good business. I suppose men will be men—your clerk included. From your description, he would not seem to have the nerves required of a spy. I would advise you to not overlook Sir Nevil. Marshal may trust him, but I've met the man. He has nerves aplenty! He seems the more likely culprit."

Millicent sighed. Mary was encouraging, but it all seemed so fruitless. She rose.

"I'm so glad you came this time, Mary. The Archbishop can be a bit…"

"Frightening?"

Millicent laughed,

"Yes, a bit."

Mary surprised her with a quick hug.

"I'll do my best to come next time you call, my lady. I find the man a little frightening myself."

Firestorm

A rough hand shook Roland awake an hour past midnight. He gave quiet instructions to the man who had roused him, dressed quickly and headed up toward the Northgate. As he emerged onto the roof of the gatehouse, he found Declan there, an eager look on his face. Without a word, the Irishman pointed out toward the enemy positions.

On most nights the campfires of the enemy were plainly visible in the distance and on a clear, moonlit night a watcher on the gatehouse roof could see the enemy sentries, keeping their own lonely watch on the city. They had waited through ten nights for the fog to return. Now there was nothing to see but a wall of grey.

"Started coming in an hour ago," Declan whispered, "thick and grey as gruel. I sent for ye when I was sure it was settlin' in for a spell." Roland nodded. Behind him on Barn Lane, he could hear the faint sounds of men quietly assembling, greeting each other in hushed voices.

The days and nights since the last fog blanketed Chester had been marked by feverish planning and careful preparation. He had gathered Patch, Declan, Sir Edgar, Thorkell and Sir James to help plan a daring attack on the trebuchets under the cover of the next fog. There had been questions and heated arguments over how the thing was to be done. In the end, all agreed that sallying out of the city, even under the cover of fog, was risky, but it had to be tried. When the debate was done and the particulars agreed upon, they presented the plan to Earl Ranulf.

"It's risky," was the Earl's first opinion.

"Aye, my lord, it is that," Roland said, "but we will have surprise on our side. They will not expect this and will be slow to react."

Ranulf pursed his lips.

"And if they are quick to react, they will slaughter my Danish archers!"

Roland had to suppress a smile. Ever since the Earl had seen the field beyond the River Weaver littered with dead mercenaries killed by the Danes, he had shown a marked regard for his new force of bowmen.

"My lord," Thorkell said stepping forward. "It should take only two minutes from the time we light the fire pots until we have finished our task. When the last arrow flies, we will turn and run. The Northgate is only three hundred yards away. I do not think they will move that fast."

The Earl nodded.

"I hope you are right, Master Thorkell, and I note that this plan has Sir Declan and the Invalid Company at the Northgate, ready to ride out should you be pursued."

"Aye, my lord. We've already been saved once by the Invalids. I trust they will not fail us."

Ranulf rose.

"If they do, it will not be from lack of courage." The Earl turned toward Declan. "Sir Declan, I will ride with you—if our services are required."

"Of course, my lord."

As Roland listened to Ranulf, he thought back to the first time he'd seen the young Earl of Chester. It had been on the great procession to London to attend the coronation of King Richard. Then, Ranulf had been surrounded by toadies and opportunists and had seemed to be a boy playacting at being an Earl. No longer. Adversity had turned the callow nobleman into a true Marcher Lord—a man worth following.

The faint noise from Barn Lane had died down as men awaited the word to march. Roland looked once more to the north. Fifty paces beyond the Northgate, the swirling grey turned to black. He whispered a command to the man beside him, who went to the trap and called quietly to the men on the floor below.

Carefully they began to crank the windlass that raised the portcullis. The thick ropes had been newly covered in a thin layer of grease and the pulley newly oiled. Only a slight groaning issued from the wooden windlass as it took the weight of the heavy iron barrier. As they worked, Roland climbed down through the hatch, exited onto the north wall and hurried down to the arch beneath the gatehouse. He would lead the archers.

When he reached the street below, Svein handed him his longbow and a bundle of arrows bound together with twine. He made a quick check and counted four fire arrows and ten bodkin-tipped shafts. The small cages behind the head of the fire arrows were already stuffed with woollen cloth and smelled strongly of resin. He nodded to Svein and moved to the front of the column.

No command was needed as he stepped out of the shelter of the gatehouse and headed north into the swirling fog. As the grey mist closed in, he kept his eyes riveted on the roadway ahead. Thirty yards from the gate, he saw the first stone, carefully placed by the side of the road.

Three nights before, in a driving rain, two farmers, Cheshire men who had worked the land where the mercenary siege engines now stood, had been lowered over the east wall. They followed the ditch at the base of the wall until they reached the Northgate, then crawled out on their bellies toward the enemy lines.

Each man carried a leather bag filled with fist-sized white stones. These they placed at intervals as they slid through the mud toward the siege engines. It took hours to lay out the stones, but before the wet dawn arrived, they had left behind markers to guide the way for the archers, even in a thick fog. The rain was finally ending as the two farmers were hauled back over the east wall.

Roland followed the trail of stones for another two hundred paces until he reached a spot where three stones formed a rough vee, pointing west. This was the sign to move off the road. He raised his head and looked to the north. For the first time, he could see a faint glow through the fog—the campfires of the enemy.

Roland slowed his steps. If the farmers had estimated properly, he was only a hundred yards from the enemy machines and the sentries guarding them. They could not risk the noise from a stumble now. He looked behind him and saw the dark shape of Svein behind him. He had made the turn at the three stones as well.

For days they had drilled for this moment. The one hundred Danish archers selected for the attack on the siege engines would turn west off the road at the three stones and move across the enemy front until their line was opposite the siege engines at a distance of one hundred paces. They had spent hours practicing with the new arrows, getting used to the heavier shaft and adjusting their draw and elevation to strike at targets exactly one hundred paces away. Each day there were fewer misses.

Every third man carried a clay pot bound up with cord and filled with tinder and pitch. In a small pouch, each had a fire steel and flint. Slowly and carefully they picked their way over the rough ground, following the man in front of them, until Roland reached a final grouping of three white stones that marked the westernmost firing position. He stopped and turned to his right. Svein copied his movement and it rippled down the line all the way back to the road.

Across the way, Roland could hear men talking. There was no way to tell what they said at this distance, but a round of laughter assured him they were not discussing a surprise attack. He turned to his right and gave a hand signal that was passed on down the line and out of sight in the darkness.

The man next to Svein knelt down beside the fire pot. He struck a spark and it didn't catch. Three sparks later a tiny flame emerged. Dimly, Roland could see fire pots igniting one after another down the line. There was still no sign that the enemy knew they were there.

***

A hundred paces north, Jan Claes stamped his feet and pulled his cape closer around him. It wasn't nearly the coldest night he'd spent on this campaign, but the damned fog brought a dampness with it that seemed to seep into his bones. He looked off to the south toward Chester and saw nothing. Even on a clear night, there was rarely anything to see in that direction and in this fog, he could barely see twenty feet in front of him.

Sentry duty in these conditions seemed pointless, but he knew better than to object. Complaints to his sergeant usually meant double the duty! Behind him he heard some of the men laughing. They'd been casting dice and gambling away their pay. That was not for Jan.

He paced back and forth and tried to think of pleasant thoughts to pass the final hour of his watch. There was a tavern girl back home in Flanders who had never given him a second look. He liked to dream of what she would think when he came home, his pockets full of silver from this campaign. She'd look then, he would wager!

He kept his eyes to the south and did not look back at the fire that burned brightly behind him. It would ruin his night vision and, while he might be bored with this duty, he was no green recruit. He knew his job and would do it like the veteran he had become. He was turning his thoughts back to the tavern girl when he saw something odd in the distance.

There were lights. He knew in this fog, no light from the city could reach him—so what could this be? There was nothing to his front but open fields. At first he saw three, then three more, then—dozens! He did not know what to make of these lights, but it could only be trouble. Jan Claes called for the sergeant of the watch.

***

All along the line, the fire pots began to blaze and men crowded around to feed the resin-soaked rags of the fire arrows. Roland heard a shout in the distance. Some alert guard had seen the yellow glow rising to the south. There was no great alarm in the man's voice, only the sound of a watchful sentry who had seen something strange.

The flames from the fire pots illuminated a dozen ghostly archers off to Roland's right. He watched them light their arrows in the pot and carefully elevate their bows before loosing their shafts into the dark sky. He lit his first arrow, brought his bow to the proper elevation and added his shaft to the hail of fire flying through the fog at the hated trebuchets.

***

The sergeant of the watch had been tossing dice when Jan Claes shouted his first warning, but the man was winning and did not want to ruin his streak of good luck. It was probably nothing anyway. At his guard post, Claes watched as the yellow light to the south seemed to grow and spread. Then, to his horror, it rose into the sky and headed toward him! He shouted another warning, then began to run. This second call forced the sergeant to put down his dice and look up. He saw flames dropping from the sky.

It froze him in place as the first volley hit. One of the men in the dice game took a blazing arrow in the chest and fell over backwards. The man next to him knelt down and beat out the flames that were igniting his comrade's clothes, but the arrow had already done its damage and the man was dead.

No one else had been hit, but the siege engines had not been so lucky. All save one had been struck by multiple arrows. The sergeant screamed at his men to pull out the arrows before the flames caught, but the barbed heads did not come out easily. As they worked frantically to tear the burning arrows from the heavy oak, a second volley fell out of the sky and began striking men and machines. The guards began to run. The sergeant pulled a horn from his waist band and blew three times, a signal that would alert the entire camp of danger.

All along the line of siege engines, the fires began to take hold as the shouts from the mercenary lines took on a new urgency. The Danes paid no mind. They lit their arrows and loosed them, trusting that their hours of practice would send the shafts true. It took less than a minute to send four hundred flaming arrows into the midst of the enemy.

By the time help arrived from the main camp, three machines were engulfed in flames and eight more were catching quickly. Men ran forward with blankets to beat at the flames. The engineers who manned the trebuchets tried frantically to save what they could, but the damage was not over.

Their fire arrows gone, the Danes began shooting bodkin tipped shafts at the mercenary lines, lowering the angle of flight to account for the lighter arrows. Soon screams began to mingle with the shouts of alarm in the murky distance, telling the Danes that they were striking flesh and blood.

Roland strained his eyes into the darkness, and saw that the glow to the north was growing rapidly. It was impossible to tell how many, if any, of the four hundred fire arrows had hit their mark, but something was ablaze in the enemy camp. He was tempted to stay and keep sending waves of arrows into the enemy ranks, but they had come to destroy the trebuchets and only morning would tell if they had succeeded. He would not risk the lives of his men just to draw more blood from the Flemings and Irish across the way.

He started to raise his arm to signal withdrawal when a dark shape hurtled out of the blanket of fog and slammed into him. The man let out a guttural cry of rage and drove his dagger down at his neck. It missed his jugular by a hair as Roland twisted frantically to his left and managed to get one arm free. The man drew back his knife hand for another thrust but Roland wrenched his body upwards and slammed an open palm into the side of the man's head, bursting an eardrum.

The man was stunned for a moment but recovered. He reached for Roland's free arm, his weight still pinning his foe to the ground. Then the horn tip of a longbow came out of the darkness and took the man in the temple. He collapsed in a heap. Strong hands rolled him off of Roland. It was Svein.

"I'm obliged, sir." Roland managed.

"We are even now, I believe," said Svein, as Roland struggled to his feet. "I did not like being in your debt."

"Consider it discharged."

A horn sounded from the north and Roland heard a horse squeal.

"I think it's time to run," he said.

He did not need to give the signal. All along the line, the Danes turned and ran for the Northgate. Roland was the furthest and had just reached the north road when he heard the rumble of hooves behind him. Some part of the enemy cavalry was reacting more quickly than he had hoped. He ran faster.

A hundred yards from the gate he heard a warning shout and leapt off the road as the Earl of Chester thundered by on his charger, followed closely by the Invalid Company. Roland stood and watched them pass. He caught a quick glimpse of Sir Edgar as he flashed by, one hand holding his reins and the other his long battleaxe. Within seconds, a fearsome din arose as the Invalids smashed into the mercenary cavalry.

He reached the gatehouse and clambered up to the roof. Off to the north, where there had been only thick grey mist fading into blackness, there was a growing light. It throbbed and swayed sending red and yellow reflections off the banks of fog. It was the line of siege engines—and some of them, at least, were burning. Below, on the north road, the clash of swords had faded and the riders had begun to return to the Northgate. Roland ran down to the street where the Danes had gathered and found Thorkell.

"Losses?" he asked.

Thorkell laid a gnarled hand on his shoulder.

"One man, Roland."

"Dead?"

"Broke his ankle stepping in a hole as we ran back," Thorkell said with a grin. "I think his pride was the principal casualty."

Roland shook his head. They had been lucky. He had expected to pay a price for striking at the enemy siege engines. Now they would have to wait for the light to see the results of their night's work.

He climbed back to the top of the Northgate and watched the glow from the north as the night wore on. He was not the only one who could not sleep. The top of the gatehouse was crowded with Danes and a goodly number of the Invalids waiting anxiously for the dawn.

First light arrived, but the fog did not lift. Another hour passed and finally the sun began to burn away the mists. A collective gasp escaped from the watchers on the gatehouse roof as the morning light revealed the blackened ruins of ten trebuchet's completely destroyed by fire, two badly damaged and one machine apparently unscathed. Men could be seen in the distance milling about the scene of destruction.

A murmur ran through the watchers. Roland turned to see the crowd parting as Earl Ranulf approached. The Earl nodded to him and peered out at the enemy lines. The lone unburnt trebuchet lifted a solitary stone toward the walls. It fell into the ditch. The people on the roof hooted and sent catcalls at the enemy. Ranulf threw an arm around Roland's shoulder and beamed.

"Well done, sir. With only one machine, it will take them a year to dent these walls!"

Roland nodded, but did not smile. They had forestalled a direct assault on the city, but the mercenary force was still there, hemming them in on all sides. He looked up into a cloudless blue sky. There was a crisp wind blowing from the west, reminding him that it was now autumn. The results of this night's work might keep them safe until the King returned in a few months, but if Richard did not return, burnt trebuchets would not save them. The city had food for three months. After that, they would starve.

And then, they would surrender.

Mare Tempestas

*T*he ancients knew. The great sea that lapped so gently at their shores in the heat of summer could turn deadly in the autumn and winter. During the season of storms, they kept their ships at anchor in protected harbours and coves and the men who sailed them stayed close to their hearths.

The King of England had been warned. He knew the danger of an autumn sea, but could not seem to extract himself from King Guy's hospitality. As was his nature, he felt compelled to inspect every fortress on the island, provide extensive counsel on administration and taxation and view countless musters of the Cypriot forces. It was nearing Michaelmas when Baldwin finally threatened to leave without him.

And so, the King's galleys left Cyprus in early October. For nine days they sailed west—passing north of Crete and south of the Peloponnese on favourable winds. They kept a careful watch for trouble brewing in the skies as the ships swung north into the Ionian Sea, bound for the Adriatic.

With supplies running low, they put in at Corfu, a notorious nest of pirates. Tensions were high as the galleys took on water and provisions for men and horses. Sir Roger and the Templars had strapped on their mail and were armed to the teeth in a show of force meant to forestall any trouble.

"Nasty lot," observed Sir Baldwin as he stood beside Sir Roger at the galley's rail and looked out at knots of evil-looking men who lounged around the docks.

Sir Roger nodded.

"Nasty to be sure, but no fools," Sir Roger replied. "They'll be looking for easy pickings and a fight with a score of Templars is far from that."

"I'm sure you're right, Roger," he said and gestured toward the Templars who were standing with hands on sword hilts, glowering at the watchers. "But keep these boys up here where they can be seen until we get the supplies aboard. I wouldn't want any of these rogues to get ideas."

Sir Roger nodded and Baldwin returned to the small nook next to the King's cabin that served as his quarters. Two hours later, the galleys pulled away from the docks unmolested, though a sharp watch was kept for any sign they had been followed out of the harbour. Turning back north, they took advantage of strong prevailing winds as they entered the Adriatic Sea. It was now the end of October and every man aboard said silent prayers for continued fair weather. As they skirted the Dalmatian coast under clear skies, it seemed that those prayers had been answered.

But the ancients knew.

They were but two days sail from their planned landfall on the northernmost shore of the Adriatic when suspicious clouds began to build behind them. As the first squall approached, the crew of the galleys took in sail and lashed down anything that needed to be secured. The rain hit as the oarsmen, who had been idle for days, returned to their benches to maintain headway in the growing seas. The shipmasters had been steering along the eastern shore of the Adriatic to avoid possible encounters with enemy ships near Venice and now that choice seemed a bad one. The lee shore was a nightmare of rocky islands and headlands with no likely place of refuge to ride out the storm.

So they ran north with it, throwing heavy lines from the stern to keep from turning abeam to the following seas. With no sails set, the wind whipping through the rigging made a strange moaning sound that added to the fear of the crew. Through the rest of the day and into the night, the men below stayed at the oars. The knights bailed the seawater coming over the rails using buckets and helmets and all aboard redoubled their prayers.

As dawn neared, there came a sight that no seaman wished to see. Ahead of them, a faint grey line of breakers stretched out of sight along a rain-swept shore. They had run out of sea. The shipmaster motioned frantically for the King to come near so he could shout over the roar of the storm.

"Lash yourself to the rail," he screamed, "and pray that is sand ahead!"

King Richard staggered to the rail on the raised stern of the galley and began securing himself, even as waves crashed over him. Seeing the approach of the storm-ravaged coast, others followed suit. One man lashed himself to the mast and others tethered themselves to whatever was close at hand.

Sir Roger looked out across the frothing sea and caught sight of the second galley. It had been caught in a cross current near shore and was now riding abeam to the oncoming breakers. It wallowed sickeningly in the swells and the knight thought of his warhorse, Bucephalus, trapped below decks.

It's every man and horse for himself today, old friend.

He staggered toward the spot where the King clung to the rail, but before he could lash himself near the man, a huge wave crashed over the side and he felt his feet fly from beneath him. As the torrent drained back toward the sea, it drew him with it, and before he could grab the port side rail he was plunged overboard. As he struck the water he gave thanks that he wore none of his armour, but he landed in a trough and plunged deep. He had started to pull hard back toward the surface when another wave lifted him high along with the galley, which was drifting away to his right.

As a boy, he had learned to swim in the Dee, but this was not the gentle river of his youth. He flailed his arms and legs to stay afloat and managed to take in a breath before the wave crested and tumbled him under again. He reached upward and, kicking furiously, broke the surface once more, only to swallow a great gulp of seawater. But in that moment at the crest of a new wave, he had seen the shore and felt a glimmer of hope. It was a sand beach—not rocks. Then he was under again.

His lungs were burning as he felt a strong current pulling him back toward the sea. He fought against it, then realized it was another great wave gathering. He pulled hard toward the shore and the wave swept him up the beach where he landed heavily on the packed sand.

Immediately, he felt the surge pulling him back out with the receding wave and dug his hand and toes into the sand. He skidded backwards, but the wave lost its grip on him. In the few seconds he had before the next onslaught, he struggled to his knees and scrambled toward a line of gnarled trees and low scrub that lay above the pounding of the storm.

The following wave struck him, but he was too far up the shore for it to drag him back. Reaching the trees, he turned to watch the galley carrying the King strike the beach at an angle. The rending sound of the keel snapping and hull collapsing could be heard over the thunder of the surf. He saw men tumble from the deck and from the shattered hull onto the sand and others, struggling against the current, being sucked back into the sea.

He staggered to his feet and looked down the beach in time to see the second galley fly up on shore and seemingly land gently upright on the sand. The vessel leaned a little to the starboard side when the following wave struck it, but did not break apart. The big knight stumbled toward the King's galley and had to stop as his gut heaved up great gouts of seawater.

When he reached the wreck, he was relieved to see Richard standing on the sand just above the crash of the waves, directing the effort to rescue survivors. Sir Roger hurried to the King's side and Richard embraced him like a brother.

"Thank God you're saved!" the King shouted above the storm and pointed toward the wrecked galley. "Help those you can!" Sir Roger nodded and edged down near the shattered wreck that was still wallowing dangerously as the waves pounded it. It was a scene of horror and chaos. Up and down the beach half drowned men were crawling forward trying to escape the waves. Others cried out as they were swept away.

Sir Roger dragged one man after another up the beach and out of harm's way. As he returned to the wreckage, he heard a shouted plea from inside the galley. The shattered ship was a deathtrap that was quickly being reduced to kindling by the relentless pounding of the sea. Carefully the knight picked his way past the accumulating wreckage to peer into the hull that had been cracked open like an egg. Back near the stern he could barely make out a man who lifted his arm in supplication.

"Help me!"

It was Sir Baldwin. The man was tangled in a web of rope and broken timbers from which he could not extract himself. As Sir Roger crept forward over jumbled benches, empty now of oarsmen, the ship gave a sharp lurch and a new opening appeared in the hull opposite him. With this pounding, the galley would soon be nothing but floating scraps of wood and anyone inside would be beyond rescue.

The big Norman began to frantically hurl benches and broken timbers aside and bulled his way through the obstacles to reach the trapped knight. As he broke loose a bench that had wedged itself between the keel and the hull, Sir Baldwin managed to struggle free.

"I'm obliged to you, sir!" he shouted, but Sir Roger didn't notice. He slung the man's right arm over his shoulder and fairly dragged him back the way he had come. But the boat lurched and rolled again and the gap where he had entered now had sealed itself on the sand.

He swerved to his right where a new hole in the hull had been ripped and pulled himself up and out, turning back to help Sir Baldwin. The knight's left arm hung limp by his side, clearly broken. Sir Roger grasped the man under his armpits and hoisted him clear. With the sea sucking at their legs, they staggered back up the beach to safety. With the rain still beating down on them in sheets, Sir Baldwin went down on his knees among the scrub and gnarled trees, and raised his one good hand to heaven, sending up a prayer of thanksgiving.

Sir Roger turned and headed back toward the wreck, but he saw no one left near the stricken ship. As he watched, a massive wave engulfed the beached galley and splintered the wreckage completely. The remnants of the King's ship were sucked out to sea leaving the beach oddly empty, as though no tragedy had happened here. Staying above the grasp of the heaving sea, the big Norman knight made his way back toward the King who was organizing the care of survivors.

"Your grace," he shouted. "I go to the galley yonder." He pointed west down the beach where the second ship still rolled with each incoming wave. The weary king merely nodded his assent.

The wreck of the second galley was but a mile away, but Sir Roger found that the storm had torn new inlets in the low lying shore. These could be waded, but only with care. It took him a full hour to reach the grounded vessel. He found the shipmaster sitting on the sand, his head in his hands, sobbing.

"Are you injured?" he asked touching the man's shoulder. The veteran seaman looked up at the knight.

"My ship! How will I get it off this beach? I am ruined...ruined!"

"Aye," said Sir Roger as he studied how far up the beach the vessel had been tossed. "Doesn't look like you'll float her off, but gather yourself, man. What's become of your crew? Did all survive?"

The man shrugged and went back to sobbing.

Disgusted, Sir Roger left him and walked closer to the vessel. He was relieved to find that most of the crew was gathered on the far side. They had rigged a ramp and were struggling to bring the horses up from below decks. A large man with a missing eye appeared to be directing the operation.

Ah, the true master of the ship.

Sir Roger approached the man and got his attention.

"You the mate?" he shouted over the wind.

The man just nodded.

"Were any of your crew lost?"

The mate raised one finger. They had lost only a single man.

"My horse is below. Let me go aboard and lead him out!"

The man at first seemed to ignore the request, but seeing the look in the knight's eyes, waved him toward the wreck. Sir Roger slapped him on the shoulder and quickly made his way up the ramp and over the rail of the galley, which lay at a difficult angle. Below he could hear horses. Some stamped at the hull and some whinnied in fear or pain.

The crew had removed most of the planks from the deck and he could see into the hull. Bucephalus saw his master before Sir Roger saw him and gave a loud snort that the knight would have recognized anywhere.

"Ho, boy!" he shouted and picked his way to where the horses were pinned in the stern. The big warhorse pricked up his ears and strained against the rope that held him fast. Sir Roger had lost his sword, but still had a small blade. He reached past a wild-eyed mare to cut the rope that held Bucephalus.

The big horse surged forward and Sir Roger just had time to pull down the pole that had served to pen the animals in before the warhorse broke it down. There was no bridle, so he grabbed the mane and led Bucephalus forward. The warhorse needed no urging when it saw the ramp. He coiled on his huge haunches and came up from the hold in a single bound, nimbly trotting down the ramp to the sand.

As the storm ebbed, the crew salvaged what they could from the beached galley. The rest of the surviving horses, only seven in all, were brought out. Food, weapons and other equipment were stacked above the reach of the waves. The shipmaster, having recovered his composure, plotted how he might refloat his ship. Sir Roger managed to collect saddles and bridles for three horses, including Bucephalus, and rode back to the King leading two riderless horses behind.

He found Richard in animated conversation with Sir Baldwin, whose left arm now sported a crude splint. The King seemed buoyed by the arrival of three healthy mounts.

"Well done, Sir Roger! I feared if Bucephalus had come to harm, you would be inconsolable. Are these three all that survived?"

"No, your grace, there are four more, but the crew has not yet recovered saddles and bridles for those. The shipmaster is a dolt, but the mate knows his business. He will salvage all he can."

"Weapons?"

"Enough, your grace."

"Will the galley float again?" the King asked.

"Possibly. Her keel wasn't cracked and the hull is intact, but she was thrown far up the beach and it will take logs to roll her back down to the water."

The King looked around at the stunted trees that bordered the sea.

"Then it will be weeks, if the thing can be done at all. As I was telling Sir Baldwin, it looks as though the Almighty must agree with my overland route, as He has seen fit to deny us any other!"

In the face of the King's bravado, the knight thought it best to allow the man to make a virtue of necessity. As they spoke, the last of the rain blew inland and the sky began to lighten. Off to the northwest, a purple line of mountains caught a beam of sunlight. The King pointed at the sight.

"There's our path home, lads. God is pointing the way!"

Sir Roger looked at the mountains and saw white on the topmost peaks. He kept his opinions to himself.

A Rising in Sherwood

Sir Robin of Loxley looked around him at the ragged men gathered at the edge of the cold woods as dusk fell. A few were trained fighters—men who had escaped with him from the doomed citadel of Nottingham—but most were simple peasants. He had watched them trickle into the vast forest of Sherwood for months, fleeing from the famine that was overtaking their villages.

Since the fall of Nottingham Castle in June, matters had grown infinitely worse for the people of the Midlands. Prince John had appointed one of William de Ferrers' confidants as the new Sheriff and Sir Alfred de Wendenal was intent on gaining favour with his new master. He was given a strong garrison of three hundred men and these he sent out like locusts to strip anything of value they could find in the land.

It was the Sheriff who had driven these farmers and herdsmen to leave their fields and homes and come to Sherwood. They had come with rusty old swords, pruning hooks, wooden staffs and hope—hope that the stories they'd heard passed from village to village were true, that an outlaw band in Sherwood was stealing food and delivering it to hungry mouths.

The first to come had found Robin with little more than a score of men, but they had kept coming. Through the summer and autumn he had brought the new men along slowly. They had raided small granaries and harassed the Sheriff's tax collectors whenever they strayed near Sherwood. They'd even carried out a daring night raid into Nottingham proper and had got away with a small chest of gold that was held at the town hall. The Sheriff had personally led the pursuit into the forest, but turned back as his casualties mounted.

It was now early November and winter was taking a firm grip on the land. Robin looked at the grim faces of the men nearest him and felt the weight of their hope. He had led men into battle many times, but those men had freely chosen the warrior's path. These men had not. They had been content to live out their days tilling the land, but could not abide their wives and children starving—not when harvests had been plentiful.

Like him, they were cold and tired, but at least their bellies were full. Poaching the King's deer had seen to that problem. But there weren't enough deer in this vast forest to feed the starving families left behind on the farms and in the villages. So they had come to the hamlet of Southwell.

Across a quarter mile of frost-covered fields lay the looming bulk of the great Southwell Minster and next to the minster was the palace of the Archbishop of York. Around these imposing structures a small village had grown up. Robin was not interested in the church buildings or the village. His attention was riveted on a large structure at the edge of the cleared field. It was a huge tithe barn owned by the church. This was no small granary. Its contents could feed a dozen villages for months, but word had reached Sherwood that the Archbishop planned to sell most of the grain for silver. The prelate claimed the funds were needed to save York from foreign mercenaries—and more importantly to save the great York Minster.

Tuck had scoffed at the claim.

"There's enough silver in the vaults beneath York Minster to keep every mercenary in the Midlands well paid for a year I'd wager. But the Archbishop has to provide for his palaces and his bishops' palaces with those funds, so he takes food out of the mouths of his flock to pay the mercenaries. Makes me sick."

Robin required no convincing.

"We'll take the grain and if York burns, it will be on the Archbishop's head, not ours."

They had scrounged and stolen ten wagons and seven draft horses to take away the grain. Some of the stronger men would have to pull the wagons without horses. His scouts had reported that the barn was well-guarded. That was expected. The church hereabouts looked to its own needs first.

The guards were hired mercenaries and, no doubt, capable fighting men. He glanced at the skinny farmer next him with his sharpened pruning hook and wondered how he would fare against such men if it came to that. If his plan worked, he would not have to find out.

The core of his band—a score of experienced men, well-armed with swords and longbows had moved into position almost an hour ago. Most of these men, he had known since his youth. As boys they'd roamed this huge forest and knew it like their mother's face. When he and his companions had grown old enough to become unruly, his father had gathered them together and turned them over to Magnus Rask, his Master of the Sword, for instruction.

Rask was a huge young Dane with a nasty temperament, but a man totally loyal to the lord of Loxley Manor. It was Rask who taught Robin and his companions how to use a blade and shoot a longbow. He had also taught them how to fight dirty in a brawl. The Dane showed no deference to any of them and was particularly hard on the son of his lord. He had happily administered many a beating to young Robin, but could never wipe the cocky smile off the boy's face. In time he'd come to admire his student, even when the boy began to beat him.

Rask and Tuck had done their best to train these new men. They drilled them every day. The farmers were clumsy but game and, until tonight, they had used them sparingly on small raids where the guard forces had been weak. They'd shown themselves to be brave enough, but if things went wrong this night, their training would be put to the test. Friar Tuck crept up beside Robin at the edge of the wood and whispered his report.

"We count five guards posted around the barn, but there'll be another twenty off duty in the village—perhaps more. As soon as someone raises the alarm they will be there in minutes."

Robin muttered a quick acknowledgement. Tuck's report confirmed earlier scouting they had done over the past two days. Their problem was not so much the men on guard as the barn itself. It was a sturdy wooden structure with only one wide oak door at ground level. A small hatch sat under the eaves fifteen feet off the ground at the opposite end. This opening led to a hay loft. If the guards managed to retreat into the barn and barricade it, rousting them out would be difficult and take time—time for reinforcements to arrive.

So the plan was simple. All the guards would be killed by his archers at the outset. Once they had been quietly dispatched, his farmers would break into the barn and load up the grain sacks as fast as they could while Rask and his archers kept watch on the hamlet. If all went well, the sun would rise over Southwell Minster and the next guard shift would find dead comrades and an empty tithe barn.

"Does Magnus have the bowmen in place?"

"Aye," Tuck said. "There are two watching each guard. When they see the signal, they will take them all down at once."

"Good."

Robin turned to look a last time on the men gathered behind him in the woods. A horse snorted and he froze, but realized it was one of the draft horses they had stolen to haul the grain away. At this distance, it was doubtful the guards had heard. He exhaled slowly and walked to the edge of the wood. In his hand was a small torch—no more than a branch with flaxen cloth wrapped around one end and soaked in resin. He took flint from a small pouch and struck a spark. The torch flared. He let it burn for no more than ten seconds—long enough for his men to see—then rubbed the flame out in the dirt.

Now it would begin.

***

Bruun Vermeulen felt ill. He thought it might have been a bit of bad pork he'd eaten for supper, but it could have been the ale he'd consumed so freely at the meal. The brew had a strange odour to it and the tavern owner was not known for providing the most wholesome of fare. He had thought about getting excused from duty, but then he would have had his pay docked, so he had taken up his station just east of the tithe barn. He was to watch for any locals sneaking up from the village to filch grain from the holy church.

He had been on duty for an hour when his stomach heaved. He bent double to retch into the grass and never saw the torch that flared at the far tree line. Nor did he see the two arrows that passed harmlessly over his bent back—but he heard them and he knew that sound. The guard nearest him made a small cry, like an animal in pain, then went silent. Bruun Vermeulen was an experienced soldier and no hero.

He dropped to the ground and began crawling toward the village.

***

The wagons were being wheeled across the open field when Magnus Rask found Robin.

"We may have lost one of the guards," he said grimly. "My boys saw him go down, but when they checked, there was no body and no blood."

Robin nodded.

"We have to expect the other guards will be roused. They'll send a rider to call out the garrison at Newark Castle. The Sheriff has three score mounted men there and they could be here in three hours or less."

"Aye," said Rask. "We'd hoped to have till dawn, but we'll load what we can by midnight. We can hold off the local boys that long. What shall we do with the rest of the grain?"

"Any that's left, they'll sell," Robin said flatly. "Not a loaf of bread will go the people who grew it."

"Not a crumb," Rask agreed.

Robin did not hesitate.

"Burn it."

***

It was just past midnight when Robin called a halt to the loading. Six wagons had been piled high with sacks and hauled out of the tithe barn into the forest. The mercenaries in the town had been roused and had, no doubt, sent for help, but they chose not to venture from the hamlet after the first man to do so fell dead with a longbow shaft in his chest.

Inside the barn, a spark was struck in the hayloft. Within minutes, black smoke began to pour out of the hatch under the eaves as the hay in the loft went up and caught the thatch of the roof. By the time Robin and his archers reached the shelter of the forest, the place was a roaring inferno.

The empty fields around Southwell Minster were illuminated by the flames as the last wagon disappeared into the trees. There was an abandoned mill deep in Sherwood that Robin had set the men to repairing months ago. Now it would be put to good use and there would be flour for bread—but not nearly enough.

Tuck settled in beside Robin at the edge of the woods. Rask had spread his archers for a mile or more along the track that the wagons had taken. It made for a lethal ambush corridor. If a mounted force came from Newark, they would not get far once they reached the woods. Riding into Sherwood with ill intent had become a deadly undertaking.

Robin looked at his good friend. Most of the men who had gone outlaw with him had managed to put back some of the flesh they'd lost in the siege of Nottingham Castle, but Tuck still looked gaunt. He'd been taking just enough food to keep his strength up for the past months and could not be persuaded to take more.

"Children are dying all across Nottinghamshire," was all he would offer in reply to Robin's entreaties.

As the creaking and groaning of the last overloaded wagon faded, the monk spoke.

"It's not enough, Robin. For every mouth we feed, there are ten going hungry."

"Aye, Tuck, it's not. But what more can be done? We can raid and ambush as long as we can get safely back into Sherwood, but we haven't the strength to challenge the Sheriff out in the open, not in daylight. With a few more men and decent weapons, we'd have a chance, but as it is, we're forced to skulk in the forest like the outlaws we are. It feels like we are alone in this, but I wonder—are there other's resisting John's madness?"

"The Queen."

"Aye, the Queen, but we don't know her plans or even if she still lives. It's been nearly a year since we gave her the King's message and most people are long dead at her age."

Tuck grunted.

"I suppose she isn't immortal, though if any woman could aspire to that, it would be Eleanor."

Robin was silent for a while.

"The King could be dead too."

Tuck nodded.

"Possible, but I doubt it. News like that would spread fast, even into Sherwood. And if he's alive, he will put an end to this within a week of his return."

Robin snorted.

"December is but a few days away and the King promised to be home by then. But you will recall how long it took him to get to the Holy Land. He is a man easily distracted and prone to dither. If he is late in returning, there might be nothing left to save."

From the village across the fields a small cheer erupted and men could be heard shouting.

"They've arrived," Tuck said.

Just then a column of mounted men burst out of the village and rode past the flaming barn. A man in front pointed to the deep ruts the loaded wagons had made in the soft earth. The lead riders spurred their horses into a trot, heading straight for where Robin and Tuck crouched in the shadows.

"They never learn, do they?" Tuck observed.

"I hope not," said Robin as he drew a clothyard shaft from his quiver.

Treason

*I*n early November, Marshal left London to meet with the Earl of Oxford. His bodyguard rode with him, all save Sir Nevil who stayed behind to deal with any trouble that might be stirred up in the city with the Earl absent. The night of the Justiciar's departure, Andrew Parrot waited until most in the house had retired for bed, then stepped out the front door and headed west. A few seconds later, Jamie Finch slipped out of the rear of the house and followed him.

The clerk took a route up Cheapside and into the teeming market district. A dozen times he cast quick glances over his shoulder to ensure he was not followed. He never saw Jamie Finch. At length, he came, as he always did, to the White Mare and tapped on the door. It opened quickly and he slipped inside. The woman who greeted him was fat and florid. She held out her palm and he placed a coin in it. She inspected it, then led him down a hallway past a large parlour where women lounged on cushioned benches.

Parrot did not give them a second look. At the end of the long hall, they reached another door and the woman opened it for him. There was a passageway there, too narrow to be considered an alley, that ran between the rear of two buildings.

Andrew Parrot stepped into the dark space and did not look back as the door closed behind him. The narrow cleft at the rear of the White Mare opened onto a broad avenue only a few steps from his destination. He cast a quick look up and down the street, crossed over and tapped on the door. It opened a crack, then swung wide. Bishop Poore's most trusted agent smiled warmly at the clerk.

"How are you, Andrew?"

"I'm well. I've brought you information—important information."

"Wonderful! I marvel at your boldness, Andrew. I truly do. What do you have for me?"

Andrew Parrot felt the familiar flush he always felt when praised this way. He knew this thing he was doing was wrong, that it would hurt a man he admired, but it was worth it if it pleased the person sitting across from him. He gave the agent a detailed report on what he had discovered.

Twenty minutes later he was at the back door of the White Mare. He knocked and the woman let him in. He hurried down the corridor and out the front door. He noticed that the night had grown colder and pulled his robes tight around his shoulders. He did not notice the man standing in the shadows who had been patiently waiting for him to reappear. The one followed the other at a discreet distance back to Marshal's house.

***

When Marshal returned to London a week later, news reached him that a force of two hundred men, sent by the Earl of Norfolk at Marshal's request to bolster loyalist forces in London, had been ambushed outside the town of Colchester with great slaughter. Marshal was aghast—and furious when word reached him of this disaster.

With barely a hundred men scattered around the capital, the forces loyal to Richard were no match for John's garrison in the Tower. Thus far, no open hostilities had broken out between the factions inside London, but Marshal knew control of the city would one day be contested. He had need of Norfolk's two hundred men.

"Barely thirty survived!" he railed. "Thirty! By God, someone will pay for this. I swear it!" His guards clustered near the entrance to the parlour office as the Justiciar stormed around the small space and cursed this latest news. He turned to Sir Nevil.

"Nevil, send word to the Earl of Norfolk that we will find and punish whoever did this! He'll know it is an empty promise, but send it nevertheless." He paused and looked at the worried faces surrounding him.

"Leave me," he commanded. "I need to think." Millicent had watched all of this from the bottom of the stairs, drawn there from her room by the Earl's loud oaths. She turned and started back up.

"Lady Millicent, a moment of your time please."

Surprised at the summons, she hurried back down the stairs and joined him in the office. He closed the door behind her.

"There can be no doubt that this outrage was done on John's orders, though he will have covered his tracks carefully. To arrange such an ambush, he had to know of our plans well in advance. Norfolk could have let the secret slip somehow, but I doubt it. That man has ever been tight-lipped. Only three men here in London were privy to that information—Sir Nevil, Parrot, who wrote out my plea to the Earl, and myself. I did not inform the Archbishop of my intentions."

Millicent saw where the Earl was heading.

"So you will now consider the possibility that one of your own *is* a spy?" she asked.

Marshal nodded wearily.

"I fear I must. Have you learned anything that would point to a traitor in this house?"

"My lord, what I have is thin, to be sure. But your clerk, Parrot, often spends time in your office on nights you are away. On other nights, when you are absent, he visits a brothel."

Marshal arched his eyebrows.

"He works late when I am gone and has visited a bawdy house?" I'll concede the latter surprises me, but even Master Parrot must need some respite from time to time! I don't see that this suggests treason."

"I agree, it proves nothing, my lord, but it is the only thing I've observed that seems…out of ordinary."

Marshal rubbed his chin.

"Keep a close eye on Parrot, then. He seems too meek a man to engage in treachery, but who knows what lies inside a man's soul. His visits to the ladies of the night might not be the only secret he keeps hidden. But tell me, you have nothing to report regarding Sir Nevil?"

"Only that he is a most boring man, who rises early, does his duty and takes to his bed at the same time every evening. I've not seen him leave the residence, save on your instructions."

For the first time Marshal smiled.

"You know, Nevil once had a wild streak. When we were younger he lured me into more than one awkward situation, but age has calmed him. I would stake my life that Nevil Crenshaw is not your spy."

Millicent wasn't so sure. If she were to exonerate every man vouched for by Marshal, her work would have been over before it had begun, but she had no further evidence to present.

"I hope you are right, my lord. I will keep close watch on both of these men and hope that one makes a mistake."

"Very well, my dear, keep me informed." He rose, indicating their meeting was over. She crossed the parlour and headed up the stairs to her room. After three and a half months of careful watching she could only say that the clerk had unexpected habits and that Sir Nevil was boring. No wonder Earl William had not taken her seriously.

I make a poor spy!

A Lion at Bay

Seven men rode into the Julian Alps on a clear and cold day in early November. In the lead was a tall knight mounted on a formidable warhorse. He wore a tattered surcoat with a rampant stag on the front over a mail shirt. A second knight rode beside him, his left arm secured with a splint and lashed to his side. Five men wearing the red cross of the Knights Templar followed the two leaders. Four were true members of that fierce band of holy warriors, but the fifth was not. The fifth was the ruler of an empire, trying to slink back home unnoticed through a land filled with his enemies.

For three days they rode hard across a low coastal plain with the mountains looming larger with each passing hour. Twice they were stopped by local officials, curious as to the identity of their traveling band. They claimed, honestly, to be returning Crusaders and invoked the Truce of God.

The Pope had declared that no Christian ruler could molest Crusaders on pain of excommunication, and for local officials this was enough to gain them passage. But every one of the seven knew that, no matter what the Pope might threaten, Richard's enemies had more concern for vengeance and profit than the salvation of their souls. The Truce of God would not save Richard the Lionheart if they were discovered.

On the fourth day it began to snow. It wasn't heavy, but even in the valleys it made the footing treacherous for the horses, and on the high peaks the white drifts crept further down the slopes. On that day, the King fell ill with a fever. His strong constitution kept him in the saddle, but he needed rest after the calamity of the shipwreck and their hurried flight north.

On the fifth day they reached Villach, a small market town in a broad valley surrounded by peaks. The summits that lay ahead were higher than those behind. The town lay in a bend of the Drava River that ran swift and deep through the entire length of the valley. The only crossing was the bridge at Villach and they made for it. They were not surprised to find it guarded. A squad of four, fronted by a fat corporal, barred the way.

"Hold! State your business." The corporal spoke in German and his tone made this more of a request than a command. He had his duty, but these travellers looked to be both of noble rank and dangerous men. The corporal's regard for his health trumped any other obligations.

Sir Roger deferred to Sir Baldwin, who spoke a bit of the language and was well known for his diplomacy.

"Captain of the Guard, my compliments. We are Crusaders returning to France. We wish only to tarry for a night in your city until this snow abates. Can you suggest an inn and stables?"

The corporal seemed to inflate beyond his natural stature at this verbal promotion.

"Ja, my lord. The Weissen Schwan keeps a good table and there are few guests this time of year. It's just across the bridge on the right."

"You are most helpful, Captain." Baldwin leaned down and placed a coin in the man's hand. "This should buy you and your men a round, once you are off duty," he whispered.

The corporal looked at the coin and realized it would buy considerably more than that and slipped it quickly into his purse.

The men need not know.

"You say you are bound for France, my lord? What route are you taking from here?"

Baldwin had hoped to avoid direct questions about their planned route—the better to avoid surprises—but to refuse to answer this friendly inquiry would raise suspicions. They had decided to strike north from Villach through the mountains to

Salzburg, then on to Saxony as the most direct route to safety, but he had no intention of revealing these plans to anyone. He quickly thought back to the maps he had studied on their voyage from Cypress.

"We plan to travel to Innsbruck," he lied, "then through the Arlberg or over the passes to Munich. From there it is but a short way to our home." This route was plausible, as it led more directly to France. From Villach, the road to Innsbruck ran due west for over a hundred miles before swinging north and over an ancient pass used long before the Romans came. It would take any pursuers far from their true path.

The corporal frowned.

"My lord, that way is finished. Winter has come early to the high mountains. I'm told that pass has been chest deep in snow for a fortnight—the same with the passes north to Salzburg." He took off his dented helmet and scratched his bald head.

"I would advise you to turn east to Vienna. That way is difficult, but still possible. From Vienna, you can follow the Danube through the mountains then turn west for France. Or, perhaps you could go back south and find passage by sea from Venice."

Baldwin tried to hide his distress at this news, but he could hear murmurs of concern behind him as the Templars and the King heard the mention of Vienna and Venice, both deathtraps for them.

"Ah, that is bad news, Captain, but better to hear it now than to be turned back at the passes. We will stay the night and decide our route in the morning."

Satisfied, the corporal waved them through and they clattered over the bridge and into Villach. The inn was snug, as most were in these lands, and after filling their bellies on sausages and black bread, the King's party gathered for a parlay in one of the two rooms they were sharing.

"You all heard the guard. Winter has come early," the King said. "It seems the fates conspire against us, so we must choose between poor choices. East to Vienna or south to Venice—either way seems equally dangerous to me. What say you all?"

Sir Alexander Barnstoke, a Templar, spoke first.

"I passed through Venice two years ago, your grace. I can tell you that the Doge has the best spy system in Europe. A dog cannot piss on the street in that city without his knowledge. So your presence would be known in a matter of hours. There is no way we could secure a ship in any event. It is winter. The Venetians are the best sailors in the world and they do not sail in this season. I would advise against Venice, sire."

The King nodded glumly. Sir Baldwin took up the discussion.

"I have no reason to believe the spy system in Vienna is any less efficient than the Doge's. And may I remind your grace that, while the Doge would love to turn a profit by holding you for ransom, with Duke Leopold, the matter is personal. He will not have forgotten what happened in Acre."

The King sat on the edge of the bed and rubbed his temples. For the moment, there seemed little fight left in the mightiest warrior in Christendom. He sighed and turned to Sir Roger de Laval.

"What say you, old soldier? South to captivity and ransom—or east to humiliation, and perhaps worse?"

Sir Roger was standing by the small window that looked down upon a cobbled courtyard. In the twilight, delicate snowflakes could be seen dancing around the flickering light of a torch. He could only imagine what conditions must be like at higher elevations.

Still...

"Your grace, I would rather try our chances with the snow of the passes than to fall into the hands of your enemies. Winter has come early, so the man said, but so may spells of fairer weather. Traders and pilgrims would not take this chance, but we are desperate men and I would rather risk freezing than being taken as prisoner."

"Have you seen the passes in winter?" asked Sir Alexander hotly. "I have. No one can cross these mountains in winter!" There were murmurs of agreement from the assembled knights.

Sir Roger's eyes met the King's.

"Hannibal did. And he did it with elephants. Perhaps we can do it with horses."

For a moment, the King seemed to rally to this new challenge. He started to stand, but was seized with a fit of coughing. When that was done, his resolve seemed to have drained away. He sat back down.

"I am not Hannibal," he managed.

"No, your grace, you are Richard Couer de Lion. Don't let your enemies put you in a cage! They will not follow us into the passes."

The King shook his head.

"Still no honey-coating, eh, Roger? Your plan is perhaps the wisest, old friend, but, even now, I shake with fever. I do not think I would survive the ordeal. We must take our chances and pass through the gauntlet of our enemies. Tomorrow we ride for Vienna, and may God watch over us all." There was finality in the King's statement. Sir Roger stepped back and bowed his head.

Better to die in a snow bank, he thought.

The next morning they gathered at the stables. The snow had stopped, and as they secured their kit to their saddles, Sir Roger noticed a sizable crowd of town folk gawking at them from the street. He nudged Sir Baldwin and tilted his head toward the onlookers.

"We attract too much attention. Sooner or later, we will come to the notice of people who mean us harm."

Baldwin nodded.

"I lay awake in the night thinking of how we might slip through Leopold's net. I believe smaller groups will attract less notice. I've advised the King that we should split the party in two and he has agreed. I will go ahead with three knights and you will ride with the King and Sir Alexander. Perhaps if there is danger, it will fall on my group first and give warning to the King."

Sir Roger could find no fault with the strategy, though it surely placed Sir Baldwin and the lead element in the most danger. But if word had been sent ahead that a group of foreigners were traveling to Vienna, then splitting up had some merit. It made the best of a bad situation.

Sir Baldwin set out at once with his group of three while Sir Roger joined the King in the inn. The snug common room where they had dined on sausages the night before was now deserted and dark, the hearth fire having burned down to bare embers. The King chewed indifferently on a slab of black bread the innkeeper had provided and looked morose. Sir Roger watched him in silence.

This fever has taken the fight out of the man.

King Richard turned suddenly toward him.

"I want you to make a promise to me, de Laval. If my enemies find us and it appears I am to be taken, I do not want you to defend me. There will be too many and you would sell your life for nothing. I do not want that on my conscience."

Sir Roger rose to his feet to protest, but the King waved him back to his seat.

"I know...I know. You would defend me to the death, man, but I need your loyalty in a more practical way. Leopold may value his grudge more than money. If he takes me, I may be put away in some bottomless hole for the man's amusement, with no one to know. It would suit my enemies' purpose to simply make me disappear. If it comes to that, I need you to get clear. Get back to England. The Queen must know of my fate. England must know!"

Sir Roger struggled for a reply.

"Your grace... I..."

"Swear it!" the King demanded.

Sir Roger bowed his head.

"I swear it."

***

It took more than a week to reach the approaches to Vienna. The weather was bitter cold and the roads frozen, but they were spared heavy snow. Sir Roger took care to keep a useful distance between the King and the party ahead, led by Sir Baldwin. The valleys they travelled through were not heavily populated, and though both groups were occasionally stopped by officials in the small villages, none chose to challenge these hard looking men. It was Sir Baldwin who first encountered a serious obstacle as they approached Vienna late in the day. Ten miles from the walled city, a barrier blocked the road. It was manned by a squad of ten, led by a tall knight in the livery of the Duke of Vienna. The man seemed to take his duties seriously.

"Who are you and where are you bound?" he demanded.

"I am Sir Philip de Croix. I return from Jerusalem to my home in Isle de France."

Sir Baldwin was a native French speaker and flew his false flag with conviction. After a few minutes of probing questions as to his route and his plans for any stops in the domain of Duke Leopold, he was waved through the barrier. He saluted the guard with relief, and spurred his horse toward Vienna.

I must get word back to the King of this roadblock.

As soon as he could find a place to stop for the evening, he would send one the Templars to circle around the guards and take word to the King to find a different route. The man at the barrier had been too observant—too devoted to his duty to risk the King's discovery. He urged his horse into a trot.

Back at the barrier, the leader of the guard patrol watched as the four knights disappeared around a bend. The man had been a foot soldier at Acre and there was no mistaking the nobleman he had just questioned—no matter what lie he told. He called one of his men forward.

"Take a message to the Captain of the Guard. Tell him Baldwin of Bethune just passed through our guard post with three Templars. They were headed for the city. Do you understand?"

"Aye, sir."

Just that morning, the Captain had reminded all of the road patrols to be on the lookout for certain knights—Sir Baldwin among them—who were thought to be traveling with the English king. King Richard had not been in Sir Baldwin's party, but what if the knight was simply scouting ahead for his master?

The leader of the guard post hesitated. The Captain of the Guard would no doubt consider the possibility that King Richard might be trailing his friend Baldwin. He would send mounted troops up the Villach road to search for the English king. The man rubbed his chin. He should probably wait for orders, but...if he took a squad back along the Villach road himself and bagged the English king, his fortune would be made. If he botched the capture he'd be sacked, but.... Squaring his shoulders, he barked out orders to his men. The prize was worth the risk.

They would go to catch the Lionheart.

***

The barking dog was the first sign of trouble. Sir Roger eased his hand to the hilt of his sword and rose quietly from the mat on the floor that had served as a bed. The King and Sir Alexander had not stirred. There was a tiny window in the second floor loft they occupied that looked out onto the cobbled road in front of the inn. He looked down and saw that it had started to snow—hard. The dog barked again and through the swirl of white flakes he saw ten men, under arms, marching down the road from the north, from Vienna.

Perhaps it was just a passing patrol, but that seemed unlikely at this hour when most folk were abed. There was a man near the front of the squad who was not a soldier—most likely a villager, rousted out to guide the men from Vienna. As they neared the inn, the villager turned to the soldier at the head of the patrol and pointed directly at the window where he watched.

"Damn!"

Without ceremony he kicked the King and Sir Alexander awake.

"Soldiers," he hissed. Both men immediately pulled on their boots and grabbed their weapons. Sir Roger scrambled down the ladder from the loft in time to kill the first man who burst through the door of the inn. As the man fell backwards, his startled companions froze. It was enough time for him to slam the door and brace a bench against it. It would not hold for long. Now the King and Sir Alexander joined him in the common room. They could hear orders being shouted and the sound of men moving to surround the place.

"Can't let them trap us here," the King said, looking around for some way out.

"Through the kitchen to the stables," said Sir Roger. "There are only ten or so and they are not mounted. We can cut our way through a few spearmen to get to the horses."

The King nodded and the three hurried through the kitchen to the rear of the inn and barrelled into the alley behind. Four men-at-arms turned the corner into the narrow rear passage and saw them. They lowered their spears and charged.

These Viennese spearmen were no match for the three hardened warriors and all four went down in a matter of seconds. There was a back entrance to the stables in the alley that was barred, but Sir Alexander kicked it down without trouble. Hurriedly, they saddled their horses and were mounting when a hue and cry rose up from the alley behind them. The King led the way through the front entrance of the stables and spurred his mount to the right. They would make for the road back toward Villach, if they could get clear.

They had hardly gone fifty paces along a narrow back street when another spearman leapt from an alley and barred their way. The King rose on his stirrups and knocked the man's weapon aside. Following close behind, Sir Alexander gave the man a savage blow with his broadsword that left him screaming on the cobbles. The three men kicked their mounts into a fast canter as they neared the main road.

Almost there, Sir Roger thought, as Bucephalus gained momentum. Then, all was chaos. The King careened into a host of mounted and armed men on the main road from Vienna. Surprised, they hesitated for a moment and Richard almost bulled his way clear, but the horsemen recovered quickly and swarmed around him. Sir Alexander, who had been close behind the King, went down fighting, a mace taking him in the back of the head.

Sir Roger put the spurs to Bucephalus and leaned forward as the warhorse pinned back his ears and slammed into the men surrounding the King. Two horses went down squealing before the bulk of the huge charger, their riders thrown. But the road to the east was filled with mounted troops from Vienna and they pressed forward, seeking to claim the royal prize.

Two men on foot came at Bucephalus from behind, one received a savage kick from his massive rear hoof, but the other managed to dodge and lunge forward with his lance. Sir Roger wore no mail below the waist and the point sliced along his thigh, leaving a nasty gash. His battle fury roused, the big knight hardly noted the wound as he turned and struck the man down, but now there was a solid mass of men and horses between him and the King.

For the moment, Richard held his attackers at bay, standing in his stirrups and swinging his long broadsword two-handed at any man who came near—but the situation was hopeless. He swivelled in his saddle, his chest heaving and for a moment locked eyes with Sir Roger, then he held out his arms to his captors and dropped his weapon. In seconds, men crowded in to seize him.

Roger de Laval did not have to ponder the King's last silent command to him. It had already been given, but it took all of his discipline to pull his warhorse's head around to the south. With a sick heart he gave his charger the spurs. Two horses stood between him and the open road. Bred for speed more than war, they reared in panic as Bucephalus bore down on them. One horse threw its rider and the man who managed to keep his saddle went down under Sir Roger's sword. Behind him, all closed in around the real prize, the King of England, the renowned Lionheart. The big knight galloped free into the night with no riders following him.

Sir Roger cursed under his breath as he pushed the horse hard to put miles behind him. When no pursuit came, he slowed. Bucephalus was built for the short, violent cavalry charge, not a long chase. He would have to husband the horse's energy for when it was needed. As he rode into the night he cursed again.

His King had been taken!

It was a disgrace that he would never live down. All that was left for him was to abide by the King's command and get to Queen Eleanor with news of her son's fate.

It would be bitter tidings for her and for his country.

***

Thirty miles south of Vienna, a tiny village clustered around the main road that ran on southward through the valley toward Graz, then west to Villach. It would be easy to miss the frozen track in the village that split off northwest toward mountains that loomed blackly in the predawn darkness. But Roger de Laval had been looking for this road. When he found it, he pulled his reins to the right and left the main road behind.

He would never be able to outrun the pursuit on Bucephalus, and pursuit would surely be coming. He looked up at the black crags that loomed darker than the night sky and patted the big horse's neck. It was snowing lightly now and a thin blanket covered the road.

It will get worse. Leaning forward he spoke to Bucephalus in a quiet voice.

"Hannibal did it with elephants, Buc, elephants!"

An hour later, twenty armed men thundered through the village heading south. They paid no attention to the small road leading up into the mountains. The tracks of the big grey warhorse had been covered by the snow.

At higher elevations, the world turned white. The sky, the road, the mountains all blended into a swirl of pure white that would have been beautiful had it not been so damned cold. Roger de Laval had seen bitter winters on campaign in France and Ireland, but there had been nothing like this cold.

He had lost most of the feeling in his feet and the breath came in steamy puffs from his horse's nostrils as they laboured upwards. If his feet were growing numb, his thigh had become a fiery agony where the lance had ripped across the muscle. He had pressed hard against the wound as he rode and the bleeding had stopped, but now the dried blood stuck to his leggings and any movement tugged at the ragged gash.

He dismounted when the drifts reached Bucephalus' hocks and led the horse on foot. For an hour, the road clung to the left side of a narrow defile that dropped off steeply into nothingness on the right. It was now near dawn, but the increasing fury of the snowstorm made the road hard to see. Sir Roger kept one eye on scattered patches of grey that marked the rock face to his left. It was all he had to guide by.

Coming around a bend, a hard wind sent ice crystals flying from the growing drifts to nearly blind man and horse. The wind-driven snow began to cake on Sir Roger's beard and the front of his woollen coat. Bucephalus whinnied and shook his massive head as the snow stung his eyes.

"Hang on, old boy—just a few more miles," Sir Roger shouted above the roar of the wind. But he had no idea how many more miles lay ahead and the road kept climbing. He thought of the night he told the King he would rather die in a snowbank than be captured.

"Brave talk in a warm inn," he said out loud. Bucephalus, hearing his master's voice, laid his massive head on Sir Roger's shoulder for a moment. The man reached up a gloved hand to stroke the horse's muzzle.

"Sorry I dragged you into this, big fella. But we are not done yet."

He bent his head and trudged on. Somewhere there was a bright sun shining in a blue sky, but here, the storm roared around him like some evil spirit, determined to sweep him off the heights to his death. He slipped and fell to his knees, but rose again. The effort to get to his feet shocked him. Some strange weakness seemed to have taken control of his limbs.

He kept climbing, stumbling into waist-deep drifts. There was no feeling left in his hands or feet. For a moment the path seemed to level and he struggled forward, only to fall once more. It felt peaceful here in the drift, but he fought to free himself. He managed to get to his knees but felt light-headed. The wind sounded like voices screaming into the night and lights danced before his eyes. He tried to rise to his feet, but this time his legs would not cooperate.

He groaned. His mind was foggy. Somewhere, he thought he heard a dog bark. Bucephalus nudged him with his nose, but he couldn't move. He had one final thought before darkness took him.

I'm so sorry, Catherine.

Part Three: An Uncivil War

The Ransomed Crown

The Old Templar

Snow was falling softly as the monk made his way at twilight through the Aldersgate and into London. He had come from the London Temple where a distracted clerk had been persuaded to tell him where Sir Bernard Waldgrave had taken lodgings. He walked another block and found himself standing at the door of a man he hadn't seen in five years. Tuck rapped on the oak and waited. From somewhere above he heard the creak of a shutter and felt himself being inspected by unseen eyes.

"If that's you, Bernard, come down and open the door," he called out. "It's Augustine."

He heard the shutter close and footsteps on stairs. A moment later, the door swung open. A tall man with a shock of white hair stood there. He leaned forward and squinted.

"Is it you? The eyes aren't what they once were."

"It's me, Bernard. Can I come in?"

The man hesitated for a moment, then stepped back.

"Yes, of course, Augustine, come in."

He followed the older man into a small room with a bench and a chair. A small fire gave off a little light, but not much warmth. Sir Bernard settled himself in the chair and looked at Tuck.

"It's been a long time, Augustine. Are you still preaching to the heathens up in the hills?"

216

Tuck looked at the aging Templar and thought back to his first days in the Order when this man had been his guide. Sir Bernard had been as tough as boot leather and breathtakingly lethal with a blade. He had taught the young miller's son from Derbyshire the mysteries of the Order and the finer points of swordsmanship. Together they had travelled to the East and had served long years on the dangerous pilgrimage route to Jerusalem.

The bond between them had been strong, but, in the end, Tuck had lost his stomach for the killing. The two had quarrelled bitterly over his decision to leave the Order and their parting had been cold. Now his old guide had retired from active service with the Templars. It seemed the years had not softened the man.

"Sorrowfully, I've had to give up that calling for a time, Bernard. My flock are dying faster than I can save their souls."

"Dying?"

"Aye, have you not heard of the famine in the Midlands? Our good Prince John is starving the people to pay for mercenaries to gain the throne."

Waldgrave grunted.

"Everyone knows about John and his mercenary army, but famine in the Midlands? There have only been rumours."

"Children are dying in the villages, Bernard. I've seen it. We try to help, but it's not nearly enough."

"We?"

"Aye. There are over a hundred men with me in Nottinghamshire, all now outlawed. We steal what grain we can, but the Sheriff has the land in an iron grip. We save some, but..."

In the firelight, Waldgrave's face grew mournful.

"Augustine...you...an outlaw?"

"What choice does a man of God really have when children are dying, Bernard? But it is going to take more than a band of outlaws and my prayers to prevent the disaster that is visited upon the people of the Midlands. John must be stopped. We need help—and soon."

Sir Bernard shook his head sadly.

"Surely these are dark times, Augustine, but you know our Order's purpose—and it is not to save starving peasants in

England. And it is certainly not to interject ourselves into a royal civil war. You'll get no help from the Templars."

The old man was quiet for a while. He leaned over and threw a stick on the fire, then spoke again.

"We did not part friends, Augustine, and I've regretted that. It pains me now to see you about to throw your life away to no purpose. John will be a terrible king, but men who are in a position to know are betting that he will have the crown by the end of the year. When that happens, bands like yours will be hunted down and you will swing—or worse. You should come back to the Order, Augustine. This doesn't have to be your fight."

The older man leaned forward as he spoke, looking into the eyes of his old comrade, but saw nothing there but calm resolution. Tuck shook his head.

"Oh, you're wrong there, Bernard. This *is* my fight. It's the fight I fled from as a young man—to my lasting shame. I found a refuge here in our Order, but I always felt I had abandoned the people out there. I won't abandon them a second time."

Sir Bernard sighed and sat back.

"Very well then. The best I can do is send you to a man who is as stubborn as you. He refuses to see that John has all but won and he'll probably swing along with you. But if there is any chance that the Prince can be stopped, William Marshal is the man who will stop him. I can give you a letter of introduction. I saved the man's life once when he made his own pilgrimage to Jerusalem."

Tuck rose to his feet.

"Marshal? Didn't he lead the relief force that tried to save Nottingham Castle?"

"Aye, and he failed. In fact, the man has never won a battle—as far as I know."

Tuck smiled broadly for the first time.

"Then perhaps he's due."

***

The snow had stopped, but a cold wind was blowing as Tuck made his way east through the centre of the city. It was late, but yellow light and the sound of revelry leaked out of tavern doors along the way. The country might be tearing itself apart, but Londoners seemed hardly troubled by the turmoil. He paid little attention as he picked his way along the street, stepping around the usual effluent and offal now lightly dusted with white. Marshal had quarters near Tower Hill and Waldgrave had assured him the Earl was currently in the city.

William Marshal.

Tuck knew of the man, though they had never met. Marshal had begun acquiring fame very young. He had been one of the great tournament knights of the age, the victor in hundreds of jousts. Such was his reputation in the lists that minstrels sang songs of him. Tuck had always considered these organized combats a ridiculous spectacle, but no one could doubt that the men who fought in them had courage aplenty.

Tuck passed by St Olave's church, old before the Normans had conquered the land, and couldn't help but cast wary glances at the white mass of the Tower rising above the hill. The thing was more than simply a fortress. William, Duke of Normandy, had ordered it built to make it clear who ruled this town and this land. For over a hundred years it had glowered down on the city of London, daring any to challenge Norman rule.

When he arrived at the place Sir Bernard had described, he noted that, from the second floor, one could likely observe the drawbridge that led into the Tower. Marshal had chosen a strategic place to call home. He climbed a short set of steps and knocked on the door. It opened almost instantly and an armed guard gazed at him suspiciously.

"What's yer business?"

"I've come to see Sir William Marshal. I have a letter of introduction from Sir Bernard Waldgrave." Tuck thrust the parchment toward the man.

The guard looked him up and down. He took the parchment, broke the seal and looked at it.

"Wait here," he said and slammed the door shut.

Long minutes passed before the door swung open once more. A tall, handsome man with broad shoulders and piercing grey eyes looked down on him.

"Father Augustine, please come in. I am William Marshal. I was about to have a late dinner. Would you join me?"

"I'd be pleased to, my lord."

Marshal led him toward the back of the house. Tuck saw stairs leading up to the second floor and wondered if there was a man at the window up there noting who came and who went from the Tower. They entered the kitchen, where there was a rough table set with cold meats and bread. A pot hung over the fire, giving off the unmistakable aroma of stew. Marshal motioned for Tuck to sit, then filled a cup from a pitcher and passed it to him.

"Wine from Aquitaine. Nothing like it here in England."

Tuck took a moment to inhale the heady fragrance of the liquid but waited for Marshal to drink first. He had not had wine in over a year and as he followed his host and turned his glass up, he felt the warmth spread in his belly. He forced himself to drink only half of the cup and set it down.

Marshal had already returned his cup to the table and waited for Tuck to speak.

"My lord, I've come looking for help."

Marshal nodded.

"Most who show up at my door are looking for help, Father. Sadly, I've had little of it to give lately. I'll confess I would have turned you away had you not had the note from Sir Bernard. Did he tell you he saved my life?"

"Aye, my lord, though he gave no details."

Marshal's eyes took on a faraway look for a moment.

"It is a long story, Father, but I was venturing in places a pilgrim to Jerusalem should not have been. Thank God Sir Bernard and his Templar brethren were nearby or I would be long dead."

Marshal blinked and seemed to return to the present.

"Sir Bernard's note says you were once in the Order but are now ministering to folk in Nottinghamshire. What kind of help are you seeking, Father?"

Tuck cleared his throat. He hoped the Earl appreciated directness.

"My lord, there is famine in the Midlands and it is no act of God. Prince John is bleeding the land to pay his mercenaries. Children are starving. Let me go right to the heart of the matter. A year ago, the King sent me home from the East with a message for the Queen. In his message, he promised that he would be home before Christ's Mass. That day is but weeks away. I trust the King's return will put an end to this madness, but we've heard no news of his approach. Where is the King, my lord?"

Marshal raised an eyebrow.

"I will tell you honestly that we've had no news of Richard since he sailed from Cyprus in early October. It is anyone's guess when or if he will return to England. I'm familiar with this message you carried. I was present at Oxford when two young knights gave the same message to the Queen."

At that, Tuck slammed a palm down on the table top and smiled broadly.

"I know those lads, my lord, and I'm right happy to hear they survived their journey home! I fought with Sir Roland and Sir Declan at Acre. They are loyal men and more deadly than they look."

Marshal returned the smile.

"Aye, Father. They gave a good account of themselves when they returned to Chester, but now that city is besieged and I expect your friends are hard pressed."

Tuck sighed.

"We knew that the mercenary army had marched west after the fall of Nottingham Castle, but had not heard much since."

Marshal frowned.

"The loss of Nottingham was my fault, Father. I tried to break the siege, but we took a drubbing at Leicester. Somehow word of our approach found its way to our enemies. The garrison had no choice but to surrender. To my shame, John made every man bend a knee and swear loyalty to him."

"Not every man, my lord."

Marshal looked at him curiously.

"After delivering the King's message, I intended to find a bit of peace and return to my flock in the mountains of Derbyshire," Tuck said. "I travelled with Sir Robin of Loxley and we were sickened by what we saw in the villages we passed. When John threatened the castle at Nottingham we knew its fall would make the Prince's grip on the Midlands stronger. So Sir Robin and I joined the garrison there."

"And after the surrender? I can see you weren't hung, but how did you avoid bending the knee?"

Tuck shrugged.

"I, and my comrades, avoided that indignity, my lord, by going over the wall and escaping into Sherwood Forest. We've been outlawed, but our numbers have grown. Sir Robin is our leader and we have over a hundred men now. But we cannot match the strength of the new sheriff who is stripping the land of everything. We have few weapons—some of the men have only staffs and pruning hooks. My lord, women and children are starving in Nottinghamshire and Derbyshire. Something must be done. Can you help us?"

Marshal stood up.

"Eat first, then we'll talk. Perhaps we can help each other."

***

They talked long into the night. Marshal offered Tuck a bed but he refused. As he left the house that looked out over the grounds of the Tower, he felt the wind press his coarse robes around his legs. It had turned colder while he and the Justiciar had discussed a way forward.

As he reached the street and turned back toward the west, he had the odd sensation of being watched. He looked down the street behind him. It was empty. Then he looked up. Someone was standing in the second floor window of Marshal's house watching him.

It was a girl.

The Ransomed Crown

A Lion in Chains

By the highest window in the tower, a woman sat and looked to the east. She had always enjoyed this view from the castle of Tancarville, perched high on a bluff overlooking a lazy bend of the Seine as it neared the sea. But now the land was grey, the last leaves had fallen from the trees and a cold wind rattled the shutters. Another winter had come, and with it a feeling of growing despair.

It had been six months since the messages from her son had stopped coming. Walter of Coutances had learned through his contacts that Richard had made an extended stop in Cyprus before sailing west in early October, but no further word or sign of his approach had reached her. Her spies had kept watch in every major port around the northern shore of the Mediterranean, but none had seen the King or heard any hint of his coming. And now, for the past month, the tattered remains of his army had begun arriving at the ports of England and Normandy.

So where was Richard?

The wind changed direction and an icy gust blew her grey hair back. She still wore it long. Men had once written poetry about Eleanor of Aquitaine—the lustre of her hair, the brightness of her eyes, the grace of her neck. She pulled a shawl closer around her bony shoulders, but did not move. Men had worshiped her beauty well into her forties, but now she was nearly twice that and men either feared her or depended on her to save them from their follies.

223

It was wearisome. She had held Richard's kingdom together against determined enemies for over two years now, but those enemies were growing bolder. John now held the royal castles at Windsor, Lincoln and Nottingham and was actively plotting with Philip of France to gain that slippery ruler's support to take the crown itself. Her short visit to England the previous winter had slowed the designs of her ambitious younger son, but had in no way ended them.

The surprise reappearance of the Earl of Chester from Wales and the recapture of his city had been a setback for the Prince and his favourite lackey, William de Ferrers—and a rare piece of good news for supporters of the King. But John had responded by sending his mercenary army to besiege the city. It had taken them six months to starve Nottingham into submission. How long could the men at Chester hold out against a force such as that?

William Marshal had been her strong right arm, but it was all he could do to keep the barons in the north and south of the country from throwing in their lots with John. This he did with veiled threats of what the King might do upon his return to those who proved less than loyal. But veiled threats didn't always prevail against the very real threats that John could muster.

And what if Richard was dead? She tried to keep that thought at bay, for in that lay the end of all of her dreams and the end of the empire she and Henry had built. John would never be able to hold it—not against Philip of France.

The shutters creaked again and a movement on the road below caught her eye. A lone man on horseback was coming down the road from Rouen—the road down which trouble always came. The rider leaned forward, his chin almost touching his chest. She wondered if he was asleep in the saddle, but then his head rose slowly and he gazed up at the castle. She sighed and rose from her place.

It was time to be Queen once more.

***

The man who entered her meeting hall was tall, pale as a ghost and gaunt. He had the frame of a powerful man and she could tell by the breadth of his shoulders that he had not always been so painfully thin. He had the look and dress of a knight, but moved with the unsteady gait of an older man. The Captain of the Guard told her that he had to help the man dismount his horse. Her visitor removed his hat in her presence to display a bald head. There were scars there. He went down on one knee.

"Your Grace," he began and seemed to struggle to draw breath. "I bring you news...of the King."

She stiffened. The mournful look on the man's face told its own story. Had her greatest fear come to pass? She steeled herself.

"What is your name, sir."

"I am Sir Roger de Laval, your grace."

De Laval...ah, yes.

"Give us your news, then, Sir Roger."

The tall knight nodded, but seemed to list to the right and fight to take in a breath.

"The King...the king...." he muttered, then toppled to the floor.

The Queen sprang up from her chair and ordered a man to fetch her physician. She moved to the fallen man's side. His eyes were open, but when she laid a hand to his forehead it was burning hot to the touch.

"Stay still," she whispered, "you are ill." But the man shook his head.

"The King...your grace, he has been taken prisoner...in Austria. The Duke...Duke of Vienna." The effort produced a long bout of wracking coughs.

The physician arrived and after touching the man's forehead murmured some of his usual nonsense. He drew forth a small bottle from his bag and forced his new patient to drink, which produced a new round of coughing. Finally the eruption ended as the man's eyes rolled back in his head.

"Physician, see that this man lives," she said. "He has done us a great service, and I believe there is a young woman in Cheshire who will be very put out should he die—as will I."

The Queen drew away, lost for the moment in furious thought. Richard was captive.

...but he was alive!

It was grim news, but not the news she had feared most. If Richard lived, there was still hope. But what ghastly price would they pay—would England pay—to free their King? And could they do it before her younger son seized the throne?

***

It took Sir Roger two days to recover from his swoon and another to get to his feet and walk unsteadily about his room. His fever had passed, but the Queen forbade him to take his leave until he recovered more of his strength. The woman had even posted a guard on his door, figuring—rightly—that he might ignore her command.

She'd visited him on the third day to hear his full account of the King's capture. She had already sent a courier in all haste to fetch Walter of Coutances. This Duke Leopold of Austria may have taken her son, but he was a vassal of Henry VI, the Holy Roman Emperor, and it was to Henry that she would dispatch the Archbishop. There was no one else with the political skills and shrewdness needed to negotiate Richard's release.

She could see that the big knight was weak, but seemed to be recovering. At her prompting, he told her of the shipwreck, the desperate flight through the mountains and the King's capture near Vienna.

"It will always be my shame that I could not protect him, your grace, but he made me swear to get to you with this news. Had it not been for a goatherd in the mountains, I would have failed at that as well."

Eleanor shushed him.

"You almost died up there in those mountains. You've done your King a great service, Sir Roger. We are in your debt."

When he had finished recounting his story, she told him the incredible news of Chester's capture by William de Ferrers and its recapture by Earl Ranulf. She wanted to tell him of his daughter's role in these dramatic events, but did not.

Let the girl or his wife tell it as they see fit.

The Queen rose to leave. She did not want to distress a sick man, but felt he needed to know the truth.

"Sir Roger, after the city fell back into Ranulf's hands last summer, my son, the Prince, sent his army of mercenaries to take it back. Chester has been cut off and besieged for four months now." She saw the stricken look on the man's face, but left him to digest these bad tidings.

Sir Roger sat on his cot and tried to think clearly. The news that the city was besieged chilled him. If Chester was invested, then outlying strongpoints like Shipbrook must have been abandoned. It meant that Catherine and Millicent would be trapped in a city that had been cut off for months. The thought made him ill. He had stood atop the broken walls of Acre and looked down into that city at the end of its siege. There were piles of dead on every street. It was a nightmare vision. The next day, he returned to see the Queen. He stood straight and fought to keep from swaying as he addressed her.

"Your Grace, I know you mean well, but I beg you to release me. If I could walk across the Alps to bring you news of your son, surely I can make it to Chester to see to my own family."

The Queen considered the tall bald knight carefully. He was still pale and was not fit to travel yet, but the look in the man's eyes was desperate. She might actually need to lock him up to hold him here. A memory came to her of a meeting she'd had with Sir Roger's wife over two years ago. She had asked the woman if she loved her husband. Catherine de Laval had made it very clear that she did and, looking at the plea in Roger de Laval's eyes, she now understood why. Nothing was going to keep this man from his woman. She sighed.

"Sir Roger, I understand your desire to get to Chester and see to the safety of your family. Against my better judgement, I'm letting you go, but I will not have you riding across the breadth of England in your condition. I will send word to one of my ships at Harfleur. It will take you into the Channel, around Cornwall and deliver you to the River Dee. You must find your own way from there. I'm sure you know the perils of trying to get into a city under siege, but I shan't try to dissuade you."

Sir Roger bowed his head.

"Thank you, your grace."

The Queen rose and stepped forward, taking the knight's rough hands in her thin, delicate ones.

"You go with my thanks and my prayers, Sir Roger. I believe you may have saved your King and your country."

***

The Bishop of Beauvais burst into the private parlour of the King of France waving a sheet of vellum.

"They have him! Merciful God they have snared the beast, your grace!" Philip looked up, irritated that his cousin had disturbed him, but curious as to what had made his usually dour kinsmen so animated. He did not have long to wait.

"It's a message from the Holy Roman Emperor, your grace. Richard was taken captive by the Duke of Austria and is now in his custody—held captive in Oschenfurt!"

Philip leapt from his chair so abruptly that it toppled over backwards. He could hardly believe the news his spymaster had brought him. He seized the document from the Bishop's hand and read through it twice before laying it on his table.

"How could the fool have ventured anywhere near Austria?" he asked incredulously. "He must have lost his wits to put himself at the mercy of the very man he humiliated at Acre."

Not a man present at the capture of Acre was unaware of the insult the Duke had suffered at Richard's hands after the battle. Philip, himself the frequent object of the English king's scorn, could only imagine the satisfaction Leopold must have felt to have his haughty enemy fall into his hands.

The Bishop rubbed his hands together like a boy who had been promised a treat.

"Not a man in Europe hates Richard more than Leopold!" he said. "He may simply kill him."

Philip raised a hand.

"No. He may hate Richard, though in truth no more than I do, but he will not kill him. The Emperor will forbid it. I expect even now they are haggling over ownership of this prize ape they have captured."

The Bishop's eyes lit up. He saw where his master's thoughts were heading.

"They're going to sell him! Of course! Henry is the poorest Emperor ever to wear that rusty old crown of Charlemagne. He needs the money to keep his own barons in line."

"Yes, cousin, they will sell him. The question is—for how much and who will be the buyer."

Philip casually stepped over and righted his fallen chair. He looked once more at the piece of vellum with the seal of the Holy Roman Emperor that had changed everything, then turned to the Bishop.

"Send for Prince John. I think it's time we talked."

***

The message from Henry VI, Holy Roman Emperor, arrived at Tancarville on the same day that Walter of Coutances disembarked at Harfleur, the port nearest the Queen's cliff-top castle by the Seine. The Archbishop of Rouen made haste to attend the Queen, given the urgency of her summons, and could see by the look on Eleanor's face that the news was not good.

"He wants us to give them our kingdom in exchange for our King," she said flatly, handing the sheet of vellum with the Emperor's seal to her spymaster. The Archbishop read hurriedly through the short document and visibly flinched when he read the final paragraph.

"One hundred fifty thousand marks? My God, it must be a mistake, your grace," was all the man could manage.

"It's no mistake, Walter. We both know Henry's hold over his barons is hanging by a thread. He has no prestige and so needs money to buy their support. He must have prayed for a miracle and my son has granted him one by blundering into his grasp. I doubt God had much to do with it."

The Archbishop found he had started to pace back and forth, so distressed was he by this calamity. It was a bad habit and one he had never revealed to his Queen. In mid-stride he caught himself and stood still.

"Your grace, that is five times what we gather in taxes in a year! There may not be that much silver in all of England." The man stopped for a moment, running figures in his head. "That would be...*over fifty tons of silver!*"

As a Justiciar, Walter of Coutances had somehow managed to keep the government of the realm operating, even in the face of John's pillaging of the Midlands. Resources had been scarce and revenue sparse, but he and William Marshal had somehow managed to scrape together the funds to pay the bills over the past two years. No one understood the magnitude of this blow more than the Archbishop of Rouen. Eleanor watched as the blood drained from the man's face. She knew he was stunned, but she needed him now more than ever.

"Walter, I want you to leave today. Go to Henry. Persuade him to lower his price. Tell him whatever you must. Promise him whatever you must, but Walter…in the end we will have to pay—somehow. I will write to the Pope. This is a gross violation of the Truce of God and I believe Celestine might threaten excommunication. His Holiness has no more love for Henry than his barons do."

The Archbishop bowed his head.

"I do not think the approbation of the Pope will sway Henry, not with this much money at stake, but it could help with his bishops and Henry needs their support almost as much as the funds. I will do as you ask, but I am concerned for my work in London, your grace.

Eleanor did not need to ask what work that was. The Archbishop controlled a growing network of agents vital to their plans. Since she'd made him her spymaster, he had shown an exceptional gift for intrigue, but those gifts were now needed elsewhere.

"Walter, I cannot leave for England just yet. If I do, we will surely lose the Vexin and likely Gisors as well. Rouen may hold. Robert, Earl of Leicester, has returned from crusade and commands there. He can be depended upon to die before giving Philip an inch of that town, but those who command elsewhere seem to require me to stiffen their spines."

"They fear you more than Philip," the Archbishop said.

"As well they should, Walter! This is no time for half measures. And as dire as the situation may be in England, we cannot afford to lose these lands. So I must stay, but Walter…we must get Richard back. If we cannot, John will surely lose it all."

230

"I will spare no effort, your grace," the Archbishop said and bowed his head.

"I know I can count on you, my friend. Come back to me after you've rested and eaten. I cannot take up the reins in London for you, but I would hear what you and your men have been up to."

"They are not all men, your grace," he replied with a sly smile. "You yourself taught me the value of women in this work."

"Ah, yes, you have that clever young woman you brought with you from Rouen—what was her name?"

"Mary Cullen, your grace. She has been instructed to keep you informed by weekly courier of any news our agents glean whilst I am away. You may count on her."

"Good. But what of your suspicions that we have a spy in our midst? This would be the worst of times to have our plans compromised."

"As you know from my last dispatch, I strongly suspect that one of the men close to Earl Marshal is a traitor, but which one I cannot say. Marshal is certain they are all innocent, your grace, but you know that the man has a trusting nature, whereas, I do not."

"Nor do I, Walter. How do you plan to catch this spy?"

The Archbishop looked sheepish.

"There again, I have followed your advice concerning the suitability of women for this work. With his agreement, I've placed an agent near to Marshal, a young woman with a keen eye and sharp wits—a girl not unfamiliar to you."

The Queen looked at him quizzically. Then it struck her.

"The de Laval girl?"

"Aye, your grace, Millicent de Laval. I sent for her just before Chester was cut off. She has been watching the men that surround Earl William since August, but has not ferreted out the traitor yet. I've urged her to be patient. Our spy is no doubt skilled in covering his tracks."

Eleanor raised her eyes to the ceiling. She was relieved that the girl's father had taken ship the day before—though she would have certainly kept this information from him. She had no doubt

231

that blunt fighting man would have bulled his way right into Marshal's home, looking to haul off his daughter.

"She's a talented girl, Walter. I hope she lives to see her family once this is over."

"I hope that for all of us, your grace, and until then, may God have mercy on England."

Eleanor frowned.

"If He does, it will be the first time He has in years! But I should not blaspheme so."

The Archbishop gave her a wan smile.

"Do not fear, your grace. The Lord loves a sinner!"

***

The day was bitter cold and the feeble sun that shone through the overcast sky offered no relief to the men who rode through the thick woods south of Paris. In the centre of his escort of heavily armed riders, Prince John eased a hand from his reins and pulled the heavy ermine robe tight about his neck, but the icy wind still found a way in. He steeled himself against the cold and tried to prepare himself for this meeting—a meeting that could decide his fate and that of England.

The summons from Philip and the news it contained had been stunning. His brother, the mighty warrior, the invincible knight, had been captured trying to sneak back home from his failed Crusade by a second rate nobleman!

He had placed spies at every port in England and France watching for Richard's return. But as the battered remains of the English army dribbled into Portsmouth and Southampton through December, there had been no sign or news of the King. He had begun to believe that his fervent wish might be granted— that Richard was dead, lost at sea perhaps. Now came this news of his capture and the urgent summons from Philip.

By midmorning they arrived at Fontainebleau, the fortified hunting lodge of the Capetian kings. Word of the Prince's approach had preceded him and a trumpeter blew a fanfare atop the gate tower as the troop thundered across the drawbridge and into the courtyard. John had hardly dismounted when Philip of

France appeared at the top of the stone steps that led up to the great arched doorway of the keep.

John hurried up the steps and when he neared the French king he went down on one knee. He looked up into the face of the man who had sworn his hatred of the Plantagenets since childhood.

"Your majesty," he said. "I come to do you homage."

***

Philip wasted no time in getting down to business.

"Will the Queen pay the ransom?"

John grimaced.

"My mother will move heaven and earth to get Richard back," he said flatly. "If she can raise the funds, she will pay. She could have me on the throne for free, but there is no love in that dried-up breast for John—only for her precious Richard!"

Philip arched an eyebrow. John's jealousy of Richard was not news to him. He had studied this family for years and knew their weaknesses. He had seduced John's late brother, Henry the Young King, into rebelling against his father, Henry II. He'd aided Richard himself when he had risen against the King. These rebellions had all failed, but they had weakened the bonds that held this warlike family together. And Philip meant to exploit that weakness to the fullest.

"Your grace, to win the crown will cost you blood or money," he said, fixing the young English prince with his gaze. "You must either seize the throne by force before Richard can be ransomed or, failing that, outbid Eleanor for custody of your brother. In either case, I am prepared to aid you."

John looked up at the King. He needed Philip now, more than ever, but he was no fool.

"How can you help me, your majesty?"

Philip smiled benevolently.

"Your grace, I think you will be the greatest English King since Canute. I am prepared to marshal my army at Wissant, where my fleet stands ready to land it on the shores of Kent."

John stifled a gasp. For a moment he saw the prize finally within his grasp. Despite spending a fortune on his mercenary host he had not managed to get his boot firmly on the neck of the English barons. Many were cowed and many more had been bought, but there was still resistance to his claims to the throne. Having a French army at his back could tip the balance. But he had known Philip since boyhood and sensed there was more to this bargain.

"What will it cost me for this support?"

"A fair price, I think you'll agree. You will give me possession of Gisors and the Vexin, which your father stole from France. You may keep the rest, but you will do public homage to me for all of the English holdings on the continent—Normandy, Aquitaine, Brittany—the lot."

John did not flinch. It was a steep price, but not unexpected. He had been prepared to do homage to Philip for the English lands in France as some of his forebears had done. That was a mere formality with little real impact on his domains. The loss of Gisors and the Vexin would be painful, for it placed Philip's forces in a much stronger strategic position should war come to Normandy. Still, he would have given up these and more to gain the crown.

"When will your army be prepared to sail, your majesty?"

Philip shrugged and waved a hand in the air.

"Of course I must be certain my men will be welcomed and not set upon by your enemies or mine when they disembark. To be certain of that, I will need certain assurances from the greater part of the English nobility, you grace. Give me written assurances of support and we will march to your aid."

John felt his heart sink. If he could muster that kind of support from the barons, he would have no need of Philip!

"And should I seek to outbid the Queen for my brother, what are you prepared to contribute."

Philip sighed.

"England is a very rich country. We are sadly poor. But I can guarantee you five thousand pounds of silver against the ransom."

John was surprised. This was a huge sum.

"And what will you gain from this, your majesty?"

Philip laid a brotherly hand on his shoulder.

"Well, there is the Vexin and Gisors," he said, "and one thing more. I want Richard."

John shrugged.

"You are welcome to him."

The Old Soldier

*T*he ship dropped anchor well into the estuary of the Dee. It was a frigid, blustery morning and the mouth of the river provided a protected anchorage out of the hard wind piling up whitecaps in the Irish Sea behind them. The master of the vessel watched as his lone passenger, a tall, worn-looking knight, climbed carefully down into the small boat that would carry him ashore.

He had wondered from the beginning of this voyage why the Queen had hired his ship to bring a single man to this remote part of her realm. He shrugged. Who could understand the purposes of royalty? He had tried to strike up a conversation as they beat down the Channel in remarkably fair weather for December, but the knight had been in no mood for conversation. He sensed his passenger had lived through something that had taken him to the very edge. He seemed fragile, but in the man's eyes there was still a fire. The ship's master decided it was best to leave Sir Roger de Laval to himself.

The small boat drove in among the reeds where the last ford on the Dee crossed the river. Sir Roger rose from the bow and stepped back onto English soil for the first time in over two years. He instinctively looked across the river toward Wales. Nothing moved there. He looked down at the trail that led up toward the higher ground on the English side. There were a few old hoof prints in the frozen mud and nothing more.

He shoved the boat back into the current and slung his sword belt over his head. His battleaxe hung at his side as he started up the path toward home. He thought he had prepared himself for the worst, but his breath caught in his throat when he topped the last rise and looked across the untended fields at Shipbrook.

"Damn…"

He cursed to himself and started across the fields still covered in hoarfrost. No one challenged him. The approaches showed clear signs of a battle, though not a recent one. The gate was down, its wood splintered. The crude ram that had done the deed stood like some strange beast in the entrance. He stepped around it and looked inside. The hall was burnt down and no living thing moved.

He could not bring himself to enter. Anything inside that might have had worth to him was destroyed—or dead. He backed out of the broken gate and looked to the east, toward the besieged city of Chester. Without a word he trudged off in that direction. He knew a mercenary army stood between him and the city, but Catherine and Millie would be there—*must be there*. The mercenaries had best stay out of his way.

***

The sentry yawned and shook his head, trying to stay awake one more hour until sunrise. It had been a very cold night and the horses had been restless. He'd walked among them during the small hours of the night and it seemed to settle the beasts down, but in the bitter cold, the fire near the picket line kept drawing him back.

Now, as the warmth seeped into his bones, his head nodded—once, twice, then came to rest on his chest. He dreamed of his mother in Antwerp. She was baking a tart. He never heard the man come out of the woods behind him or saw the flash of the sword as the heavy hilt took him in the temple. His mother and the tart dissolved into utter blackness.

***

A guard at the Northgate saw it first. Just as dawn arrived there was movement to the northwest. A rider was coming toward the town and moving fast. The man on the horse had got clear of the tree line by a hundred yards when more riders burst from the woods. The guard atop the Northgate counted five riders trying to close on the one.

"Sergeant of the Guard!" He called.

Sir Edgar Langton had just left the gatehouse to conduct his dawn rounds of the city walls when the call came down to him. He instinctively looked to the north and saw the rider, his horse at full gallop heading toward the city gate. The riders who pursued him were whipping their horses to close the gap, but the man in the lead looked sure to beat them. But the gate was closed and barred. He knew it could be a trick, but something told him it wasn't.

"Open the gate!" he roared. "Call up the archers."

This last command was hardly needed. At each of the city gates four longbowmen were assigned to each watch and they had heard the sentry's first alarm. The four were already scrambling up the ladder to the top of the barbican.

"Archers," Sir Edgar ordered. "Cover that man!"

The fleeing rider was within two hundred yards of the gate and coming hard when his horse stepped in a cleverly concealed hole in the road covered over with hide and dirt. The Chester garrison had pocked the approaches to the city with these traps to slow any approach to the walls.

The beast lunged forward, its leg snapping like a twig. The rider was catapulted over the animal's head and onto the roadway. Sir Edgar thought he might be dead, but saw the man lurch to his feet, his left arm hanging limply at his side, and begin to stumble toward the safety of the now open Northgate. Behind him the riders slowed—made cautious by the fate of the horse in front of them—but they were closing quickly on the lone figure staggering up the road.

Atop the barbican, the archers took aim. Four arrows flew and two men toppled backwards off their mounts. The other three had had the presence of mind to fetch their shields before giving chase. They had seen far too much of the deadly Danish archers that manned Chester's walls. Another flight of arrows rained down and a horse was struck in the head. He bucked off his rider and fled back toward the woods. Still, two men refused to let their quarry escape.

Sir Edgar hurried down from the wall walk to the street. A group of guards quartered near the Northgate had been roused by the uproar and were pouring out of their barracks.

"Follow me!" he bellowed.

The portcullis had been raised at the first command and a half dozen men followed Sir Edgar through it, but there was no way to reach the man before he would be ridden down by the two horsemen. The lead rider closed in, leaning forward, his sword raised for a killing stroke.

The man on foot must have heard the hoof beats draw near. He stopped abruptly, fumbled for an instant at his waist then twisted violently to the rear. It was too late for the rider to check his momentum as he saw a gleaming battleaxe rise up in a vicious arc toward him. It took the horse in the jaw and the animal fell as though its bones had turned to water. The rider screamed as he fell under the horse's bulk.

The last rider fended off another hail of arrows from the Northgate and reined his horse to a stop twenty paces from the man who now stood facing him, his battleaxe hanging loosely in his right hand. It took him but a moment to decide the chase was over. He sheathed his sword, swung his horse's head around sharply and flipped his shield over his shoulder to protect his back before whipping his horse toward the safety of his own lines.

The man standing in the road swayed from side to side as he watched the last of his pursuers flee. His head swam and he felt his knees start to buckle. As he went down, he felt strong hands catch him, then the world turned black.

**

It was a dream he'd had before—many times. Catherine was sitting near him, speaking softly. He strained to hear what she was saying but couldn't quite make out her words. But the simple sound of her voice was like a balm. He started to drift off again.

"Roger!"

His eyes flew open. It took a moment for him to focus and in that moment nothing made sense. He saw grey stone and a high ceiling. He blinked and looked down He prayed he wasn't dreaming, because Catherine, his Catherine, was there—right in front of him. Her brow was furrowed as she looked at him with concern. And her hair—it had wisps of grey!

"Roger!"

He sat up. He felt a sharp twinge in his arm, the pain confirming that this was not a dream. After two and a half long years—he was home.

"Cathy…"

A sob escaped Catherine de Laval's throat as she wrapped her arms around him.

"Oh God, Roger" she croaked. "You've come back. I'd almost given up…"

He sat there in this dream that was no dream and smelled her hair. It smelled the same as it had the first day he had ever held her close. He reached to return her embrace, but his left arm would not move, so he wrapped his good right arm around her waist. She shuddered and buried her face in his neck.

"I promised I'd be back, Cathy," he said gently. "Have I ever broken a promise to you?"

She lifted her head and looked at his face, so gaunt and worn and dear. She kissed him on the lips.

"No, Roger de Laval, you haven't. And I'll have your promise right now that you'll never leave England again—no matter where the King may wish to take you."

He managed a weak smile for her.

"I promise it."

She drew back.

"I'll hold you to that, Roger. Now that the King has returned, there are more than enough things to set right here in our own land."

He gave her an odd look, then realized there was no way the news could have reached Chester yet.

"Catherine, the King has not returned," he said in a pained voice. "He has been taken as a captive in Austria. To my shame,

I...I couldn't protect him. I was sent to give word of it to the Queen. God help us if she cannot get him back."

Catherine felt a sick feeling in the pit of her stomach. So much of their hopes had rested on Richard's return and now what hope was there? Since they had burned the trebuchets in the autumn, the mercenary army had settled into a deliberate siege. With extra mouths to feed among the refugee Danes, the city had been on half rations since the Feast of All Saints. Even so, there was little more than a month of food left. After that, the city would be forced to surrender—a grim prospect, but...Roger was home and that was enough for now. She touched his cheek.

"I've no doubt you did your duty to the King. Now, you need to rest a little more. You've broken your arm it seems."

He looked at the wooden splint on his upper arm and gave a little snort. Then he looked past Catherine.

"Millie..."

Catherine had been dreading this question.

"She's in London, Roger, and as safe as she would be here. There is so much to tell you. She has done extraordinary things since you've been gone. I believe you will be proud."

He started to speak. Questions swirled in his head. London? What was Millie doing in London? He opened his mouth, but Catherine put a finger to his lips.

"I know you have questions, husband, and I will answer all I can, but for now you must rest."

Her words made him aware of the crushing weariness he felt. He was helpless against it and slid back down onto the bed and back into darkness.

***

It was morning when he woke once more and Catherine was still beside his bed. He reached to her with his good arm and she took his hand.

"You have visitors, Roger."

He turned his head and saw his two former squires standing across the room, anxious looks on their faces.

"Ah, my boys!" he said and hoisted himself up in bed.

"My lord!" they said at the same time and rushed forward.

241

He hadn't seen Roland or Declan in over a year and neither had much the look of a boy any longer. Both visitors to his bedside began to talk at once, words tumbling out in a rush.

"Gentlemen, please," Lady Catherine said, stepping in. "All can't be told in a single breath." They both stepped back sheepishly. "My husband knows nothing of what has happened here and at Shipbrook since you all took your leave. It is time he did."

For an hour the three sat beside Sir Roger's bed and told the story. Lady Catherine spoke of the summons from the Queen, her recruitment of Millicent to spy on Ranulf and their daughter's role in saving the young Earl from sure execution at the hands of Prince John and William de Ferrers.

"Millie a spy—you allowed this?" he asked his wife, shock written on his face.

"Roger, do you not recall your daughter's nature?" she asked gently. "She has grown into a young woman while you were away. She was asked by the Queen and did not seek my permission. It was her decision. And please consider, had she not been there, Ranulf would be dead. Where then would our family be?"

The big Norman knight shook his head, trying to digest this dire news. It was as though he had returned to a world turned on its head. Catherine took his hand and continued the tale. She told of their exile in Wales, kept safe by the young Welsh rebel, Llywelyn, how they had languished for months in the wilderness—until things changed on Christ's Mass day. She glanced at Roland, who took up the thread of the story.

"My lord, Master Sparks and Boda saw us safely home to the Dee. It was the day before Christ's Mass. We found Shipbrook burnt and occupied by de Ferrers' men. We saw them off, but feared the worst. Then Sigbert, the swineherd, found us and gave us hope that Lady Catherine and Millicent had fled safely into Wales. We went looking for them."

"Good lads!" Sir Roger said and laid a big hand on Declan's shoulder. "Though landing at the Dee seems an odd route to get to the Queen in London."

"My lord, the King did not specify a route, but cautioned us against being waylaid—as so many of his messengers had been. We thought it was unlikely that the King's enemies would be watching the west country."

"And you thought you should visit my family before going to the Queen…" Sir Roger's voice grew husky as he realized that these two young men had found a way to honour their loyalty to his family without violating the orders of their sovereign.

"Aye, my lord. That's what we figured. The Dee would be a clever landing place and, as it happened, Shipbrook was on the way to London."

Sir Roger allowed himself a small smile.

"Go on."

"We found Lady Millicent and she was determined to reach the Queen to seek aid for Earl Ranulf. We rode with her to Oxford where the Queen was holding court. She did not know that Ranulf had survived the fall of Chester, but was heartened to hear it. She gave us what aid she could—a troop of men who had come home wounded from the Crusade. They call themselves the Invalid Company and they are men to be reckoned with, my lord. With those men and with the help of Prince Llywelyn, we were able to take back the city. Now, we just have to hold it!"

Sir Roger had been listening intently and when Roland paused, he spoke.

"Alwyn…you've not spoken of Alwyn," he said, his voice anxious. "I saw what they did to Shipbrook…"

Declan shot a quick glance at Roland, who gave a short nod. The Irishman cleared his throat. He wanted some gentle way to say this, but there was none. As he spoke, his voice was near to breaking.

"We were crossing the Dee, my lord, when Baldric hailed us. He told us what happened at the ford." He paused for a second to gather himself, then plunged on.

"My lord, when the Earl and your family fled into Wales, Alwyn guarded their retreat across the Dee. He slowed the pursuit at the ford and killed many of de Ferrers' men. But there were too many. My lord,…Sir Alwyn died at the ford and is buried on the far side, on the high ground there."

For a moment Sir Roger looked like he did not understand what Declan had said, then a look of inconsolable grief played across the big man's face. He sat up in bed, then tried to rise but could not find his balance. He slumped back down.

"Alwyn…," he moaned, "Alwyn." Tears poured from his eyes. They were tears for Alwyn and for Shipbrook and for all the evil that had happened while he was away serving his king. After a time he grew quiet.

"Once this is over," he said gesturing toward the east window of the room. "Once this siege is broken, you will take me to his grave. A part of my heart is buried there."

Both of the young knights nodded, too choked up to speak.

"And after that, we will find William de Ferrers—for he is a dead man."

***

It was the eve of Christ's Mass and Roland had duty as Captain of the Guard. As he moved along the wall walk between the guard posts he could hear singing coming from inside the town. It surprised him that, with their poor rations, anyone would be celebrating, but then he recognized the hymn and the voices. It was the Danes. He stopped near the Bridgegate to listen for a while. The Danes might be hungry, but they were happy to be alive this Christmas.

"Sir Roland."

Roland startled, unaware that anyone was near. He turned to see Sir Roger approaching.

"They told me I would find you somewhere along the wall near here," the big knight said.

"Aye, my lord. Please join me. I've just finished my rounds."

Roland was pleased for the company. It had been three days since Sir Roger had managed to get past the mercenary army and into the city. Lady Catherine had fussed over him and forced him to rest, but the man could only stay abed so long. Roland had fretted over how gaunt his old master had looked the day he arrived, but had seen the knight's strength come back with remarkable speed. Before long, he would be his old self.

Sir Roger leaned on the crenelated battlement and looked out over the River Dee.

"It's a pretty spot. You can see the water boil as it tumbles over the weir—even at night. Never cared much for city life, but always enjoyed the view of the river from these walls."

Roland thought of the many times he and Millicent had stood in this very spot and watched the water.

"My lord, Lady Catherine has told you about Lady Millicent's summons by the Archbishop."

Sir Roger nodded.

"Aye, she did. I won't pretend to approve, but the thing is done. You can be sure that the moment we find a way to break this siege, I will be on to London to see for myself what these great lords are up to with my girl."

Roland took a deep breath and screwed up his courage.

"When that day comes, I will do the same. My lord, you should know that I love your daughter. I know that you and Lady Catherine expect her to marry well and I have nothing, but she loves me as well."

He had a hundred other things to say, but he had said the things that summed up all the rest. He stopped talking and waited. Sir Roger pushed back from the battlements.

"My wife told me of this but an hour ago. She also reminded me that *I* had nothing when we met and that her family had hoped for a better match." He paused and looked at his old squire.

"You are a lucky man, Roland Inness."

"Lucky beyond compare, my lord."

Sir Roger laid his good hand on Roland's shoulder.

"And she's a lucky girl."

A Christ's Mass Gift

It was Christ's Mass when Friar Tuck reached the edge of Sherwood Forest. He sat on a bench atop a large wagon piled high with a stinking mass of hay and manure. Over the past ten days, as he plotted a circuitous path northward from London that avoided the larger towns, he had grown used to the stench. The four mules that pulled the wagon over the frozen road seemed untroubled by the smell.

In his meeting with William Marshal in London, the Justiciar had listened carefully to Tuck's plea for help and had offered what he could. It had taken time to arrange, but on the eighth day a messenger arrived at the house of Sir Bernard Waldgrave where Tuck had been given a place to sleep. The promised aid was waiting in a barn outside of the Aldgate.

He bid a quick farewell to his old mentor and hurried through the city. In a barn just a stone's throw from the Aldgate, he found a wagon and a team of mules. In the wagon were weapons—broadswords, dirks, spears and some old dented shields—enough to arm twice Robin's band in Sherwood. There was a tarp drawn over this precious cargo and at the far end of the barn there was a reeking mound that had been mucked out of the stalls.

Tuck did not hesitate. He reached for the pitchfork that was stuck, tines-first, into the mix and began to scoop the hay and manure onto the tarp. It took an hour of hard labour, but in the end he was certain no one would be anxious to inspect his wagon too closely.

On his journey north, he had avoided the most direct route to Nottingham through Leicester and headed due north on Ermine Street, the old Roman road that ran from London, through Lincoln, and on to York. This route ran to the east of Derbyshire and Nottinghamshire. Just north of Sleaford, he turned west onto rougher roads. He skirted Newark where the Sheriff of Nottingham still maintained a strong garrison and made his way, unmolested, into the deep woods north of Nottingham that had become his home. He did not have to go far before being challenged.

"Ho there, fat friar, what stinking mess have you brought into our beautiful forest?"

Tuck hauled in on the reins and the team of mules stopped in their tracks. He looked around and was not surprised to see no one. The leaves were off the oaks here, but there were cedar and other evergreens that provided ample places to watch the forest path unseen. But he didn't really need to see who had hailed him. He had come to know that voice well.

"I've brought you a present for Christ's Mass, Magnus Rask, and I'd wager my load smells more fragrant than you!"

Immediately, the big Dane stepped out from behind a fir tree and trotted down to meet the friar. Two other men broke cover but kept watch on the road. When Rask reached the wagon he wrinkled his nose.

"A shit wagon for a present, Tuck?" he asked with a grin. "Well, I suppose it's exactly the sort of thing our friends in London would think suitable!"

Tuck grinned back.

"Oh, I think you will find this present most suitable, Magnus, but let's get it into camp before we unwrap it."

Rask crawled up beside him on the bench.

"Fair enough. The smell will hardly be noticeable amongst all the other fragrances of the camp. We've had another twenty men come in since you left and the place is getting ripe."

Tuck snapped the reins and the mules obediently leaned into their traces.

***

Wagons were not often seen this deep in the forest and men began drifting into the clearing at first sight of it, their leader, Robin of Loxley, among them. Tuck reined in the mules at the edge of camp and Rask immediately singled out some of the youngest men to begin clearing away the dung and hay. With a good deal of loud groaning and complaining, four of them went to work. Bystanders offered encouragement and suggestions until the work was done. The filth cleared away, Tuck ordered them to pull back the tarp.

"Good God!"

Under the concealing mound of stable muck, Robin saw what William Marshal had sent them.

"Proper weapons, by God! No more staffs against lances. This *is* a most excellent gift for Christ's Mass!" He turned to Tuck. "How many?"

"Over two hundred of various sorts, by my count."

Robin's eyes gleamed as he rummaged through the lances and swords. He saw an odd wooden handle protruding from the stack and dug out a single crossbow and held it high. The men who crowded around the wagon hooted and laughed.

"Does the Justiciar think we have a Genoese among our men?" Robin shouted gaily. Tuck smiled at the sight. After all they had endured since returning to England, it was good to see the young knight laugh again. Robin handed the crossbow to one of his men and turned to Rask.

"I leave it to you to issue these, Magnus. I will be considering how to make good use of them."

Rask nodded and turned to the men.

"Clear away, all of ye. I'll pass these out after I've made an accounting." The men started to move off.

"Raymond Langum, you can put that sword back where you got it!" The miscreant sheepishly removed the blade he had tucked in his shirt and dropped it in the wagon.

Robin turned to Tuck.

"Tell me of your visit to London, Tuck. This gift is most welcome, but how stands the country? What is Marshal doing and what will he want from us in exchange for these weapons?'

Tuck nodded.

"It's about as bad as we feared. The barons in the far north are staunch for the King as are the Earls of Norfolk, Oxford and Chester. Those in Yorkshire and Lincoln are fence sitters, though they are apparently buying peace from the Prince. Most of the Marcher Lords, with the exception of Earl Ranulf, are committed to John. We know where the Earl of Derby stands."

"Up the Prince's arse, when last I looked," Robin said, dryly, "but what other news do you have? If we are to be proper outlaws, we should be better informed."

Tuck laughed.

"This news will please you. Marshal tells me our two young comrades from Cheshire made it safely home with their message for the Queen."

"Roland and Declan? I'd wondered about those two! It good to know they are safe and sound."

"Well, sound enough, I'm sure, but safe is another matter. It seems the Earl of Chester was charged with treason soon after we took ship for the Holy Land. He lost his city to William de Ferrers, but somehow got it back with help from our two young friends. Now the army that bottled us up in Nottingham Castle is besieging Chester."

They had heard rumours that, when the mercenary army marched west out of Sheffield, they had ravaged the high country and then turned southwest toward Chester. They had assumed Chester might be the target, but now that was confirmed. Both men had keen memories of the suffering that went with a siege.

"God watch over our friends and the people of Chester," Robin said.

"Amen," said Tuck.

The two men had been walking across the clearing as Tuck reported on his journey to London. The burly monk noticed that the camp had grown in the month he had been gone.

"They are still coming," he said.

"Aye, a few more every week. Another fortnight and we'll be two hundred strong. And with these weapons, we may be able to do more than just raid grain barns, but tell me—what does Marshal want in exchange for his help?"

Tuck shrugged.

"He wants us to make mischief for John's men here in Nottinghamshire."

"Well that will be easy enough, but surely there's more."

"Aye, there is. Marshal asked me, if the crown were in the balance, would we come to his aid, if summoned."

"And you said…"

"I said yes, of course."

The King's Ransom

Walter of Coutances stepped off the sailing cog at the dock in Harfleur to find a carriage and driver waiting for him in the port town. It was the first day of January in the Year of our Lord, 1193. The driver had been ordered to wait for his arrival and to fetch him whenever he should return from Germany. In two hours he was standing before Eleanor.

"The bargaining was hard, your grace."

"I expected no less, Walter. Tell me."

"The ransom has been reduced to one hundred thousand marks—still a ruinous sum, and the Emperor wants Richard to provide a fleet and an army to help him take Sicily back from the usurper Tancred."

Eleanor felt her shoulders sag. The outrageous price for the King's return had been reduced by a third, but it would still pauper the kingdom. As for the Emperor's ridiculous demand that Richard help him take Sicily, she cared not a whit. It was a promise easily made and just as easily broken once the King was released..

"Very well, Walter. You've done as well as could be expected with that greedy German. Prepare me a proclamation to be sent to every nobleman, merchant and bishop in the realm. You may handle the details of the assessments, but I want the silver brought to London and I want it there by the feast of Saint Matthias."

The Archbishop gasped.

"Your grace! That is but six weeks from now."

Eleanor fixed him with a withering look.

"I can count, your excellency. The more time we give them, the more they will find ways to shirk their duty. You must give them no time and brook no excuses. Our realm cannot afford any delay in this. I fear we may already be too late."

Walter of Coutances had no answer for that. The Queen was right. Any delay in getting the King released would begin to raise suspicions that he would not be freed at all. John, who had been proclaiming that Richard was dead for a year, now was spreading the rumour that the Emperor would never let his brother go. Time truly was no friend of those loyal to the King. He bowed his head in submission.

"It shall be done, your grace."

Eleanor nodded. She felt sympathy for the man. The task she had given him was grievous and would win him no friends, but it was at times like this that a man's loyalties were truly tested. She knew that the Archbishop would not flinch.

"Have the ransom deposited in the crypts beneath Saint Paul's. It's the most secure place in London, next to the Tower, which my younger son currently occupies. Advise Marshal that I hold him responsible for keeping it secure. I will return to London a week before the final collection is done and will sail with the silver to the Emperor's court in Speyer. You will arrange for a ship and crew."

"As you wish, your grace."

Eleanor stood, signalling the end of the session. The Archbishop bowed and turned to go, then heard her speak softly.

"We must all hang on a little longer, Walter."

***

From one end of the Angevin Empire to the other, there was an outcry over the Queen's proclamation. Never had such a demand been made on the coffers of the church or the purses of the nobility and there was resistance. But Eleanor was unmoved. Reluctant princes of the church and resistant barons were browbeaten and threatened and by the middle of January the silver began to flow into London from every part of the realm.

The Ransomed Crown

By the end of the month, the crypt beneath Saint Paul's held the greatest treasure ever assembled in England. Wagons from Cornwall and Essex, ships from Bordeaux and Nantes had all disgorged a staggering fortune—all of which would be needed to buy back Richard from the Holy Roman Emperor. Only a final shipment from York remained. When it arrived, the ransom would be complete.

***

A mile to the west of Saint Paul's cathedral, Archdeacon Herbert Poore listened to the report of his agent.

"They have twenty-six tons of silver in the crypts, your excellency, with nine more expected from York. The Queen is still expected to arrive in three days—to count it herself, I suppose. She intends to sail with the ransom to Germany."

The French spymaster shook his head.

"I wouldn't have thought it possible. One hundred thousand marks! That she wolf Eleanor has so frightened the church and the nobles that they have actually raised the entire sum! The Prince is in a panic and I can hardly blame him."

"What will he do, excellency? If this silver reaches the Emperor, John is finished."

"You are quite correct. I have advised him to break off the siege of Chester and bring his mercenaries to London. Chester can wait. If the ransom is delivered and Richard returns, John will be lucky to keep his head."

"And what of us, excellency? I am not suspected and as for our clerk, they have not managed to track him past the brothel—or so say our watchers. Could we not survive Richard's return?"

"You were not here during the days of King Henry's rule. Now there was a man who knew how to be a king! It was a miracle I survived those days. I lost a dozen agents right here in London. And if Richard returns, I fear those dark days will as well. We need John to forestall that. We have worked too hard to place a crown on that weak limb of the Plantagenet tree to see it all fail now." The man paused and wiped a thin froth of spittle from his lips.

"Eleanor is the key. Without her, the resistance to John would have long since collapsed. Come back to me on the day she arrives in London. There is a man who has been waiting to make history. I think his day has come round."

***

Walter of Coutances had spent the month of January sending off harsh demands to nobles both rich and poor, while William Marshal took on the task of protecting the growing hoard of silver. The Lord of Striguil ordered every man who owed him allegiance to come to London armed and ready for a fight. He worried that he had stripped his defences along the Welsh border to the bone, but there was no help for that.

Loyal men such as the Earl of Arundel and the Earl of Norfolk sent what troops they could spare and by the middle of the month, Marshal could count on over three hundred knights and men-at-arms within the walls of London to secure the growing ransom. This force maintained an uneasy balance with the large garrison of the Tower that was loyal to John, but hardly a day passed without some provocation in the streets and alleyways of the capital. Men died on both sides, but open warfare had not erupted—yet.

On the last day of January, the Queen arrived as promised from Tancarville. Marshal met her at the Billingsgate docks with a hundred armed men.

"Your grace, it is good to have you home again."

Eleanor pulled her cape tight around her as a nasty wind blew off the waters of the Thames. As she stepped onto the gangplank she looked around at the show of force on the docks, then took the Justiciar's hand as she set foot back in England for the first time in a year.

"It's good to see you, William. You've no doubt heard that Philip has officially declared war on us. He sent a letter directly to Richard letting him know. He must have gloated over every word. He will no doubt take the Vexin, but there is nothing to be done about that now. How stand things here in London?"

Marshal shrugged.

"Difficult, your grace. I have just enough men to keep John's garrison from doing anything rash regarding the ransom, but not much more than that. With your permission, we will be lodging you with the Archbishop. We decided last night that it would be safer there. His house is within sight of Saint Paul's and can be more easily guarded. The palace at Westminster would require half my men to secure."

The Queen was unruffled.

"I spent fifteen years locked up in a nunnery, William. All I need is a bed and a place to sit, but before I settle on the nest, take me to the church. I want to see it."

Marshal knew she had no interest in admiring the great cathedral. The woman wanted to see with her own eyes what was being stored in the crypts beneath.

"Of course, your grace."

He helped her into her carriage and mounted his horse. At his command, the armed escort began the short trip up from the river to the higher ground occupied by the church. Marshal led the column of men around to the north side of the building. The entrance to the crypts was here. The Queen didn't wait for Marshal to help her as she stepped out onto the street, narrowly missing a great mound of horse dung.

Marshal dismounted and extended his arm. She took it and together they crossed the church yard, passing through a phalanx of armed men left there to safeguard the silver. All bowed as she passed. As they made their way down the short flight of stone steps to the underground chamber, Marshal saw how the lines in her face had deepened in the months since he'd last seen her. William Marshal might have spent his adult years amid the intrigues of the royals, but he was a simple man with a happy family of his own. He couldn't imagine what this aging Queen endured having her two remaining sons at sword points.

Inside the crypts were more men, their weapons stacked by the entrance for easy retrieval. Men did not go armed in the house of God, even into the crypts. Marshal slipped off his sword belt and handed it to one of his men. Behind them, a bishop came hurrying down the steps, hastily adjusting his robes.

"Your grace, God be praised your journey was a safe one," he managed as he fought to catch his breath.

"Thank you, your excellency. Your King will not forget the good service the clergy of Saint Paul's has done on his behalf."

"Of course, your grace, of course. He is the anointed of God!"

Marshal thought he heard a quiet snort from the Queen, but couldn't be sure. Two of the guards appeared with flaming torches and led them further into the gloom. Huge pillars loomed up on either side supporting the foundation of the massive structure above. The floor was earth and in the shadows, where the torchlight couldn't reach, small creatures scurried about.

The Queen paid no attention to such. At length, they reached the southern end of the long subterranean chamber. Stacked against the wall were dozens of large chests, all closed and sealed with the wax emblem of the Archbishop of Rouen. Marshal leaned in close and whispered to Eleanor.

"Walter weighs and records the contents of each before sealing them."

The Queen nodded.

"How close are we?"

"We have only one shipment left. It is to depart York in three days under heavy guard."

"I confess, William. I wasn't sure it could be done. Open one."

Marshal motioned to one of their escorts who secured his torch in a notch in the wall and broke the seal on the nearest chest. When he drew back the lid, torchlight reflected off stacks of silver chalices and ciboria—the instruments of communion.

"How will they perform the Eucharist?" she asked.

Behind her a new voice spoke up.

"Tin plates and wooden cups I suppose, your grace." Marshal and the Queen turned to find Walter of Coutances standing behind them, slightly out of breath.

"I doubt Jesus will mind."

***

The Ransomed Crown

On the day of the Queen's arrival, Archdeacon Poore's agent informed him that Eleanor was not staying, as expected, at the Palace of Westminster, but would take residence with the Archbishop of Rouen. Lodging her near Saint Paul's and the ransom would make executing his plan more difficult in some ways, but simpler in others. His mind was already sorting through the possibilities. He would need time to gather information—there must be nothing left to chance! But it would be over a fortnight until the last of the treasure reached London. He had time.

"What of our man close to Marshal," he asked his agent. "Can he be of use?"

"Excellency, I think that the clerk would faint if Eleanor of Aquitaine blinked at him."

"Very well. You understand that when this deed is done, there will be no stone unturned to ferret out our network. From your description, your clerk would not stay silent under torture."

"I will attend to it, excellency."

"See that you do." The elderly prelate rose and beckoned for the agent to follow. "Now, I want you to meet the man I've chosen to kill the Queen."

***

The day after the Queen's return to London, a rider on a worn out horse arrived from the north with urgent word for Walter of Coutances. It was a message from his spy in York. The Archbishop sent a courier to fetch William Marshal and when his fellow Justiciar arrived they called upon the Queen.

"There is treachery afoot, your grace," the Archbishop said. "I have a man close to the Sheriff of Yorkshire. This man has embarrassing secrets—secrets that, if known, would ruin him. I keep his secrets—as long as he does my bidding. He has been my eyes in York ever since and his reports have all proven accurate and useful. I've just received his latest message."

Marshal furrowed his brow. For not the first time, he recognized what a ruthless man Walter of Coutances could be. His fellow Justiciar unfolded a piece of vellum.

257

"My man writes: 'Your excellency, etcetera, etcetera. Sir Alfred de Wendenal, Sheriff of Nottingham has been ordered by his grace, Prince John, to seize a shipment of silver leaving York for London. Sir Hugh Bardolf, the Sheriff of Yorkshire is aware of this order and has been persuaded to turn over the treasure without resistance. They will blame the theft on the outlaws of Sherwood." The archbishop carefully refolded the message and slipped it into his pocket.

"There are other details concerning the exchange, but that is the gist of it."

He turned to Eleanor.

"I have no time to get a warning to loyal men in York to stop this shipment before it leaves the city, your grace, and de Wendenal has more than enough men in his garrisons at Nottingham and Newark to take the silver, even if that bastard Bardolf was inclined to fight for it."

The Queen turned to Marshal.

"My lord, I presume you could not march your men north in time to secure these wagons."

Marshal shook his head.

"No, your grace. Most of my men are foot soldiers. Even if I was to march today, I could hardly reach Leicester by the time the column from York enters Nottinghamshire."

"How much do you reckon is in this shipment?"

The Archbishop sighed.

"Nine tons of silver I've been told, your grace. It's the gleaning from all of the northern regions and a quarter of the whole. To replace that would take months—if it can be done at all."

The Queen turned back to her advisors.

"What then are we to do, my lords? We do not have months! Are we finished? Has John won?"

"No!" William Marshal slapped the table in front of him. "I cannot get my men there in time, your grace, but if they intend to blame this outrage on the outlaws of Sherwood, then we will turn this lie on its head. These 'outlaws' are loyal to the King and they owe me a debt."

The Queen looked at him sceptically. She had not heard of any loyal forces in that county—not since the fall of the Nottingham Castle.

"Who are these outlaws you wish to entrust with the King's ransom, William?"

"I believe you know their leaders, your grace. Sir Robin of Loxley and Father Augustine brought you a message from the King over a year ago. They fought to defend Nottingham Castle and managed to escape its fall. They have raised a band of peasants in the forest of Sherwood and I have sent them weapons. They are obliged to answer my summons when I send it."

The Queen's eyes widened.

"I remember those two! The young one was handsome and the friar was stout. The message they brought from Richard was distressing and I'll confess that, beset as we were, I practically invited them to turn outlaw and make life difficult for John in the Midlands! It was a terrible thing to suggest, but I was desperate. I never thought they would take my words to heart."

Marshal shook his head.

"Your grace, I've spoken to the friar. They are loyal men, but this uprising of theirs is not for you or the King—it's for the starving people of Nottinghamshire."

Eleanor scowled.

"I'm not fond of peasant insurrections, William—for any reason. They too often end with people like us torn apart by mobs, but these outlaws of Sherwood appear to be the only tools at hand."

"Aye, your grace."

Eleanor gave a little sigh.

"Send your summons."

William the Marshal

Prince John sat in the round tower keep his father had built at Windsor and listened to a chill wind howl around the battlements. The mournful sound matched his mood. Just three months past, the crown had been within his grasp and now it all seemed to be slipping away.

Philip, that most devious of allies, had failed to honour his promise of troops to help him seize the throne. Without the French army at his back, taking the country by force was not going to be possible. His mother had rallied just enough of the barons to thwart him in that ambition. If that fool de Ferrers had been able to retake Chester, it would have been a needed boost to his finances and his prestige, but six months of besieging the place had not forced Ranulf to surrender.

As the end of January approached, the unthinkable appeared to be happening. His mother, against all reason, was on the verge of raising the enormous ransom needed to free Richard. The thought of his brother's return made him shiver more than the cold that seeped into the stones of the castle. He had no doubt Richard knew of his treason and would be thirsting for vengeance. The best he could hope for if he fell into his brother's hands would be a quick beheading.

There were worse ways to die.

Another gust caused one of the shutters to bang, startling him. He stood and paced around the room, thinking furiously.

Philip had suggested that they outbid Eleanor to gain custody of Richard, had even pledged five thousand marks of his own, but the price was one hundred thousand and his own coffers held barely enough to keep paying his mercenary army. There was only one source for that sum—the ransom itself.

The idea had been tumbling around in his mind for weeks now. His spies had kept him informed as William Marshal scraped together a force to guard the silver under Saint Paul's. He had been tempted to have his garrison assault the place and seize the hoard, but the numbers were too even and the outcome too uncertain. If he were going to snatch Richard's ransom away, he would need an overwhelming force in London and there was only one such force at his command.

He called his servant and sent for a courier. Within the hour, his order was making its way toward Chester. This would be his last chance and he would stake all on the outcome. If he could gain the ransom, he would gladly pay the Emperor his asking price and just as gladly turn Richard over to Philip. It would be the death of his brother, but there would be no blood on his hands.

***

Earl Ranulf flushed, embarrassed as his stomach growled loudly, the sound amplified inside the stone chamber. Chester had been on half rations since the feast of All Saints and the Earl had set the example, scrupulously taking his meagre ration of bread, the same portion as the meanest stable boy or washer woman. He had kept a brave face, but his stomach was not impressed. It was now the third day of February and he was hungry.

The sight before him was distressing, though not surprising. Lady Catherine had requested his presence that morning and, together, they had gone to the granary where the last of the barley was stored. He looked into the gloom and could see that the stone coffer that had been overflowing in August, now had a forlorn drift of grain in one corner.

"How long?" he asked.

Lady Catherine did not hesitate. She had kept careful watch over the food supplies for over six months and could tell at a glance what a day's half ration would consume.

"Three days, my lord."

The Earl's shoulders slumped for a moment, but he recovered.

"I will not see my people starve, my lady."

"You will surrender, my lord?"

"No, I will fight."

***

The Earl of Chester held his council of war that night. Sir Roger de Laval, Roland Inness and Declan O'Duinne were there along with Patch and Thorkell.

"In three days, there will be no bread. I will not surrender the city without striking a blow. Tomorrow, we will march out and offer battle to the mercenaries. Perhaps we will win and the siege will be broken. Perhaps we will lose and our enemies will march over our bodies into an undefended city. God only knows. But I will not turn over this city to William de Ferrers while there is breath in my body. How say you?"

"Aye," said Sir Roger.

"Aye," said Roland.

"I'd like a go at 'em," agreed Declan.

"The Invalids will not surrender, my lord," said Patch.

"The Danes will not be slaves," said Thorkell. "We will fight."

Ranulf rose to his feet.

"It will be my honour to lead you. We will assemble at the Eastgate an hour before dawn."

***

The plan was straightforward. At first light, the Earl would lead his mounted force through the Eastgate and strike the mercenary positions that guarded the road beyond the open fields there. Once the cavalry had cleared the gate, the infantry would follow and form a defensive line a hundred yards from the walls. On the walls above, the longbowmen of the Danes would stand ready to make any force attacking the defensive line pay a heavy price.

Ranulf, backed by the Invalids and his other mounted men, would continue to attack and inflict damage on the enemy until they organized themselves to counterattack. Then all would fall back to the defensive line outside the walls of the town. It was hoped that the mercenaries, seeing the entire garrison marshalled in the open, would mass and attack. The men of Chester would be greatly outnumbered, but the eight score bowmen on the walls would even the odds a bit.

It was still dark when the horsemen gathered in a thick column that stretched back from the Eastgate to the centre of town. All through the night, the temperature had been dropping and clouds had rolled in from the west. Sleet began to fall in flurries making a sound on the steel helmets of the riders like small beads bouncing off a marble floor.

"Good weather for a dawn attack," said Sir Roger, more to himself than to anyone nearby, but Roland heard him and turned to look at his old master.

"They'll be snug in their huts, my lord," he said with a smile.

"Cuddled together, they'll be!" added Declan O'Duinne who sat his horse beside them in the column.

Both young knights were grateful to have Sir Roger de Laval back. His broken arm was not fully healed, but he had regained most of the strength he had lost during his ordeal with the King. He looked ready for a fight.

During Sir Roger's month-long convalescence, they had slowly drawn out the story of the King's capture and his own escape over the passes of the Alps. He had been found, collapsed in a snow bank, by a goatherd looking for a lost member of his flock and dragged back to a mountain hut. He'd spent a week there fighting off a fever that left him weak. When he had finally recovered enough to continue his journey, the goatherd had demanded compensation.

"He demanded Bucephalus!" Sir Roger said, as he told the story. "Thought he could use him in the spring for ploughing in the valley! I was not fit to walk, so he offered a swaybacked mule in exchange for the greatest warhorse ever sired." He stopped, his eyes shining when he thought of his horse. "But the man had saved us both, so I had little choice. And I thought Buc might like living out his days eating dandelions up there in the mountain pastures. So I made the trade."

On this morning he sat astride a fine mount, but thought wistfully of his great warhorse in the faraway mountains. Earl Ranulf came down from the Eastgate where he had been talking to Thorkell and mounted. Roland glanced back down the line of Invalids. He nodded to Sir Edgar and to Patch and Sergeant Billy. They sat easy in their saddles, talking quietly and jesting. The Invalid Company was ready.

It was very dark in the narrow street, but the sky above, despite the storm, seemed lighter. The Earl gave a quick signal and the great oak gates swung open. He rose on his stirrups and turned back to the column of men behind him. All were leaning forward in the saddle. He drew his sword and led them out into the storm.

The column moved up the road at a canter. As they neared the tree line, the Earl put the spurs to his warhorse and the animal went to a gallop. His movements rippled back through the column as men urged their mounts to more speed and drew their swords. The hurtling mass of men and horses reached the spot where mercenary sentries had kept watch on the town since summer and found—nothing.

***

Five days after the Queen's arrival in London, word came that the mercenary army at Chester had broken off the siege and was marching on the capital. When Marshal informed the Queen, she seemed unsurprised by the news.

"He's missed his chance to take the crown by force, William. He'll try for the silver now. I know John. We almost match his strength in London. He won't risk his garrison against your men—not when he has another card to play. That's why he's recalled his mercenaries from Chester. He's going to seize the ransom."

"Your grace, if over a thousand mercenaries enter the gates of London, I won't be able to save the ransom. The Emperor won't care a whit where his money comes from—and if it comes from John, Richard will never see the light of day again."

After three years of struggle it had all come down to this—who would control London and the treasure that lay beneath Saint Paul's? Attempting to stop John's mercenaries short of the city held enormous risks. Marshal could scrape together no more than four hundred men to face three times that number somewhere northwest of the capital, but waiting until they reached London seemed even more perilous. Trying to defend the walls of the city with John's garrison at his back would be folly.

So they had marched.

Four days later, William Marshal stood on the crest of a long slope that rose up from a shallow valley below. In the first light of morning, he could see a river there, marked by a line of trees. He did not know its name. There would be a ford where Watling Street crossed the stream. Behind him, on the far side of the ridge were three hundred foot soldiers and seventy mounted men. His scouts had reported that John's mercenary army was marching southeast on the same road. They would meet soon, and this spot looked promising.

Down near the river, the frozen ground was cleared, with only a few forlorn stalks of wheat straw poking above the thin layer of frost. The slope down there was gradual and the ground firm—good ground for cavalry and it was cavalry that worried Marshal.

His scouts had counted a thousand infantry and over four hundred mounted men in the host heading his way. Most were Flemish and Irish mercenaries, but these had been joined by mounted knights in the service of William de Ferrers and other barons who had cast their lots with John. It was a force that, on an open field, would overwhelm his own. But as he looked at the slope below, he saw that this ground offered some advantages.

While the land near the river was ideal for cavalry, that changed as the road climbed to the top of the ridge. Here the slope steepened and open fields were hemmed in by thick woods. By the time the road reached the ridgetop, the forest had encroached to within fifty paces on either side. Attackers would be forced in on themselves the closer they got to the crest. He would place his men, like a cork in a bottle's neck, across this narrow front and stand his ground.

As the sun grew brighter, he noticed that there was little frost where he stood. The ground near the river bottom was still frozen, but days of clear skies and afternoon sun had thawed the higher parts of the slope. He stepped off the road and felt the ground give—mud.

Mud would be his friend.

He heard a quiet curse behind him and turned to see Sir Walter FitzWilliam, his sworn man, extracting a boot from the clutching muck.

"Sir Walter, tell me what you think of this ground."

He took a moment to scrape mud off his boot before looking up and carefully scanning the slope running down to the river.

"Good ground. Best I've seen. Shall I set the line, my lord?" Walter FitzWilliam was a bluff man of few words, but a veteran with a keen eye.

"Aye, Walter, I think we'll fight them here."

***

Fifty paces from the top of the ridge, men were hard at work, sharpening stakes and pounding them into the ground. Beneath six inches of mud, the ground was rocky and Marshal could hear his men curse when it refused to yield. Still, by noon, a triple line of stakes bristled from tree line to tree line, with the only gap being the Roman road with its worn stone paving.

For a moment, Marshal pictured what it must have been like when this road was new and the soldiers of Rome, their ranks perfectly dressed, had marched north to put down one rebellion or another among the wild tribes of Britannia. He had heard legends as a boy that the wild Queen Boudicca had met her end somewhere near here in a battle of annihilation with a Roman legion.

Rome might have long ago abandoned this outpost of empire, but it seemed the Britons were still warlike enough to trouble the King's peace. His scouts had been shadowing the mercenary army from the moment they had broken off the siege of Chester. As the hired Flemish and Irish soldiers made their way, first south, then east, they had been joined by scores of Englishmen, ordered into the field by those barons who had calculated that John, Prince of England, would prevail in this fratricidal war.

A rider had reached him at mid-morning to report that the head of the enemy column would reach the river by nightfall. They would see his preparations and would likely wait until first light to make their attack. It would make for a restless and fearful night for his men on the ridge.

The scout said the enemy column was miles long. Marshal had known since he marched from London that he would be outnumbered when he met John's forces, but he had hoped that some loyal men would heed his urgent calls for help. The Earl of Hertford had promised to meet him with another two hundred men at Towcester. When they'd marched through that village in the small hours of the night, there had been no sign of the Earl or his men. Perhaps he was late—or perhaps he had reassessed the chances of victory. Marshal sent a rider east down the road to search out any help that might be coming, but the man had not yet returned.

As the long afternoon drew to a close and the early winter sunset approached, he saw riders come out of the woods on the far side of the valley and rein in as they saw his position on the ridge. Minutes later, a solid mass of cavalry appeared, filling the road. In the cold winter twilight, sound travelled well and Marshal could hear officers shouting orders. Men peeled off to both sides of the road and began to dismount. For the next hour, foot soldiers entered the valley as the first occupants got their evening cook fires started. As the night grew dark, the fields across the river flared with hundreds of fires. It was a grim sight.

Marshal walked out beyond his line of stakes and looked back up the ridge. It was good ground and he had prepared his defence well, but in the end he knew he would lose. The men he faced were professionals and outnumbered him four to one. The mud might slow them and the stakes hinder them, but it would not be enough to stop such an overwhelming force. Yet he had to make a stand somewhere.

After a last look at the campfires filling the opposite side of the valley, he turned back toward his own lines. To the men he passed, he showed no hint of fear, but he was afraid—not of death. Death had never frightened William Marshal.

He was afraid to lose.

***

The Earl of Derby sat on a small stool in front of his tent as his servant tended the fire. William de Ferrers was in a black mood. Here in the bottom land by the river, the cold settled in, damp and clammy, and the flames barely fended off the chill. They had been marching for five days and he was sick of living like a primitive. He looked across the valley at the glow on the opposite ridge and the sight cheered him a little. Their scouts had reported at midday that the great Earl William Marshal, Marcher Lord and Justiciar of the realm, had come out from London to meet them—with barely four hundred men!

William Marshal.

He had only met the man twice and did not like him. Any man who guarded his virtue as carefully as Marshal, had to be a fraud. And that such a man had risen from being a lowly household knight to become Lord of Striguil and Justiciar of the Realm was an insult to men of more noble birth.

A de Ferrers had fought with Duke William at Hastings. Marshal's greatest forbearer had been hardly more than a groomsman for the Conqueror's horses. He failed to see what made Marshal suitable for high office beyond his prowess in tournament and joust. It certainly was not his breeding! But the morning would see an end to the man's pretensions. If Marshal survived the day, his reputation would be in tatters and his decision to support an absent king would likely cost him his life. Either way it would be the end of this up-jumped pretender.

Marshal's defeat would leave the road to London open to them and the Prince's orders had made it clear that they must reach the city in all haste. He had been stunned when the order came to abandon the siege of Chester. They had been so close! The city had to be on the verge of starvation and he had pictured many times his triumphal entry and Ranulf's humiliation.

Things were moving in ways de Ferrers did not fully understand, but instinct told him that these were the final moves in a deadly game. He consoled himself with the thought that when John took the crown, he would get Chester back and Ranulf would surely hang for treason. Once more, he would be the most powerful man in the Midlands.

There will be scores settled then.

He held his hands out toward the fire to warm them. His black mood was gone.

***

Marshal moved among his men as night fell—joking with them and bucking up their courage. Many of these men had been his loyal retainers for years. Their deaths would be on his head. Finally, he found a quiet spot and fell into a fitful sleep. Around midnight someone shook him awake.

"My lord," a man hissed. "Get up!"

It was Sir Walter. Marshal threw off the cape that he'd drawn around him to fend off the dew and felt for his sword.

"What is it?" he asked, slightly groggy with sleep.

"My lord, it's a miracle!"

"Is it Hertford? Has Earl Richard joined us?"

"Nay, my lord."

"Then what, damn it all!"

"It's Ranulf, my lord," said FitzWilliam with a huge grin, "come all the way from Chester!"

Marshal scrambled to his feet and saw the Earl of Chester striding down the slope toward him. The two Marcher Lords embraced as though they were long lost kin. Marshal had only met Ranulf once, at Richard's coronation, and the man before him bore little resemblance to the boyish Earl he had been introduced to over three years ago. He wore rusted mail and a dented helmet and could have been mistaken for an itinerant knight. But the mail was otherwise well maintained and the man wore a sword like he was used to it.

"My lord, you are an answer to my prayers!" he said as he drew away. "I had not expected to see you here."

Ranulf nodded.

"I had not expected to be here, my lord. Chester was starving, but when we rode out four days ago, the enemy was gone. I sent out my scouts and they met one of your own. He told us you were marching from London to meet these foreign bastards, though he did not seem to know why. For our part, we did not care why—we cared only that you were going to fight. I have watched my people go hungry and seen my city bombarded. Every man here is ready to get some of our own back. We've marched day and night to get here ahead of those people," he said, gesturing westward into the darkness.

"And you are a most welcome sight, indeed, my lord," Marshal said, slapping the young Earl on the back. "What have you brought me?"

Ranulf turned and gestured toward three men standing behind him.

"I bring you the Invalid Company, now one hundred strong and commanded by Sir Roland Inness and Sir Declan O'Duinne." Roland and Declan stepped forward and gave a short bow.

"I remember you lads from Oxford!" Marshal said, clasping hands with each in turn. "The day you two rode off with the dregs of London's gutters behind you, I feared I was sending you to your deaths. Praise God I was wrong!"

"I could not have taken back Chester without them," Ranulf said. "I also bring Sir Roger de Laval, commander of the King's heavy cavalry in the Holy Land and the man that brought us news of Richard's capture. I cannot help but think that much of the mischief visited on Cheshire these past years could have been avoided if Sir Roger had been there to advise me."

Marshal looked at the tall, worn knight with a big frame and a fringe of greying hair around a bald pate. He stepped forward and clasped Sir Roger's hand.

"Your reputation precedes you, sir."

"As does yours, my lord." Sir Roger paused. "I'm told by the men who escorted her to London that you have played host to my daughter since August. Is she well?"

Marshal had not expected this—had not known that Sir Roger de Laval had survived the crusade and had somehow got home to Cheshire—the girl didn't either. He could see the man

270

was desperate for news of his daughter, but afraid of what that news might be.

"My lord, Lady Millicent was well and healthy when we marched four days ago. Your daughter is an extraordinary young woman. You and Lady de Laval can be proud. She bearded me on the day we met about the burden she and her mother had suffered with you gone, but she never shirked her duty to the King. My wife bore me a daughter a year ago," he said with a sigh. "I've only seen the babe twice in all that time, but I hope that one day she will grow to be something like your Millicent."

Sir Roger fought to speak, overcome by this news of his daughter.

"She was just a little girl when I left, my lord. It's hard for me to picture her otherwise."

"She is a fine young woman now, and beautiful, I would add. She will make some young noble a handsome wife."

Sir Roger shot a glance at Roland Inness who was standing beside Declan.

"I believe, my lord, she's already been spoken for."

Marshal gave Sir Roger a small bow and turned back to Ranulf who pointed to a cluster of men gathered around in the darkness. All looked weary from long days and nights of hard marching,

"My lord, I bring you eight score archers from the mountains of Derbyshire," Ranulf said with a flourish.

"There are no better men in a fight than the Invalids, my lord, but my Danish longbowmen might be their equal. I have seen what they can do against even armoured knights and so have those bastards across the river. They will not rejoice to face these men again."

William Marshal looked past Ranulf at the ranks of bowmen standing tall despite the forced march they had made to reach this field. Each had a longbow that reached from the ground to above its owner's head. Every man had a full quiver.

The odds were beginning to even.

Robin Hood

*T*here was a small tavern in Beeston that stood beside the road running north from Leicester to Nottingham. The tavern keeper was a jolly man with a bulbous nose who sold ale that wasn't sour and stew that had a little meat in it. He was a good-natured man who was slow to anger and quick to forgive, but he hated the Sheriff of Nottingham.

Sir Alfred de Wendenal had inflicted various injuries to his coin purse and to his pride over the past year and he nursed a grudge. He was not the sort of man to take up a sword, but he had chosen to fight back in his own way. Tavern keepers hear things—rumours and such—and every few days he was visited by a man from Sherwood Forest. He told this man all he had learned about events in Nottingham and the activities of the Sheriff. By prior arrangement, it was to this tavern that a rider had come from London with an urgent message for the outlaws of Sherwood.

William Marshal had sent his summons.

***

"Nine tons of silver?"

"Aye, Rob," Tuck replied. "That's what the message says. It's the last bit of the King's ransom. They are to have it 'stolen' near Newark on the road from Blythe. We're to be blamed."

Robin laughed.

"Your friend Marshal must have found that amusing."

"I expect he did, but what he wants of us is dead serious."

"Indeed it is serious, old friend. Nine tons of silver could feed every man, woman and child in Nottinghamshire for the rest of their natural lives. If we can get our hands on it, why should we turn it over to Marshal?"

Tuck looked at his friend, unsure whether Robin was serious or jesting.

"We will turn it over because we are not truly outlaws. We will turn it over because it will get Richard back and put an end to this chaos. And if that is not enough reason, we will turn it over because if we don't, whoever is King will come to Sherwood with an army and hunt us down like dogs."

Robin threw an arm around Tuck's shoulders.

"Then I suppose we will have to turn it over. Let's have another look at that message. We need a plan!"

***

The Sheriff led fifty horsemen out the main gate of Newark Castle at dawn. His orders from Prince John had been explicit. The last of the King's ransom was being shipped south under guard from York. It must not reach London. He was to seize the wagons hauling the riches of the north and secure them at Newark. The men from Yorkshire escorting the wagons would be expecting them. He was to show them the seal of Prince John and they would not resist when he took the silver.

It had all been arranged.

The Sheriff absently reached down and touched the leather bag holding the Prince's seal as he rode. He was nervous. The theft of silver intended for the King's ransom was far different than stealing a few pigs from a peasant's sty. It was the sort of thing that could cost a man his head—if the King ever did return. Three months ago, he would have been unconcerned. Back then, most of the nobles had concluded that Richard was dead—drowned somewhere at sea. John's star was rising and his own star had risen with that of the Prince. But then came the stunning news that the King was alive and uncertainty had begun to seep into his gut.

He was the oath man of William de Ferrers who was wholly in thrall to the Prince, but the Earl had not been himself since he had taken the blow to his head at Chester. And with the new year had come a frightening increase in the strength of the outlaws of Sherwood. It was all troubling—but he had his orders.

***

The road from Blythe to Newark skirted the northern edge of Sherwood Forest. It was no Roman road and could be almost impassable in the spring when the rains turned the deep ruts into muddy quagmires. But in the dead of winter, it was solid enough to support wagons heavy with silver. Five miles south of the tiny village of Blythe, three huge wagons, each pulled by a team of eight oxen laboured along the road.

Thirty heavily-armed mounted men rode to the front and rear and on each wagon a man with a drawn sword sat beside the driver. Anyone within a mile of this procession could hear the bellow of the oxen and the snap of the teamster's whip in the cold air. This was their fourth day on the road and the man at the head of the column was tense.

His instructions from the Sheriff of Yorkshire had been clear. Somewhere, a few miles outside of Newark, they would be challenged by a large band of 'outlaws'. To insure there were no mistakes, the outlaw leader would produce the seal of Prince John as his bona fides. Faced with overwhelming odds, he was to surrender the wagons without a fight. His men would not be told that this outcome had been planned. The fewer who knew the truth, the better.

The orders were simple enough, but any transaction that involved an exchange of tons of silver was enough to give a man a case of the nerves. Still, they were a good half a day's march from Newark, so he tried to relax. Just as he was beginning to calm himself, he looked up to see ten men on horseback blocking the road. He raised his arm to call a halt. This was supposed to happen much nearer to Newark, which was ten miles further along. Had he misunderstood his orders?

He had also expected a much larger force—one that would justify him surrendering the wagons in the eyes of his own men.

Ten men were hardly overwhelming! Behind him, his mounted guards nervously laid their hands on the hilts of their swords. Upset at this unexpected deviation from the plan, he rode forward to meet the men blocking his path.

"Are you from the Sheriff of Nottingham?" he asked quietly, once he was out of earshot of his own men.

Sir Robin of Loxley nodded, then urged his horse forward and showed the man the seal of Prince John. Robin watched the man's face. His woodcarver had laboured over this seal for three days. Would it pass inspection? The captain of the guard detail gave it a long look, then reached out to inspect it. Robin brought the flat of his sword down on the man's wrist.

"Don't you trust us?"

"You were supposed to bring enough men to make this believable!" the man hissed, rubbing feeling back into his numb wrist. "I can hardly surrender to ten men!"

"Of course not," Robin said and raised his left hand. Like ghosts, a hundred men emerged from the woods on both sides of the road. Robin moved the point of his sword to under the man's chin.

"Is this convincing enough?"

All along the column, the riders from York drew swords. From the trees, a dozen arrows struck the sides of the wagons. The message was clear—resist and die.

"Give the order, captain!"

The captain of the guard swallowed hard. This was more than convincing.

"Throw down your weapons!" he called over his shoulder.

***

Eight miles further down the road toward Newark, eighty men, dressed in peasant garb hid in the bushes and waited. They had been there since noon and had expected the wagons to arrive before sunset. But the shadows were growing long with no sign of the column from York. The Sheriff of Nottingham paced in a clearing near the road. Something did not feel right. He had placed a man with a fast horse at an inn in Tuxford, a mere twelve miles up the road. The rider had returned at noon to report that the column of wagons had passed by the place a little after first light.

They should be here by now.

As the light began to die he decided he could wait no longer. He called two of his men forward and ordered them to head northwest up the road toward Blythe and find the damned wagons. It was full night when his men returned. The story they told made the Sheriff of Nottingham sick to his stomach.

***

Deep in Sherwood Forest, men were breaking the seals on the heavy chests and loading the silver into bags. These were packed in smaller wagons drawn by horses and covered with a mound of hay and manure, carefully collected over the past three days from every farm within ten miles. It had been Tuck's idea.

"You can be sure there will be a hue and cry from one end of the Midlands to the other when they learn of the theft," he said. "Every man the Prince can spare will be looking for three ox carts. We wouldn't make it out of Nottinghamshire with these beasts," he said gesturing at the nearest ox that was bellowing loudly. "I brought our weapons from London in a wagon full of barnyard waste and no one troubled me the entire way."

Robin had agreed, but insisted that the treasure not go entirely unguarded. There would be a dozen wagons, all taking different routes from Sherwood and rendezvousing on Ermine Street north of Stamford. Each would have a sole driver. But trailing well out of sight behind each would be five men or more on good horses—enough to see off any curious local constabulary. A wagon or two might be lost if it had the bad luck to fall into the hands of a curious searcher with enough force at his back, but most should get through.

As the last of the bags was covered in dung, Robin shook his head and turned once more to Tuck.

"Are you sure we can't keep it?"

A Reckoning on Watling Street

As men rose in the cold predawn darkness to ready themselves for battle, the night sky was ablaze with stars. Out of old habit, Roland looked up and found the north star. It shimmered in the clear freezing air and made him think of Rolf Inness, the man who had first taught him how to find the seven points of the Plough and follow them up to the star that always told true north.

As he stamped his feet to get feeling in them, he wished that finding his way in life was as easy as following a single star. As a boy, his father had been that for him, but William de Ferrers had ended that. He looked across the valley and wondered if the Earl of Derby was over there—with the paid soldiers of a treasonous Prince. He prayed that he was. There was still his blood oath to fulfil.

Nearby, he saw Sir Roger climb to his feet. The big man moved slowly and stiffly. As he cleared his throat and began relieving himself in the grass, a small smile came to Roland's lips. The first time he had seen the big Norman knight was on the road to York, where he had been doing the same thing. As Roland had learned during the crusade, Sir Roger never missed an opportunity to sleep, eat or piss.

"Never know when you'll get another chance," was his simple explanation of this rule.

As he watched, the big man finished his morning business and stretched his back. The arm he'd broken on the day he had fought his way into Chester was not fully healed and it had taken him weeks to feel strong enough for sword drill. There was no doubt that Roger de Laval showed the ill effects of three years of war and the trials of his journey home.

But then the big man leaned down, picked up his helmet with one hand and his great battleaxe with the other. He straightened up, took a few easy swings with the axe to limber up and shoved the helmet on his head. In that moment, he was no longer a convalescent. Everything about the man signalled danger.

With his father dead, Sir Roger had become the star Roland guided by. The big Norman had saved his life and given him a path to follow. That path had made him a knight and had led him to Millie. He took a last look at the heavens and the star that all the others circled around. For however long he had left in this life, Millicent de Laval would be the star he guided on. He prayed she slept safe in bed at this hour.

"Form up!"

The command came from somewhere to the front. Roland grasped his shield and pulled his steel helmet on. A few feet away, Declan yawned and buckled on his sword belt. They would join Sir Roger and Earl Ranulf at the centre of Marshal's defence, where the one hundred men of the Invalid Company would anchor the line at the Roman road. These veterans, like all of the mounted men, had picketed their horses on the far side of the ridge.

The arrival of Ranulf gave Marshal a little over six hundred men, which he packed tightly into a line three deep that stretched from one wood line across the road and anchored itself in the trees opposite. In the centre of the line, the Invalid Company formed an inverted vee at the gap in the stakes where the stone road passed through.

Thirty yards behind this line, one hundred sixty Danish archers under Thorkell's command formed up. If the men to their front, behind a few sharpened stakes, could hold back hundreds of heavy cavalry and over a thousand foot soldiers, the longbows of the Danes would make the mercenaries pay. If the lines broke—it would be a massacre.

During the siege of Chester, the Danes had not been idle. Roland sat often with Thorkell and Svein and talked of what they had learned in the long retreat from the mountains. Some of the lessons were not new—if infantry or cavalry closed on the archers, they would be slaughtered. The mercenary infantry had never been able to get to close quarters with the Danes who used every sheltered patch of woods to strike at their pursuers, leaving many a dead Fleming and Irishman in the fields of Cheshire.

But the heavy cavalry that caught them north of the River Weaver would have annihilated the bowmen, had Earl Ranulf and the Invalids not arrived in time. In that fight, the surprise appearance of friendly cavalry had kept the mercenary mounted troops at bay long enough for the Danes to wreak havoc on them.

In the small hours of the night, Roland sought Marshal out and told him what had happened during the Dane's retreat from the mountains to Chester. The Earl listened carefully. He had never seen the longbow used in battle, though he had heard the Welsh used masses of them in their constant civil wars. If what this young knight told him was true, these eight score bowmen would be worth far more than their numbers.

It was still dark as the line of men finished sorting itself out. In the moments before a battle, men take special care to have trusted comrades to their left and right. After a few minutes, the ripple of movement quieted as men found their places. Marshal had positioned his own troops on either flank of the Invalids and was the only man on the ridgeline who remained mounted. He sat his horse just behind the centre of his line and looked into the valley.

There was mist in the low ground, but movement was visible in the enemy camp. Then a horn sounded three blasts. The mercenary army was forming up into attack formation. Above the ridgeline where Marshal's men waited, the sky began to lighten.

***

"We should wait," said Pieter Van Hese, the commander of the mercenary army. "If we go in at first light, the sun will be in our eyes."

William de Ferrers clinched his fists.

"We cannot wait! The Prince has made it clear we must reach London in all haste. He will not appreciate us wasting half a day over a bit of glare from the sun!"

Van Hese stared at the Earl of Derby with his one good eye. The man was an ass and quite possibly a coward, but he paid their wages. He shrugged his shoulders. It looked to be a very uneven fight, regardless of the angle of the sun. He had noted that there were more men on the ridge than he had seen at sunset, but no more than five hundred were visible on the slope across the valley. He had four hundred heavy cavalry alone. They could put their sharpened sticks in the ground as they wished. It would not stop what he would throw at them.

"Very well, my lord." He turned to one of his lieutenants.

"Have the skirmishers and the crossbowmen advance and engage."

"Aye, my lord!" The man ran off to give the orders. De Ferrers nudged his horse forward and watched as a line of foot, mixed with two hundred Genoese crossbowmen, began moving forward. They marched in column until they crossed the shallow ford, then spread out on either side of the road.

"Infantry forward," Van Hese ordered.

In the mercenary camp, a drum began a steady beat to mark the cadence of march as rank after rank of foot soldiers, some with lances and others with swords, moved toward the ford. De Ferrers turned in his saddle and saw that horsemen were already moving forward. As they rode past, the great warhorses snorted and stamped as they sensed a fight brewing.

Armoured cavalry had been the weapon de Ferrers' Norman forbearers had used to conquer half of France, bits of Italy and all of England and he was eager to witness the carnage it would inflict on the thin line of men on the ridge. That it was Marshal who they would crush this day made the prospect all the sweeter.

"When will the cavalry attack?" he asked, excitement in his voice. Once more Van Hese had to bite back the urge to tell this meddler to shut up.

"My lord, after the crossbowmen wear down the men up there, and before I send the infantry to close on them, our cavalry will ford the stream. At my signal, the infantry will stand clear of the road and the cavalry will move forward. Once they form their line, we will sound the charge." He pointed to his bugler standing nearby at the ready. "Do you wish to join them?"

De Ferrers blinked. He glanced across the valley as the line of crossbowmen mixed with skirmishers climbed up the slope. Thicker lines of infantry followed. Right in front of him, the cavalry was beginning to ford the stream. For a moment, he felt a strong urge to take up Van Hese's challenge, to join these men who were about to smash through the enemy line and slaughter the men on the hill.

He looked back up the ridge and saw the morning sun reflecting dully off hundreds of steel spear points. Victory might be certain, but not without losses. Perhaps it was best to let the mercenaries ride up toward the men on the ridge with the sharp spear points. After all, that is what he was paying them for. What did he care what some paid cutthroat like Van Hese thought of him?

"It's best I stay here, where I can better control events," he said and stared at Van Hese. The Fleming looked back impassively.

"As you wish, my lord."

***

With the morning sun at their backs, the men on the ridge watched as the mercenary host formed up and advanced to meet them.

"They're sending in their crossbowmen," Sir Roger said as they watched the Genoese professionals spread out at the foot of the slope.

"They don't know we have the Danes with us," said Roland. "Those men will never get close enough to touch us."

Sir Roger nodded.

"If those lads can shoot as well as you, it will go badly for the Italians."

Behind the line of infantry, they heard Thorkell's voice bark.

"Make ready!"

The Genoese were three hundred yards from the stakes. Behind them, four thick formations of infantry had crossed the ford and were forming up for the assault. At the ford, the first horsemen were crossing, with hundreds on the far bank waiting to join them. The first rays of the sun now shone above the ridge, flashing off steel helmets, gleaming breastplates and polished mail. It was a daunting sight.

The Genoese reached two hundred paces from the stakes, urged on by the pounding of a drum somewhere near the river.

"Draw!" Thorkell ordered, his voice loud but calm.

The cadence of the drum grew faster and the crossbowmen surged forward.

"Loose!"

One hundred sixty arrows leapt across the distance in less time than it took to take and release a breath. Roland heard their buzz as they passed overhead, but did not look up. He was watching the men who were marching unawares into hell. The arrows struck with devastating accuracy. Skirmishers and crossbowmen alike fell in bunches onto the frozen ground.

Shocked, the Genoese loosed a ragged return volley, their quarrels falling harmlessly short of Marshal's line. Sergeants screamed at them to advance and they did—into a second volley from the Danes. More men fell. A brave few ran forward and loosed their bolts. Four men along Marshal's lines fell. The ranks closed up to fill the gaps.

As the third volley of arrows rained down on the Genoese, they began to break—first in ones and twos, then in a general rush to the rear. The infantry skirmishers followed them back down the hill. On the far side of the river Van Hese watched his first wave break and fall back in panic. He cursed under his breath.

"What's happening?" De Ferrers called to him.

The Flemish commander had needed only a moment to recognize what had befallen his archers.

"I believe it's your damned Danes, my lord! We chased them into Chester, but it seems they have followed us here. Those are longbows on that hill."

The Danes!

De Ferrers felt the hair rise on the back of his neck. He looked up toward the line of men on the hill.

And if they've come from Chester...

Was Roland Inness up there? He felt his heart start to pound in his chest. He wanted to turn his horse around and ride away, but he stayed frozen to the spot, afraid to show his fear to Van Hese. Behind him, a trumpeter blew a blast and he saw the line of infantry part and edge away from the road. The magnificent heavy cavalry poured through the gap and spread out across the base of the slope.

De Ferrers felt his hopes rise. No force had stood against the mercenary army for over two years and these armoured horsemen were the mailed fist of that army. The trumpet blew again. He watched the riders start toward the hill, first at a walk, but slowly gathering speed.

***

Roland watched them come. He looked to his left. Sir Roger was there, his great axe dangling from a cord around his right wrist. He had no shield, as his left arm would not bear the weight. A little further on, Sergeant Billy and Patch flanked the Earl of Chester. Ranulf caught his eye and gave him a short salute, then lowered the visor on his dented helmet.

Looking back to the front, he saw the heavy cavalry cross the low land of the river bottom and gather speed as they started up the gradual slope. They came in two waves with lances held aloft and pennants waving. It was a sight to quicken the heart, had they not been coming to kill them.

Roland glanced to his right. Declan stood there, calm and ready. The Irishman gave him a wink and pointed his sword toward the approaching line of horsemen.

"A pretty sight—pity we have to kill them."

He was about to reply when he heard a commanding voice from behind.

"Steady men!" It was Marshal, still sitting his horse right behind the centre of the line.

The cavalry had reached a canter and men were beginning to whip the flanks of their chargers, urging them toward a gallop. As they moved up the slope, great clumps of thawed ground were thrown up as the footing became softer. Roland heard a sound behind him and saw that Marshal had dismounted. The Lord of Striguil squeezed through the rear ranks and joined Ranulf in the centre of the road. He drew a long broadsword and waited.

The heavy cavalry were now three hundred yards from the sharpened stakes in front of Marshal's position. The men in the line could feel the ground tremble. Only a handful of them had ever faced such a charge.

"Steady!" he heard Marshal call again.

Roland saw a horse lose its footing on the slippery soil and go down, taking another animal with it. The riders disappeared under a blur of hooves as the irresistible momentum of the charge surged up the slope.

At two hundred yards Roland heard Thorkell give his command and a black cloud of arrows arced overhead. A handful of riders toppled from their mounts, their horses continuing to bound, riderless up the slope. Other horses were struck and fell, disrupting the cohesion of the charge. It hardly seemed to matter. There was no turning back now. The riders came on.

***

Sir Connaught Kilbride dug his spurs into the flanks of his charger as he felt the big beast begin to labour up the steepening slope. The tall Irish knight was in the front rank, just to the left of the Roman road. He had watched men on either side go down under the first storm of arrows and felt his gut tighten. He'd seen this before.

He was no longer senior commander of the mercenary heavy cavalry. His failure to destroy the Danes as they fled from Derbyshire had left him in disgrace and cost him that position. Now he was just another hired sword. Kilbride had hoped to distinguish himself this day and win back a bit of his reputation. Now he simply prayed he would survive the fight.

He looked up, trying to see when the next hail of arrows would descend on them, but the morning sun rising above the ridge line was blinding. He raised his shield above his head just as the second volley struck. He felt arrows shatter on the steel and all around him horses and men were hit. The horses squealed and fell or threw their riders. Men screamed as longbow shafts pierced their mail. Kilbride's mind flashed back to a day in July when he had ridden over a field littered with the bodies of his men, most felled by these damned longbows.

He looked down the line and saw other men—men who had faced these weapons before—raise their shields high. But that did not save their horses. He wanted to look over his shoulder—to see how many they had lost, but there was no time. The sharpened stakes and the line of men were less than a hundred yards away now. He lowered his lance and sent up a prayer.

Swarm after swarm of arrows pelted the men charging up the slope, the incoming volleys nearly invisible as they dropped out of the bright glare of the morning sun. The ranks of horsemen were thinned—but still they came on. Behind the line of stakes, a man felt his bowels turn to water as this wave of steel and horseflesh drew near. A cry of pure terror escaped his lips and he broke for the rear, elbowing aside the men behind him. A man in the third rank clubbed him to the ground.

"Lances!" Marshal commanded, and men drove the butts of their spears into the ground and lowered their points to join the sharpened stakes in front of the line. They braced for impact.

***

Kilbride sensed that the decisive moment in the fight had come. Many of their men had gone down under the hail of arrows that had greeted them as they charged up the hill, but there looked to be more than enough left to smash right through the enemy line.

He had seen the gap in the solid wall of stakes at the Roman road. Others saw it as well and riders to the left and right of the line began to angle in toward the centre. He knew the defenders would have their best men there to protect the gap, but no foot soldiers could possibly stand against the sheer impact of the cavalry charge thundering toward them. As he neared the gap he saw two score knights converging into a tightening wedge of steel. He found his place just behind the lead riders and felt his heart rise.

Nothing could stop them.

***

The horses were on them. They struck all along the line, some dying impaled on the stakes, their riders flung over their necks to land, stunned and helpless, on the ground in front of the waiting defenders. Those men died under a swarm of axes and long daggers that found gaps in their armour. Some of the horses and riders were pierced by the braced spears while others shied away at the last minute from the hedgehog of sharp steel.

But many found gaps and slammed into the defensive line, trampling men under steel shod hooves. Off to Roland's right, a knight wearing a long mail coat and an armoured breastplate drove his big black warhorse through all three lines of defenders and spurred toward the hated archers a few yards away. He never reached them, as men in the rear rank turned to drag him from his saddle and cut his throat.

In the front line now, the fighting was brutal. A burly knight on a grey charger picked his way through the stakes and spurred his horse at Roland, a mace in his right hand raised to strike. But the horse had lost momentum avoiding the sharp points and Roland grabbed its bridle, dodging to the right and coming up on the rider's left. He drove his sword up under the man's ribs and the mace fell limply to his side as he toppled backwards from the saddle.

In the empty space left by the downed rider, he saw the mercenary infantry marching up the ridge to join in the fight. The foot soldiers were falling in bunches as the Danes continued their devastating volleys, but still they came on.

"Down!" he heard Declan scream behind him. He dropped into a squat as a lance passed over his head and impaled the man behind him. Declan leapt forward. The mounted knight had dropped the lance and drawn his sword, but his parry had no chance against the speed of the Irishman. Declan's broadsword sliced upwards through the man's armpit and emerged bloody above the knight's shoulder. He had to jerk the blade twice to withdraw it as the wounded man twisted off the horse and onto the churned up ground. All around them now was chaos.

Half of the mounted men who had charged up the hill were down, killed by arrows or impaled on the stakes and spears at the defensive line. But the rest were now in among the defenders and nowhere was the fighting hotter than at the Roman road. The first riders through the gap impaled men with their lances, then drew swords and maces to hack at the defenders who pressed in from both sides. Warhorses reared and struck out with their massive hooves, crushing skulls and breaking limbs. They, in turn, went down as Marshal's men struck back with spears and swords.

More riders pressed into the gap, their horses leaping over the bodies of the fallen. The Earl of Chester managed to raise his shield an instant before a lance would have run him through. The impact knocked him to the ground and left his shield arm numb and useless. The man who had struck Ranulf spurred his horse forward, seeking to ride through the gap left by the downed nobleman.

Sir Roger, seeing his liege lord down, stepped to his left and straddled the Earl. The charging rider saw the gap had closed. He stood up in his stirrups and raised a long handled axe over his head to clear the way. Sir Roger's axe was quicker. The big knight leapt forward and swung it viciously, slicing through mail and muscle and into the rider's rib cage.

Roland had seen the Earl fall and Sir Roger defend the downed nobleman. He edged left over the bodies of two of the Invalids to cover his master's flank. More riders, impeded by the sharpened stakes elsewhere along the line were pressing into the gap at the Roman road and the carnage there was appalling.

The Invalids fought with their customary ferocity but were taking casualties and being pressed back by the sheer weight of the armoured knights pushing into the gap. Roland saw Sergeant Billy go down, dead or wounded he could not tell. Through the space where he'd fallen three riders burst through and into the rear of the formation.

They made straight for the archers further up the slope. This time the men in the ranks were too hard pressed to come to their aid. Thorkell saw them break the line. It was a thing he had hoped not to see, but one he had prepared for.

"Svein!" he shouted.

Svein and ten other Danes dropped their bows and picked up the axes that had been used to cut stakes for the defensive line. They swarmed around the three riders on all sides. Four Danes died, but the three mercenaries joined them, brought down in a flurry of axe strokes. Thorkell ordered his men back into line and looked past the melee to the slope below.

The mercenary infantry were now only one hundred yards from Marshal's line. Scores of their bodies littered the hillside but they pushed on. Those that had shields held them aloft to ward off the longbow shafts. Thorkell directed his men to target the men struggling up the hill. If they reached the fight it could tip the balance.

The Danish bowmen drew and loosed as fast as they could. The advancing foot soldiers looked as though they were leaning into a windstorm as they marched up the slope with shields up and heads down. The lines of foot soldiers grew ragged as men were hit or slipped and fell on the slippery ground that had been churned into a quagmire by the charging cavalry. More and more arrows got through, striking thigh and foot and arm. More men fell.

Near the top of the slope, the fighting on the Roman road was a nightmare of blood and death. Exhausted men hacked at one another. Horses stumbled over the dead bodies of the fallen. Men screamed and cursed and prayed to God, but they fought.

Connaught Kilbride drove his sword into the neck of a man who tried to drag him from his saddle with bare hands. A tall knight swung at him with a wicked axe, forcing him to throw himself backwards to avoid the arc of the blow. He saw three of his comrades finally break through to the rear, only to be hacked to pieces by men with axes.

The vee formation that had been waiting for them as they burst through the gap in the stakes was now a bulge barely holding back the mass of armed horsemen within it. One more push and they would be through! He drove his heels into his mount and charged toward a singular figure in gleaming mail standing in the middle of the road.

William Marshal saw him come and did not wait to be ridden down. Before the man's horse could gain any speed, he darted forward and slashed the animal across its nose. There was mail there, but the blow stunned the beast and it reared back. Kilbride tried to keep his saddle, but the horse lost its balance and fell backwards over its hind legs. The Irish mercenary flung himself to the side as his horse toppled onto its back. He found himself atop a pile of dead men and horses.

He lurched to his feet and saw the tall knight coming for him. Even brave men have their breaking point. He turned and ran, scrambling over the dead and wounded as he fled back toward the gap. Other men who had lost their mounts saw him and the contagion began to spread. Panicked men tried to turn their horses and some succeeded. Others dismounted and ran for the gap. Below, the foot soldiers were still slogging uphill under the galling rain of arrows when Kilbride, trailed by five unhorsed comrades, came staggering down the hill. Men saw them come and hesitated. If the armoured cavalry was in retreat, then what were they to do?

Veteran sergeants screamed at the men, ordering them to advance, but the contagion of fear could not be contained. Men in twos and threes began peel off to follow the knights back down toward the ford. As he passed through the line of foot soldiers and saw the ford beckoning ahead, Connaught Kilbride tried to get control of his terror. On the far side of the river, Pieter Van Hese would be waiting and he would need a good explanation for why he had fled the battle.

He began to think furiously of what he would say to the grim one-eyed commander. But his thoughts were cut short when a longbow shaft struck him between the shoulder blades and penetrated his heart. He fell face-first into the mud and thought of Ireland as he died.

***

High on the ridge, men sensed the battle turning. The scores of mounted mercenaries that had forced their way into the deadly vee at the Roman road were packed so tightly together that it made it difficult to bring their weapons to bear. As the foot soldiers down the hill began to break and turn back toward the river, the Danes turned all of their fury on the mounted men only fifty yards to their front. They made easy targets.

Roland and Declan stood beside Sir Roger. All were gasping for breath. Earl Ranulf had regained his feet and, for the moment, no riders pressed them. Sir Roger moved forward to where the Justiciar stood alone in the centre of the road and the men who had once been his squires came with him. Marshal's beautiful coat of mail was spattered with mud and gore and his sword was bloody. When Sir Roger reached him, he cleared his throat and shouted above the din.

"They are breaking!"

Marshal saw it too. In front of them, more riders were wheeling their horses around to join the growing rout. He turned and saw Roland Inness.

"Sir Roland, get the Invalids to the horses! I don't want these bastards to escape to trouble us further."

"Aye, my lord!" Roland shouted back. He backed off the line and screamed at the top of his lungs.

"Invalid Company! To me!"

Men all along the centre of the line had been standing, exhausted, watching the mercenary tide recede. Roland's call snapped them back to attention. As he ran to the rear with Declan at his side, the Invalids fell in behind him, stumbling in their fatigue. They did not have to be told where to go. The enemy had broken and was fleeing the field. It was time to pursue.

The last of the mercenary infantry had reached the ford when the Invalid Company came over the crest of the ridge. They trailed horses for Marshal, Earl Ranulf and Sir Roger. The three mounted hastily and joined the pursuit as Roland and Declan led the column through the gap at the Roman road and down toward the ford.

Ahead, a cry of alarm went up as the men crowding down toward the ford saw the horsemen coming. Some plunged into deeper water to escape the crush of men in the shallows. Their mail dragged them under. A few of the foot soldiers, with no hope of gaining the far bank, turned to face the oncoming men of the Invalid Company. They too died.

On the far side of the ford there was bedlam as men bolted in any direction that might offer escape from what was coming. These men had pursued many a routed enemy in their day and they knew that to falter meant death. They whipped their horses in a frenzy to stay ahead of the pursuit.

***

"What...?"

William de Ferrers had trouble forming his question. The thing he was seeing on the far ridgeline did not seem possible. The force that had been sent against Marshal's thin lines should have broken through easily. Instead, he saw men running back toward the ford. As he watched, the trickle of fleeing mercenaries turned into a flood.

He felt a hand grip his arm and he flinched. It was Van Hese.

"I suggest you leave the field, my lord. The day is lost." He said this in the same flat tone he might have used if he was discussing the weather.

"Lost? How can it be lost?" de Ferrers demanded, feeling the panic start to rise in his chest.

"It's a battle," Van Hese sneered. "One side always loses. Today we have lost. Do you see those men coming down the ridge there, my lord? They are coming to kill us." With that, the man turned his horse's head around and slapped its flank with the loose end of his reins. The horse headed northeast, away from the river—away from the death.

De Ferrers watched him go. He wanted to follow, but seemed rooted to the spot. Then he heard a man down by the river scream in agony and the panic that had been building in him took control. Nothing mattered now, but to get as far away from this disaster as possible. Leicester lay to the northwest and Derby only thirty miles further on. He spurred his horse and headed up Watling Street.

***

Roland and Declan hit the ford side by side and splashed through it. Ahead of them riders and men on foot were scattering in every direction. His own men were veterans and knew what had to be done to crush a defeated army. They peeled off, a dozen or more to a group, and thundered after the fleeing mercenaries. Roland reined in near the centre of the deserted camp, Declan beside him. Near the finest tent in the encampment flew a banner—a white shield with six horseshoes. Both men knew the banner of the Earl of Derby.

"De Ferrers!" Roland spit out the name. He looked around frantically. The entire camp was abandoned. He turned to Declan.

"He'll head for Derbyshire!"

"Then so shall we!" Declan cried.

They kicked their horses into motion and headed up Watling Street. Somewhere along that ancient road was William de Ferrers.

***

William Marshal and Sir Roger de Laval splashed across the ford in time to see Roland and Declan spurring their horses up the road to the northwest, though most of the mercenaries were fleeing to the east. Sir Roger saw the banner of the Earl of Derby fluttering in the abandoned camp and knew in an instant what was drawing his former squires away from the battlefield. He dug his spurs into his horse's flanks and started after them. He had his own accounts to settle with William de Ferrers. The man had to answer for Alwyn Madawc.

The roads the Romans left behind were still the best in Britain eight hundred years after the last centurion climbed aboard ship to sail for Gaul. But they were not immune to the ravages of time and Watling Street was no exception. A mile from the field of battle, the flat pavement was missing a stone and William de Ferrers, made incautious by fear, did not see it. He was whipping his horse and looking over his shoulder when the animal stepped in the hole in the pavement. The horse's foreleg snapped and de Ferrers was pitched forward into space.

Luck was with the Earl of Derby on this otherwise unlucky day. He landed hard, but just missed the stones of the roadway. He lay on the verge, stunned and gasping for air while his unfortunate horse flailed a few feet away. Catching his breath, he staggered to his feet. Nothing seemed broken, but in the distance he heard a sound that chilled him. Horses were coming—and fast.

He looked around frantically. There were open fields on both sides of the road, but a small strip of woods ran beside the river just fifty yards away. He ran for the concealment of the trees. He was less than halfway there, when two riders came around the bend.

***

Roland saw the downed horse first, then caught movement off the road. A man was half running, half stumbling, across the frozen field that led down to the river. There could be no mistake—it was William de Ferrers. Roland swung his horse's head to the left and went after him.

De Ferrers saw the horse veer off the road and knew he would never reach the safety of the woods. He stopped and drew his sword. Roland guided his horse to a spot between the Earl and the trees and was out of the saddle before the animal came to a full stop. He drew his sword.

"Roland!"

Declan O'Duinne reined in his own mount and swung down onto the frozen ground. He had never seen William de Ferrers up close before and as he ran to catch up to his friend he studied the young Earl. There was something in the way the man stood and held his sword that gave the Irishman pause. As he drew even with Roland, he whispered out of the side of his mouth.

"He looks like a skilled swordsman. Perhaps I should do the honours."

"No!" Roland snarled. Many men might have reason to kill William de Ferrers, Declan included, but Roland had no intention of ceding pride of place for this task. He watched de Ferrers standing there, twenty feet away, and could see what Declan meant. The man might be afraid, but the way he stood, with his weight balanced and his sword resting at ease by his side, spoke to his experience with the blade. Roland turned back to Declan and spoke quietly.

"If he beats me—kill him."

Declan nodded.

"It will be my pleasure."

***

William de Ferrers watched Roland Inness come for him and felt his heart hammering in his chest. He had lived this moment many times in a recurring nightmare that had plagued his sleep for over three years. But something was different now and it gave him hope. Inness was coming for him with a sword, not the longbow that had troubled his dreams. Without a bow, Roland Inness was no nightmare at all. He felt his gut unclench. He flexed his wrist and began to move the sword in shallow circles.

He just might escape this trap after all.

He had been trained to the blade since he was a boy and had a reputation as one of the finest swordsmen in the Midlands. Surely he would overmatch some peasant who was more accustomed to killing with a longbow from ambush. But as he watched Roland close the distance, a nagging thought struck him. In all his years of training, he had never faced a man who meant to kill him. His gut began to clinch once more.

***

As Roland closed on his old enemy, he felt years of pent up rage prodding him into an all-out attack. He wanted to cut the guts from this man who had brought so much death and sorrow to him and to those he loved. Caution against a better swordsman might be the more prudent tactic, but he knew prudence had no place here. The words of Sir Roger's old Master of the Sword came back to him.

"When swords are crossed, lad, technique alone is not enough," Sir Alwyn had said. "Ye' must have the battle fury—the will to kill the man in front of ye'!"

He came straight in and swung at de Ferrers head. The man parried the blow easily, but the power of it forced him back a little. Roland bore in, taking a scything stroke at the Earl's midsection, then a sweeping backhand slash toward the man's chin. Like the berserker rage that had gripped his Viking forbearers when they had gone into battle, a reckless anger drove him. He left de Ferrers no time to go over to the offensive as he kept up a relentless attack.

For long minutes de Ferrers used his superior skill to turn aside every killing blow. He saw openings where his enemy was vulnerable, but the fury of Roland's attack kept him off balance and unable to launch an attack of his own. There was no grace in the blows he was parrying, but the power in them began to sap the strength in his right arm. He switched to his left. His breath now came in tortured gasps as the unrelenting assault continued.

Roland saw the scene in front of him in a red haze of murderous hate. He felt de Ferrers' strength starting to falter. Over the man's shoulders he saw riders coming. He kept up the rain of blows as the Earl's parries grew more laboured.

Across the frozen field, William Marshal and Sir Roger de Laval spurred their mounts to where Declan stood watching the unfolding drama. Both men dismounted. Declan turned to them, excitement in his voice.

"Roland has him!"

***

William de Ferrers saw William Marshal arrive on the field. There was no mistaking the most famous knight in the kingdom. He shielded himself from another overhand blow, his left arm shuddering from the impact. A few more such and he would be finished. But the arrival of Marshal gave him hope. He leapt backwards and threw his sword down, stretching his empty hands wide. He looked past Roland to where the Justiciar of the Realm now stood and shouted to him.

"I throw myself on the mercy of the King!"

To Kill a Queen

Millicent de Laval felt worse than useless. It had been four days since William Marshal had scraped together his small force and marched out of the Newgate and up Watling Street to decide the fate of the kingdom. The Earl had left behind only Sir Nigel, Andrew Parrot and one of his bodyguards when he had marched out, so the house seemed empty and, for her, the days had been much like all those that had gone before—full of fruitless watching for a spy who had yet to reveal himself.

She had considered visiting Saint Paul's and putting a coin in the beggar's cap, but knew that the Archbishop was gone, dispatched by the Queen to the Emperor's court to make final arrangements for the exchange of the ransom and release of the King. Mary Cullen, she was certain, would be wholly taken up with attending to the Queen, who was being quartered at the Archbishop's house. This was no time to add to the young woman's burden.

She walked to her window and looked out on the afternoon sun shining off the white ramparts of the Tower and wondered what the garrison might be planning, now that Marshal had stripped the city of men loyal to the King. Sir Nevil had told her there were no more than a hundred men now guarding the ransom in the crypts of Saint Paul's. She was lost in thought and jumped when she heard an urgent tapping on her door. She hurried across the room and opened it. It was Jamie Finch.

"My lady, the clerk, he just passed me in the hall and went right out the front door. He looked...agitated."

Millicent did not hesitate. She reached for her winter cloak hanging behind the door. Finch looked at her sceptically.

"My lady..."

"I'm sick of sitting in the house, Jamie. I will follow your lead, but hurry, we don't want to lose him."

Finch nodded and sprinted down the stairs. He did not wait for her and bolted through the door. Millicent hiked up the front of her skirts and ran after him. As she reached the street she slowed. She could see Finch a block ahead of her. He had stopped running and appeared to simply be a man going about some urgent business. The clerk was not in sight.

She picked up her pace to match that of Finch and followed him. It was cold and windy, but a good number of people were on the street. She took care to keep her eyes fixed on the young man ahead of her, who she presumed had eyes on Andrew Parrot. As they neared the market at the heart of the city, the streets grew more crowded and Millicent walked faster, afraid that Jamie Finch would turn a corner and be lost to her.

She saw him glance over his shoulder, then turn into an alleyway. Millicent forced herself not to break into a run. It was best not to draw notice. She walked faster and reached the opening to the alley. It curved around between buildings and Finch was not in sight. She ducked into the passageway and hurried along, trying to avoid stepping in the disgusting mess that nearby residents had deposited there.

The passage was narrow and, as it was nearing sunset, the shadows were deep. When she came around the curve of the alley, she saw a figure stopped ahead. It was Finch. He looked over his shoulder and motioned to her. She hurried to join him. He stood in the shadows at the far end of the alley. The passage opened onto a small courtyard with three buildings facing inwards. He turned, pointing to the one directly facing them and whispered to Millicent.

"The White Mare."

Millicent nodded. This was where Parrot had been coming for months. It had always been a dead end. While she had never ventured down this alley or seen this courtyard, she recognized that they were very near the Guildhall. After a while, she pointed to the door and whispered to Finch.

"Is that the only way in or out?"

Finch blinked, as though he didn't understand the question. Then comprehension hit him.

"Shit! Oh, beg pardon, miss, but I am a stupid ass! There is a back door—opens onto another alley. I shoulda' thought of that!"

He grabbed Millicent by the wrist and bolted out of the shadows and across the courtyard. He rapped on the door of the White Mare, and turned to Millicent.

"This is the quickest way."

A large woman opened the door a crack and tried to close it just as quickly, but Jamie Finch inserted his foot in the jam. He put his shoulder into it and the woman staggered backwards.

"Jamie Finch, you....!"

"Sorry Girt, no time to talk of old times. We're just passin' through!" He dragged Millicent down the hall and past the women lounging in the parlour. He reached the end of the passage and flung open the door, pulling her behind him.

"I shoulda' known that little clerk was not a patron of this place! It's been a blind all along. I'm a damn bad spy, my lady!"

The door opened onto an alleyway so narrow one could barely walk without touching the sides. The sun was now behind the walls of the city and it was dark as night as they hurried through it. Millicent could see light ahead over Finch's shoulder and finally they burst out onto a broad street.

It was Wood Street. Parrot was nowhere in sight, but directly across from the passageway was the meeting house of the Archbishop. Finch and Millicent looked at each other. This could not be a coincidence. Together they crossed the street and climbed the stairs. Finch started to knock, but Millicent grasped his wrist and shook her head. He nodded and slowly turned the lever. The door was not locked. He pushed it open. In the light left from the dying sun, they could see into the front hall.

Andrew Parrot lay there, face down. There was a small pool of blood beside him. Millicent knelt down by the clerk and rolled him over as Finch drew his knife and hovered over them.

"He's alive—barely!"

Andrew Parrot's eyes snapped open. He gave an odd cough and a little blood frothed at the corner of his mouth. It took him a moment to focus.

"You...how?"

"Andrew, who did this to you?"

He coughed again and more blood came up. Millicent looked up at Finch who shook his head.

"Who did this, Andrew?"

"The priest..."

"Priest?"

"She said...she said she loved me. She promised..."

Millicent felt the hair rise on the back of her neck.

"Who, Andrew—who said this?"

He looked at her and there was a lifetime of longing and pain in that look.

"Mary...Mary Cullen."

He coughed again and the breath seemed to catch in his throat. There was a small retching sound and his chest went still. Andrew Parrot was dead. Millicent saw he had a piece of vellum clutched in his hand. She pulled it free and looked at it. It was a poem. This was what he had been scribbling late at night, afraid for anyone to see—love poems to the woman who had led him like a lamb to slaughter.

Millicent turned to Finch, stunned.

"Mary Cullen is the French agent! Oh dear God, the Queen is in that house!" She grabbed Finch's collar. "Run! Get to Marshal's house and tell Sir Nevil to come at the run to the Archbishop's. The Queen is in grave danger!"

Finch did not hesitate. He bolted out the door and sprinted down Wood Street, dodging idlers and tradesman as he ran. Millicent was out the door a moment after him. She gathered up her dress and ran west, toward Saint Paul's and the Archbishop's house, oblivious to the stares the people on the street gave her.

Millicent knew there was ample security around the perimeter of Saint Paul's square to protect the ransom and the Queen, but guards would not stop or question the Archbishop's trusted servant. Perhaps Mary Cullen was not planning to harm the Queen, but the corpse of Andrew Parrott suggested otherwise. And she had help. Who this priest might be she did not know, but he had already committed one murder this day.

She reached the northeast corner of Saint Paul's and ran along the northern border of the churchyard. She saw armed men loitering at the entrance to every road and alleyway. These were the few men Marshal had left behind when he marched out to meet the mercenary army. They watched her run past, a curious sight, but hardly a threat to the treasure in the crypts or to the Queen. Millicent did not stop to raise an alarm. These men didn't know her and there was no time to persuade them of the danger she feared threatened the Queen.

They'd think me daft—or drunk.

She reached the northwest corner of the churchyard and turned south. A block away, she could see a guard standing at the door of the Archbishop's residence. He seemed untroubled and she prayed that he had no reason to be. She ran up to him, breathless. He watched her come, curious at the sight of a young woman running as though pursued by demons. He started to ask her if she needed assistance, but she cut him off.

"Listen to me carefully," she said, gasping for breath. "I am Lady Millicent de Laval. I am an agent of the Queen, and I believe her to be in grave danger. I need you to take me to her—now!"

The man blinked, then smiled at her.

"Miss, how am I to believe a young girl like yerself is an 'agent of the Queen'? But don't trouble yerself. The Queen is safe and sound. I've been here all morning and no danger has got past me!"

"Is Mary Cullen inside? If she is, then a world of trouble has got past you, man."

The mention of Mary Cullen, by name, set the man back a bit.

"Miss Cullen just came in a minute ago, Miss, but she lives here. The Queen sent her to fetch a priest."

"Mary Cullen is a French spy," Millicent said, in a fury, "and if she's brought someone with her, you can be sure he is no priest! Now take me to the Queen, or be known as the man too thick to protect the King's mother!"

The man blinked again. He wanted to dismiss this girl as a lunatic, but something in her manner told him not to. For if her story was true.... He frowned, but turned and worked the latch.

"Come along then, miss, but if all is well inside, you will have to answer to me!" He led her into the entrance hall and saw immediately that all was not well inside. The man who stood guard inside the door was lying in a pool of blood, his throat cut.

There was no time to contemplate this horror, as the sound of footsteps came from the landing above. The guard brought his lance up to the ready and ran up the stairs, with Millicent right behind him. When they reached the second floor, Millicent saw Mary Cullen standing at the door at the end of the hall, her hand on the latch. Beside her was a tall priest in black robes. He turned at the sound behind him. It was Father Malachy.

Mary Cullen saw them as they reached the top of the stairs and cursed aloud. She twisted furiously at the latch that led to the Queen of England, but the door would not open. Malachy turned to face this new threat and drew out a long dagger from his robes, blocking the hallway while the woman continued to try to force the door. The guard edged forward, poking the lance in short jabs, forcing the priest back toward the wall at the end of the hall.

Millicent saw Malachy look right past the guard and meet her gaze with a cold stare.

"I should have strangled you in your sleep in Chester," he said calmly, keeping his eyes on her and the point of the lance as well.

"I should have cut your throat when I heard you lead Lady Constance into treason," Millicent replied. The guard took another pace forward and Malachy took a half step back then lunged to his right, quick as a snake. He grasped the lance behind the steel head and forced it down. The guard fought to free it for a killing thrust, but could not. He dropped the weapon, lowered his shoulder and bulled his way into the priest. They both crashed to the floor.

At the end of the hall, Mary Cullen saw them go down. She turned back to the door and raised her foot. She kicked twice and the latch gave with a rending crack. Millicent watched the two men flailing at each other on the floor of the narrow hall and, when they rolled to one side, sprinted by them.

Mary Cullen turned to meet her. Her face, always so full of good humour, was now contorted in fear and rage. She reached into the loose sleeve of her dress and was drawing a knife when Millicent grasped her wrist and drove a fist into her jaw. The blow staggered her, but she did not go down.

She tried to wrench her knife hand free, but Millicent had it in an iron grip. She brought her free hand up and tried to grasp Millicent by the hair, but it never got that far. Millicent drove her fist once more into the centre of the girl's face and heard bones break, whether hers or Mary Cullen's she could not tell. The girl fell backwards, dragging Millicent with her to the floor, her nose gushing blood, the knife skittering out of her hand and through the railing. It clattered on the floor of the hall below.

Behind her, Millicent heard wood splintering. She drove her fist once more into Mary Cullen's mangled nose and the girl's eyes rolled back in her head. She turned to see the guard down and Malachy shoving the shattered door open.

Millicent scrambled to her feet. She reached down for the dagger her father had taught her to always keep in her boot and followed the false priest through the door. On the far side of the room Eleanor of Aquitaine stood with a fireplace poker in her frail hand, ready to put up a defence—even if a feeble one.

Malachy raised his blade to strike, but instinct warned him of danger. He swung around—but too late to ward off Millicent's blade. She drove it with all of her might into the man's chest. He flailed with his own blade and it raked across her shoulder, but she hardly felt it. The man staggered backwards and gave an odd cough. He reached for the handle of the blade that still protruded from his chest, but could not seem to get his hands to obey his commands. He looked at Millicent, venom in his eyes.

"Damn all the English..." he said and toppled backwards, landing at the feet of the Queen. He jerked and tried to rise. Eleanor of Aquitaine brought the iron poker down with authority on the man's head. His movements stopped. Millicent felt her head swim. She heard the Queen calling for help. She sank down to the floor, just now feeling the pain in her wounded shoulder. Eleanor rushed over and sat on the floor beside her.

Outside, in the hall, Millicent heard shouts as the two dead guards were discovered. There was thunder on the stairs and she heard the Queen call for a physician. Someone was ripping the sleeve from her dress and binding up her arm. She thought it was Jamie Finch. Then everything went dark.

Thirty Five Tons of Silver

It was nearing midnight when William Marshal called a halt. His bone-weary column of men had been marching since dawn and the weaker among them had begun to fall by the side of the road. Those who had remained in ranks now stumbled off the road and simply curled up on the ground to fall into exhausted sleep. They had reached the outskirts of Dunstable, still a day and half march from London.

Marshal had sent a rider ahead to inform the Queen of his victory over John's forces near Towcester. It had been a complete rout, with no little slaughter of the mercenaries that had plagued the Midlands for three years. After the battle, Marshal's men counted over six hundred enemy dead. Most of the bodies lay on the muddy slope below the defensive line, pierced by longbow shafts.

Marshal had called off the pursuit by late in the day. Killing mercenaries was a useful endeavour, but he did not know how things stood in the capital or if the precious silver in the crypts of Saint Paul's was still secure. So they had let the remnants of Prince John's great mercenary army slip away.

Marshal ordered the wounded who could ride, Sergeant Billy among them, to be mounted on the tired horses and began the long march back to London. They had pushed hard for two days, from dawn to midnight, and the strain was showing on every man.

Near the rear of the column, William de Ferrers staggered off the road and sat down. His hands were bound and his legs felt like dead weights. He had never walked this far in his life. The two guards who had watched him all the long day and night sat down facing him. One had a hook for a hand and the other was missing an ear.

Invalids.

He wished he had never heard the word. To be under the control of creatures like these two was an insult hard to tolerate. He was the Earl of Derby! Still, being taken prisoner was better than the alternative. During the march, he had tried not to dwell on the terror he had felt in that frozen field when he realized that all of his skill with the blade would not be enough to save his life.

When he had seen Marshal appear, he had fallen back on an ancient law of the realm. Any noble, accused of any crime, could insist that his case be heard by the monarch. It had been a custom of the English since the days of Alfred the Great. He had prayed that Marshal's well-known reputation for honour would not allow him to ignore his plea—and his prayer had been answered.

But now he would have to face the judgment of Richard himself and that gave him little comfort. He had seen men lose their heads on Tower Hill and the thought that he might join them made his stomach turn. Still, he was alive for now rather than dead at the hands of Roland Inness. He curled up on the cold ground and tried to find sleep.

***

Sir Geoffrey Kent was in a quandary. He was Constable of the Tower of London and commander of the garrison, made so by Prince John the year before. For most of his year in command, the Prince had made his residence in the White Tower. That suited Sir Geoffrey. He was a competent soldier, but had no sense of politics at all. The fickle moods of the Londoners and the shifting factions within the nobility of England were a mystery to him. He had been happy to leave such things to Prince John and simply follow the man's orders.

Now the city was awash in politics and it had been two months since the Prince had decamped from London to Windsor.

To be sure, he received frequent instructions from his master, but with John not on the scene, these orders often seemed at odds with what Kent was seeing in the streets of the capital. And now he had received an order from the Prince that chilled him.

He was to seal off the city and, under no circumstance, was he to allow William Marshal and the men under his command to enter its walls. Further, he was to use whatever force necessary to seize the silver currently stored in the crypts of Saint Paul's.

Kent could understand the timing of this order. As the silver had begun to accumulate through January, William Marshal had called in every loyal man he could to guard it. But a week ago, the Earl had stripped his forces in the city to the bone to march off and meet the Prince's army on the road from Chester. There were now less than one hundred men loyal to Marshal left to guard the treasure. Without doubt, the thing could be done. He had over three hundred men—more than enough to do it, but the politics of it had him tied in knots.

Word had reached him that Marshal had beaten the mercenaries and was marching back to London. There were also rumours that an assassination attempt on the Queen had been foiled. In the city, crowds seemed to be congregating wherever two streets met. The merchants of London might be for John, but the lower classes still seemed to revere Richard. The situation was simply too complex for him to sort out. So he fell back on duty. The Prince was his master and had delivered an order. He would follow it.

Sir Geoffrey dispatched a hundred men to secure the seven gates of the city and mustered two hundred fifty more to march on Saint Paul's. He formed them up in a column, four abreast and led them out of the Tower and into the streets of London.

***

"They are coming, your grace."

The Queen nodded to Sir Nevil.

"How many?"

"Two hundred fifty. Kent has sent the rest to secure the gates."

"Any news of Marshal?"

"Aye, your grace. A rider made it through the Newgate not ten minutes ago. The Earl was at Dunstable two nights ago. He could be here by late in the day."

"So, he won't be here in time."

"No, your grace."

"Very well, can you stop them with what you have?"

"My men will fight to the last, your grace, but if they are determined to have it, they'll be dragging that silver out over our dead bodies."

Millicent sat next to the Queen. It had been two days since the assassination attempt. She had lost considerable blood from the knife wound she'd received that day, but had rebounded quickly. The man who had stabbed her, Father Malachy, did not fare as well. He'd been tossed in an unmarked pauper's grave across the Thames. As for the girl, Mary Cullen, she had been questioned under duress and had not revealed the names of any other French agents.

"It turns out the girl is the Archbishop's illegitimate daughter—the product of a young man's indiscretion," the Queen told her with a world-weary sigh. "The Archbishop is mortified. He thought he had done right by the girl, but he never acknowledged to anyone that she was his own—for understandable reasons. It seems that ate at her, so she betrayed him."

Millicent was stunned. Mary Cullen had completely taken her in. That the Queen's own spymaster had been equally cozened did not make her own failure any easier to accept. It was a failure that had come within seconds of costing the Queen her life. But Eleanor seemed not to have lost confidence in Walter of Coutances or her. Now, faced with a new crisis, she turned to Millicent.

"What shall we do, my dear?"

"What else is there to do, your grace. We fight."

***

Sir Geoffrey Kent's column marched west on Tower Street until it intersected with Watling Street. He turned right and headed northwest toward the city centre and Saint Paul's. From the moment they tramped out of the Tower, crowds of Londoners had gathered to gape at them. Women leaned out of second floor windows to watch them pass and small boys marched along pretending to be soldiers themselves.

As they passed through the market district, the taverns emptied out and the lower classes of London began to hoot and make rude noises as they passed. A few, already in their cups, thought to go further. One man leapt out of the crowd and grabbed a helmet from the head of a man in the outer file. A sergeant knocked him senseless with the butt of a lance and retrieved the helmet. A ripple of angry murmurs ran through the crowd.

As the column passed Bread Street, the magnificent spike of the Saint Paul's steeple was visible above the buildings ahead. Sir Geoffrey was relieved. The crowds were growing and he did not like the mood of these Londoners. Shouts and insults rained down from all sides, though no one was bold enough to try to halt the advance. At last the column emerged onto the square where the great cathedral stood.

Sir Geoffrey saw a double line of men, bristling with pikes, arrayed in an arc to protect the entrance to the crypts. He had no doubt that more men were inside. He had held out hope that his display of overwhelming force would make bloodshed unnecessary, but that hope died when he saw Sir Nevil Crenshaw standing at the centre of the line. He knew the taciturn knight and thought it likely he would die before surrendering.

So be it.

He nodded to his two sergeants and they began bellowing orders. Files broke off in both direction and began to form up to attack. Sir Geoffrey marched across the square and stopped ten feet from Sir Nevil.

"Stand aside, sir!" he demanded loudly. Behind him, he could hear the buzz of the crowd grow. Sir Nevil met his gaze.

"Or what, sir?"

"Or I will order my men to attack. As you can see, you have no hope of stopping us. If you resist, we will take the silver and your men will have died for nothing."

"Except their honour!"

This was a new voice that came from somewhere behind Crenshaw. The men at his back edged aside and from the steps leading into the crypts, Eleanor of Aquitaine emerged. She wore a splendid, shimmering robe of purple silk and a coat lined with ermine. Atop her head was a crown. The buzz from the Londoners grew into an excited roar.

"Do you know who I am Constable?" she asked.

Kent swallowed hard. Eleanor of Aquitaine had been Queen since before he was born. She stood there, withered with age, but with eyes that were not old. They had the cold look of a raptor. Behind him, the crowd began to chant the Queen's name.

"I do, your grace."

"Good, then you will explain to me why you have come to steal the ransom money intended to free your rightful King?"

"I...I...the Prince..."

"My son. Yes, he is a prince—but not a king. I speak for the King. Do you doubt it?"

Sir Geoffrey swallowed hard. The chant from the crowd made it hard to hear.

"Eleanor! Eleanor! Eleanor!"

His shoulders slumped.

"No, your grace."

"Good! Now, it would please me if you would march your men back to the Tower and stay there until I give you leave to do otherwise."

Sir Geoffrey Kent bowed his head. If John wanted the treasure in the crypts, he would have to deal with his mother himself! He turned to his sergeants.

"Form 'em up!"

The crowd cheered.

***

Late the following day, Marshal's column staggered into London through the Newgate. Sir Nevil had turned out a small guard of honour to line both sides of Watling Street just inside the gate. When the last man passed through, the Earl called a halt. The Queen, who had repaired to Westminster Palace after the threat to the ransom had been eliminated, was there to greet them. Beside her stood Millicent de Laval.

As the dirty column of men trooped into the city, Millicent saw a tall man walking beside Sir William. It took her a moment to realize it was her father. She had known that Sir Roger had survived the Crusade and had escaped capture with the King. The Queen had told her as much. He had sailed for home with Eleanor's blessing, but there had been no further news of him. She had not expected to see him here.

Sir Roger looked up just in time to see a young woman, who bore a remarkable resemblance to his wife, launch herself at him. Millicent threw her arms around his neck and began to sob. Sir Roger wanted to comfort his daughter, to tell her that his heart was so full it felt like it would burst, but he was reduced to sobs along with her. For a long time they clung together. Finally he drew away.

"Ye've grown, lass", he said through tears.

"And you've turned grey," she said with just a hint of sadness in her voice, "but still the handsomest man in England!"

"And you—you've become a spy?"

Millicent laughed at that. She saw Marshal standing to the side watching them. She turned to the Earl.

"It was Parrot, my lord. Your clerk was the spy, though now he's dead."

"Parrot, a spy?" Marshal asked, incredulous, "and dead?"

"Killed by one of his own. But don't feel you've been the only one cozened, my lord. Speak to the Archbishop. It was the spy he harboured that had yours killed!" Marshal just shook his head and left the two of them to their reunion. He had to report to the Queen.

On down the column, sergeants were issuing orders as men fell out of ranks, some simply sitting down in the street. Sir Nevil had organized provisions for the men and servants with ale and bread and sausages moved among them. Roland gratefully took a cup of ale and wound his way through the ranks of the Invalid Company toward the head of the column.

They saw each other at the same moment. He let his cup fall. She turned to Sir Roger.

"Father..."

He nodded.

"Go on, Millie."

They met in the middle of the Invalids. The sweating, blood spattered men who had fought at Watling Street gave back respectfully, as the man who led them and the young woman they revered clung to each other.

***

Five days after Marshal's column entered the Newgate, a column of another sort passed through the Bishopsgate. Twelve wagons, laden with the wealth of the north and freshly cleansed of dung and hay rumbled into the city, escorted by the outlaws of Sherwood and the men of the Invalid Company who Marshal had sent out to find them. Roland Inness and Declan O'Duinne rode beside Sir Robin and Tuck as they passed beneath the arch of the gate. For a week, the men of Nottinghamshire would be the toast of every tavern in London.

***

The bellowing of three score and four oxen disturbed the dawn and echoed off the north wall of St. Paul's Cathedral. Eight huge wagons stood in the street just north of the church. Each of these wagons were stacked high with chests that now bore the seal of the Queen of England, with two armed men in front and two in back. Every street and alleyway between the cathedral and the dock at Billingsgate was guarded by well-armed men—some of whom, a fortnight before, had been outlaws.

With a snapping of bullwhips, the wagons lurched forward, the column led by twenty men from the Invalid Company. Roland and Declan rode in front with drawn swords. Sergeant Billy and Jamie Finch brought up the rear. After a long cold spell, the weather was clear and almost spring-like in London as the wagons rumbled over the cobblestone street. It was early morning, but the sound had roused a considerable number of Londoners to watch the procession move the greatest treasure ever assembled in Britain down to the docks.

With the hard looking men of the Invalid Company challenging any man who might wish to impede the march, the trip down to Billingsgate went quickly. The Queen and Marshal had preceded them and were seated on high-backed chairs on the forecastle of the cog that would transport the silver to Speyer. There was no mistaking this vessel.

It was the *Sprite*.

Master Sparks stood proudly by the steering oar at the stern and waved at the two young knights as they dismounted. Both hurried to the edge of the dock and vaulted over the railing to the deck.

"You two should wipe yer boots 'for fouling up me deck." The voice came from below. They looked into the hold and saw Boda preparing to supervise the proper storage of the silver.

"Boda!" both shouted in unison.

"I am the very same. Now tell me, will you lads be joining us on this voyage? I'll want to keep a pail handy if Master Inness will be on board. I recall he loses his breakfast if the seas are not calm."

Roland laughed, remembering his misery the first time the *Sprite* had encountered swells in the open ocean.

"That won't be necessary Mister Boda. We are staying on dry land, but twenty of my men will be along and I cannot vouch for the strength of their stomachs."

Boda climbed out of the hold and slapped each of the men on the shoulder.

"Come along. Master Sparks will want to see ye'."

They made their way to the sterncastle where Sparks stood— a man fully in his element.

"My boys!" he shouted. "Well met indeed. Are ye signin' on for another voyage? I've room for two more on the crew."

"No, Master Sparks," Roland said as he clasped the man's meaty hand. "We've other duties to attend to. Just see that this cargo gets where it's bound."

Sparks hooted.

"When have I ever failed to do that?"

***

It took an hour for the crew of the *Sprite* and the Invalids to move the treasure chests from the wagons and position them properly in the hold of vessel. Patch had been given command of the score of men from the Invalids who would guard the treasure until it was delivered to the Emperor.

The loading complete, Roland and Declan climbed back over the railings and on to the dock. Marshal stood there patiently, waiting for the ship to cast off, ever a slave to duty. A moment later Sparks gave the order and the bow of the Sprite caught the current and began to drift downstream. Lining the railings were the men of the Invalid Company, armed to the teeth. Watching over it all was Eleanor of Aquitaine.

She was going to get her son back.

The Earl in the Tower

Roland had seen the Tower of London years before when he had come to King Richard's coronation with Sir Roger. It seemed a lifetime ago when he and Declan had stood on the half-finished stone bridge over the Thames, transfixed by the sheer size of the thing. Illuminated by torches on the walls, it had loomed over the taverns and merchant houses that edged toward it from the centre of the city.

On this day, he was standing atop Tower Hill near the site where condemned men were taken for executions. He wondered why it was called a hill. For a man who had spent his boyhood in the high Pennines, this small swell in the land hardly qualified. At its highest point, he still had to crane his neck to look up at the huge bulk of the Tower itself. The sight still awed him a bit.

As he walked down the low hill, he noted that a new curtain wall had almost been completed around the original keep. He wondered if King Richard or Prince John had ordered the defences strengthened. Given the uncertain loyalties of Londoners, he would not have blamed either. In his hand he clutched a scroll signed by Earl William Marshal, Justiciar of England, granting him audience with the prisoner William de Ferrers.

On the long march back to London, he had avoided Marshal, still furious that the man had ordered him to stay his hand against William de Ferrers. In truth, he would have disobeyed that

314

command had it not been seconded by Sir Roger. Marshal had sworn to them both that Richard would have de Ferrers' head for treason. He also pointed out that Roland could lose his own if he killed the nobleman after he had thrown himself on the King's mercy.

So the Earl of Derby had been spared that day. When they reached London, he'd been led through the streets with his hands bound and turned over to Sir Nevil Crenshaw, the new Constable of the Tower. Roland would have to wait to see justice done.

For a month they had lingered in London, waiting for word of the King. Marshal had taken up headquarters in the Guildhall, the better to keep a close eye on events in the capital as they waited for the King's return. With the dispatch of the ransom, the English barons had quickly fallen in line, with many hastening to the capital to assure the Justiciar of their steadfast loyalty to Richard. Marshal received these assurances graciously, but ordered them all to dispatch grain to the Midlands to relieve the famine there. Sir Robin and Tuck departed London for Nottinghamshire with twelve wagons of wheat, taken from supplies John had stored at Billingsgate for shipment to France.

In mid-March, word came that the King had been released, but was making a leisurely progress back towards his realm with lengthy stops at Cologne, Antwerp and Barfleur. It was from Barfleur that news came of Richard's reconciliation with John. The King's younger brother had spent a fortnight after the destruction of his mercenary force frantically trying to rally the barons to his cause. Failing that he had fled to the dubious protection of Philip in Paris. In the end he had raced to Barfleur and flung himself at Richard's feet, begging for mercy.

To the shock of many, Richard forgave his treacherous sibling. It was an act that set a precedent for the judgments he would hand down for other nobles who had been less than loyal to him. With these traitors, the King's justice had been merciful indeed To Roland, it was a punch in the gut.

"Banishment? For four years? It is not enough—not nearly enough!"

Roland stood in Marshal's office in the Guildhall, called there to hear from the Earl's own lips that the King had decided the fate of William de Ferrers.

"I agree, damn it all," Marshal shouted, his face reddening as he rose to his feet and slammed a hand down on the table. "I should have turned my back and let you kill him. Had I foreseen this, I would have. I will take that regret to my grave."

"You said the King would execute him!"

"Aye, the bastard should have been marched up Tower Hill and had his head lopped off. They should have stuck it on pole by the city gates. He was a traitor to his King, and, by God, he should pay, but...but the King cannot very well execute an Earl—if he lets his brother, the Prince, live."

"These politics makes me want to vomit, my lord," Roland said, venom in every word. "Good men have died and we've impoverished the land to get Richard back and *this* is the kind of justice he brings with him?"

"He's the only King we have, my young friend, and were it not for you and others like you, we would have John instead. Then you would see what true misrule looks like."

The two men stood there glaring at each other.

"I want to see him."

Marshal shook his head.

"I don't think that wise. He will be gone in two days. You should let it go, Sir Roland. Nothing good can come of you seeing de Ferrers."

Roland did not move.

"He killed my father, my lord. I ask you to grant me this request."

Marshal sat down heavily. He owed this young knight much. It was against his better judgment, but he would not refuse him this. He took out a piece of parchment, scratched out a few lines and signed it.

"Now, before I give you this, you must promise two things or this goes right into the fire." He jerked his head toward the blaze in the hearth behind him.

"If I can, my lord."

"You must promise to keep your views of our King to yourself. Your words are close enough to treason they might land *you* on Tower Hill. I would not want that, Sir Roland."

Roland was about to give a hot retort, but he saw the look of deep concern on William Marshal's face and caught himself. He did not, after all, wish to lose his head. He met Marshal's eyes.

"Agreed, my lord. I will hold my tongue. And God preserve us if John ever becomes king. What is your second condition."

Marshal gave him a hard look.

"You must give me your word not to kill William de Ferrers when you meet him."

***

Roland reached the bottom of Tower Hill and came to the drawbridge that spanned what passed for a moat. There was a foul-looking trickle passing underneath the span, but otherwise the ditch was dry. The new curtain wall still had scaffolding at the end nearest the Thames, but was complete otherwise. There was a square stone tower that housed the main gate and it was now guarded by loyal men. Most wore the livery of the Earl of Oxford, but other noble arms could be seen on tabards. The Captain of the Guard stopped him at the entrance. Roland handed over the scroll.

The Guard Captain studied it carefully.

"What's yer business with de Ferrers?' he barked.

"Personal," Roland replied. "Earl William has authorized it."

"I can see that," the man growled, but then shrugged. "Well, if the Justiciar has no problem with you talking to a traitor, I'll not object, but ye'll have to get the approval of the Constable."

"Thank you," Roland said and was waved through, though one of the men-at-arms followed as escort.

Inside the curtain wall, the great square keep loomed, its bulk almost blotting out the sun. His escort led him across a small courtyard, past a narrow tidal inlet that showed nothing but mud and flotsam at low tide and through an archway that pierced a low inner wall running from the southwest corner of the tower to the curtain wall by the river. When he emerged into this inner courtyard he saw a flight of wooden steps leading up from ground level to a narrow, first floor entrance.

Roland had seen enough fortifications to appreciate the cleverness of this design. If pressed, defenders could simply retreat to the keep and destroy the wooden stairs behind them. Any attacker would have to reach the entrance by ladder or some other device and then force an entry where only one man at a time could advance. No place was impregnable, but it would take some serious time and engineering to breach the Tower of London.

He followed the soldier up the wooden steps and into the arched entrance at the top. The walls of the place were over ten feet thick here and this long narrow passage into the fortress would have been a death trap for any attacker. Once through the entrance, Roland almost gasped at the size of the room he had entered. It stretched to the far side of the building, though the space was filled with all of the necessary gear for the garrison.

The Constable of the Tower had the luxury of a small chamber of his own, carved out of the larger room. After a quick rap on the wooden door, the guard entered and announced the visitor.

"My Lord Constable," the man intoned. "Sir Roland Inness of Kinder Scout, here to see the prisoner, de Ferrers."

Roland looked at the man who was seated behind a small desk pouring over some sort of ledger. Sir Nevil Crenshaw was a stockily-built man with powerful shoulders and an impassive face. He was William Marshal's sworn man and had stood with the Queen in the streets of London when the King's ransom had been threatened. He had the look of a constable.

When the guard had begun his announcement, Crenshaw had not lifted his eyes from the ledger, but his head shot up when he heard the name of Roland Inness.

"Inness? Are you the commander of the Invalid Company?"

Roland bowed.

"I am, my lord—at least for the moment."

The Constable scrambled to his feet and came around the desk.

"Sir Roland, I knew those men of yours when they were fit for nothing but the bawdy houses and gutters of this town and now they are the toast of London! Well done! Well done, indeed, sir, but you must tell me—how did you get drunks and cripples to fight like that? Extraordinary!"

Roland searched the man's face for any hint of mockery there—and found none. The Constable was genuinely pleased that these veterans had redeemed themselves.

"My lord, the Invalids are men like you and I. All they needed was for someone to believe in them and to give them a cause to fight for. They did the rest."

"And you believed in them?"

"My lord, in truth, I had no one else available to believe in, so, yes, I did. And they have repaid that belief many times over."

"I should say! My lord William tells me they held the centre of the line against the mercenary cavalry. I should have liked to have seen that!" This last he said a bit wistfully.

"And I heard you faced down twice your number to protect the ransom, Sir Nevil."

Sir Nevil waved off the praise.

"It was the Queen that done it. Frightening woman, the Queen. I wouldn't want to cross her."

"Nor I, my lord. Now, if you please, I have been granted permission to see your prisoner, William de Ferrers." He handed the scroll to Sir Nevil who read it through quickly.

"It is fortunate you came today, Sir Roland, for I've just been told the ship that will bear away our traitor to Brittany has come early and will be at the Billingsgate docks in the morning. May I ask what your business is with the prisoner?"

Roland met the man's eyes.

"It's personal, my lord...personal."

Sir Nevil arched an eyebrow.

"Very well, young sir, but you must give me your word of honour."

"For what, my lord?"

"That you will not kill him. I do not like that look in your eye, sir."

Roland blinked.

319

"You have it, my lord, as does Earl William."

"Very well, I will take you to him."

The Constable buckled on his sword belt and led Roland back out into the great hall. They walked the entire length to the opposite corner of the keep where a spiral stair led to the upper floors and to the basement. Sir Nevil headed down.

"We have ensconced him under the chapel. There's no window, but it's dry and better than he deserves, I daresay." The Constable led Roland through another large room that mirrored the one on the floor above, but was filled from one end to the other with every sort of weapon. Lances, swords, pikes, axes and crossbows were lined up with precision.

Finally they reached a heavy wooden door with a small grate at head height. The Constable inserted a massive key in the lock and swung the door open.

"Look lively, you swine," he roared. "You've a visitor."

William de Ferrers had been reclining on the lone cot in the room. He leapt to his feet, staring anxiously at the visitors. Sir Nevil looked at the Earl of Derby and thought, for not the first time, how forlorn the high and mighty seemed when residing in the Tower.

"He jumps every time he hears the key in the lock," Crenshaw said with disdain. "Thinks the King might have a change of heart and..." the Constable grinned and drew a finger across his throat.

Roland barely heard him. He was watching the man in the cell. It took de Ferrers a moment, but then a flash of recognition and fear played across his face. As the Constable began to back out of the cell door he barked a command.

"Stay! You there, Constable—you will stay here! This man intends to murder me and I am not armed."

"Sir Roland isn't armed and I have his word he will not kill you, though you richly deserve it," Sir Nevil said as he stepped back into the hall, leaving Roland alone in the doorway.

Roland took a step into the cell and de Ferrers retreated, looking frantically around the bare room, but there was no exit and no weapon to grasp. He stopped and watched balefully as Roland came closer.

"I have taken a blood oath to kill you, de Ferrers, but I have given my word that it will not be today," he said. "Would that I had not missed the chance, that day on Kinder Scout."

It took a moment for William de Ferrers to comprehend that Roland had not come to kill him here alone in his cell. A bitter smile came to his lips.

"You Danes are all the same. You're all cowards—afraid to meet your betters, face-to-face! You shoot at men from hiding!"

Roland stepped closer and de Ferrers edged backwards.

"I used no bow when we met a month ago on Watling Street. We both know I could have killed you then."

For a moment, de Ferrers met the challenge in Roland's eyes, then dropped his own and turned away.

"You Danes have skulked like rats up in those hills for too long. My father should have driven the lot of you out years ago, but he was too soft. It took me to do it. Me!"

"And look what it has got you," Roland said, gazing around the barren cell.

De Ferrers barked a laugh.

"This? This will not last. I leave tomorrow for my estate in Brittany. It's lovely there in the spring you know." He gave Roland a sly smile.

"Or did you not know my family has lands in Brittany? Of course you wouldn't. And those lands are bountiful, *Sir* Roland." The Earl of Derby spit out the honorific with complete scorn. "They will allow me to give generously to good King Richard and he will, no doubt, appreciate my financial support for the wars he will be waging against Philip. Don't you think?"

Roland felt the grip he'd held on his anger begin to loosen.

"All you say may be true, de Ferrers, but you have a debt to pay—for Rolf Inness, for Alwyn Madawc, and for all the Danes you've killed. Four years in exile does not begin to pay it. That debt *will* be paid one day and I will be the one to collect it. It could be the day you set foot back in Derbyshire, or the day after that, or perhaps I will visit your lovely lands in Brittany."

As he spoke he walked calmly across the room. As he approached, de Ferrers backed away until he could retreat no further. Sweat broke out on his brow, despite the chill in the cell.

"Constable!" he called. No one responded.

Roland grasped de Ferrers by the collar and twisted it beneath his chin. The man tried to jerk away, but Roland pressed him against the dank wall of the Tower, fifteen feet thick here in the basement. There was nowhere to escape.

Roland drew his face close to his old enemy.

"Remember this, my lord. One day, when you are in a place you think safe, I will be nearby. I will be unseen, and I will put an arrow into your chest. No one will know who struck you down, but you might just live long enough to know it was Roland Inness who killed you."

He released his grip and de Ferrers slid down the wall to the floor.

"Constable," he wailed.

Roland turned and walked away.

The King's Peace

*T*he bans were posted at Easter and they were married in May. Earl Ranulf had offered the chapel of Chester Castle for the ceremony but Millicent chose Saint Mary's on the Hill. Father Augustine was invited to provide the official blessing of the union and arrived a week in advance with Sir Robin of Loxley. Together they made the acquaintance of every tavern keeper in the city.

A box from the Queen arrived in Chester on the same day as the men from Nottinghamshire. In it was a beautiful silver chalice and a note from Eleanor. Millicent read it aloud.

"To Sir Roland of Kinder Scout and Lady Millicent de Laval, please accept my wishes for a long and happy marriage and this small token of my esteem. I pilfered it from the Germans after they weighed the ransom and thought it an appropriate gift."

On the day before the event, Griff, the taciturn Welsh archer, arrived with gifts from Lord Llywelyn for the bride and groom. He carefully read the message that the young Prince of Gwynedd had sent.

"To Sir Roland Inness, champion archer, commander of the Invalids and friend; and to Lady Millicent de Laval, champion rider, intrepid spy and friend—please accept this first foal sired by Llamrei, the finest stallion in all of Wales or England."

On a lead was a colt, a young stallion with a distinctive roan coat.

"My word, it's the son of The Surly Beast!" Declan declared. Llywelyn had coveted Roland's bad tempered warhorse, known to all, save the Welsh Prince himself, as The Surly Beast, from the moment he saw the animal. Roland had given it to him for his help in retaking Chester. The Irish knight stepped forward to take the lead and the young stallion first backed away, then lurched forward and tried to bite his hand.

"I see he was bred true!" Roland said to Griff. "Tell your master it is a wonderful gift and remind him that he will always find friends on this side of the Dee."

Roland turned to Sir Roger who was standing nearby.

"My lord, I have never been suited to fighting atop a horse. Even your daughter could not make me a decent cavalry man. A horse with this spirit would be wasted on a clumsy rider such as myself. I would be honoured if you would take him, as I believe your previous mount has been retired." Roland took the reins from Declan and offered them to Sir Roger.

He took them and the colt shied away, but the big knight held them firm, looked the young horse in the eye and spoke to the animal softly but firmly.

"There'll be none of that, now, young one. It appears you are to be mine, like it or not." He stepped forward, keeping the reins taut, and reached out with his free hand to gently touch the stallion on its nose. The horse jerked its head back once, but seemed to settle then as Sir Roger spoke quietly into its ear.

He turned back to Roland and Declan, his eyes shiny.

"It's a fine gift, Sir Roland," he said. "I thank you."

Roland nodded and felt a tightness in his throat. He loved Sir Roger de Laval, not simply for having saved him when he was a hunted boy, but for what the knight was. Tuck had begun that lesson, but it was Sir Roger who showed him that a man must be judged by his actions, not by what tribe he was born into. He had arrived at Shipbrook hating Normans, but Sir Roger had given the lie to that hate. Roland had found a new home at Shipbrook, but now everything was changing. He had been summoned by Earl Ranulf in the days before his wedding for a private meeting. The Earl was blunt.

"In four years, the Earl of Derby will return from exile. I was surprised once by that ass and will not let that happen again. I need a loyal man out along my border with Derbyshire to keep an eye on de Ferrers. I think a nice, small fortress by the Weaver ford might be in order, with a platoon from the Invalid Company posted there under your command. The Danes will be settling near there. Who better to help them make a new life for their families than one of their own?"

He hadn't known what to say. His mind saw the logic in this, though his heart would have been happy to stay at Shipbrook.

"I am the sworn man of Sir Roger, my lord," was all he could muster.

The Earl nodded.

"I've not made this offer without speaking to your master first. He agrees with me."

Roland rode back to Shipbrook and found Sir Roger and Declan labouring beside a score of farmers and men-at-arms as they hoisted a huge roof beam into place with pulleys. The burned-out keep of Shipbrook was rising from the ashes. Millie and Lady Catherine stood under an awning that shaded them from the afternoon sun and were supervising the preparation of the evening meal.

The two men paused in their labours as he rode up and dismounted.

"My lord, there is no one I would rather serve than you."

Sir Roger gave him a sympathetic smile.

"And there is no one I would rather have in my service, Roland, but I've known, even in those earliest of days, that you were meant for greater things. I am content with Shipbrook, but it is too small a stage for you, I think. And besides, our Earl needs you elsewhere and I will still have good men in my service. Sir Declan here has agreed to be my Master of the Sword."

Roland turned to his closest friend and slapped him on the shoulder.

"Well done, Dec! I trust you will not go easy on the squires under your instruction." He pointed to the sky. "Sir Alwyn will be watching!"

Declan nodded happily.

"I will do my duty, but how will you get along without me? Millie may keep you proficient in sitting a horse, but without me, you will not know which end of a sword to grasp."

Roland grinned at his friend.

"Oh, I'll muddle through, but I will miss you, Dec. We will always be clan."

"Gad, Roland, we will only be a long day's ride away, once you settle up there along the Weaver."

Roland had only seen the land the Earl was offering him twice, when he had passed that way with Sir Edgar and when he had been fleeing from mercenaries, but he recalled that it was a good place for a fort—and a home. He gazed around at Shipbrook. It was hard to say goodbye. He turned back to Sir Roger.

"Then I am to give my oath to Earl Ranulf?"

"Aye, lad. If you are willing. I have served the Earls of Chester for twenty years and have not regretted that service."

Roland took a deep breath.

"Millie?"

"She's known of this since you rode out this morning. She will go where you go."

***

Roland Inness stood perfectly still in the shadows of the deep glade. He saw a hint of movement out of the corner of his eye, but did not stir. He had found a well-used game trail here two days before and had come to this place well before dawn. Now there was something on the trail. He waited.

He saw the antlers first, as a large fallow buck lowered its head to browse on some berries along the trail. Moving with elaborate slowness, he nocked an arrow. The deer, engaged with its breakfast, did not see the longbow rise slowly as Roland drew the bowstring back. The animal was only fifty paces away. He let his breath out slowly—and the deer bolted.

Roland could not find a clean shot as the animal's rump disappeared back up the trail. He looked back and saw that a hare had blundered onto the path right in front of the fallow deer and had startled it.   The hare seemed unconcerned by all the excitement and sat there, chewing on a little sprig of greenery.

Roland lowered his bow—no venison for supper tonight. He looked up at the sky, now showing a touch of gold as the sun rose, and started back toward the small forest lane that lay a mile behind him. It was a beautiful autumn day and it felt good to be in the woods, but there was work to do back by the River Weaver.

An hour later, he left the forest behind and walked through fields green with new winter wheat. Just ahead on a small bluff, a wooden palisade was rising. The structure would look more like Bleddyn's rude fortress in the Clocaenog than Shipbrook, but he and Millie had already envisioned replacing the logs with stone one day. The new fort looked down on the ford where the road crossed the river. Out of sight, in the valley beyond, he could hear the sound of axes felling trees.

On the bluff, he saw three men, his brother Oren among them, muscling a log with a sharpened point into its place in the new wall. Sir Roger had offered Oren a position as squire, but the young Dane had chosen to return to farming. He had claimed a good patch of ground a few miles away from the ford.

Roland started up the gentle slope and saw Millie emerge from the small house that was serving as their home until a more proper keep could be built. A small, golden-haired girl trailed behind her. He and Oren had ridden together to Saint Oswald's Priory to fetch Lorea six weeks after the battle on Watling Street. The brothers at the priory were heartbroken to see her go, but in Millie, Roland had found the ideal guardian for the child. The two had formed an instant kinship and were practically inseparable. Lorea waved and Millicent called to him as he drew near.

"No meat for the table, my lord?" she said with a smile.

"None, my lady. I could have taken a fat little hare that ruined my shot, but I feared it would distress Mistress Lorea," he said, laying a gentle hand on the girl's head. "She has a soft spot for rabbits."

The girl blushed at that and disappeared around the side of the house. She had been raising a baby rabbit in a hutch back there since spring.

Roland slipped an arm around his wife's waist and looked down into the river valley. He could see where men were downing trees near the banks. Sir Edgar would be there, the finest axeman of them all. He had agreed to be Roland's Master of the Sword and like everyone at this new outpost, he lent his hand to building it.

Millicent leaned against Roland.

"This is a good place to make a home," she said, looking out over the valley, its sides a blaze of autumn colours. "Do you think we'll be happy here, Roland? Will we have peace?"

He turned to look at her. Over her shoulder and twenty miles away was the border with Derbyshire. In four years William de Ferrers would be back. Four years…it had been four years since he had killed the deer on Kinder Scout. It felt like he had lived a lifetime in those four years. He looked into Millie's eyes and thought that four years of peace, with Millicent Inness by his side, would be worth whatever came after. He pulled her close.

"Yes, Millie. I think we will."

The Ransomed Crown

Peace finally comes to England with King Richards ransom, but across the border in Wales a vicious civil war continues. Prince Llywelyn calls in an old debt owed him by the Earl of Chester. In payment he wants Sir Roland Inness and the Invalid Company. Follow the new adventure!

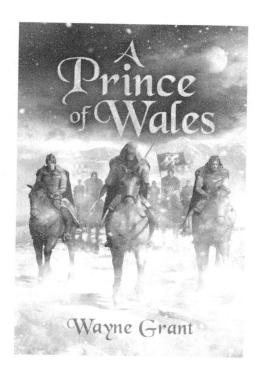

Order on Amazon, Amazon UK and Audible

US: https://www.amazon.com/Prince-Wales-Saga-Roland-Inness-ebook/dp/B077CF71GY

UK: https://www.amazon.co.uk/Prince-Wales-Saga-Roland-Inness-ebook/dp/B077CF71GY

Audible: https://www.audible.com/pd/A-Prince-of-Wales-Audiobook/B07BNTCQY5

Historical Note

Many of the events depicted in *The Ransomed Crown* are fictional, but this story was built around a core of real events. The period from King Richard's departure on Crusade in December, 1189 to his return from captivity in March, 1194 was truly a time of troubles for his kingdom.

Prince John, rightly maligned down through the ages, did try mightily to usurp his brother's throne. Queen Eleanor did have to fight a two front war—against Philip of France and her own youngest son to keep the kingdom whole. Richard was captured and ransomed for thirty-five tons of silver. Castles were besieged, towns sacked and mercenary armies hired.

In *The Ransomed Crown* I have tried to tell a good story about one young man caught up in this fratricidal war. In telling that story, I've tried to stay faithful to the basic events of the time, but have taken license where I thought it necessary. Here are some key points on what is fact and what is fiction in this final chapter of Roland's story.

≈ Richard did tarry overlong in the Holy Land and was shipwrecked on his voyage home. He was trying to find a route overland to Saxony when he was captured by his archenemy, Leopold of Austria and essentially sold to the Holy Roman Emperor. He was eventually ransomed for one hundred and fifty thousand marks, but the final fifty thousand marks were forgiven. The one hundred thousand marks equalled thirty-five tons of silver and was stored in the crypts of Saint Paul's before being shipped to Germany.

≈ Prince John was granted the revenues of the Midlands by Richard to try and keep him loyal, but part of a kingdom was never going to be enough for his younger brother. John used his revenue to hire a mercenary army that dominated the Midlands and beyond from 1191-1193.

≈ To my knowledge, Chester was not besieged during this period, nor was the town of Sheffield sacked, though many towns were. The depredations of John's mercenaries were quite real.

≈ John actually did homage to Philip for all of the Plantagenet lands on the continent in a desperate bid to gain his support to grab the crown from Richard. Philip managed to gain Gisors and the Vexin region before Richard could return and defend his realm. He also had an army prepared to land in England, but decided it was too risky.

≈ William Marshal and Walter of Coutances were Justiciars during this period and were instrumental in keeping John in check. Walter of Coutances actually went to Germany and agreed to be one of the hostages required as guarantors of payment after the King's release.

≈ Queen Eleanor who was in her seventies (an extraordinarily old woman for the times) fought to keep the kingdom whole for Richard throughout his absence and was the true hero of this bit of English history.

≈ The battle described outside of Towcester was fictional, but was intended to be a foreshadowing of how the longbow would eventually (in 150 years or so) be used so effectively by English armies against the French.

≈ To my knowledge, there was no unit of wounded Crusaders known as the Invalids, but there should have been.

≈ I will concede that Robin and Tuck are fictional, but they have thrilled millions of fans for hundreds of years and that makes them real enough for me.

≈ A final note on the actual historical characters referenced in these books:

— I found no evidence that my villain, William de Ferrers, was any more evil than any other nobleman during that period. He just happened to be Earl of Derby during the period of this tale, so was, more or less, in the wrong place at the wrong time. In an interesting irony, when he finally married, he was wed to Lady Agnes De Kevelioc, sister of Earl Ranulf of Chester.

— Archdeacon Herbert Poore was not a spymaster for the French—that I know of.

— The Bishop of Beauvais was King Philip's spymaster.

Books by Wayne Grant

The Saga of Roland Inness
Longbow
Warbow
The Broken Realm
The Ransomed Crown
A Prince of Wales
Declan O'Duinne
A Question of Honour

The Inness Legacy
No King, No Country

ABOUT THE AUTHOR

Wayne Grant grew up in a tiny cotton town in rural Louisiana where hunting, fishing and farming are a way of life. Between chopping cotton, dove hunting and Little League ball he developed a love of great adventure stories like Call It Courage and Kidnapped.

Like most southern boys he saw the military as an honourable and adventurous career, so it was a natural step for him to attend and graduate from West Point. He just missed Vietnam, but found that life as a Captain in an army broken by that war was not what he wanted. After tours in Germany and Korea, he returned to Louisiana and civilian life.

Through it all he retained his love of great adventure writing and when he had two sons he began telling them stories before bedtime. Those stories became his first novel, Longbow. The picture above was taken outside the Tower of London.

The rest of The Saga of Roland Inness, which includes *A Prince of Wales, Declan O'Duinne* and *A Question of Honour* are now available on Amazon.

To learn more about the author and his books check out his website: www.waynegrantbooks.com or his Longbow Facebook page: www.facebook.com/Longbowbooks/

You can also follow him on BookBub: www.bookbub.com to get information on when his books go on sale and on Goodreads www.goodreads.com.

If you think these books have merit, please leave a review on Amazon or Goodreads. For a self-published writer this is the only way to get the word out. Thank you!

Made in the USA
Monee, IL
26 November 2020